Y0-BQX-230

BRACED FOR MURDER

A BEANIE AND CRUISER MYSTERY

Braced for Murder
Introducing Calamity, Cruiser's Canine Partner in Crime

Sue Owens Wright

FIVE STAR
A part of Gale, Cengage Learning

GALE
CENGAGE Learning®

Detroit • New York • San Francisco • New Haven, Conn • Waterville, Maine • London

LIBRARY OF CONGRESS CATALOGING-IN-PUBLICATION DATA

Wright, Sue Owens.
    Braced for murder : a Beanie and Cruiser mystery introducing Calamity, Cruiser's canine partner in crime / Sue Owens Wright.
— First edition.
        pages cm
    ISBN 978-1-4328-2689-5 (hardcover) — ISBN 1-4328-2689-1 (hardcover)
    1. Women private investigators—Fiction. 2. Dogs—Fiction. 3. Murder—Investigation—Fiction. 4. South Lake Tahoe (Calif.)— Fiction. 5. Mystery fiction. I. Title.
PS3623.R565B73 2013
813'.6—dc23   2012051191

First Edition. First Printing: May 2013
Find us on Facebook– https://www.facebook.com/FiveStarCengage
Visit our website– http://www.gale.cengage.com/fivestar/
Contact Five Star™ Publishing at FiveStar@cengage.com

Printed in Mexico
1 2 3 4 5 6 7 17 16 15 14 13

This book is dedicated to all the found hounds and the people who open their hearts and homes to them.

CHAPTER 1

Writing an exposé on a dog pound can be beastly work, especially for someone like me with an animal attraction. That was the case with a story I was covering for the *Tahoe Tattler* about Lakeside Animal Shelter. Since accepting this freelance assignment, I found myself involved not only in a conflict about the overcrowded, mismanaged facility but also rescuing homeless basset hounds for Found Hounds, a local organization that's dedicated to saving as many bassets as they can from shelters. No one was braced for the pack of trouble about to be unleashed on South Lake Tahoe, at least not until I discovered the corpse.

I'd already helped place several dogs in their forever homes and had volunteered to help out on July 14 at the upcoming Bassetille Day Basset Waddle, a fundraiser for a new no-kill shelter in South Lake Tahoe. My own found hound, Cruiser, who until recently had enjoyed being an only dog, was learning to tolerate living in a hound dog hostel, otherwise known as my mountain cabin in the Tahoe National Forest.

While waiting for a call from a fellow rescuer, Jenna Fairbanks, about another homeless basset that had turned up at the shelter, I busied myself with putting the finishing touches on a raffle prize basket to raise money at the Waddle for Found Hounds. Cruiser was naturally curious about my activity. As always, the slightest crinkle of paper or aluminum foil alerted him to the possibility of treats. A moment later, he was nosing into the contents of my basket for something, anything, tasty to eat.

"Sorry, Cruiser. These goodies aren't for you, boy." I nudged his muzzle aside before he could douse my cleverly arranged basket in drool. You might say that expert basketry runs in my family. Intricately woven baskets from the Washoe tribe are highly prized among collectors of Indian artifacts. Though my gift basket was not one I'd woven myself, I hoped that it would raise some generous bids in the silent auction, assuming a certain treat-nabbing hound didn't claim the prize first.

Cruiser took the hint but didn't stray too far to keep an eye out for anything that might drop within range. I tried my best to ignore "the look" I was getting from The Lord of the Glance. We both knew if he kept up the doe-eyed, pitiful pup act long enough I'd crumble like a soggy dog biscuit and offer him something from my stash of goodies. I have to go easy on the treats with Cruiser or he'll become a round found hound. There's nothing he likes better than to eat. Fortunately, the phone's ringing interrupted the test of wills between Cruiser and his faltering food slave.

"Hi, Elsie. It's Jenna." Her voice sounded hollow on her cell phone, like she was talking into a soup can in a seventh-grade science experiment. "I have more information for you about the dog at Lakeside. Got a pen and paper?"

"Go ahead."

"This one's a tricolor female, about a year old. Her name is Calamity."

"Cute name."

"She was wearing a name tag when she was picked up, but there was no other I.D. on it."

"Probably another tourist lost his dog." Cruiser was one of the few lucky abandoned summer strays that had found a permanent home.

"No doubt," Jenna said. "People come up here to visit the lake and forget how important it is to put a current address and phone number on their dog's collar."

"Too bad. A little thing like a microchip can save owners and their dogs a lot of distress."

"Especially the dogs!"

"No microchip on Calamity?" I was glad I'd had Doc Heaton implant one in Cruiser during his last visit to the clinic. He could still be the happy wanderer if I didn't watch him closely, and I didn't want him ending up a jailbird. Given half a chance, he'd follow that keen nose of his to the ends of the earth.

"I'm sorry to say they don't routinely check for them at the shelter, but you can have the vet check for one. No one has come to claim her in three days, and no one adopted her over the weekend. Time's up for this dog, unless you can take her until she can be placed in a permanent home."

"I'll take her!"

Cruiser cocked his head and gave me a quizzical look. If there were a cartoon thought bubble over his head, it would have read, *Uh-oh. Better start stashing my treats for a rainy day. Mom's takin' in another refugee.*

"Oh, good. She's in a pen at the rear of the facility. They'll hold her until ten A.M. If she's not adopted by then . . ."

"I get the picture, Jen."

"When you get to the shelter, look for A . . . body."

"What? Look for a what? You're breaking up. Jenna, you still there?"

"Hold on. . . . driving through Cave Rock."

"Speak up. I can barely hear you." It wasn't the first time this Native American sleuth had encountered trouble because of Cave Rock. My first involvement in Tahoe crime-busting had been over this rock of ages, which is still a sacred site to the Washoe tribe.

9

All I heard was dead air for a few moments, and then Jenna's voice came through again. "Can you hear me *now?*"

"You sound like a TV cell phone ad. What did you say before?"

"I said look for Amanda Peabody. She's on the staff, but she's sympathetic to our rescue efforts and will help you with Calamity."

"I thought Rhoda Marx usually handles all the adoptions at the shelter."

"She does, but as you know, she's been making it difficult for the rescue groups to do their job."

"Too bad." Rhoda Marx had become a pet adoption road-block ever since taking over as manager of the shelter. The handling, or mishandling, of stray pets by Round 'em Up Rhoda, as she was known by animal lovers in the community, angered more than local rescue groups.

"Fortunately for Calamity, Rhoda didn't turn up at work today," Jenna said. "Didn't call in sick. A no-show."

"That doesn't sound like the *über* efficient Rhoda I know."

"The stalag probably won't miss having that mutt matron goose-stepping around there for one day."

Even Rhoda's co-workers had occasionally called her Mengele Marx and made other derogatory cracks about the shelter being an animal Auschwitz. She was commonly referred to as a "euthanasia expert." From the numbers of animals destroyed there each year, it appeared she was proud of her reputation. Those comments were well deserved. The fact that she resembled a dreary character from an Edward Gorey cartoon didn't help matters much. Although many of the problems at the shelter were also due to a faltering national economy and efforts to stretching the dollar until the eagle screams for mercy, by Rhoda's failure to implement at least some positive changes at the shelter within a limited budget, she had rightfully earned her reputation.

What had sparked the recent media focus on the shelter was a case in which a basset had been rescued once from the shelter and placed in a loving home, only to end up back at the same facility and destroyed before the rightful owner could claim her pet. Tahoe pet lovers and animal rights groups were outraged over the incident, and it had become the canine cause *du jour.* Letters of protest besieged the *Tattler* when the article ran with the ill-fated hound's sad face on the front page. My editor, Carla Meeks, has never been one to downplay such ready-made drama. Community chaos makes sensational headlines, and that sells newspapers.

In light of the uproar, I wasn't too surprised to hear Rhoda had taken a sick day, unannounced or not. She'd become a public scapegoat over the shelter problems, thanks in no small part to the spotlight trained on them in the paper and on TV, not to mention the efforts of the Tahoe Animal Impoundment Liberation Society (TAILS), a militant group that had staged several protests outside the shelter since the story broke.

A band of activists with roots in the Bay Area, TAILS members were not above proving their point through acts of violence if need be. There had been some incidents at research labs in Northern California, where primates had been freed from their cages to run amok in the community. All were quickly captured, but it could have been disastrous because some of the monkeys were infected with highly contagious diseases.

Cruiser sidled up to me and planted his drool-doused chin on my knee. As any writer and her hound dog knows, perseverance eventually pays off, except in this instance. He wasn't getting any of these Bacon Beggin' Strips. They were reserved for the raffle winner's dog.

The furrows in his brow made him look more pitiful than usual. How can a basset hound look any other way? No botox for bassets. I sensed that this forlorn expression wasn't about treats, though. He knew something was up. It was as if he had understood every word of my conversation with Jenna about the stray basset.

More likely, he was reading my body language and knew I was excited about something, but Cruiser knew all about strays. He'd been one himself before my husband found him abandoned by the side of the road one summer. At first I thought it was a stroke of luck for Cruiser when Tom brought him home, but now I know it's really the other way around. I never saw anyone bond with a dog the way my husband had with Cruiser. They were inseparable, and Cruiser was never happier than when they were doing guy stuff together out in our garage. So was his idol, Tom. Cruiser kept vigil on the world, greeting an occasional passerby or barking at a sassy squirrel while Tom tinkered on projects and the radio played his favorite '60s hits.

I didn't grow up around dogs and neither had my daughter, Nona. Truthfully, I wasn't too receptive at first to the idea of our adopting a stray dog. I'm so glad I didn't say no. My long-eared friend and I have been through a lot together and have provided each other with much-needed solace since Tom died so tragically in a forest fire. I'd have been too lonesome without Cruiser's company, especially since Nona's visits have grown infrequent, with her blossoming career as a fashion model. This cabin of mine can be a bit solitary sometimes, even with a howling basset around.

I didn't know if my slobbery sidekick would adjust to another four-legged guest at the MacBean lodge. Cruiser's an easygoing guy, as his name implies, but he'd made it clear enough in the past that he prefers being an only dog, especially after I brought a golden retriever named Buddy home. Then there was the mischievous Scottish terrier and a pampered Pekingese that took up residence with us briefly during the Sirius murder case, which really messed with his leader-of-the-pack status.

He'd been pretty tolerant of my basset rescue activities thus far, as long as I didn't become a foster flunky and make this a multi-dog household for good. I decided to take Cruiser along with me to the shelter, so he and my new charge could get acquainted away from his home turf and avoid any potential dominance issues that might arise.

I grabbed Cruiser's leash and he followed me to my Jeep, known around here as the BUV, or Basset Utility Vehicle. I boosted his heavy canine caboose onto the passenger seat and belted him into his safety harness. Lifting seventy pounds of hound gets harder as I get older. I may have to get one of those dog ramps so he can waddle right up into the car. Cruiser settled into cruising stance and we were off, headed straight for Calamity at Lakeside Animal Shelter.

Chapter 2

A cool alpine zephyr zipped through the car windows. Despite the season, the weather was nippier than a border collie among a herd of unruly sheep. At the topmost elevations, linen clouds draped towering tables of granite. It was the kind of Tahoe summer day I so love, cool and pleasant with a sapphire sky to rival the lake, a royal blue crown jewel of the Sierra. Still, there were clouds gathering on the horizon that signaled a storm in the making, but I'm not just talking about the weather.

As we approached Lakeside Animal Shelter, a cacophony of yips, barks, and howls could be heard a good distance away. I've never liked going to the shelter. It's hard not to come away in tears. Cruiser bayed his answer to the lament coming from within the cold cinderblock walls of the shelter. Several placard-carrying protesters from TAILS circled in the parking lot. Painted in blood red letters on the signs were slogans like LAKESIDE KILLING KENNEL and LAKESIDE, THE ANIMALS' ABU GRAIB.

They spotted me driving up with a dog in the car, and I sensed I was about to be confronted. One protester broke from the group and approached me as I got out of the car.

"You're not surrendering your dog to this place, are you?" Her voice was husky, and so was she. She appeared to be in her early twenties and wore combat boots dyed to match the color of her spiky, purple hair. I counted thirteen piercings, and those were just in her left ear.

"Heavens, no!"

Her icy blue gaze conveyed that she didn't believe me. I had to admit it's all too common at pounds and shelters to see people dropping off an old dog with costly health issues or the grown puppy Santa left last Christmas, or the dog whose owners didn't have time for him anymore or couldn't take him along with them to wherever they were moving. I knew the usual assortment of shelter stories; so does every animal shelter worker in America. Everyone wants a puppy, but cute little puppies grow up into dogs that need food, care and attention, and usually don't get spayed or neutered. As dogs age and associated health problems arise, their upkeep gets more expensive. Old Dog Tray ends up dumped at the pound or shelter and usually doesn't get re-homed.

"Trust me, ma'am, you don't want to leave your dog here. It's anything but a shelter. This isn't a fit place for any animal." I knew she was right about that, which was why I was here.

"Trust me, Miss, I'm not planning to drop off my dog."

"The name is Victoria Thatcher. People call me Tori. I'm with TAILS, which stands for . . ."

"I know all about your group. I'm Elsie MacBean. I'm working with Found Hounds to place basset hounds in foster care until they can be adopted."

Her demeanor softened. "Elsie MacBean. Of course! I know who you are. You're a reporter with the *Tattler,* aren't you?"

I nodded. Gee, I didn't even have to flash my press card anymore. People knew me, mostly because of my dog and our past escapades into crime-solving at the lake. Maybe Cruiser and I would have to start wearing disguises in public.

"And this fine fellow here must be the famous Cruiser." She reached in the window and stroked Cruiser's head. He leaned closer so she could scratch his ear. What a pushover.

"That he is. So you see, I'm really here to make a withdrawal, not a deposit."

She laughed. Kewpie Doll dimples creased her cheeks when she smiled, which wasn't often. Tori was sure no Kewpie.

"Great. I wish we could get more people coming in here to adopt dogs and cats from this place."

"Best not scare them away then. Some people are a little nervous about crossing picket lines, you know?"

I'd struck a chord. Hackles rose, and her militant tone resumed.

"We're here to raise public awareness about the problems at this facility and ensure necessary changes are made to improve conditions for the animals."

"Me too, but I prefer to do it in writing."

"Different strokes."

"Precisely."

She was right, of course. Still, I worried that her mutt militia might have the opposite effect intended by discouraging potential adopters. There had already been some graffiti and other vandalism at the shelter that had been attributed to TAILS.

Tori made no excuses or apologies for any troubles at the shelter. In fact, for the sake of free publicity, she was happy to claim responsibility for them, whether or not her group was the cause. Anything to aim the spotlight of public scrutiny on the shelter, more specifically on Rhoda Marx, was fine and dandy. I suspected she'd only been nice to me in the hope of getting some coverage in the *Tattler*. I would have been happy to do an impromptu interview, but right now a dog needed rescuing.

I left Cruiser in the Jeep in case someone else might assume I was here to surrender him to the shelter. Entering the kennels to search for my latest rescue hound, I could see and smell plenty of cause for complaint. The cages were overcrowded and filthy. There was no food or fresh water in the dispensers. The kennels had not been cleaned recently, and the shelter had already opened to the public for the day. I could only assume that these cages were not intended for public viewing. If they were, it was doubtful anyone would adopt any of the animals impounded in them. In one cage I counted half a dozen dogs of all ages and breeds. There was the usual assortment of discarded pits and Chihuahuas. Puppies ambled playfully between the legs of a Rottweiler, which snarled and snapped an occasional warning.

As I passed another cage, a kennel-crazed Husky paced in circles while an Aussie shepherd gnawed in futility at the chain link fence. One dog had a torn, bloody ear from a fight that had probably erupted with a cellmate. The smell coming from the cages was so bad I held a handkerchief to my nose. For a moment I thought I might be sick.

"Need some help?" I heard a man's voice behind me. I turned to face a kennel attendant with Conan the Barbarian biceps. Did guys pump iron in dog prison, too? A cigarette dangled on his lip under a shrub of mustache. The label affixed to his shirt pocket said REX. Good name for a dogcatcher, I thought, trying not to laugh. At least *he* had an ID tag.

"I'm looking for Amanda Peabody. She's a volunteer here."

"I haven't seen her yet this morning. We opened a few minutes ago."

"Looks as though these cages could use a good cleaning before the public arrives. The smell is kind of off-putting for potential adopters."

"You with that bunch of animal-rights kooks outside?"

"No." I thought it best not to mention I was doing an exposé in the *Tattler* about the shelter, or he'd have kicked me to the curb with the rest of the animal-rights kooks.

"Good. We've got enough to handle around here without a bunch of troublemakers making things harder for us. What can I do for ya?"

"I'm looking for a dog."

"You've come to the right place, lady. We got plenty of those."

"Too many, from the looks of it."

"We only have so much space for all these strays and not enough funds to keep 'em here for long. You lose a dog?"

"No, someone called and told me you have a basset hound. Female, about a year old."

"Basset hound? Oh, yeah. I remember that one."

"Where is she?"

"In a holding pen . . . at the end of the gray mile." This guy was as bad as Skip with his gallows humor. "This way."

I followed Rex through row upon row of cages, trying not to notice the sea of searching, hopeful eyes that followed me. Every cage held packs of dogs in all sizes and breeds, longhaired, shorthaired, purebreds and mutts, all wanting liberation and love. If I were *bow*lingual, their desperate barking would have translated to "Get us out of here!" I wanted to take them all, but of course I couldn't. I didn't have enough space to start my own kennel. Besides, Cruiser wouldn't hear of it.

Finally, we came to the last row of cages, and like every animal in the shelter, I instinctively understood what awaited them beyond that last wall. A palpable pall of fear and death intermingled with the foul air. I would not be bringing Cruiser inside to meet Calamity. They would have to be introduced elsewhere. I knew it would be far too traumatic for him to enter this place.

"Here she is," Rex said, pointing to a smallish tricolored basset cowering in a far corner of the cage. She had the longest ears I'd ever seen and couldn't have weighed more than thirty pounds. I could count every single rib beneath her dull, dirty coat. If I'd had thimbles I could have played them like a washboard. I tried coaxing her to me with a treat I had stashed in my pocket.

"Calamity. Come, Calamity." She started to respond to me

and made a move to approach me until she spotted Rex. Her lips curled in a warning snarl. Clearly, she was afraid of men. I surmised she had been abused by one at some time or other. Not Rex, I hoped. One often never knows the history of a stray, and with some of the stories I'd heard from members of rescue groups, sometimes it's better not to know. "Can you let me inside the cage with her?"

"I'm not really supposed to, but okay," Rex said. "Be careful, though. She's as snappish as a crocodile."

He unlocked the cage and I stepped inside. Calamity still cowered in the corner, refusing to come to me. Her eyes were fixed on Rex, not on me. I wasn't getting a warm and fuzzy vibe from him, either.

"Would you mind leaving us alone for a while? She seems wary of you."

"Yeah, sure. I've got plenty of other work to do."

I didn't ask what kind of work. I only hoped it was cleaning kennels and feeding and watering the hungry inmates at Lakeside Shelter.

I knelt down so I wouldn't appear so overwhelming to the short-legged dog. Ever viewed the world from the knees up? It must be scary. Coming down to her level instantly seemed to ease her apprehension. After a lot of coaxing, Calamity finally came closer to me. She peered into my eyes with hers, which were the rich color of Hershey's dark chocolate. She edged closer. I held the tidbit far enough out so she could get a good whiff. She sniffed it, snatched the treat, along with nearly a finger or two, and retreated to her corner to devour it.

Under the circumstances, it was hard to tell whether she was exhibiting fear aggression because of being caged or if she would display the same behavior on the other side of the fence. She might require a lot of training and socialization before she could be placed with a family, but that's why I was here—to give her a second chance.

I went to fetch Rex and then had him get a leash so I could spring Calamity from pup prison.

"Here, let me have it." He handed the leash to me. I managed to lasso her before she could slip past me.

"They'll handle everything for you up at the front desk. Then she's all yours. Good luck!" Rex seemed glad to be rid of this thirty pounds of tri-trouble.

Despite her small size, she was as strong as an ox. The little, long-eared locomotive dragged me the length of the shelter toward the double doors leading to the exit. Hunkering as close to the ground as she could get, and with a white stripe down her back, she looked more badger than basset. She instinctively knew the way out of the place and wasted no time in getting us there as quickly as possible.

"Be right back!" I managed to yip to the woman at the front counter before Calamity yanked me out the front door, through the picket line, and across the parking lot. She wanted to get as far away from that death camp as she could. I managed to steer her toward the Jeep, and before she could outmaneuver me, I thrust her into yet another wire cage.

Quickly shutting the door of the sky portable kennel before she could realize where she was and try to escape, I slipped her another tasty treat and tried to reassure her everything would be fine now. She seemed to understand I meant her no harm, although she wasn't too happy about being inside a cage again. I'm sure she was glad to be anywhere else but in the shelter. So was I!

Cruiser was curious about what was going on in the back of the Jeep, but my good dog stayed put. This wasn't the first canine hitchhiker we'd had in the car, so he knew the drill.

"You're okay, Calamity. I'll be back in a few minutes." I gave her another couple of treats to distract her, tossed one to Cruiser too, then went back to the checkout counter to complete the paperwork.

While waiting at the counter, I noticed a very large white German shepherd dog curled in a battered basket beside a desk. Then I noticed the name on a brass nameplate on the desktop, Rhoda Marx. He looked up at me when I approached the desk, then sighed and tucked nose to tail again.

"Sorry to keep you waiting," said Amanda Peabody, who had finally materialized after Rex told her I was looking for her. "Busy day."

"Looks like you have your hands full around here."

Amanda looked flustered as she leafed through files searching for the right form. I attributed her anxiety to the demonstrators outside, and her boss's unexpected absence.

"Yes, we're short-staffed, and people are dropping off way too many animals. It's hard to keep up with everything else there is to do here every day."

"That always seems to happen in the summer at Tahoe."

"The usual problems of kitten season and tourists losing or dumping their dogs don't help matters."

"Beautiful dog," I said. "Whose is he?"

Amanda glanced in the direction of the sleeping shepherd. "Oh, that's Spirit. He belongs to Miss Marx. He's sort of the mascot around here. Good watchdog, too. I feel safe with him around, especially with all the troubles lately."

"I imagine so. He must weigh a hundred twenty pounds at least."

"More like a hundred fifty."

"Puts away a lot of dog chow, I'll bet."

"Yes, but he hasn't touched a drop yet today. It's not like him."

"Thank goodness my rescue dog isn't *that* large."

"I'm glad Jenna sent you, Elsie. It didn't look like this little basset was a good candidate for placement, especially after she failed most of her socialization tests. But I understand you have some experience with rescue dogs, so you might be able to rehabilitate her."

"What kind of tests did they give her?" Amanda didn't know that I was interviewing her too, testing her to see if they really did thoroughly test the dogs for their people skills before giving them a thumbs-up or -down for possible adoption. It was hard for me to stop being a reporter, even for a minute.

"We evaluate how they react to being approached, petted, held down on their back. Do they struggle and squirm or submit when you hold them down? It's a good test for puppies, too. If they struggle, you have a dominant dog that might be difficult to train or control. Also, you want to see if they will respond to any of the basic commands—sit, stay, down. Of course, any demonstration of aggression is considered an automatic elimination. We can determine that pretty quickly by squeezing the tender part of the paw. If the dog tries to nip or bite, that's it. They're pretty strict about that rule here."

It seemed a bit unfair to make life-or-death decisions this way. Dogs might perform better on such tests away from these stressful surroundings.

"So, how'd she do?"

"She didn't react very positively to any of our tests."

"I already noticed that she has some behavior issues. How on earth did you get her exempted for fostering?"

"Again, just lucky. The shelter manager has final approval on all adoptions. If she'd seen how this dog reacted to the tests, it would have been curtains for her. Rhoda didn't show up today, though, so I slipped this one through without her knowing about it. She's such a pretty little girl, and I think she could be a good dog in the right home. Don't blow my cover, okay? I'd lose my job for sure."

"Don't worry, I won't."

"Good, I have a few papers for you to sign, then Calamity is yours." I don't think I imagined the tone of relief I heard in Amanda's voice.

I had finished signing the last of the release papers when my ears were assaulted by a woman's scream that echoed from the far end of the kennel. It could be heard above the frenzied barking and howling of every inmate at Lakeside Animal Shelter.

Amanda and I dashed through the corridors to the source of the hysterical screams. The dogs barked and lunged at the cage doors as we ran past them. Several fights broke out. Even as we reached the far end of the facility, I was still unsure where the sound had come from. Rex abandoned hosing down kennels and the canine combatants inside them and joined us in our search, but the screaming had stopped by the time we arrived. We stood there, listening for another clue of where to look for the source. Someone moaned.

"Did you hear that?" I said.

"Yeah," Amanda said.

Rex pointed to the euthanasia room. "It came from in there."

I'd never before been through the door marked "Kennel Personnel Only," but I knew what went on behind it. Inside the small room was the CO chamber, where the unwanted and the unclaimed met their fate daily. A female kennel attendant was lying motionless beside the death machine. I knelt and felt for a pulse.

"She's okay. She just fainted."

"Why did she faint?" Amanda said.

"She must have seen this," I said, pointing to the viewing panel on the euthanasia chamber.

Inside the chamber lay the lifeless body of Rhoda Marx.

CHAPTER 3

From the time I placed the call, it took Sheriff Cassidy ten minutes to arrive at the crime scene. The protestors froze when they heard the sirens and saw the law arrive. They no doubt assumed the shelter had called in a complaint and the police had come to break up the protest; however, there was far worse trouble at the shelter than anyone could have guessed.

Skip's attractive new deputy, Rusty Cannon, had come along to assist him. What is it with Skip and redheads? First that flirty waitress, Rita Ramirez, and now Rusty. From the look on her face, I could tell this was her first murder detail. In this case, green wasn't a good complementary color for red. *Hope you brought barf bags, Skip.*

Rusty had a name like a pole dancer and a figure to match. She filled out every inch of her uniform. Where was Skip doing his recruiting for the force, Vegas? Knowing Skip, I'm sure he didn't mind having a bodacious crime-scene partner, but right now I had a different kind of body for him to size up.

"What took you so long, Skip? Stop for coffee and Krispy Kremes on the way?"

"Very funny. Where's the stiff?"

"Over there." I pointed toward the euthanasia chamber.

"This is a first. The victim goes to the gas chamber before the killer does." Skip's black brand of humor invariably surfaced at times like these. I was surprised when Rusty didn't laugh at her boss's joke. I would have taken her for the type who would shine up the brass to get ahead in the force. But she seemed more intent on the fact that there was a corpse in the room with us—her first, I surmised as the color drained from her peaches-and-cream complexion. When she clapped a hand to her mouth, I thought she was going to lose it.

"We're not going to need a cleanup on aisle four, are we, Rusty?" Skip said.

She gulped. "No, I'm fine, Chief." Brushing a stray lock of claret hair from her eyes, she slipped on the Latex gloves and got down to the unpleasant business at hand. Perhaps I had misjudged Skip's rookie.

"You found her this way?" Skip said to the still wan-looking kennel attendant who'd had the displeasure of discovering her employer's corpse. She nodded. I could tell he felt empathy for her. He studied her face a few seconds and then glanced down at her name badge, or so it appeared to anyone who doesn't know him as well as I do. Skip is such a pushover for a shapely female. On the other hand, he may have been observing her more as a possible suspect, noting her reaction, her body language, and other behavior.

"Nothing's been touched here. Right, Beanie?"

"Everything's the way we found it."

"I didn't think they still used these contraptions in animal shelters," Skip said as he flipped the latch on the chamber with a gloved hand. When he opened the door, Rhoda's left arm flopped out. It sounded like a wet trout slapping the cold concrete floor. Skip was unperturbed by the sound. He's a veteran fisherman, after all. More than one rainbow trout and Kokanee salmon has met its fate at the end of a hook on one of his many fishing expeditions on the lake in the ol' *Trout Scout*.

"Most don't," I said. "Unfortunately, many municipally funded ones still do."

"We hoped to change over to injection, but it was too

expensive," Amanda said. "There just isn't enough money to do everything you'd like to do."

"Did you know that *euthanasia* means 'good death' in Greek?" Skip liked to make small talk while he was investigating a crime scene, especially if there was a murder victim. It wasn't exactly like whistling while you worked, but the effect was the same. It kept you emotionally detached and allowed you to remain objective. He opened Rhoda's gaping mouth wider. "This definitely wasn't a good death."

"I know," I said. "Death by CO suffocation is cruel, according to the Humane Society of the United States. Sodium pentobarbital is the preferred humane agent for the euthanasia of companion animals."

"Isn't that the same thing they use on death-row inmates?" Rusty asked.

"You're thinking of sodium pentothal, the first of three drugs they administer," Skip said. "It's quick, but some argue it's not painless."

"Who would do something like this?" Amanda said. "I didn't like Rhoda, but she didn't deserve to die like . . . like a dog."

"Some might disagree," I said.

"I don't know who, but it was some dirty dog who had a bone to pick with her," Skip said. "Better secure the crime scene and start lifting some prints off this thing, Rusty."

"Right, Chief."

"Speaking of dogs, I have two waiting for me out in the car," I said. "I'll leave you two to your work. Call me later, Skip? I'll need details for the *Tattler*."

"Sure thing, Beanie."

As I headed for the car, I heard a canine chorus coming from my Jeep. Cruiser and Calamity were trying to out-howl each other. Cruiser was clearly ready to go home. My new adoptee had no more clue where home was than any of us had about why Rhoda Marx met her end the same way Calamity would have, had I not come in time to rescue her from Lakeside Shelter. How could anyone call such an Auschwitz for animals a shelter, anyway? A shelter should be a *no-kill* facility, and everyone at this murder scene would no doubt have agreed that goes for humans and animals alike.

CHAPTER 4

Calamity howled all the way over to the vet clinic, and with Cruiser's baying I had surround hound sound. I understood that she was frightened. She had no idea what else lay in store for her, and if she'd known, she wouldn't have been too happy about it. She needed to have a complete checkup before I took her home. She had soiled her cage in transit. I only hoped this mistake was due to anxiety and not one of the diseases that breed at overcrowded shelters like Lakeside.

By the time a dog arrives in a shelter, it's already been through a lot of trauma. It's been separated from its home, its master, and has probably dodged a few speeding cars, as I'm sure Cruiser had before Tom found him. How he managed to survive life on busy Tahoe streets without becoming road kill, I'll never know. I've seen some strays actually wait for traffic lights to change before crossing streets, but basset hounds aren't known for their road sense. Once a hound sets its nose on the trail of its quarry, be it bunny or bagel, he is oblivious to any possible danger he might encounter along the way.

"How's everything looking with Calamity, Doc?" I said.

"She certainly has a good set of teeth." When Doc Heaton gave Calamity the onceover, she'd tried to nip him twice. Once when he poked her fanny with the thermometer and once when he tried to look down her throat. Fortunately, he was accustomed to uncooperative patients and took her attitude in stride. Once he'd nearly lost the tip of his pinky to a testy terrier. There are worse battle scars to bear than those inflicted by a fearful stray in need of medical assistance. At least those were for a good cause.

"I expect you're not the first to discover that," I said.

He laughed. "This little lady's already been spayed, so you won't have to worry about her giving birth to more little piranha pups."

I love a vet with a good sense of humor.

"She looks to be in good shape, but I did a blood panel and took a stool sample to be sure. Hopefully, she doesn't have heartworm or any other parasites. She's definitely underweight for her size, but with some TLC and a good high-protein diet, she should be back to normal in no time. I expect you'll have her all prettied up in time for the Waddle."

"Cruiser and I will take care of that. He won't mind sharing some of his treats with her." Sure he wouldn't. Who was I kidding?

"I think you'd better hold her head while I give her a couple of little jabs here, Elsie. She's a snappish one."

"I hope that won't cause problems in finding her a good home."

"She'll probably settle down after you get her home."

"I expect so. She's been through a lot." I held Calamity close and braced her head firmly so she couldn't do any more damage to Doc Heaton's fingers. A moment later, she was back in her stinky crate. The vet tech had washed it out, but it still reeked. Fortunately, I had a few spares at home. Once back in the car, the doggie duet resumed. Who needs a boom box when you have two bassets howling in the car?

When I veered into the driveway of the old homestead, the howling stopped. Cruiser was only slightly more relieved to be home than I was. I think we both sensed that some challenges lay ahead for us with this newest rescue dog. Calamity was much more high-strung than the other bassets I'd fostered so far. I already knew that much from her behavior in the shelter and in the car. I could only hope she wouldn't live up to her name. In fact, I had to wonder how she got it in the first place. I cut her some slack because I knew she was scared and had most likely suffered some abuse in her past.

She obviously didn't like men, but I didn't live with one, so that wouldn't be a problem. There was just the occasional visit from Skip and Nona's assortment of boyfriends. What would Nona think of her? She was coming up to Tahoe in time for the Waddle. I was glad, not only because I hadn't seen her in a while, but also because I could use an extra pair of hands to help me manage two dogs in a one-dog household.

I opened up the rear door of the Jeep, hefted the sky kennel out and set it down as gently as I could. Calamity's squirming around made it too difficult to carry her in the cage. Besides, it smelled too bad to take in my house. I hesitated to open the cage door, but I had to in order to slip the lead on her. She could have easily slipped my grip, run away, and ended up right back where she started. Like the other unfortunate basset, she probably wouldn't be so lucky a second time. But she didn't try to get away from me. She was just happy to be out of the cage.

The moment she was out of her crate, that nose started sniffing the trees and bushes. I let her have her head, following her around the yard at the end of the leash. Who was leading whom here? Anyone observing us could tell right away. Cruiser made his customary mark on the old piddling pine tree and shot straight to the back porch. I heard the flap of the dog door and knew I had one less dog to worry about for the moment. I knew he would make a beeline for his raining cats and dogs quilt at the end of my bed. He was already claiming his territory, in case the newcomer might have any confusion as to who was top dog around the MacBean house.

After Calamity had finished her sniff and squat tour of the backyard and rechristened Cruiser's pine tree, I led her inside. She seemed calm enough, so I decided to let her off the leash to explore her new surroundings. I realize only in retrospect that this was my first mistake with Calamity. It was important for her to feel comfortable in my home, but I shouldn't have given her free reign yet. I was accustomed to calmer hounds like my easygoing couch spud, Cruiser. Once released, she hurtled through the house, looking for the quickest way out. I dashed over to Cruiser's dog door, flipped down the security panel and locked it in the nick of time before Calamity found her escape hatch.

Perhaps it was the scent of Cruiser and the lingering aura of other rescued dogs that set off her full-scale panic attack. Or maybe she was looking for her other master or perhaps a sibling or two. Who knows what was going through that pointy little noggin of hers? When she saw there was no escape, she flopped down on her haunches and began to bay mournfully.

To my dog-loving ears, hearing her howl that way was like hearing a lost child crying for its mother, and perhaps that's exactly what it was. I had no doubt she was a puppy mill dog that had been separated from her mother at six weeks of age or even younger. How could anyone at the shelter have expected her to be socialized when all she'd probably ever known in her life was the inside of a cage? Her lament tore at my heart like a pup with an old leather slipper. Only another basset could manage to look any more pitiful than Calamity did at that moment. I tried to soothe her, to distract her with another treat, but it did no good. She wasn't having any of it.

Cruiser came running from my bedroom to see what was the matter. When Calamity saw him coming toward her, she took off in the opposite direction. Thinking this was an invitation to play, Cruiser chased after her, barking and baying his excitement, which only made things worse. Each time they rounded the table, I tried to intercept Calamity or Cruiser, with no success. Between the two of them they upset my furniture and knocked over lamps and broke a couple of vases. By the time I could lasso her again with the leash, the whole place looked like the result of a smash-and-grab home invasion robbery. What had I gotten myself into with this nutty dog?

Exhausted, I sat down on Tom's chair to catch my breath after the doggy decathlon in my living room. The dogs had finally worn themselves down. Cruiser climbed up on the couch and perched on his hair-coated pillow.

"Sit, Calamity!" She had no idea what that command meant, but she was so pooped from the chase she sat anyway. About the time everyone was all settled down, the phone rang. Calamity shot up like she'd gotten another needle jab from Doc Heaton.

"Easy, girl. It's only the telephone." She leapt onto the ottoman, in case Cruiser decided to start chasing her again.

"Hi, Mom. It's me."

"H . . . hi, Nona."

"You sound out of breath. Been out exercising with Cruiser on the mountain trails again?"

"No, I was doing a little indoor exercising with Cruiser and Calamity."

"Calamity? Don't tell me you've taken in another basset boarder."

"Yes, and I think this one's going to live up to her name." I sighed as I surveyed the wreckage in the living room.

"A female this time?"

"Yep."

"That should make Cruiser a happy camper."

"Not thus far. Besides, he's neutered and she's spayed. What's he gonna do?"

Nona laughed.

"You coming up for the Waddle?"

"That's why I was calling you. I'm taking some vacation time. I wanted to be sure you don't mind putting up with me for a while."

"Are you kidding? The question is, will you be able to put up with us?"

Nona's laugh sounded melodic to my ears. As light as wind in aspen trees. "Don't I always?"

"When are you coming?"

"I'll be up late tomorrow."

"No boyfriends tagging along?" Neither of us had forgotten Medwyn's visit one deadly winter.

"Don't sweat it, Mom. It'll be just me this time. Sounds like you have your hands full enough there with Cruiser and Calamity."

I didn't mention the other business at the shelter over the phone. Nona would find out about it soon enough. It would be good to have my lovely daughter here with me again, at least for a little while. She was so busy these days with her modeling career, which often took her abroad, it seemed she came to visit less and less. In years past, she'd spent all her time swimming in the lake, or water skiing on it, and flirting with the beautiful boys of summer. No matter how far away she journeyed, Nona would always return to Tahoe each summer as our Washoe ancestors did.

Since her father had passed away, I was grateful for her company, even if it was only the occasional visit. She is the only family I have left other than Cruiser. Like him, Nona is always there for me, no matter what kind of *calamity* her mother gets mixed up with.

CHAPTER 5

The dogs had finally calmed down, and I started cleaning up the mess they'd made of my house in their mad dash around the place. Fortunately, they'd only broken an inexpensive vase and not any of the priceless Washoe artifacts I keep displayed on shelves in my living room. Good thing bassets are too short to reach very high up, but those long, perpetual-motion tails can do some damage if you're not careful. I keep most of my valuables above tail-wagging level. It's also a good thing Tom left me a little nest egg and the *Tattler* keeps me busy writing articles. At this rate, rescuing rascally hounds could get expensive.

Calamity had conked out on Tom's old ottoman. Her long, long ears enveloped her like a silken blanket. I suspected she was either worn out from the morning's events or she was having a mild reaction to the vaccinations Doc Heaton gave her. I'd seen Cruiser go through this before with his booster shots. Watching her curled up there reminded me of the night Tom arrived on our doorstep with a thin, forlorn-looking stray hound dog. I remembered Cruiser lying on Tom's lap that night and two pairs of sad eyes staring at me with a look that said, "Can I please keep him?" I was powerless to refuse, and I've been a pushover for basset hounds ever since, even when they were the ones doing the pushing over, as they'd done to my furniture during Calamity's calamitous homecoming.

I righted the upset lamp and then busied myself scooping up

shards of broken glass. I feared I might be scooping much more than this after my new adoptee had finished adjusting to her new abode. I didn't even know whether she was house-trained. She'd already had one accident in the car on the way home. *Just tackle one problem at a time, Beanie.*

As I headed to the front closet for the broom, I spotted Skip striding up to my porch. I met him at the door before he could ring the doorbell and get the dogs all riled up again.

"Hi, Beanie. What happened in here? A home invasion?"

"You could say that."

The moment Calamity heard Skip's voice she barked her alarm, launched from the ottoman, and shot down the hallway. I didn't have the energy to chase after her again, so I let her go. Things could have been worse; at least she wasn't attacking my houseguest. It was clear to me by now that she had some serious issues with men. Cruiser, on the other hand, looked up, saw it was Skip, thumped his tail twice on the sofa, then went back to snoring and his dream of chasing rabbits in an alpine meadow.

"At least one dog here is happy to see me. Sort of."

"Don't mind Cruiser. Our new houseguest wore him out. It's been a stressful morning for all of us."

"You can say that again." Skip sat down next to Cruiser and stroked his head. I was glad Cruiser still had a male influence in his life. It was clear that despite the slobber, Skip didn't mind being his step dog-dad. Cruiser grunted his pleasure at the attention he was getting and rested his chin on Skip's knee for better stroking advantage.

"Finished up at the shelter, Skip?"

"Yeah, this was my first experience with euthanasia."

"Lucky you," I said. "I only wish it was the same for Lakeside Shelter. I agree with TAILS. Lakeside doesn't deserve to be called a shelter. They destroy far more animals than they place in homes, and the rest go to research labs. A shelter should be a no-kill facility. Period!"

"You can never call it that now. Not after today."

"That's for doggone sure." Skip may have his black humor as a release valve for defusing tense situations, but I have my canine quips.

"So, any ideas who might have had a grudge against Rhoda Marx?"

"You mean besides every animal lover in Tahoe?"

"Made a few enemies along the way, huh?"

"Yeah, thanks in part to the *Tattler* and a certain reporter who shall remain nameless."

"I guess it kind of goes with that line of work. Nobody loves the dogcatcher."

"It's a hard job, I'm sure. I couldn't do it, that's for certain. It's tough enough going down there to rescue the dogs. If I worked there, I'd end up with my own animal shelter full of stray dogs and cats. Not to mention the bunnies that get dumped after Easter."

"I'm sure Cruiser would love for you to adopt bunnies. He's not allergic to them like I am."

"I didn't know you were allergic to bunnies, Skip. Does this mean you've cancelled your subscription to *Playboy*?"

When Skip blushed, his freckles were like seeds on a strawberry. Embarrassed, he quickly changed the subject. "People who work in shelters get a bad rap sometimes, kind of like peace officers do. We're just doing our jobs, after all."

"Yeah, nobody likes the dogcatcher, but they're only cleaning up the mess left by folks who don't spay and neuter their pets or who buy pets on a whim without considering the responsibility that goes with caring for one. Sometimes the rap is well deserved, though, as in Marx's case. She's handled things badly with the public, shelter personnel, and especially rescue groups, and the animals have paid for her mistakes."

"So did she." As Skip talked, Cruiser turned belly up for a tummy rub. No point in wasting an opportunity for a full body massage.

For some reason, the talk of Playboy bunnies brought Skip's new partner to mind. "How'd Rusty do at the crime scene this morning?"

"I don't know. I'm still trying to decide."

"What do you mean?"

"We had a disagreement about proper procedure, and I had to step in and take over. She didn't appreciate being dressed down on the job."

"That's too bad." I felt immediate empathy for Rusty. I'd had bosses who did the same thing and made me feel foolish in front of my peers. "Couldn't you have talked to her about it later?"

"If a rookie is doing something wrong, I can't let her foul up evidence. She needs to learn to check her ego at the door when we enter a crime scene."

"I suppose you're right. What was the problem, though?"

"At first I thought she was missing evidence, but she insisted she'd done it correctly. I guess she was, because when I dusted the chamber for prints, I got the same result."

"What?"

"We found those of Rhoda Marx and a couple of other shelter personnel."

"That's not surprising. They work there and have probably operated the machine."

"I know that, but there were other prints we couldn't explain."

"What prints?"

Skip had a funny look on his face, and at first I thought he was jerking my choke chain when he said, "We found dog prints."

"What other kinds of prints would you expect to find at an animal shelter?"

"The thing is, the prints weren't inside the thing. We found paw prints on the outside, even on the door handle."

"I'm not sure what you're suggesting."

"Neither am I. Perhaps we'll know more when the full report is in and we've been able to question some of the shelter staff more thoroughly. Rusty is signed up for a training class for the next couple of weeks."

"Sending her back to rookie school already?"

He laughed. "No, it's one of those employee relations things they make us all attend to keep Internal Affairs happy. I was hoping maybe you can help me out a bit in her absence, if your busy writing schedule allows."

"Sure. Actually, it should fit right in with my busy writing schedule. I have to keep Carla at the *Tattler* happy, too. Let me know the medical examiner's findings on Rhoda when you get them, will you?"

"Will do. I expect his report should be on my desk soon. Hope so, anyway. The caseload has been getting backed up lately with all the summer drug activity."

"I've never understood why people would need drugs at Tahoe. This scenic place is all the drug anyone could ever need."

"What was that stuff your grandpa used to smoke in that ceremonial pipe of his?"

"Watch it, paleface. I'll have to sic our tribal watchdogs on you."

"Please, these two watchdogs are enough for me. Besides, I suppose everyone has to have his drug of choice. As for me, I'll take caffeine."

"I'll brew us a fresh pot of coffee if you like."

"Don't bother. I really should be getting back. I'll grab some java on the way back to the office."

"You're going to leave me here with this vicious beast? Some public protector you are, Skip."

Skip laughed. "Don't forget you have your trusty sidekick, Cruiser. He's been known to back you up in a tight spot from time to time. And now you have Calamity, too."

"Yeah, double trouble." I wasn't sure if Cruiser was going to be much help to me in taming the little four-legged, long-eared shrew I'd rescued. Like Skip, Cruiser is a pushover for a pretty face.

"This is quite a mess you have here to clean up," Skip said, surveying my disheveled room. "Are you sure you haven't gotten in over your head with this new dog of yours?"

"Could be." Skip is a master at stating the obvious, but what he had told me about the evidence surrounding the death of Rhoda Marx promised to be an even bigger mess to clean up. "I need to get this place tidied up before Calamity makes another one. Besides, Nona's coming up soon for a visit, and I don't want the place looking like a wreck."

"Whew, it's a wreck all right, I've seen tidier smash and grabs."

A smash from the back bedroom accented Skip's words as though he'd cued the action.

"What was that?" Skip instinctively slapped his holster, ready to draw his weapon.

"Calamity!" I yelped, dashing down the hallway with Skip and Cruiser hot on my heels.

CHAPTER 6

"It's a smash and grab, for sure," I said when I saw the basket I'd painstakingly assembled for the Waddle overturned on the floor. The perpetrator was still at the scene of the crime, gutting the basket of its yummy contents. Calamity had torn open the bags of carob-chip cookies, gobbled them down and was proceeding to rip apart the one filled with Cruiser's favorite, Bacon Beggin' Strips. And in case any canine crime scene investigator might wonder who had perpetrated the deed, her carob-coated muzzle was evidence enough of having committed the offense. "Caught in the act, Calamity!"

"I see now why you named her that."

"I didn't. She came with the name."

"It's perfect for this dog." Skip eyed this scene in the same way he assesses any other crime scene, including the one he encountered at the shelter, noting every minute detail. Was he going to dust for paw prints here, too? I halfway expected him to pull out his handcuffs and read Calamity her rights.

"That's really all I know about her, though. I have absolutely no information about her health history or where she came from, but from what I've seen thus far, I suspect she's probably damaged goods. She may have been abused in her former home. I think I really have my work cut out for me."

"How could anyone ever think of mistreating a basset hound? I mean, get a load of that innocent face."

"I suspect you'll find a pair of devil horns poking up beneath that hound halo of hers.”

Despite visible evidence to the contrary, Calamity was the picture of innocence, all right, but I knew from past experience that inside the head of the basset is a cunning mind that will stop at nothing to obtain the desired objective, which is usually food. I had no doubt she was plotting her next domestic exploit as we spoke.

“I can’t imagine how a beautiful dog like this could end up dumped at a shelter.”

“It happens more often than you’d care to know, Skip. Mostly, people can’t deal with that hound stubborn streak. Bassets are single-minded when in the pursuit of a scent trail.”

“Like pursuit of a stash of treats, you mean.”

“I’ll say! It does make them a bit harder to train than some breeds, and folks too frequently mistake a basset’s stubbornness for stupidity. Some don’t like their howling, either. It’s not music to everyone’s ears like it is to mine.” When I reached for the Beggin’ Strips, my gesture was met with a warning growl.

“Careful, Beanie. I think she means to keep her prize.”

“Uh-oh. Looks like we have some food-guarding issues, too.” In spite of Calamity’s threats, I called her bluff and managed to nab the last bit of evidence away from her before she ingested it bag and all, with a finger or two for dessert. I didn’t need more vet bills for an attack of pancreatitis.

“It’s my fault. I shouldn’t have left the basket within easy reach. She’s probably starved. I should have offered her some kibble right away when I brought her home, but I got distracted.”

“She does look a little underfed.”

“I know. She’s underweight for her size, so she’s not been getting enough food. Someone probably dumped the poor girl in the backyard and forgot about her. It’s going to take a little creativity at mealtimes, though. I have two dogs with different dietary needs, and I can't keep kibble available for Cruiser all the time or he'll inflate like a zeppelin."

"He's sure come a long way from when you first got him."

"Amazing what a little TLC can do, isn't it? After a few weeks with us, he was a different dog. He looked more like Calamity does now when he first came here. I hope I can work the same magic with this dog. It's going to take more than a new diet, I think, to make a new dog out of *her.*"

"I'll leave you two to your tug of war. I have a mounting caseload waiting for me back at the office and a new deputy to break in. As if I really needed a murder investigation on top of it all. And I think this one is going to be a real dog."

"I suppose that's to be expected with a murder at the dog pound."

CHAPTER 7

Mealtimes at the MacBean house kennel had suddenly become more complicated, as I discovered on the morning following Calamity's arrival. Now there were two mouths to feed different canine cuisine. Cruiser and I were on a low-cal diet, but my anorexic adoptee needed a dietary regimen to help her quickly put on weight and get prettied up for possible adoption at the Waddle. Judging from the raffle basket incident, she wasn't a picky eater. Is there any such thing in Bassetdom? If there was, I hadn't yet encountered one.

All I had at the house was Cruiser's diet kibble to feed her that morning, which she gobbled with gusto, but I'd have to pay a visit to the pet store to pick up some special food for my new boarder. I decided to leave the dogs behind this time, but I couldn't trust Calamity not to get into trouble again. I tried to coax her into the crate, but she wasn't having anything further to do with cages of any kind. After her experience at the shelter, I can't say I blamed her. So I left her locked in the spare bedroom. Only this time I made sure there was nothing else she could get in to.

The moment I led her into the room and shut the door behind me, she began barking her head off. Calamity's bark was nothing like Cruiser's, which was deep, melodious, and pleasant to the ear. Hers was a sharp, hysterical yelp. *Oh, great,* I thought. *Separation anxiety, too.* This dog was a furry funhouse of troubles. I assumed that she'd settle down after I left. I was so wrong. I

43

could still hear her yapping as I backed out of the drive and drove down the street. Poor Cruiser. He wouldn't be getting any sleep while I was gone.

Sally Applebaum, the owner of the Haute Hydrant, is active in all the local pet causes, including Found Hounds. She was donating a lot of merchandise to our upcoming fundraiser and would be providing numerous raffle items, including dog beds, coats and sweaters and, of course, plenty of treats. Sally is a whole lot of woman with a super-sized heart to match.

"Hello, Beanie!" Sally chirped her usual friendly greeting as I entered the shop. Summer roses flowered on her full cheeks when she smiled. Fabian, Sally's adored Yorkie and official store Welcome Waggin', trotted over to me and sniffed the bouquet of basset on my pants leg. He recognized Cruiser's scent from past visits to the store, but the new Eau de Calamity made him linger a bit longer than usual.

"Hi, Sally. How's the pet biz?"

"It's been quieter than usual, but then Sundays are always a bit slow." I knew Sally was being her cheery, optimistic self, although a little positive thinking never hurts in hard times. The economic slump hit small shops like hers hard. Less money in people's pockets meant less money to spend on their pets, and the Haute Hydrant wasn't the only one in Tahoe feeling the crunch. Even chain stores like the new Petropolis on the North Shore were tightening their collars a few notches to make ends meet. "Need more diet kibble already for that chow hound of yours?"

"No, he's got plenty of that. I need to add some weight, not take it away."

"I know you don't mean Cruiser, so I'm guessing you must have taken in another foster." Sally motioned for me to come with her. I followed her to the aisle where she kept the dog food. There were so many brands to choose from, I'd have never been able to make a choice as quickly as she could. Sally knows more bits about kibble than anyone. I trusted that she'd pick the perfect nutritional food for my new foster dog. I didn't want to stay away too long, in case Calamity was getting into any more mischief in my absence.

"Yep. This one's going to be a handful, I can tell. It's no wonder that no one had adopted her yet at Lakeside Animal Shelter."

"It's a wonder anyone ever adopts a pet from that place. And they don't give people half a chance to adopt the ones that are adoptable."

"I always thought they held them a couple of weeks."

"Most people assume that, and they don't want the public to know the truth. Much of the time animals are destroyed before they can even be evaluated and put up for adoption."

"I had no idea."

"Some animals are only in there for a few hours. No one even has a chance to see them. Small dogs and purebreds stand a better chance of adoption, but bully breeds are dead on arrival. No one adopts the pits and Rotties. Cats stand hardly any chance at all."

"That's a crying shame, Sally."

"Sure is. Something has got to change. There are too many pets coming in, too little space, and too few personnel. That's why volunteers are so important, but they can't even keep volunteers there for long. Not now, anyway."

"Why is that?"

"Things changed for the worse after that horrid Marx woman came on board as manager. She's a cold one."

"You can say that again." Sally didn't know just how cold Rhoda was now.

"If you dare to offer a dissenting opinion, Medusa Marx can turn you to stone with a glance. I volunteered there for years, but finally I couldn't take it anymore. From what I hear, things haven't improved any since I left. In fact, they even have a hard time keeping paid employees on the staff for more than a few months at a time. I don't know how people can stand to work there day in and day out and see what goes on behind closed doors. It's a disgrace."

"Things are even worse there now."

"What do you mean?"

"Someone died."

"What happened? Don't tell me someone finally gave Rhoda Marx her comeuppance?"

"That's exactly what I'm telling you. Her death is being investigated as a homicide. How did you know the victim was Rhoda Marx? It hasn't even been reported in the papers yet."

"Lucky guess. Everyone who ever worked with Rhoda hated her like poison."

"Sounds like you didn't like her much, either." It took me by surprise to hear my friend even utter the word *hate*. It was so un-Sally-like.

"I'm just saying that she could be very unpleasant when she wanted to be, which was most of the time, according to her co-workers. I once saw her reduce one of her female employees to tears, then say to her, 'I'll have no crybabies on my staff.' "

"Who was that?"

"Can't recall. She left the shelter shortly afterward."

"I'm sure there are disgruntled employees in every office, but who would hate Rhoda enough to want to kill her?"

Sally didn't look up from the cash register as she punched in the price code for my bag of Wholesome Hound kibble. "Who wouldn't?"

CHAPTER 8

As I drove back to the cabin, Sally Applebaum's comments roiled in my brain like the summer storm clouds on the horizon. The cool breeze wafting through my car window had grown cold and, like Sally's words, sent a chill clattering up my spine like a row of kennel doors clanging shut. I had seen a dark side of my friend, who for as long as I'd known her had always kept her sunny side up.

Perhaps her uncharacteristic negativity was also a symptom of our troubled times. Too many people. Too little money. Too much traffic, noise, and pollution. Too many animals and not enough homes for them all. But no one ever expects things to turn deadly, even when they do.

Seeing Nona's bright yellow Volkswagen beetle parked in my driveway scattered my depressing thoughts like the V of geese fleeing the gathering storm. Hooray! Nona was here! Things would be better now. Like Cruiser, I am always happier when the pack at the MacBean house is complete.

The first drops of rain drummed a lively tattoo on the car roof as I hefted from the car the bag of dog chow and other goodies I'd bought at the Haute Hydrant.

"Need any help with that, Mom?"

"No, thanks, honey. I've got it."

"Better hurry, it's starting to rain."

"Coming!" I made it to the front door as the first rumbles of thunder volleyed overhead and the heavens opened up. I could think of nothing better than Nona and me chatting over some hot tea during a summer storm. We had some catching up to do, but first things first. Some introductions were in order. I only hoped Calamity would be more congenial to Nona than she'd been to Skip.

"Come give your mom a big hug, Papoose."

Nona and I gave each other bear hugs. She felt like a sparrow in my arms.

"Have you given up eating altogether? You can carry that skinny model stuff too far, you know."

"It's hard finding time to eat on my crazy schedule."

"Well, you've got some time off now, so I'll put some meat on those bones while you're here."

When Nona didn't reply, I knew I was in danger of crossing the badger barrier, so I changed the subject. I didn't want to chase her off the moment she arrived. This time I wanted her here for a good, long stay.

"How was your drive up the hill?"

"Fine, except for the usual traffic hang-up at Placerville."

"Why do you think they called it Hangtown? Have you already met Cruiser's and my new roomie?"

"Yeah. She was shrieking like a teakettle when I got here. She calmed down after I let her out of the back room, though."

"Oh, no! You let her out? And she didn't tear the place apart?"

"No, she's fine now. I gave her the rest of the sandwich I had left over from lunch. She wolfed it down, then fell sound asleep."

"Where is she?"

"She's lying on your bed, where Cruiser usually sleeps."

"Uh-oh. His Lordship may not take too kindly to that. I expect I'll have to come up with other sleeping arrangements while she's staying here."

"Speaking of teakettles, how about brewing us some tea, Mom?"

"Sure, as soon as I restock the pup pantry. Earl Grey okay?"

"Perfect."

I stashed Calamity's kibble beside Cruiser's low-cal variety in the Yum-Yum Nook. You can always tell when you're in the home of a dog lover. There's more food and treats stored in the larder for the pets than for the people. My pantry resembled the shelves at the Haute Hydrant. The bottom shelf held a variety of canned food in nearly every flavor, from trout to turducken, to appease Cruiser's discriminating palate. On the second shelf I kept all the sundry canine remedies: ear washes, sprays, ointments, pills and such. And on the top shelf, out of basset-raiding range, were the treats.

So far, Cruiser hadn't discovered how to use a chair to reach the uppermost shelf, although I've heard of bassets that have. One dog pushed a chair up to the kitchen counter one Christmas, climbed atop it, and not only demolished a standing prime rib roast but also tossed holiday hors d'oeuvres onto the floor for the rest of his low-slung cohorts in crime.

Satisfied that everything was stashed safely away, I brewed some tea for Nona and me. By the time the kettle whistle shrieked, arrows of rain pelted the kitchen window. I flicked on the kitchen light when the storm's full fury blackened the skies to obsidian.

I handed Nona her special cup with the cross-country skiers on it. "Here's your tea, dear."

"Thanks." She took a long, slow sip and smiled at me. I noticed that her gingersnap eyes didn't have quite the same spice to them as I remembered. "I'm so glad you were able to find another cup like the one that broke. I loved that cup."

"I know. You'd had it since you were a child. Your grandma let you use it when we used to come up and visit. That's why I tried so hard to search for another cup just like it. Finally found one at a thrift shop."

"Gosh, it feels good to be here again. Sitting down with you over tea and chatting about old times is so comforting."

"I'm glad you're here. It gets pretty lonely here sometimes without you."

"If only Dad were here too, everything would be perfect, like it was before . . ." Nona's eyes misted. "I sure do miss him sometimes."

"Me too, honey. I still expect to see him sitting in that old easy chair reading his paper, or sometimes, when Cruiser barks and runs to the door, I think it must be your father coming home for supper, but of course, it never is. Usually, it's Skip, which is almost as good in Cruiser's estimation."

"He loves Skip nearly as much as he did Dad."

"I know. That's why I keep him around." I laughed.

"Who? Cruiser or Skip? They're both your partners in crime." Nona didn't know the half of it.

"You might as well tell me what's going on, Mother. I'll read all about it in the *Tattler,* anyway." There was no fooling Nona. She could read her mom like a dog-eared book. "Please don't tell me you're mixed up in another murder investigation."

"All right. I won't tell you."

"Be serious. You know I'll ask Skip if you won't tell me."

"If you want to play Truth or Dare, Nona, I'm game. I'll tell you the truth about what's going on in my life, but I dare you to tell me the same about your own." There's more than one way to nose into my daughter's life.

Nona picked up her cup of tea and took another sip before answering. "Okay, but you first."

I took a few sips of my cooling Earl Grey before our mother-daughter powwow commenced. For several minutes the room was silent except for the steady drumbeat of rain on the roof and the click of toenails on linoleum. One way or the other, calamity was about to befall me.

CHAPTER 9

I was actually relieved when Calamity charged into the kitchen, looking for more trouble to get into. She was a welcome distraction because I knew Nona wasn't going to like what I was about to tell her. Namely, how another newspaper assignment for the *Tattler* had gotten her mother involved in much more than researching and typing an article. I know she worries about me almost as much as I worry about her when we're apart.

Before I could stop her, Calamity made a beeline for Cruiser's Yum-Yum Nook. I had left the door ajar and her keen nose led her straight to the third shelf, the treat treasure trove. Far more agile than Cruiser, she stretched her full length, easily reaching the bag of Bacon Beggin' Strips she'd ripped open before.

"Oh no you don't!" I intercepted the bag mid-snatch as she snapped at empty air. I held the bag high over my head, shifting it from hand to hand as she leapt repeatedly to gain the prize. For a moment we must have looked like a pair of basketball players scuffling there in the pantry, with me guarding the home cupboard advantage. Only when I dropped the ball, or in this case, treat, did she retreat from her offense. Game won, Calamity trotted off with her bacon strip.

Exhausted, I flopped down in my chair. "Now, where were we? Oh, yes . . ."

Nona listened without comment while I told her about my activities at the shelter and the discovery of Rhoda Marx's body. I think Nona is secretly proud of her mom's reputation in Tahoe

as not only a stringer for a newspaper but a respected and intuitive crime-solver.

"All right, Nona, I've told you everything. Now it's your
turn. So spill." My mind raced faster than the wind in the pines
outside my cabin as I wondered what my daughter was about to
tell me. Was it a new boyfriend? Was she dating a nice man this
time? Could she even be getting engaged to be married? Then
my mind wrapped around all the negative possibilities. Was she
finally migrating across a vast ocean to Europe to pursue her
blossoming career as a supermodel? Was she pregnant? Nothing
I imagined could have prepared me for what my only daughter
was about to say.

"I found a lump, Mom."

A lump clotted in my throat at the mere mention of the word.
Finally, I managed to squeak out, "A lump? Where?"

"Right here." There was a lump all right. It felt about the size
of a pea.

"Did you have a mammogram?"

"Yes. And an ultrasound, too. Inconclusive. Next up is a
biopsy."

"When?"

"I was supposed to go next week, but I decided to come up
here instead. I wanted to talk to you about it first, Mom."

Nona rarely asked for my advice in her life decisions. I was
honored that she was asking now; I only wished it had been
about anything but this. I hadn't known how to respond when
my own mother had told me she had cancer. All I could recall
about that terrible moment, still frozen in my memory, was feeling like I'd been trampled by a herd of buffalo. I felt the same
way now.

Neither of us dared utter the "C" word, but it hovered in the
room with us like the blackest thundercloud.

"Try not to worry. It might be nothing, dear. Not all lumps

are malignant. False-positive mammograms are pretty common. You've been under a lot of stress with your career. It could just be a clogged gland or a cyst." I knew even as I said it that I was trying harder to convince myself than her that everything was okay.

"You're probably right." The furrows of worry in Nona's brow could have rivaled a basset hound's.

"Maybe you should have gone ahead and had the biopsy, to be certain. At least you'd know one way or the other. It's best not to delay too long with these things."

"I know I probably should have, and the doctors were pressuring me to have it done. I guess I'm afraid of what they might tell me. If it is malignant, I'm not sure what course I would pursue. White man's medicine is bad. You've said it yourself."

"I know." I remembered how my mother had suffered toward the end of her illness. The standard slash, burn, poison method of cancer treatment hadn't worked for her. The cancer returned despite every painful, invasive procedure the doctors subjected her to. Only when in desperation we turned to the old ways was she able to find any relief from her affliction and live out what time she had relatively pain-free. Her final days had been spent peacefully in her own home surrounded by the familiar things of her life and her loved ones, instead of at a cancer clinic undergoing endless grueling treatments. But Nona was young, too young to be diagnosed with cancer.

"I want to see a tribal doctor, Mother. Can you arrange it for me?"

"Of course, honey." Naturally, I understood that this meant I'd have to seek help from my old rival, Sonseah Little Feather, but I'd do it—for Nona's sake.

Chapter 10

It wasn't only the sultry summer storm that kept me awake that night, tossing and turning until I was wrapped in a cocoon of covers. Poor Cruiser grunted his displeasure about having to shift his position every time I did. My mind raced with worry. If thoughts about what Nona had told me weren't enough to keep me wide awake, there was always my restless rescue and an unsolved murder.

At bedtime, I had to dose Calamity with some Rescue Remedy because the thunderstorm was freaking her out. She shivered and shook with fear until the herbal cocktail began to take effect. I began to wonder how many more issues came in this little basset basket case. Perhaps I'd take a dose of the stuff myself, since it also works to soothe stressed-out humans. I tried coaxing Calamity into her crate, first with a Beggin' Strip, a spoonful of peanut butter, even a sample of imported cheese. It was useless. She refused to set one paw inside it. I knew it wouldn't work to have her sleep with Cruiser at the foot of my bed. He wouldn't stand for it. Besides, with two big basset hounds stretched across the bed, where would I sleep?

I understood that she was disoriented and confused. After being shuffled around so much in her short life, how could she possibly know where home was, or even *what* home was? People have no conception of the harm they inflict on these sensitive, domesticated creatures when they tire of the puppy they got for Christmas or the one they fell for in the pet store window, then toss them aside like yesterday's broken toys. By the time a dog has spent time chained in the backyard and ultimately surrendered and impounded, they truly are broken, in body and spirit.

I prepared a bed on the floor in my room for Calamity and she stayed there, for a little while. Next thing I knew there was a cold nose nudging my hand. Apparently, not even natural herbs were a sure remedy to completely soothe her nerves tonight. Or mine.

"Go lie down, Calamity!" She did, for a little while. Then she began exploring the bedroom for something to get into. I heard the rustle of paper and knew she'd found the trashcan. I led her over to her bed and stroked her, talking softly, trying to get her calmed down and more relaxed in her surroundings.

"Now, stay. Go to sleep, girl." She obeyed my command until I had slid under the covers, then she was up like a shot, nosing into something else. I began to think I was fostering a ferret. She was certainly more nocturnal than Cruiser, who was snoring blissfully on his quilt at the foot of the bed. Even when a volley of thunder crashed, he never flicked an eyelash. Calamity, on the other hand, was terrified. I managed to calm her down again, but when she wouldn't stay in her bed, in desperation I took her bedding out to the living room and got her settled out there. I went back to bed and shut the door. It was quiet, at least for a moment or two. I had just closed my eyes when I heard her scratching and whining at my door.

"*No!*" I repeated it once or twice and then I heard nothing more from her. With the house finally silent, I soon slipped off to sleep, snoring in concert with Cruiser . . .

My mother and I were hiking up the trail together behind the cabin, as we often did when she was alive. Night blanketed the mountain as we headed for a tribal gathering. Mom held my hand, as she had from the time I was a child, guiding me, leading me, always in the direction I should go in life. Cruiser was there too, trudging along beside us while sniffing and marking the wild scents among the scrub.

Somewhere along the trail, Nona emerged from the pines and joined us. She wore the ceremonial costume young girls of our tribe are dressed in when they die. Her pristine white buckskin dress shimmered like a ghost in the moonlight. She clutched a shield of beautiful Washoe basketwork to her breast. We climbed to the crest of the mountain, where a bonfire was blazing. The glow could be seen from a great distance. Then I heard coming from far off the criers, women who moaned and cried night and day for the dead. Their mournful wails echoed through the forest.

When we arrived at the campfire, Nona handed the basket to me. It was the finest of basketry, expertly woven, like the baskets of Dat-so-la-lee, whose work is still prized for its intricacy and beauty. My mother and I filled the basket with healing, medicinal plants, and then handed it back to Nona. She set it on a rock beside the fire and the three of us danced around the fire while the singers grunted, as the Washoe call the singing on such tribal occasions.

The wailing of the women grew louder and louder, then suddenly it was not women I heard crying but a cacophony of dogs howling. It seemed like I was at Lakeside Shelter, walking down the aisle that led to the euthanasia chamber. Every dog in the place was howling and yapping. Something was terribly wrong, but what was it? What were they trying to tell me? In my dream and even when I awoke drenched in sweat, my heart thudding in my breast like a drumbeat, I understood that this was a warning of danger.

CHAPTER 11

Morning came too quickly. My bloodshot eyes matched Cruiser's. Drooping red haws, typical of the basset hound, always make him look like someone's been spiking his water bowl. Spending a restless night in my bed with me doing a war dance sure hadn't helped matters any.

"Come on, boy. Time to rise and shine." Cruiser groaned his displeasure at my wakeup call and eased off the edge of the bed. Suddenly, I remembered that there were now two hounds in the house. Where was the other one? Oh, yeah. I'd locked her out of the bedroom so Cruiser and I could get some sleep. Heaven only knew what she'd gotten into in the rest of the house during the night. I was afraid to find out, but I opened the bedroom door, ready to face the damage. No Calamity. Cruiser ambled past me toward the kitchen to seek out the next most important thing in his world besides sleep . . . food.

I followed my hungry hound down the hall and into the living room but found neither hide nor hair of Calamity. Had I forgotten to lock Cruiser's dog door after he went out at bedtime? If so, my new foster was no doubt long gone, and the way I was feeling this morning I wasn't sure I'd have been too broken-hearted about it. It's not that I minded having more than four paws pattering around the place. I've had several dogs at once before, and I say the more the merrier, and the hairier. What does it matter that furballs the size of Sasquatch lurk in every corner of my house? That's the price of puppy love.

Nonetheless, I had to admit that this dog was far more of a challenge than I was accustomed to. Cruiser had blended right into our lives as though he'd always lived here. Not so, Calamity.

The dog door was secured, so I felt assured that she hadn't escaped. I crept back down the hall and peeked in the open door of the guest bedroom where Nona slept whenever she visited. She was turned away from me, facing the mirrored closet door. Her luxuriant chestnut hair draped the pillow like a red satin ribbon. I could see in the reflection that she was still sound asleep. No sign of my adoptee, though, or at least that's what I thought until I glimpsed two russet heads instead of one poking out from under the duvet. Calamity was tucked under the covers right beside Nona with her pointy noggin resting on the fluffy feather pillow like a princess. When I clucked my tongue in amusement, and mild exasperation at the drool I was sure to find caked on my brand new duvet, a shiny black nose popped out from under the covers. Calamity reared up and cast me a coy backward glance, no doubt gloating at me for having succeeded in worming her way into someone else's warm bed for the night.

I tried without success to coax her out of the bed without waking Nona. I beckoned in a whisper, "Calamity, come," but she wasn't about to budge an inch from her cozy cocoon. I couldn't really blame her. She'd probably known little enough comfort thus far in her young life, so I wasn't about to deny her that for the sake of a washable bedspread.

I had resigned myself to let them both sleep undisturbed when the phone jangled an alarm. I hurried to snatch it from the cradle before it rang again. I knew Nona needed her beauty rest, and Calamity, too.

"Hello?"

"Hi, Elsie, it's Jenna. I just got a frantic call from Amanda Peabody at the shelter."

"What's wrong?"

"She says someone broke into the shelter last night. All the dogs are gone!"

"Gone? How strange. Any idea who might have done this?"

"She's pretty sure it's the TAILS activists."

"Seems likely, since they've been threatening to take action if conditions at the shelter don't improve. What can I do to help?"

"See if you can find out for sure who's behind this, and if you should see any strays running loose around town, let me know right away. We'll take them in, and I'll try to get them fostered instead of letting the dogcatcher take them back to the shelter."

"How many fugitives are we looking for?"

"A couple dozen. I'll get descriptions of the dogs from Amanda. She'll help us out as much as she can. She's been working on building an adoption Web site to find homes for strays."

"Okay, I'll keep an eye out."

"Thanks, Elsie." The line clicked.

"Who was that?" Calamity plodded at Nona's heels when she came into the kitchen.

"Jenna Fairbanks, one of the volunteers with Found Hounds."

"Oh, yeah. That's the rescue group you got this dog from."

"Right." My rescue remorse was growing worse by the day.

"Got any coffee brewed, Mom?"

"Not yet. I'll start some. Did you sleep well last night with your furry friend?"

"Snug as a bug in a rug."

"Don't you mean like a basset in a blanket?"

Nona laughed. "She would have whined at the bedroom door all night if I hadn't let her in. It was the only way to shut her up."

"I know. Cruiser and I thank you, even if my new duvet is ruined."

"Sorry. I invited her onto my robe at the foot of the bed, but she obviously had other ideas."

"That's okay. I don't have anything around this house that isn't washable because drool rules here. I'm just glad we all finally got some sleep."

"Once she curled up next to me, she settled right down."

"It was probably the beat of your heart that calmed her."

"I never thought of that. That must be why they always say to put a ticking clock and a hot water bottle in with a new puppy. The pup thinks it's his mother."

"It's even better if they wrap the heated bottle in an old piece of fur. They settle right down. If she's like most rescues, she is probably a product of a puppy mill. They are taken from their mothers and litter mates at far too young an age, and all kinds of health and socialization problems result from it."

"Poor things. Gosh, you don't think she thinks I'm her mother, do you?"

"Could be. You're not very furry, though." Nona giggled and stroked Calamity. "She appears to be bonding with you much more than she has with me thus far. And she didn't take to Skip at all. Doesn't seem to like men, from what I've noticed."

"Smart dog." Nona's experiences with men hadn't been much better than Calamity's had. Perhaps they had more in common than she thought. The dog rested her chin on Nona's knee. "She sure is a needy little girl, isn't she? I guess her whole life has been a calamity up until now."

"Unfortunately." At the mention of her name, Calamity tried to jump in Nona's lap.

"Tell her 'off.' Good a time as any to start teaching her some manners."

"Why don't I just say 'down,' instead?"

"Because when you teach her to lie down, you'll use that command. She would get confused if you used the same command for both behaviors."

Nona said the word in her soft, sweet voice. "This one isn't working, either." They looked like they were in a boxing match as she tried to push the dog away. Calamity kept coming at her, sparring to gain the upper paw. I grabbed a couple of treat tidbits and placed them in Nona's hand.

"Now, repeat the command again, but this time say it louder and stronger. Be like an eagle, not a sparrow. The moment she obeys, give her a treat and praise her like crazy."

It took a few more tries, but finally stubborn Calamity obeyed Nona's command and stayed put. "It worked!"

"Well done. Maybe I can persuade you to take her to obedience school for me while you're here."

"Ha, ha. Very funny, Mother."

"Why not? She obviously likes you, and she'll need to pass obedience training before she can be placed in a permanent home."

"I'm no dog trainer. I've never even had a dog before. You know that."

I blamed myself for neglecting to introduce my daughter to a puppy when she was little. Dogs teach a child so many valuable lessons a parent can't. "You never know, you might meet some handsome young dog at the class." I could almost see the manhunt gears engage in Nona's brain. That suddenly put an entirely different spin on things.

"I'll think about it. By the way, I overheard some of your conversation on the phone earlier. Is there more trouble over at the shelter?"

"I'm afraid so."

"It's not another . . ."

"No, no. Not that. Someone broke into the shelter last night and released all the dogs."

"Released?"

"Or stole them."

"Who'd steal a bunch of stray mutts?"

"Hard to say. Possibly someone looking to turn a profit."

"Huh? How?"

"Not all dogs in shelters are mutts, as most people think. There are plenty of purebreds that could be sold to pet stores or research labs. Purebreds get stolen all the time from owners, too. Especially toy breeds, which are always popular."

"Maybe it could be some weird religious cult or something. There are so many creeps nowadays who might do harm to animals."

"Possibly. More likely it's the animal liberation group that's been picketing at the shelter."

"If that's true, then why did they only take the dogs? Why not the cats, too?"

Nona had a valid point. If TAILS was the group responsible for this, they would have freed the cats *and* the dogs, and probably the rabbits and hamsters, too. Heaven knew what Cruiser and I might find running loose in the forest on our next walk.

"Here's your coffee, Nona. Keep a close eye on Calamity for me, okay? Make sure she doesn't get into any trouble while Cruiser and I are gone."

"Will do. Where are you going?"

"To see who let the dogs out."

CHAPTER 12

In tailing the troublemaker who had unleashed havoc on Lakeside Animal Shelter, there was no better place to start than with Victoria Thatcher, the activist I'd met in the shelter parking lot. Something about her manner had sparked in me an instant aversion, and it wasn't just the purple hair or body piercings I'd found off-putting. At least I'd like to think it wasn't the obvious generation gap between us that was tainting my perception. Thank goodness Nona had never gone through a Goth phase like some youths do. She is much too beautiful to drape in black. When I'm an old woman, I may wear purple, but I vow that it won't be my hair color.

From what Tori had said to me that day, I deduced that she would have no qualms about rattling a few cages, or even cracking them open, in order to drive home her radical agenda for change at the shelter. Whether or not her tactics included murdering Rhoda Marx, no one had intimated as yet, but in my mind the possibility certainly existed.

TAILS headquarters wasn't easily found by letting your fingers walk through the Yellow Pages. The whole place had a subversive air to it, right down to its location, which was hidden behind a little-frequented mini-mall at the "Y" where Lake Tahoe Boulevard meets Highway 50. An outline of the word "NAILS" could still be discerned in the weathered wood beam above the door where lettering for the previous tenant, a nail salon, had been removed. I had to wonder why they hadn't substituted a "T" for the "N" and just kept the sign, but they clearly didn't want their whereabouts known to the general public. They might find people picketing on their own doorstep, especially when word got out about what had happened at the shelter.

Left to their own devices for very long, those released strays would form packs that might resort to preying upon livestock or pets for food, much like the coyotes that roam the forest behind my cabin. A pack of feral dogs could even attack a child! That wouldn't be good PR for TAILS if it turned out they were responsible for the break-in.

When I entered the anteroom with Cruiser in tow, I spotted a woman at a desk answering phones and asked her to direct me to the top dog. She spotted Cruiser and offered him a biscuit, which he eagerly snarfed, sliming the receptionist's hand before I could persuade him we weren't here to raid the cookie jar. She had to wipe the drool from her hand with a tissue before answering the next phone call. Occupational hazard. Like a four-legged snail, Cruiser left a glistening trail of slobber behind him as he meandered down the hall at his leisure, searching for more biscuits and sniffing where other dogs had left their mark, itching to leave his own pee-mail message. I'd taught him better, though. All piddling was to be done outdoors.

I found Tori Thatcher holed up in a cramped, paper-strewn office at the rear of the shop working at her computer. A large, tortoiseshell cat was curled beside the keyboard, trying to distract the typist with an occasional tail twitch. I hated to admit that, except for the cat, this space looked like my own office, wall-to-wall chaos. I couldn't quite make out what was on the computer screen, but when Tori saw me, she clicked on another window to hide whatever information wave she was surfing.

"Hi, Tori."

"Elsie MacBean. What brings you here?" She eyed me with her usual intensity. I didn't know if she was scowling because she had been concentrating and was annoyed at being interrupted, or if she was disappointed that I'd so easily ferreted out her secret lair. Perhaps both.

"I'd like to ask you a couple of questions. Got a moment?"

"I'm pretty busy right now, as you can see."

"I won't take up much of your time."

About then, Cruiser moseyed into the office. Tori's brow smoothed like an ironed sheet when she spotted him. She coaxed him to come to her, which he did. I was glad I'd brought my doggy diplomat along to break the ice.

"Hmm . . . okay. I guess I could use a break anyway. I've been at this for hours. Working at the computer too long makes my neck ache."

"I know the feeling. What are you writing?"

"An article for our next newsletter, *TAILS from the Front.*"

"Is this it?" I said, pointing to one of the piles on her desk. The cat took this as a cue to abandon her post beside the computer and drape herself across the desktop, right on the newsletter pile.

"Yup. Go ahead and take one."

"Thanks." I slipped a copy from under the office kitty and flipped through the eight-page glossy leaflet. It contained some graphic color photos of animals rescued from deplorable conditions. You'd have thought the shots were taken in a third-world country. They weren't. I set it back down on the splintered, coffee-ringed desk. "Nice quality newsletter you've got here." I didn't comment on the content. "Must cost a lot to produce."

"We believe the organization's funds are better spent on educating the public about animal welfare than on fancy office furniture." Looking around her office at the cat claw—shredded chairs and thrift store tables, I had to agree there was nothing fancy about the decor.

"I guess you must have heard about what happened over at Lakeside."

"Oh, you must be referring to the shelter manager's death."

"It's being called a homicide. I assumed you already knew about it."

"Why would you assume that?" Her brows knitted again. Someone needed to acquaint the hirsute Tori with the miracle of electrolysis for that unibrow of hers. Fortunately, she hadn't dyed her eyebrows purple, too. They'd have looked like an exotic caterpillar inching across the white page of her broad forehead. A lip wax wouldn't hurt either, but I was no one to talk. Growing a goatee is one side effect of being a middle-age woman that I hadn't anticipated.

"You read the newspaper, don't you?"

"I read them online. As you can see, I already have enough paper to wade through."

"Indeed you do."

"So, are you going to tell me what happened at the shelter or not?" Tori drummed her fingers on the desk. I knew I was in imminent danger of overstaying my welcome. Either that, or I'd struck a nerve. Perhaps there was really no need to tell her what I was about to.

"There was a break-in at the shelter last night."

"What do you mean?" She stopped drumming her fingers when the cat began batting at them. "A theft?"

"You could say that."

"What was stolen? Money?"

"Dogs."

Her caterpillar brow arched in surprise. Whether feigned or not, I couldn't tell. "Oh, I see. And you obviously think we had something to do with this."

"Isn't that what your group is about? Animal liberation?"

"Of course we are, but we wouldn't just release animals from a facility without assuring they'd be properly cared for. That would be irresponsible and harmful to the animals and to the community."

"So you're saying you would liberate them if you *did* have the means to care for them?"

For the first time since I'd met her, the cat had Tori's tongue.

CHAPTER 13

My chat with the TAILS ringleader hadn't been nearly as productive as I'd hoped. I'm usually a good people reader, but Tori Thatcher would be a perfect Stateline card dealer with that poker face of hers. For all I knew, she moonlighted at Caesar's when she wasn't breaking and entering animal facilities.

TAILS headquarters seemed to be the logical place to begin my search for the person responsible for unleashing havoc on the shelter and the community at large. What better suspect than a fanatical animal liberation group, more specifically their lead dog? In my mind, it wasn't much of a leap from some of their malicious acts committed at animal facilities to murdering a reviled shelter manager.

At any rate, my ensuing investigation provided Cruiser with a nice, long car ride. There's nothing he enjoys more than hanging his head out the car window, ears flapping in the breeze. As we drove west on Lake Tahoe Boulevard, I scanned the roadside for any sign of stray dogs, as Jenna had asked me to do. All I spotted were dogs being led on leashes. At least I felt assured that those dogs would never end up in a shelter or under the wheels of a car on a busy South Tahoe thoroughfare. Then I thought of the millions of dogs who aren't so lucky, but I had to put them out of mind, at least for the moment. I had only begun to sniff around on this case, and who better to help me do it than Cruiser? As if in response, I heard the familiar snuffle of my sleuth's nose sampling the air for scents as we approached the shelter.

Lakeside Shelter looked quiet—too quiet for a workday. I saw only one or two cars in the lot I didn't recognize as belonging to the staff. No cars meant no adoptions, but that's because there were few animals left at the shelter to adopt, at least until more strays were rounded up, as they surely would be. A couple of people had come to adopt kittens. There is always a surplus of kitties in the summertime.

I also noticed that there were no demonstrators congregated outside the entrance of the shelter today. Perhaps they were lying low for a while, either because they were responsible for the break-in at the shelter or were afraid that people would assume they were responsible for it, and worse. A murder rap wouldn't do their cause much good . . . or would it? There was something about Tori Thatcher that made me believe there was nothing she wouldn't do to focus public attention on their cause. Even if her group could prove they had no involvement in the Marx murder, spotlighting the mismanagement of a shelter and animal overpopulation issues would be furthered in the bargain.

When Cruiser and I entered the shelter, we were met by Amanda Peabody.

"Hey, Cruiser, how are you, boy? Want a treat?" *Ask a silly question.* Funny how dog lovers always greet the hounds before the humans. Amanda reached into the biscuit jar on the counter and offered Cruiser a tidbit. He snatched it up and then begged for another.

"At this rate, I'll never have to feed him again. He can beg for treats everywhere we go. He just scored some at the TAILS office."

"I heard you went there. Did you get to talk to Victoria Thatcher?"

"Yes, but how did you know I was going there?"

"I overheard Jenna talking to you on the phone."

"Is she still here?"

"No." Amanda offered Cruiser another treat and proceeded to quiz me. "What did Tori have to say?"

"Not much."

"Maybe the tongue ring got in her way."

"Something had hold of her tongue, that's for sure. She's one cool cookie."

"She's just a San Francisco snob who thinks she can come to our community and stir up trouble."

"Hey, back up the cable car, Amanda. I'm from San Francisco, too."

"You are? Sorry, I didn't know that."

"That's okay. You couldn't have known. I don't like to make rash judgments about people, not even Tori Thatcher. Maybe she's not so different from you and me."

"How so?"

"She also does what she can for the welfare of animals, only she does it in a more confrontational manner."

"Murdering a shelter manager is pretty confrontational, all right." Amanda slipped Cruiser another treat.

"What makes you so certain she's behind Rhoda Marx's murder?"

"Who else would it be? You know TAILS has been causing trouble here because of her. I even overheard Tori threaten Rhoda one day."

"You did? What did she say to her?"

"I don't recall her exact words, but it was something like, 'It's you who should be gassed, not the animals.' "

"Wow! What did Rhoda say?"

"She said nothing, but that's how she always responded to people who were angry with her. Her silence only served to make them angrier. It wasn't the first time someone threatened her."

"Really? Who else has made threats against her?"

"A better question would be, who hasn't?"

"She was really that terrible to work for?"

"Yes, she was. I knew one day somebody was going to get even with her somehow, but I always thought it would be one of her co-workers, not an outsider."

"How do you know it wasn't a co-worker?"

"I don't know, but I'd like to think I haven't been working side by side with a murderer all this time."

Rex suddenly came to mind. If anyone looked like trouble, it was he.

"Who is the newest employee at the shelter?"

"I'm not sure. There's a high staff turnaround here."

"You must keep employee records."

"Sure."

"If it's on a computer file, can you e-mail it to me? I'd also like to know who's been here the longest and who was the last person to leave your employ. I'd like a list of volunteers, too."

"I don't know if it's filed on the computer. We're a little behind in technology here. Anyway, I'm not authorized to release that information to the public, Elsie."

"I'm sure you can give it to Sheriff Cassidy, then. This is a murder investigation."

"I still can't believe something like this happened here at our little Tahoe shelter."

"Tahoe isn't immune to crime, not even murder. No place is."

"I probably shouldn't say this, but things have been much better here since Rhoda's been gone. There'll be a replacement soon, though."

"Why don't you apply for the opening, Amanda?"

"I doubt if I'd ever be considered for the position. The City Council will probably make another appointment."

"Is that how Rhoda got her job?"

"Yes. It's always who you know. I don't think she'd have been appointed on her merits alone. I only hope the next manager will be an improvement on her."

"From what you've told me, sounds like whoever it is couldn't be much worse."

"I hope not."

"Well, Cruiser and I had better get going . . . Cruiser, where are you?" As usual, he had done his disappearing act while I was distracted. It wouldn't be hard to find him, though. All I had to do was follow the drips of slobber on the concrete, like a track of breadcrumbs in the forest. There were so many different scents in the shelter for him to explore, it was no wonder he'd wandered off. Amanda trailed me as I followed the drool down one corridor then the next until I came upon Cruiser frozen in front of an empty kennel marked 9. The kennel door was the only one on the corridor opened wide. Cruiser stood in front of K-9, holding to a point like a dog that is trained to hunt more than biscuits and Beggin' Strips. His hind legs were a-quiver with excitement or fear, or both. I'd seen him do that before, always when danger lurked nearby. Then, he lifted his nose to the ceiling and let out the most sorrowful howl.

CHAPTER 14

The trail of red paw prints began in one corner of Kennel 9, led out the kennel door and down the corridor. Amanda and I both stood staring at the bloody prints. We were frozen in place like Cruiser, who seemed to sense something we couldn't. Amanda's face was whiter than Cruiser's belly in a snowdrift.

"You look as though you've seen a ghost," I said.

"I'm not sure I haven't."

"What do you mean?"

"Every time anyone comes down this corridor, the kennel door is thrown wide open like it is now."

"What's so unusual about that?"

"It's always locked."

I looked at the latch. There was a lock hanging on the door, but it was unlatched. It hadn't been jimmied.

"It's not locked now. Who has the keys?"

"We keep them on a big O-ring. Rex carries it around with him most of the time. But no dogs are kenneled in this cage. We haven't used it since that terrible incident with Gilda."

"I remember it well. Poor Gilda." I could still see the headlines of the article I had written in the *Tattler*. Gilda, also a basset hound, was the unfortunate victim of Lakeside policy that had been the catalyst for all the troubles going on at the shelter in the past few weeks. After her sad, wrinkly countenance appeared in every newspaper in the Tahoe basin and beyond, she had become the poster pup for raising public awareness about poorly run shelters. Gilda was one of many dogs that never came home.

"We've had problems with other dogs who were kept in the kennel, so we've become a little superstitious about it," Amanda said.

"What kinds of problems?"

"We've had several dogs go kennel crazy after spending only a few hours inside. That usually happens over a longer time. One bitch killed her pups after we put her in there. And now this."

"So, what are you saying? This kennel is haunted?"

"I don't believe in ghosts, but I do believe in curses. I think it's cursed because a bad thing happened here."

"I'll buy that." I am no stranger to the world of the unseen. This wasn't my first experience with strange occurrences in and around Lake Tahoe. With me, it's as hereditary as Cruiser's long ears and keen nose. Like him, I can sense things that aren't immediately evident. Some signs come to me in dreams and visions. The Washoe believe in all manner of things most people don't, like water spirits of the lake and ancient, fearsome creatures. Tahoe is not without its share of ghosts and curses. However, this was my first encounter with a cursed kennel at the local animal shelter, bloody paw prints and all.

Cruiser was behaving very strangely, even for a nosy basset hound. His noggin' was bobbling the same way it does out in the woods when he's caught the scent of a squirrel or some other creature with that super-sniffer nose of his. As in the field, I had no choice but to follow his lead.

He waddled down the corridor of the shelter in the direction of the ominous crimson paw prints. What could it mean? I had seen many strange phenomena in my lifetime that couldn't be easily explained away, but I had never seen bloody prints appear out of nowhere. They were usually accompanied by a corpse, which made me wonder what horror we might discover at the end of this bloody trail.

Amanda and I followed close behind Cruiser as though we were at the end of an invisible leash. He led us straight through the kennel, past the string of empty cages. We trailed him down the gray mile all the way to the euthanasia chamber, where the paw prints abruptly ended. The prints at the end of the trail looked fresher and wetter than the ones near K-9.

"This is really strange," Amanda said.

I bent down and dipped my forefinger in one of the prints. "Something strange is going on here, all right," I said. "Your bleeding ghost has two legs instead of four, Amanda."

"What do you mean?"

"This isn't blood, it's red paint."

CHAPTER 15

The fake bloodstains at the shelter had me befuddled. Who put them there, and why were the prints leading from Kennel 9 to the place where the lifeless body of Rhoda Marx had been discovered only days before? What was the connection? Could it be a warning of more trouble to come? The threat of another murder about to be committed? Who would be the next victim?

Clearly, it was some kind of spoof or scare tactic from someone who had an ax to grind with the shelter. I assumed it was the handiwork of one of the TAILS activists, who might have opened all of the cages for the animals to escape into the adjoining woods. If that had been the idea behind the break-in, it certainly wouldn't benefit the animals.

It could also be a disgruntled employee or volunteer who worked in the shelter or had worked there at some time in the past. It was clear that someone was intent on causing more trouble at Lakeside Shelter. Perhaps that's what Cruiser really sensed. Trouble. The question was, from whom, or what, would it come?

Of course, with Cruiser it could have been the lingering bouquet of some hot little bitch that had set him to sniffing around the shelter, not that my neutered male would know what to do with one if he found her. Speaking of little bitches, I began to wonder what trouble that naughty Calamity was getting into behind Nona's back in my absence. I decided it was time to go find out.

Cruiser and I made tracks for the MacBean cabin, but we weren't the only ones. As I drove past the sheriff's office, Skip's patrol car veered out right in front of me. I laid on the horn, and he scowled at me in his rearview mirror. I knew he was wondering who would be brave enough or stupid enough to honk at The Law to get out of the way. When he spotted me with my co-pilot, the fuzzy orange caterpillar mustache on his upper lip handle-barred in a big grin. He pulled over and waved for me to come up alongside.

"Hey, Beanie. What a coincidence. I was just heading over to your place."

Now, that was a big surprise. It was almost high noon, and this lawman always seemed to end up at my place right around mealtimes in the hope I was cooking up some veggie chili. He was in luck today. I'd cooked and frozen a big batch of it because I knew Nona was coming up. She loves my chili too, like her dad did. All that was required was a little defrosting in the trusty microwave.

"Why, what's up?"

"I have some new information on the Marx case. Feed me lunch, and I'll tell you about it."

"All right, Skip. Follow the bouncing basset."

"Lead on."

I drove ahead and Skip pulled in behind me, giving a playful retaliatory blast on his siren. Cruiser bayed in response. Now I was the one shooting daggers at Skip in my rearview mirror. "Smart alec sheriff," I muttered. "Just for that I'm putting an extra shot of Tabasco in your chili."

Driving back to my place, I began to wonder what Skip was going to tell me about the Marx case. What new piece of evidence had turned up? Had he already made an arrest? And if he had, was it the right person? After all, he's the law in these parts. I'm just a reporter who moonlights as a private investigator, although these days it seems more like the other way around. But Skip isn't always as intuitive as he might be. He tends to rely more on hard evidence than gut feelings, and that's his job. Evidence is important and can't be ignored, but you can also get a sense about things and people that is often every bit as conclusive—a psychic fingerprint. In that way, I'm a lot like Cruiser. He uses all his senses.

When I drove up to my cabin, I had a pretty strong sense about what I might find when I entered the front door. All Nona would have to do was get distracted for a little while, and Calamity would get into trouble. But when Cruiser and I entered the house, everything appeared to be in order. No upturned wastebaskets or shredded paper were strewn about the house. Nona was reading a book, and Calamity was lying at her feet, sleeping peacefully. Of course, the moment she saw us come in, that was the end of the serene scene. She raced over to greet Cruiser and me.

When she tried to jump up on me, I pushed her back down. I told her to sit and then rewarded her with a tidbit before giving her the attention she craved. She didn't jump up again. Slowly, I felt like I was making some progress with my new foster.

Basset hounds are much brainier than they get credit for. Beneath that nonchalant, innocent exterior is a cool, calculating intelligence. Like a mystery novelist and the criminals they write about, bassets are forever plotting and scheming their next caper while their owners are usually clueless. Calamity was no exception. I had no doubt there were plenty of behavior hurdles left for us to surmount before she could be considered adoptable.

"You were gone quite a while," Nona said.

"I had a few things to attend to. Did you have any trouble with Calamity?"

"Not at all. She's been as quiet as a mouse the whole time you were gone."

"That's what worries me."

"What's for lunch, Mom? I'm starved."

"How's chili sound?"

"Yummy!"

"Good, Skip's joining us. He should be pulling up pretty soon. I don't know where he is. He was right behind me."

"Maybe he got a call or something."

"Could be. I'll go ahead and warm it up."

"Good. If he doesn't show, that means there'll be more for us."

CHAPTER 16

Skip drove up half an hour later.

"What happened to you? I thought you were right behind us."

"I stopped to grab a cold brewskie to wash down that famous five-alarm chili of yours."

"Your beans await you, Sheriff. Have some fresh garlic bread, too." Skip sat down at the kitchen table to delve into his bowl of red.

"Please, don't say beans," he said.

"Why not?"

"Because it reminds me of the bean counters who are cutting back our funding for the next fiscal year. We were long overdue for a raise and some new crime lab equipment, but now that's all down the tubes."

"The economy is bad everywhere, Skip. They're having the same troubles at the shelter."

"I may even have to lay off some staff. That means more work for you-know-who."

"I thought you seemed a little stressed out lately. What about your new rookie, Rusty? She'll be some help to you, won't she?"

"I don't know. She's still pretty wet behind the ears."

"Looked like she was handling things pretty well on the Marx case."

"It's just that there are guys who have been with the department longer who might resent her advancing too quickly in the ranks."

Seems like I'd bumped my head against this glass ceiling myself plenty of times in the past on the job. "Why? Because she's a woman? And pretty, too?"

"There're laws against discrimination on the job, Beanie. You know that."

"Yeah, but it still happens anyway. And you know that!"

"I have to admit the fact that she was a *Playboy* centerfold doesn't help matters."

"She was? How do you know that?"

"I caught one of the guys with her pin-up in his locker."

"Did you make him take it down?"

"Of course."

"You didn't put it up in your own locker, did you?" Skip has always been a pushover for a pretty face or a shapely figure, as he'd proved many times before. Rusty Cannon had both.

"Don't be ridiculous. I threw it in the trash."

"What difference does it make what this woman did before she joined your department or does after hours on her own time?" Nona interjected. "There are lots of women and even some men who have modeled for men's magazines to get through college or whatever their goal might be."

Nona had that right. I only hoped none of her Victoria's Secret work was taped inside a locker at some police station.

"It doesn't make a bit of difference to me, but it might to some," Skip said, shifting in his seat. I noticed a rolled-up piece of paper poking out of Skip's hip pocket. About that time Calamity wandered into the kitchen, investigating the source of the aroma of food. She edged up to Skip and snatched at the corner of the paper in his pocket. Out it came. Skip slapped at his pocket but he was too slow on the draw this time. "Hey, bring that back here!"

"Calamity! Drop it!" I commanded. She didn't, of course, but began shaking the paper like a terrier with a rat. I managed to grab it away and began to smooth it out as best I could. Then I saw what it was. I unfolded a foldout of the voluptuous redhead, Miss March, none other than "Busty Rusty" Cannon. "Threw it in the trash, huh?"

Skip snatched the paper away. When his face flushed, it wasn't because of my spicy chili but something a lot spicier. "I forgot it was in there. I really did intend to throw it away."

"No time like the present." I wasn't sure, but I thought I saw a tear roll down Skip's cheek as he tore up the tattered centerfold and threw it in the trash container.

"What's wrong, Skip?" His complexion was nearly the color of the chili. Sweat beaded on his temples.

"What did you put in this stuff? Lava?" Skip mopped his brow with a corner of my tablecloth.

"It's a lot spicier than your usual, Mom." Even Nona was breaking a sweat, and she never does. "Trying out a new recipe on us?"

"I added some jalapeno peppers and a couple of other secret ingredients to the mix. Too hot?"

"Was the Angora firestorm too hot?" Skip said, chugging down his beer.

"Be glad I left out the extra Tabasco sauce in yours. I was going to get even with you for blasting Cruiser and me with your siren."

"Don't worry, you did." I wasn't sure if he was referring to my chili or the shredded centerfold.

Nona was doing okay, but then she had been reared on the red stuff at the MacBean house. "You really ought to think about competing in one of those chili cook-offs, Mom. This is the best batch you've ever made."

"Yeah, and now it's the hottest, too," Skip said as he polished off the last of his bowlful.

"Maybe someday when I get tired of selling my words and snooping around crime scenes, I'll sell chili. Anyway, I'd rather make it for my friends and family."

"Yeah, 'cause we're your guinea pigs." Skip leaned back in his chair and heaved a contented sigh. "Whew, I'm stuffed!"

"Well-fed guinea pigs, though." I playfully patted Skip's rounded belly.

"Gee, thanks." I could tell Skip didn't appreciate my comment. He'd never let on, but I know he is sensitive about his thickening waist and thinning hair, especially around pretty young gals like Nona and Rusty.

I didn't like hurting Skip's feelings so I changed the subject. "You said if I fed you you'd tell me what you have on the Marx case."

"That's right. I did, didn't I?"

"What did you find out from the M.E.?"

"Well, the autopsy showed . . ."

"Hey, if you guys are gonna talk crime and cadavers, I'm outta here," Nona said. "Come on, Calamity, let's go keep Cruiser company." Calamity's toenails clicked like castanets on the kitchen floor as she trotted along behind Nona.

"Looks like Nona has a new friend."

"It's funny how dogs choose their people. This little dog bonded with Nona from the first moment, like Cruiser bonded with Tom. It was only after Tom died that Cruiser and I became close. Until then, he was Tom's dog."

"Yeah, I remember how much Tom loved Cruiser."

"It was mutual."

"And now it's the same for you and Cruiser."

"I think dogs know what we need better than we know

ourselves. Maybe that's why Calamity has chosen my daughter. Nona needs a good friend. She's kind of like her mother, a bit of a loner."

"She lives in a big city. How can you be alone in a big city? That is, unless you breathe on someone after eating a whole loaf of garlic bread." Skip popped a Tic Tac in his mouth.

"It can be a lot lonelier in a big city than in a small town. In a small town, everyone knows who you are, and people are more inclined to reach out to one another. You can get lost in a metropolis like San Francisco. I should know."

"That's right. I forgot you grew up there. As it so happens, so did Rhoda Marx."

"Maybe that's part of the reason no one around here liked her much. She was an outsider."

"Could be." When Skip scratched his mustache, it looked like he was tickling a caterpillar.

"Someone disliked her enough to kill her. That's got to be about more than being an outsider."

"Wrong, Beanie. More than one person hated Rhoda Marx enough to murder her."

"What do you mean?"

"Because she was already dead before somebody put her in that chamber and turned on the gas."

CHAPTER 17

What Skip told me over chili and garlic bread had me stumped. He explained that a blow to Rhoda's skull had killed her, not the gas in the euthanasia chamber. That's why the tissue inside her mouth wasn't the color of cherries (or my chili), as it would be if she had died from CO poisoning. But if she was already dead, why put her in the gas tank? Had her murder been a team effort? She clearly had made plenty of enemies in the community, including some on her own staff. And of course there was TAILS, always lurking about, raising my suspicion about these activists' motives. Had she been killed elsewhere and her body placed in the chamber to make a point about animal cruelty? None of it made any sense. Not to me or to Skip, either. Meanwhile, Marx's murderer was still on the loose, and the trail was going colder by the day. And perhaps there was more than one stray suspect unleashed on the community.

Besides the death of Rhoda Marx, other matters closer to home were weighing on my mind. I was worried about Nona. After what my daughter had told me about discovering a suspicious lump, I understood why she had decided to take a hiatus from work, particularly at a time when her career was going so well. Nona is too much like her mother sometimes. She's as driven to succeed in modeling as I am to succeed at writing.

Some traits skip generations, and Nona's head-in-the-sand reluctance to find out for certain whether the lump was really anything to worry about was very much like her grandmother's had been. Unfortunately, my mother should not have ignored her symptoms as long as she did. In retrospect, I should have noticed her crushing fatigue when we walked in the forest together, instead of discounting it to advancing age. Perhaps we were both in denial about her failing health. You don't like to think about the possibility of losing someone you love. I vowed not to make the same mistake with Nona.

I certainly could understand her trepidation and why she was distrustful of the standard invasive medical treatments, should she have a malignant tumor. I'd seen my mother go through that agony to no avail. While her life may have been prolonged, her quality of life was dubious.

No one has yet discovered for certain what causes cancer. Whether it's a virus, faulty genes, poor lifestyle choices, environmental pollution, or a combination of all these, I have no doubt that stress is also an often-overlooked factor in human diseases. The negative effect of prolonged stress upon any living organism is undeniable, and Nona's life has certainly been stressful the past few years. I'm not just referring to the demands of making her mark in the world of supermodels, constantly striving to achieve physical perfection by whatever means. At least Nona hasn't had any part of her body surgically altered for the camera. She's so naturally gorgeous it isn't necessary, but she has struggled constantly with her weight, like her mother and even her mother's dog. I also can't discount the fact that she's been unlucky in love, nor can I ignore the effect that her near-death experience at the hands of the murderous Medwyn that terrible winter of the Tahoe Terror might have had on her. I couldn't help blaming myself in some measure for Nona's problems. She would never have been in harm's way if it weren't for her meddlesome mother who is always getting involved in crime.

In my experience with rescuing dogs for Found Hounds and

having seen what long-term stress can do to dogs, including cancer and other health and behavior problems, I understand that we have more in common with our canine brethren than we might imagine, as research scientists are discovering in their studies of human diseases like cancer. I had always believed it wasn't an accident that Cruiser appeared when he did, just before the most devastating time in my life—Tom's death. Perhaps it was also no accident that Calamity had come along at a time when Nona was facing her greatest life challenge. I am certain that Calamity sensed Nona needed a friend, and there's no doubt that Calamity needed one, too.

My greatest challenge at the moment was the prospect of having to deal with Ms. Littlefeather, tribal elder and media darling. Wherever there was a TV camera, you'd find her right in front of it. She's no shrinking violet, that's for sure, and it's good that someone like her speaks for our people's interests in the community. That aside, I knew that having to ask her for advice was going to stick in my craw like a pinecone, but I'd do anything for my daughter, even make nice to my old rival.

I caught up with Sonseah that afternoon as she was leaving the local TV station, where she had just talked with newscasters about the Washoe tribe's growing contention over a large tract of native land on the West Shore being threatened by development. If there was one thing Lake Tahoe didn't need more of to sully its cobalt blue waters, it was more land development. The struggle to preserve tribal land in the Tahoe Basin is ongoing, and I felt bad that I hadn't been right there with Sonseah on TV to help her defend our heritage, but I had too many irons in the fire already, and they were heating up fast.

"Elsie MacBean, what brings *you* here?"

She said it like I'd never had any previous experience with the media. Didn't she know what I do for a living? Her arrogance apparently knew no bounds. At least she wasn't festooned in her usual ceremonial regalia, which made her appear haughtier. For Nona's sake, I swallowed my pride.

"I need to talk to you. Can you spare a moment?"

"I have some time before my next personal appearance. There's a little coffee shop around the corner. We can talk there."

I followed Sonseah to a cozy little coffee shop. Perk Up was a retro java joint, with no fancy coffee drinks or screeching cappuccino machines. Sonseah had always seemed to me more like the Starbuck's type. She looked like someone with exotic tastes in everything, including her caffeine, but to my surprise she ordered straight black coffee. Gosh, did anyone really serve that anymore in cafés? Only at places where waitresses with red beehives, like Rita Ramirez, pour the coffee. I treated Sonseah to her coffee, since she was taking time to schedule me between TV spots.

"Now, what did you want to talk to me about?"

"It's about my daughter, Nona."

"Such a beautiful girl."

"Thank you. Yes, she is beautiful." The way Sonseah said it, she almost sounded as though Nona and I couldn't possibly be related. She had never seen photos of me when I was Nona's age. We could be twins, even if Nona was a bit taller and slenderer. She got that from her father.

"There's nothing wrong with her, is there?"

Was Sonseah a mind reader? No, she was probably just reading my body language, much like Cruiser does. I'm sure that my concern about Nona was practically oozing from every pore. Could she scent pheromones of fear like a dog can?

"Yes, she's found a suspicious lump."

"Oh, I'm so sorry, Elsie." Sonseah's tone was suddenly entirely different than I had ever heard come from her until now. With her next words, I understood why.

"My mother had breast cancer."

"So did mine." I didn't mention that she hadn't survived it. I didn't want to speak the words aloud for fear it might jinx Nona. I also didn't want to entertain thoughts of another disastrous prognosis.

"Believe me, I understand what you're going through. Is there anything I can do to help?"

Unlike when I'd heard some people mouth such well-meaning platitudes, I believed that she really meant it.

"Yes, there is, Sonseah."

"Why don't you call me Sonny? Everyone does."

Everyone but me until now. "Sure. Sonny it is." I didn't even know this woman had a nickname or would even want to be referred to by anything other than her formal name. Perhaps that was just her public persona. I was seeing a new side to my old nemesis I hadn't ever known existed. Sometimes people wear masks, letting you see only what they want you to see. Not everyone is an open book like I am.

"You may as well call me Beanie, too."

A warm, empathetic smile softened her angular features. It was a different smile from any I'd seen on Sonseah's face— when she smiled at all. "Just tell me what you need, Beanie."

"Nona wants to have a healing ceremony with the tribe. Do you think you could arrange it for us?"

"Yes, I'd be glad to do that. When did you want to do it?"

"As soon as possible."

"Okay. I'll give you a call when it's all set up. Keep it under your hat, though."

"Of course. Thanks so much, Sons—"

"It's Sonny, remember?"

"Sonny." Boy, I must be in Sonseah's inner circle now. Sarcasm aside, it felt good to talk with someone of my own tribe who really understood what we were possibly facing. Hav-

ing a family history of the disease made the odds of Nona having a malignancy much greater. Like Scarlett O'Hara, I wouldn't
think about that now. I'd think about that tomorrow.

CHAPTER 18

Cruiser can be pretty demanding about his walks. I try to limit him to two a day, but he sometimes has other ideas. Often I feel like I should be earning my living as a professional dog walker. He's not a young dog, so I don't like to overdo a good thing, especially at nearly 7,000 feet altitude. Like some other dog breeds with deep chest cavities, bassets can be candidates for bloat and gastric torsion, which can be fatal, so when I exercise him, I'm very careful not to feed or water him within two hours before or after.

However, Calamity was a young dog and full of energy that needed to be expended at regular intervals so she didn't get into mischief. Keeping her active might help prevent her from wreaking havoc in my house. I only hoped I had the energy to keep up with her. Having Nona with me would be a big help, especially since she and Calamity appeared to have bonded like peanut butter and jelly from the get-go. You never know who a dog will form an attachment to, but they choose their human companions as surely as we choose them.

The setting sun filtered through the dense stand of pines behind the cabin, and a cooling breeze brushed the treetops. It was time for a last walk up the hill with Cruiser and Calamity before darkness fell.

"Ready for a walk, guys?" Silly question. All I had to do was make a move for the leashes, and Cruiser was up and in formation for his evening excursion. Dogs are experts at reading our body language, and Calamity was already an apt pupil of Cruiser's. She knew something good must be about to happen if Cruiser was getting so excited about it. Nona's getting up to join the outing was all that was needed to spark the new dog's interest in going for a walk.

The only trouble was that I knew she had no leash training. Calamity's paw pads were so pink and smooth I doubted if she had ever been outside a cage in her life. I guessed she was probably a puppy mill dog, which could certainly account for her lack of socialization and fearfulness of every new situation. Being in a poorly run pound hadn't helped improve her puppy mill issues any. A walk in the forest was no doubt going to present a whole new challenge for her, and for us. But inhaling some fresh mountain air before retiring for the night would help me sleep better.

This certainly wasn't the first time I'd walked more than one dog at a time in the woods, but it was the first time I'd ever walked one with no clue about the purpose of a leash. If this were a field trial, I could let my brace of two bassets range free to sniff at will, but if I did that with Calamity, she'd probably head straight for the hills. I made the mistake of using an extendable leash to walk her in the forest. This was like threading the leashes through an agility course as the dogs wound through the scrub brush and pine trees ahead of us, getting more tangled by the minute.

Of course, Cruiser has never been above playing bread and butter with trees, light posts, or anything else you can wrap a leash around. It's the nature of a stubborn, scent-driven basset to head in the opposite direction you have a mind to go. When you feel a firm tug on the line with a seventy-pound hound at the other end, it's usually you who gets reeled in, not the dog. At least I had Nona along with me to help untangle the leads as we went along. I could tell she was losing patience, though.

"This is impossible, Mom. I think Calamity needs some leash training before we attempt another walk."

"I think you're right." Of course, I wasn't doing much better with Cruiser, who wanted to sniff every tree and shrub in the forest. "It's getting late. We'd better head back to the cabin before it gets too dark."

The forest was enveloped in shadows as the sun made its final stand against the purpling peaks of Mount Tallac. The rising crescent moon looked like a dog's tail wagging on the eastern horizon. Just when we managed to point the dogs in the direction of home, I heard a thudding on the ground among the trees to my right. I glanced in time to see a pair of deer, a buck and a doe, dashing through the forest.

The buck's antlers clattered among the pine branches as the magnificent animal crashed through the thick woods. Velvet brown eyes were wide with fear as the deer fled a predator or some other imminent peril. Other than coyotes, they had few natural predators left at Tahoe. I had heard no coyote packs since we'd been out in the forest. That left only the hunter or a forest fire to account for the deer bolting through the trees. At least that's what I imagined until I heard the sounds of distinctly canine yips and barks that trailed the fleeing deer down the mountainside.

Both Cruiser and Calamity froze in their tracks. Cruiser lifted his muzzle to the cool night air, sniffed the subtle scents carried upon the wind currents, and bayed. His novitiate, Calamity, emitted a few tentative barks before her pendulous lips formed a perfect "O" and she joined Cruiser in a true basset chorus. By now, I understood every nuance of Cruiser's utterances and what they meant. I knew he wasn't begging for Bacon Strips. This was a warning!

"Mom! Look over there!" Nona pointed toward a stand of pines from which the deer had emerged moments before. Among the shadows of the pines on the forest floor, I could make out the silhouette of the pack of wild canines chasing after the deer. It was not a sight foreign to me. I had spent much more time hiking these mountains than my daughter had, so the appearance of coyotes was not cause for alarm. I had often seen packs of coyotes tracking their prey in the waning hours of day and heard their cries echoing from deep in the woods on moonlit nights. I had no fear of them. Attacks upon humans are rare. They are usually more afraid of us than we are of them, although I understood that the coyote's howl could make the hair on a tenderfoot's neck spike like a dog's ruff.

"It's a coyote pack chasing the deer. They won't bother us." The words had no sooner left my mouth than one of the animals stopped short in his pursuit and stepped from the shadows into a silver beam of moonlight. It was then I realized that this was no coyote pack tracking deer but a pack of feral dogs. We all stood frozen in place as the large, white German shepherd dog edged closer to us. Fur bristling, his lips curled over sharp fangs in a menacing growl. I recognized the animal from a previous less-threatening encounter. It was Spirit, the shepherd I had seen at Lakeside Shelter the day I adopted Calamity.

Now Spirit looked like a ghost dog with his coat glistening like fresh fallen snow in the moonbeams. I had been impressed with the sheer size of the animal when I first saw him at the shelter and thought he was beautiful, but my perspective was now very different out here in the forest surrounded by a pack of wild, hungry dogs.

Several of the other dogs abruptly ceased their pursuit of the deer and joined the shepherd at the forest's edge. We weren't running away like frightened deer, so I suppose we looked like easier prey to them than the buck and doe. We didn't have sharp antlers to attack them with, either. In fact, we had nothing to fight them off with, not even a walking stick, which I often carried when hiking. Nona and I were as frightened as the deer. The trick was not to let the feral dogs know it.

"Don't move a muscle, Nona." If we turn to run, they'll be after us in a flash. We don't stand a chance of outrunning them." I knew we stood even less chance of escaping the pack with the two slowpokes, Cruiser and Calamity, tagging along with us. They couldn't fend off an attack from the dogs. They'd be killed for sure.

Half a dozen other dogs of various breeds flanked the large, powerful shepherd. Most were mixed breeds, but I could make out a couple of purebreds in the group. All were medium-sized to large animals. Spirit, the largest among them, was clearly the alpha of the pack. Like a general commanding his troops, he growled his commands to them to stand their ground. None were backing down.

"They aren't rabid, are they, Mom?"

"No, I don't think so. Just a bunch of starving strays."

"What are we going to do?"

"If we can somehow scare off the big guy, the rest will probably follow suit."

"Good. How do we do that?"

"I'm thinking, Papoose. I'm thinking."

"Think faster!"

Chapter 19

The wind had picked up and was howling through the forest like a pack of hungry coyotes, but it wasn't a coyote pack that confronted us now. The feral dogs were becoming harder to discern among the shadowed pines in the enveloping night. Was that shape moving out there in the darkness an animal, tail erect and quivering, ready to pounce, or merely a sapling waving in the breeze? The imagination plays tricks on you when you're scared, and I confess that I was scared silly. So was Nona. I couldn't tell if the knocking sound I heard was her knees or mine, but we both heard the threatening guttural growls of the wild dogs and the crunch of pine needles beneath their paws as they closed in on two frightened women and a brace of bassets.

"Back away slowly, but don't make any sudden movements. Avoid any direct eye contact. They'll perceive that as a threat."

Nona followed my lead. We both stepped backward a couple of paces, but when we retreated, the pack advanced. We inched back a few more feet, slowly trying to reel in Cruiser and Calamity as we did. Calamity finally responded to the tugs on her leash, but Cruiser wouldn't budge. My foolishly stubborn dog was determined to stand his ground.

Calamity began to tremble and whine, but a deep rumble rose from Cruiser's throat that seemed to come from the tip of his tail and resonated in his barrel chest. He was alpha of his pack and prepared to defend it, come what may. His challenge was answered by the menacing snarl of Spirit and his cohorts.

In the moonlight I could see the shepherd's muscles tensing up for an attack.

"Cruiser, hush." I knew if he continued his growling, the confrontation could quickly escalate and we'd be in big trouble. He'd given a good account of himself in the past against a lone canine adversary, aptly dubbed the Tahoe Terror, but he'd never manage to fend off an entire pack. Yet I knew he'd die trying to protect us in an ear-tearing fight, and I couldn't let that happen to my brave boy. What to do? What to do? There were no rocks around nearby to use as weapons. As a last resort, I picked up a large pinecone lying at my feet and hurled it at the shepherd, hoping to scare him away. It had no effect. Spirit didn't even flinch. He only growled louder as he began to draw closer, his posture stiffening for the assault.

"What are we going to do, Mom?"

I didn't answer, because I really didn't know what else to do. "Mother?"

I thought of my own dear mother and how we often used to walk together in these woods from the time I was a child. I always felt so safe with her close beside me. I remembered how Mama taught me the secrets of nature and unlocked a magical spirit world for me, as her ancestors before her had done for their children. She knew every tree, rock, and rivulet of the Tahoe landscape like the deep creases in the palms of her own weathered hands.

As I visualized my beloved mother, I fancied I heard her calling my name in the wind that moaned through the forest. "El-si-nore." When I heard her strong, reassuring voice on the wind, I felt my fear melt away, and I instinctively knew we'd be all right. She would protect us . . . somehow.

Just then, a powerful wind gust ripped through the topmost branches of the pines towering above us. The trees waved and whipped wildly in the gale. I heard an explosive crack from somewhere close by, and I knew what that meant. I had heard those sounds echo through the woods before in a storm, but there was usually no one around to shout out a warning, "Timber!"

"Nona, look out!"

An instant later, one of the legion of beetle-rotted pine trees crashed to the ground right in front of us, creating a sharp, splintered barrier between the pack of dogs and their intended prey. Spirit yelped in shock and surprise, then tucked tail and ran off into the woods like a frightened pup. The rest of the dogs followed suit. Nona and I sighed our relief as we heard their yipping chorus fade off in the distance.

Exhausted, more from stress and fear than our hike through the woods, we trudged back down the mountainside in the dark with only a new moon to help light our way. Occasionally we paused, still alert for signs that our attackers might have returned. We heard nothing but the helpful wind soughing through the pines and the occasional muffled sound of pinecones dropping to the needle-strewn forest carpet below.

At last, I spotted the comforting sight of lights shining through the windows of my cabin. Home had never looked as inviting to me as it did now. I'm sure Nona and the dogs were as happy as I was when we were finally safe inside my cozy alpine abode.

"You unleash these two hounds, Nona, and I'll put on a kettle."

"Good. A hot cup of tea is just what I need after that. Where did all those stray dogs come from?"

"Escapees from Lakeside Shelter, no doubt."

"How did they escape from the shelter?"

"Someone had to have let them out, of course."

"But why? Don't they know how dangerous that could be to the public?"

"Whoever did this didn't care about that or didn't think about the consequences of 'freeing' the shelter dogs."

"I don't understand why anyone would do something like that."

"To make a point, perhaps." I saw Tori Thatcher and TAILS written all over this dog prison breakout. Who else but an activist group like hers would pull such a stunt?

"But what if they attack a child or kill someone's pet? Those animals could easily have hurt us, or Cruiser and Calamity."

"I know."

"We were lucky that rotten log fell over when it did or we'd all have been done for."

I knew that luck didn't have much to do with the tree falling when or where it did. I believed it could only have been my mother's benevolent spirit in the woods intervening for our safety. Speaking of a Spirit in the woods, we still had a big problem on our hands. A pack of feral dogs wasn't something you wanted roaming free in an area heavily populated with summer tourists. A disaster was bound to occur. The strays would have to be trapped as soon as possible before any damage was done, but that would be difficult with the animals running loose in the forest. The terrain would make it much harder for the dogcatcher to apprehend those furry fugitives. Where was Round 'em Up Rhoda when you really needed her?

CHAPTER 20

The articles I wrote for the *Tattler* about the break-in at the shelter and the feral dog pack we encountered in the forest were intended to alert Tahoe residents and tourists of possible danger, but it didn't prevent the inevitable from occurring. Days later, a five-year-old boy was bitten by a stray dog. Whether or not it was one of the shelter dogs or another stray wandering in the community no one knew for sure. The culprit had successfully eluded all attempts to capture him.

Fortunately, the child was only bitten on the hand, and although he did have to undergo precautionary rabies treatment, the bite was not too severe. No stitches were required, and there was no permanent damage done, except perhaps that of a psychological nature. I hated the thought of a young child being bitten by a dog, not just because of the physical injury but because he would no doubt grow up suffering from cynophobia. Someone who is afraid of dogs is one less person who is going to adopt a homeless dog, and there aren't enough homes to go around as it is. So, whoever was responsible for the shelter break-in had unleashed problems more far-reaching than a bunch of stray dogs wreaking havoc in the community.

Meanwhile, there were problems of a murderous nature still unsolved, namely, the Rhoda Marx case. The most obvious perpetrator of the crime was the same person or persons who broke into the shelter and released all the dogs. My best guess was that TAILS was wagging this dog of a case, but there was no conclusive evidence to support my hunch. The killer could be any number of people who had it in for Rhoda Marx. She certainly wasn't the most popular gal on the canine cellblock. In talking to her co-workers and even her casual acquaintances, I sensed the animosity they felt for "Mengele Marx," as she was best known to those who loathed her, and that went double for the animal lovers on the list, as I was about to discover.

"Mom, telephone for you."

"Coming. Say, have you seen my favorite earrings lying around here anywhere?"

"You mean the ruby ones Dad gave you?"

"Yes. I've lost one."

"Oh, no! Are you sure?"

"I found one of them on the nightstand, but I can't find the other one."

"I'll search while you take this call."

"Is it Skip?"

"No, Jenna Fairbanks."

"Oh, all right. I hope she isn't going to ask me to foster another crazy dog." I went to answer the phone and spotted Calamity in the living room with Cruiser. She looked as innocent as a lamb, which made me wonder what she'd been up to. When she saw me heading in the direction of the kitchen, she ceased her industrious gnawing of a rawhide chew. The only time she wasn't into some kind of mischief was when she had a chew toy to occupy her. She was still a young dog, and with her nervous nature, chewing something seemed to provide an outlet for all that pent-up energy. Cruiser had long since outgrown his need to chew. He was more into power napping when he wasn't on a crime beat with me. I was glad to see Calamity busy with something that was on my approved list of chewies. I knew it couldn't last, though. I heard the tap of toenails on hardwood as she abandoned her pacifier in the hope of acquiring something more palatable from Cruiser's stash.

I picked up the phone, keeping a wary eye on Calamity.

"Hello."

"Hi, Elsie. How's it going?"

"All right, Jenna. And you?"

"Fine. Say, I know you're busy, but can you possibly find time to lend a hand with the preparations for our Bassetille Day event?"

She wasn't asking for me to make more room at the inn for another incorrigible basset, so who cared if there was another item added to my endless to-do list? Never mind that the one at the top of my list was a real killer.

"What do you need me to do?"

"I'm scheduling a meeting this afternoon for volunteers to form some planning committees for the event. Can you come to my house at two?"

"I'll be there. By the way, have you found anyone to adopt Calamity?"

"No, not yet. Is she giving you trouble?"

"Let's just say she's living up to her name."

"I can try to find another foster home for her if it's not working out."

"No, that's okay. It's nothing I can't manage. Maybe someone will adopt her at the Waddle. It's only a couple of weeks away. We can last that long." I tried to keep the doubt from creeping into my voice, but Jenna picked up on it like a hound on a hunt.

"Are you certain?"

"Uh-huh. Calamity's scheduled for her first training class next week, and she's already gained some weight, so she should be looking good in time for the Waddle."

"That ought to help matters. If only people would take the

time to train their dogs, fewer would end up in shelters in the first place."

I suspected that Calamity's problems went far deeper than a lack of training classes, although classes certainly would have helped. "She's a beautiful little dog, but she has some issues, as you know."

"Don't we all? I can think of a few people I know who could have used some basic training."

"So true, Jenna." That was another list of mine that seemed to grow longer all the time. We'd have to compare lists sometime. When I hung up the phone, I realized I had more company in the kitchen. While I had been talking to Jenna, Cruiser had joined Calamity in launching an all-out assault on the yum-yum nook. While I was distracted, she had managed to open the cupboard door and was standing on her hind legs to reach the shelf where I kept the primo treats. I was frankly surprised that she wasn't balanced on Cruiser's back in a pantry-raiding pyramid to reach the topmost shelf. Stretched full length, her slender body reminded me of a child's Slinky toy. She snapped at empty air as she desperately tried to nab the edge of a bag of Beggin' Strips. "Calamity, no!"

She yelped her alarm and obeyed my command, but only because I had surprised her.

"Caught you in the act, didn't I? All right, you two. I'll give you a tidbit, then it's out of the kitchen with both of you."

Before I could grab the bag, it fell from the shelf and the contents spilled out on the linoleum. Quicker than a flea can jump, Calamity had gobbled up every last bacon strip. Cruiser didn't stand a chance. Who needed a Dyson "Animal" with her around to vacuum my floor?

Nona heard Calamity's yelp and came running on the double from the bedroom. She looked genuinely distressed, as though she expected to find something far worse than two dogs pillaging the pantry. I interpreted her distress as worry about me, but I couldn't have been more wrong.

"What's the matter?"

"It's just Calamity."

"I heard her cry out. Is she all right? Cruiser didn't snap at her again, did he?"

"Of course not, but I wouldn't blame him if he had. She was the one doing the snapping at Cruiser's treats."

"Maybe she's hungry."

"That dog is always hungry. If I didn't know better I'd think she had a tapeworm. Everything is fair game for Calamity. She's liable to get hold of something she shouldn't eat if we're not careful. Which reminds me, did you find my missing earring?"

"No. I looked everywhere."

"Did you check under the bed?"

"There, too. Are you sure you left them on the nightstand?"

"Yes. I always remove my earrings last thing before I go to sleep."

"Unless you lost the earring someplace else, it's bound to turn up here sooner or later."

"It's not likely I lost it elsewhere. Those earrings have a safety latch, so they don't come off easily."

"Don't worry, Mom. I'll keep an eye out for it. I know how much they mean to you."

"Can you stick around this afternoon? I have to go to a meeting, and I'd rather not leave the dogs unattended, especially you-know-who."

"Sure, I can stay with them. I don't have any plans except for some reading I want to catch up on."

"Thanks, honey. I shouldn't be too long."

"Take your time. We'll be fine." I always felt bad about asking Nona to dog-sit whenever she came up to visit me. Despite her affection for Cruiser, she hadn't acted very enthusiastic about it in the past, but something was different this time. I expected her to be out on a manhunt, like she usually is when she comes to Tahoe, but she preferred hanging around the cabin with the dogs and me this time. I hoped it wasn't because Nona was sicker than she was letting on. We never talk about health issues much. Neither of us likes to complain about our aches and pains or likes hearing about them, either. Until now neither of us ever had anything much to complain about. It was obvious that she seemed to enjoy being around Calamity. Was it because Calamity was fiercely independent and kind of a wild child like Nona? Or was my daughter finally becoming a dog person like her mother? Whatever the reason for the change in Nona, I had to give at least some credit to Calamity, doggone her mischievous hide.

Chapter 21

Jenna's place was located near Fallen Leaf Lake, not far from where my ancestral home once stood before it was destroyed in a forest fire. Her house didn't look much different than ours had, with its rustic rock fireplace and foundation. Driving down the long road that meandered through the pines and aspen groves, I pulled off the road a moment to admire the lake, one of several smaller bodies of water surrounding Lake Tahoe that were formed eons ago in this alpine region.

Like the other lakes, Fallen Leaf was not without its rich collection of legends and lore. Author John Steinbeck and numerous others who have found creative inspiration beside the various lakes of this region had traversed the potholed road I jostled down now. Some people think Fallen Leaf Lake was so named because of its distinctive shape, but when viewed from the summit of Mount Tallac, the nearly four-mile-long body of water, which appears as richly sapphire in hue as the bigger lake and is situated eighty feet higher in elevation, more closely resembles the shape of a human foot. Ancient man might have thought some giant creature left its footprint here, which later filled with water to create the lake.

I passed the ruins of Anita Baldwin's rustic cabin on the two thousand acres she inherited from her father, Comstock millionaire Lucky Baldwin, along with half his twenty million-dollar estate, when he died in 1909. Photographer Dorothea Lange summered there with her family. While the children who came along with Dorothea and her husband ran around wild and naked all summer on the secluded property, pretending to be Indians in the sweat house the family built while they were visiting, Dorothea busied herself shooting forms of nature— pine trees, stumps, and the golden sunlight filtering through broad leaves—though she achieved her fame from photographing people during the Great Depression.

None of Fallen Leaf Lake's history was as rich in my mind as the Tahoe history of my own family. The idyllic summers of Steinbeck, Baldwin, and Lange held no power over the memory of ours. I looked back with fondness and bittersweet longing upon all the happy times we spent there together each summer when my grandparents and parents were still living. I remembered fishing with my grandfather beside the lake, catching trout by the boatload. I could see the rainbow-striped scales of the fish glistening in the sun as they danced on the end of the line. Somewhere deep inside, I was still that little pigtailed girl who delighted in wading in the shallows and leaping from stone to stone. I could almost feel the cool, smooth rocks of the lake bed beneath my bare feet.

I recalled the time I was wading in the lake and slipped on some mossy stones. Next thing I knew, I was underwater. When I surfaced for air, looking like a drowned rat in my soaking wet clothes, I realized that my mother was filming the event for posterity with her movie camera, laughing her head off. At least I know where I get my warped sense of humor. Looking back on it now, I have to admit it was pretty funny. That was a lifetime ago, but the memories are still as verdant in my mind as the summer greenery that surrounds this hidden lake.

Jenna met me at the front door before I could ring the bell.

"Beanie, come on in. We've been waiting for you."

"Sorry. I got a little sidetracked on the way here."

"That's okay. I was just making some coffee. I think you

already know everyone, except for my good friend, Roberta Finch. Everyone calls her Bertie."

"We haven't actually met before."

"I'll let you go ahead and introduce yourselves while I finish up in the kitchen."

Even TAILS couldn't have boasted a collection of any more dedicated animal advocates than were assembled in Jenna Fairbanks's spacious living room, which was occupied by another collection of rescued canines and felines. Now I understood why she hadn't let me ring the doorbell. Chaos would surely have ensued. Several bassets, mostly hard-to-place seniors, snoozed comfortably in fleece snuggly beds. The cats made themselves comfortable wherever they wanted. I hoped the kitchen was off limits. I don't care for cat hair in my coffee. Dog hair is okay, of course. Jenna's home was considerably roomier for housing rescues than my two-dog-capacity cabin, although it had accommodated three on occasion.

Besides Jenna, who along with Bertie was the driving force behind this Bassetille Day event, Amanda Peabody and Cruiser's and my old friend, Sally Applebaum from the Haute Hydrant pet store, were there. Amanda was in charge of games and contests for the dogs, and Sally was to provide the contest prizes and solicit donations of items for the silent auction. Since I was the only writer in the group, it wasn't hard to guess who was to be in charge of advertising and promotion. Bertie had volunteered to handle any adoptions of homeless hounds at the Waddle. In fact, she had insisted on it, and everyone understood the reason why. It was Bertie's dog, Gilda, who had been tragically killed before she could be redeemed from Lakeside Shelter, despite the fact that she was microchipped. Gilda had become the cause célèbre of this fundraiser. Everyone blamed Rhoda Marx and her rigid pound policies for the dog's needless death. Bertie was still furious about it.

Jenna returned from the kitchen with the coffee and poured us each a cup.

"What kind of turnout are you expecting for our event?" I asked her.

"We've got about three hundred people registered so far. Your online ads have really helped get the word out."

"That's a decent number for our small community."

"I doubt we'll have the kind of attendance they do at some Basset Waddles, like the ones held in Michigan and Illinois, but people will travel a long way to waddle with the bassets. We have several registrants from Canada, and even a few from abroad."

"I'm sure the location of our waddle is an added attraction. People from all over the world come to visit Lake Tahoe."

"How are we doing on donations for the silent auction, Sally?" Jenna said.

"People have been very generous so far. We've had a lot of support from Petropolis and other businesses in the area."

"I guess we aren't the only ones who want to see Tahoe have a state-of-the-art animal shelter," I said.

"The sooner that terrible place is demolished, the better," Bertie said. "Gilda's spirit won't rest until every last rotten brick of it is razed to the ground."

"I'm so sorry about your dog," I said. "It was such a terrible tragedy."

"Delicious coffee cake, Jenna," Sally said. "You must give me the recipe."

"Of course. Happy to. It was my mother's favorite."

I noticed Sally giving me a funny look. I realized that she and Jenna were trying their best to change the subject, but it was too late. I'd evidently said the wrong thing. The floodgates opened.

Bertie began to sob uncontrollably. "My poor, poor Gilda.

I'll never get over losing her. Never!"

"I'm so sorry. I shouldn't have brought it up."

"No, I'm glad you did."

"How did she end up in the pound, anyway?"

"I was called away on a family emergency, and my neighbor, who was watching her, accidentally let her get out. Gilda was a wanderer, so you had to watch her very carefully or she'd give you the slip when your back was turned."

"Most people don't know the nature of these hounds," I said. "They'll follow that keen nose anywhere. That's how we ended up with Cruiser. He was wandering loose on the streets when my husband saw him. If Tom hadn't found him, I don't think Cruiser would have had a happy ending, either. I still have to watch him when he's off leash or he'll do his famous disappearing act."

"Gilda had a microchip. There was no need for my darling girl to end up the way she did. She wasn't sick or homeless. That evil Rhoda Marx killed her, and I'm glad she ended up the same way all her helpless victims did."

"I know you're still hurting over Gilda's loss, but that sounds pretty cold-hearted, Bertie," Jenna said to her grieving friend.

"No colder than that horrid woman was, and you know it, Jenna. She deserved the same treatment she gave so many innocent animals that could have found homes if they'd only been given half a chance."

No one here was going to disagree with that statement. The room was dead silent, except for the sound of snoring bassets. It was what Bertie said next that gave us all cause for concern about her state of mind.

"Care for some more coffee, Bertie?" Jenna asked.

"No, I'd better not. I haven't been sleeping well lately."

"You, too?" I said. "Those night sweats are murder."

"No, it's not that. It's Gilda."

"Oh, did she used to sleep with you?" Amanda said. "I can't sleep a wink without my canine comforters, either."

"Me, neither," I said. "Even if Cruiser snores. A snoring dog is white noise for a dog lover, though. Lulls me to sleep every time."

"You don't understand," Bertie said. "Something wakes me up every night. I feel a pressure on my chest."

"You should see a doctor, Bertie." Jenna said.

"Gosh, that sounds like there could be something wrong with your heart," Sally said.

"There's something wrong with my heart, all right. It's been broken to bits. But what I'm feeling is nothing like that. It feels like a pair of paws resting on my chest. That's what Gilda used to do. Sometimes, if I was having a restless night, she would crawl up in the middle of the night and place her paws gently upon my chest, and she always did the same thing every morning to wake me."

"You must just be dreaming, dear," Jenna said.

"It's no dream. I'm fully awake when it happens. I know it's Gilda's ghost. I've even seen her! She's come back to haunt me for letting her die." Bertie buried her face in her hands. It was hard watching someone suffer so over the loss of her pet.

"Oh, Bertie, please don't do this to yourself. You didn't let her die. It was an accident. I know you're distraught over her death, but you have to stop grieving so for her. Gilda wouldn't want you to be in such pain. She loved you too much to ever want you to hurt this much."

Bertie looked up at Jenna and then at the rest of us. I don't know what emotion was registering on my face, but I hope I didn't seem as patronizing as the rest of the women in our group.

"I know you all think I'm insane, but I know what I saw. I didn't imagine it. Gilda has come back, and her ghost will never rest until Lakeside Shelter and everyone who had anything to do with her death is history." With that Bertie abruptly stood up. In so doing, she spilled her coffee all over Jenna's coffee table. She didn't pause to apologize but stormed out the front door. The sound of the door slamming woke up the snoring bassets.

We were all dumbfounded until I finally said, "I guess this meeting is officially adjourned."

CHAPTER 22

Driving home from the committee meeting, I kept thinking about what Roberta Finch had said about Gilda. Was she having worse menopausal symptoms than most women her age, a candidate for the nearest psych ward, or had she really experienced a hound haunting? I have heard of people who have recently lost a beloved pet claiming to have heard the sounds of toenails clicking on the floor or the jangling of dog tags. Some feel Fuzzy the cat circling their ankles, as it would have when it heard the sound of the can opener at feeding time.

Others claim to experience the sensation of the bed's edge dipping as though the animal is climbing up as it did in life, and the same thing Bertie felt, paws pressing upon her chest. It's not that uncommon for people to claim they see an apparition of their pet after it has passed. Whether this is all wishful thinking on the part of grieving pet owners or whether the animal's spirit really does come back to visit the human it was so devoted to in life is certainly debatable, but I have no doubt that every animal has a spirit, like any other living, breathing creature.

Who's to say where that spirit goes after death? If for some reason the animal's spirit is not at rest, it's not unreasonable to believe that it could come back to comfort its owner as it did in life, or perhaps even help that owner avenge its untimely death, as in Gilda's case. It was clear Gilda's owner had no doubts about that.

What concerned me even more than Bertie's obvious distress

over the tragic loss of Gilda was her animosity toward the person who was responsible for her demise, Rhoda Marx. From everything I'd heard thus far, it was clear that no one liked Rhoda, but Bertie's feelings went far beyond dislike. We'd all heard her say she was glad Rhoda was dead and that she died the way she did. I suppose I might say the same thing about anyone who hurt my dog. I don't think I'd go as far as someone had to get even with Rhoda Marx, but Bertie's enmity toward Rhoda begged the question, Had she somehow been involved in her death?

I was met at my front door first by Cruiser and then by Calamity, who charged past him to greet me, probably because she smelled traces of other bassets and the lingering aroma of Jenna's yummy coffee cake on my clothes. That move was a big mistake on the newcomer's part, because Cruiser quickly put her in her place as only an alpha dog can. He whirled on Calamity, let out a gruff admonition and gave her a good gumming on the ruff of her neck. Calamity cried out her surprise at Cruiser's unexpected reprisal. There was no harm done to her except for a generous dousing of slobber, but she got the message right away. The rule of the pack is supreme, even for the normally laidback basset hound. So far, Cruiser had been more successful at behavior modification with Calamity than either Nona or I. We might have to recruit Cruiser as her trainer.

"How did your meeting go?" Nona said.

"It didn't. We didn't accomplish very much this afternoon. We kind of got off track."

"I know how that goes. It's hard to keep meetings focused sometimes."

"Oh, this one was focused, all right. It just wasn't what I expected we'd be focused on."

"Which was?"

"One of the ladies was very upset about her dog." I didn't go into more detail. I didn't want to get into further discussion of the Rhoda Marx case with Nona for the moment. Besides, I could tell from her tone of voice that something was amiss on the home front and needed my immediate attention. I was right.

"I think you'll be very upset with your dog when you find out what she's been up to, Mom."

"Calamity is not *my* dog." That was wishful thinking on my part. Potential adopters weren't exactly beating down my front door to take her off my hands. I was almost afraid to ask my next question. "What's she done now?"

"Come with me. I'll show you."

I followed Nona to my bedroom, fearing what I was about to discover when I opened the door. I'd certainly taken on a load of trouble when I agreed to foster Crazy Calamity, and with a murderer still on the loose, there was already plenty of trouble to go around.

Calamity followed close on our heels, but she turned tail and shot back down the hall when she heard the ire rise in my voice as I gazed at the canine crime scene that lay before me. My white duvet was smeared top to bottom with stains. It was like one of those paw paintings you see at animal rescue benefits. "What's that brown stuff all over my duvet?" I wasn't sure I really wanted to know.

"It's chocolate."

"Chocolate! Where did she get chocolate?" Around my house that was like asking where Willy Wonka hides his golden tickets. There was always a stash of chocolate hidden somewhere on the MacBean property, if you knew where to look. Sometimes I hid my treats so well I forgot where I put them myself. Calamity had evidently discovered my private reserve. She was so good at breaking and entering that lockbox, which held not only Cruiser's goodies but also mine, I was surprised she hadn't been able to spring herself free from Lakeside Shelter.

"Apparently, Cruiser's treats weren't good enough for her. She went for yours instead." Nona tried not to laugh when she said it but couldn't contain herself. She burst out laughing at the Jackson Pollock—inspired painted canvas that was once my bedspread.

"This is no laughing matter, Nona. Chocolate is harmful to dogs, and it looks like Calamity got a pretty good dose of it here. Chocolate has theobromine in it, and there's more of it in dark chocolate like this. It can kill a dog if they get too much in their system."

"How would you know if they got too much?"

"The dog would act agitated, for one thing."

"How could you tell with Calamity? She's always agitated."

"Point taken. This dog has a stomach of iron, but I think I'd better get her to the vet right away, just in case."

"I'm afraid she has something else in her system, too."

"What?"

"I finally figured out what happened to your earring."

"You did? What?"

"Calamity has been eating our earrings. She ate mine, too."

"How do you know?"

"I found some that had obviously been gnawed. A few of the mates are missing, so I can pretty much guess where they went. She must have gotten into my travel case."

About that time, I heard a suspicious noise down the hall in the kitchen. Calamity was probably back in the pantry looking for something else to get into. I caught her before she nabbed a whole box of Ding Dongs.

"No you don't, young lady! It's off to Doc Heaton with you." I snapped on her leash and hurried out the door with Calamity, her muzzle still smeared with the evidence of her latest escapade. Evidently, there was more than one chocoholic residing at the MacBean cabin.

CHAPTER 23

If I thought life with Calamity couldn't get any more difficult, I was wrong, as I was about to discover on our next visit to the veterinarian. Why do dogs always seem to know when you are taking them to the vet? Calamity had been to Doc Heaton's clinic only once before, but the moment I turned the car into the parking lot, she freaked out, bouncing around the car like she was spring loaded. It could also have been the chocolate in her system causing such extreme behavior, but since she had already yarked up most of the offending substance on my living room carpet before we left the house, I doubted that was entirely the case. I know chocolate is harmful for dogs, and I thought I had put my stash in a dogproof place, but it was hard to put things far enough out of reach to keep them from Calamity's greedy little paws. I kept thinking, "Why did it have to be my expensive gourmet Godiva chocolates and not the Hershey's candy bars I sometimes carry in my purse?" Fortunately for her, she hadn't gotten into my dark baking chocolate, which would have been more harmful and possibly deadly. It doesn't take much of that to kill a dog. Calamity's size was also in her favor. The dose she got could quickly have killed a smaller dog, but I had no doubt I was going to have this crazy hound around for a while to come.

As I dragged Calamity into the veterinarian's office, she actually latched onto the doorjamb with her front paws like a willful child. I was engaged in a kind of canine taffy pull and fast losing the battle with the belligerent basset until one of the vet techs intervened. She gave Calamity a shot of sedative to calm her down so that the staff could do an ultrasound on her and treat her for the chocolate overdose, if need be.

I waited in the examining room for what seemed like hours while Calamity was being treated. I realized that I was waiting in the same room as when I nearly lost Cruiser to poisoning of another kind during the Sirius case. I still had bad memories of that terrible day. The prospect of life without Cruiser was too horrible to imagine. Doc Heaton had been put through his professional paces on that case. Cruiser's guardian angel also lent a helping paw. I found myself feeling almost as worried about Calamity's welfare now as I had then about Cruiser's.

I hated to admit it, but this dog was starting to grow on me in spite of my every effort not to become too attached to a foster dog. Not as much as she was growing on Nona, even though I knew my daughter was enough like her father to not want to admit her sympathy and increasing affection for a home-less dog. Calamity needed a friend, and she was fast finding one in Nona. The fact that she slept with Nona at night was conclusive enough evidence to me that their bond was becom-ing stronger with each passing day. I knew Nona was worried about Calamity too, and she had wanted to come with me to the vet. I was wishing now that I had brought her along to help me with the dog, but I was fairly confident Calamity hadn't devoured enough of my chocolates to do her any permanent harm. I also wanted someone to watch Cruiser for me while I was away. Although he was no longer a curious pup inclined to chew things he shouldn't, it wasn't unknown for him to get into his own brand of mischief when left to his own devices for too long.

I had run out of pet magazines to read and veterinary wall charts of dog and cat anatomy and canine periodontal disease to study when the door to the waiting room finally opened and a groggy Calamity ambled in, led by Doctor Heaton.

"How is she, Doc?"

"Fine. Fortunately, she didn't ingest enough chocolate to do her any lasting damage. We gave her some fluids and did a gastric lavage to get the rest of the stuff out of her. She should be back to her old self as soon as the sedative wears off."

"You couldn't send some of that sedative home with me, could you? This is the calmest she's been since I brought her home from the shelter."

Doc Heaton laughed.

"Did the ultrasound show anything?"

"Nope. It was all clear. Not a diamond earring or tiara in sight. Apparently, whatever she swallowed went straight through her system without any snags. Better keep this material girl out of your jewelry box from now on, though."

"Don't worry, I will. I'm not planning to have multiple piercings on those long ears of hers to accommodate all my earrings." I thought of Tori Thatcher's piercings. "Now that would be a sight, wouldn't it?"

"Sure would. I think once this little girl gets settled someplace permanent and has a few training sessions, she'll calm down and stop causing so much trouble." I knew from his smile that he was hinting I should adopt Calamity, but he didn't know her like I did.

"I hope so, Doc. She's a real handful. My daughter has promised to take her to her first training class next week."

"You're a lucky girl," Doc Heaton said, giving his patient a friendly pat on her rump. If cats have nine lives, you must have at least half that number working in your favor. Not many animals at Lakeside Shelter have been as fortunate as you."

"That's for sure," I said. "She is certainly a lot luckier than Roberta Finch's basset."

"Yes, Gilda was a patient of mine. I was very upset with the manager of the shelter over that unfortunate incident."

"So was her owner. Still is."

"I microchipped Gilda myself, so all they needed to do was scan the dog for the presence of a chip to identify her owner. The dog's death was unnecessary and inexcusable."

Doc Heaton was visibly upset. I couldn't ever remember seeing him so emotional about one of his patients, except for when we nearly lost Cruiser. Normally, he seemed rather detached. I suppose it's something you have to do in his line of work, or you'd have a hard time doing your job day in and day out. Kind of like Skip and what he encounters in the line of duty. I'd never have made it as a veterinarian. Perhaps in my next life.

"Did you know Rhoda Marx well?" I asked.

"I did a lot of the spays and neuters at the shelter for the lucky few that were claimed in time. I knew her well enough to know she was in the wrong line of work."

"From what I've heard about her, she might have been of more use at Gitmo than at Lakeside. She ran the shelter like a prisoner of war camp, according to her staff."

"Between you and me, Beanie, I was trying to persuade the city council to get rid of her before she could do any more damage. She was bad news for the entire animal care community, and the community in general. That kind of PR isn't good for Tahoe. The council was about to take action, but apparently someone saved them the trouble."

"Apparently." The question still was, who?

Day was done by the time we left Doc Heaton's office. The drive back home with Calamity was much quieter than the one on the way to the vet's office. She didn't fight my putting her in her carrier this time. The moment she was inside she curled up and fell asleep. I would gladly have slipped Doc Heaton a few bucks under the examining table for some of that miracle potion of his. For the first time, Calamity was acting like a normal basset hound. Like Cruiser, she was now calm and laidback. Of course, I knew it couldn't last, and I wouldn't seriously keep the dog drugged to live peacefully with her, but I planned to enjoy this peace and quiet while I could. Calamity didn't even wake up when I steered the car into my driveway. Only when I opened her carrier door did she open her bloodshot eyes, which I would swear were more chocolate brown in color than they were before the infamous Godiva escapade. She'd been lucky this time, but I'd have to be much more watchful of this naughty dog in the future. I wanted her to survive long enough to find her a new home.

I could tell Nona was happy to see us come in the front door. She greeted Calamity first, who gave her a gentle lick on the hand, instead of trying to climb all over her, as she usually did.

"Are you sure this is the same dog you left here with? What did the vet do, clone her? She's so sedate."

"Exactly. She's sedated, so don't get used to this new version of Calamity. I expect the old one will return to us soon enough after the drug wears off."

"She's going to be okay, right?"

"Yes, she was lucky this time. I must be more careful in the future where I store my chocolate, though, and everything else she shouldn't get into."

Calm Calamity lay down at Nona's feet and rolled over on her back to receive a tummy rub. Nona was happy to oblige.

"Did Doc Heaton find any of our earrings in here?" Nona said, stroking Calamity's soft, white belly.

"The ultrasound was clear. No sign of any missing jewelry."

"I think I may have found some of it out in the yard, Mom."

"You did? Where?"

"Guess."

I didn't really have to guess. After talking to Doc Heaton, I already suspected where I would find the mate to my precious ruby earrings Tom gave me on our twenty-fifth wedding anniversary. Sure enough, when I followed Nona outside, there among the pine needles, glinting in the sun was The Jewel of the Pile. I'll spare you the details of our treasure hunt, but suffice to say that Nona and I got our jewelry back and after a thorough sanitizing, most of it was as good as new.

CHAPTER 24

Calamity didn't even blink when the phone rang that evening. She was still conked out from her ordeal at the vet's office. Lying side by side with Cruiser on the living room rug, they looked like bookends. This was something of a breakthrough because Cruiser hadn't tolerated her in close proximity to him until now. But when she lay down beside him, there had been no signs of disapproval from the top dog. He looked up once when she flopped down beside him and then resumed snoring. Perhaps he sensed the ordeal she'd been through at the vet, or maybe it was simply resignation that she was one of the Mac-Bean pack, at least for now. Both dogs must have been chasing the same rabbit in their dreams because their paws paddled in unison. Synchronized swimmers could never outstroke these two.

Who knows what dogs really dream about? We assume they chase rabbits or squirrels in some verdant field of their subconscious, but with rescued dogs like Cruiser and Calamity, one never knows what terrors they might actually be fleeing from in their slumber. Are they escaping monster cats with foot-long razor-sharp claws, or Dr. FrankenHeaton wielding giant hypodermic needles? Unless I am reincarnated as a dog in my next life, I'll never know for certain, but if I am I hope I come back as an adored, spoiled hound like Cruiser. What a cushy life that would be!

When I answered the phone, Carla Meeks from the *Tattler* was on the other end of the line.

"Hey, Carla. What's up?"

"I have an assignment for you if you want it. I need someone to cover the town hall meeting tomorrow night. They'll be discussing proposed changes at Lakeside Shelter. Interested?"

"Sure am."

"Great! I'll expect an article draft by the end of the week. Deliver it sooner, and I'll add a bonus to your usual fee."

"Done." It was high time I'd been offered a raise at the *Tattler*. Actually, considering the current economic downturn and the effects of computer technology on the printed word, Carla was being very generous by offering me more money for this assignment. I suppose it was mostly because I had been writing for the *Tattler* such a long time. Also, she figured I might be retiring from reporting one of these days, and she wanted to keep writers she could depend on to deliver the goods on a tight deadline.

This job couldn't have come along at a better time for me. Not only would I have some extra income, but I'd have a front-row seat in the shelter dispute. With any luck, this controversial event might even draw Rhoda Marx's murderer out of the woods. It was certain that anyone who had any investment, either monetary or emotional, in this hot-button shelter issue in our community would be present. It wasn't quite the same as the killer returning to the scene of the crime, but it was close enough.

My clothes reeked of sweat from the backyard excavation for lost treasure along with that unique mixture of disinfectant, flea spray, and frantic pets at the vet clinic. Although most dog people wouldn't mind the aroma, it was quite a pungent blend, and I doubted it would ever be bottled for sale to the public at large. Of course, I'm still eagerly waiting for Victoria Stillwell or some other celebrity dog trainer to design her own signature fragrance and call it *Puppy Breath*. Forget Liz Taylor's White Diamonds or Chanel. There would probably never be any fragrance manufactured that could capture the essence of another Victoria I had come to know of late. A perfume called Purple and Pierced? For some perhaps, but not for *moi*.

I'd immerse myself in canine cologne that was named for the essence of puppies. For a dog lover like me, there's no aroma on earth that compares to the incomparably innocent odor of a pup's moist, slightly sour, milky breath. When you hold a tiny puppy in your hands and he puffs his momma's milk scent of unconditional love into your face to be inhaled and savored, nothing is sweeter. Perhaps it's even sweeter because that innocence of puppyhood is so quickly and completely lost, never to be regained. It's a love they know only for eight weeks of their life, sometimes even less, but despite what people may think, I believe it's a love they remember forever. If you have ever watched a dreaming adult dog suckle in its dreams, even when it's very old, you know this to be true.

No one ever forgets Mother, and Mother never forgets us. She never stops loving us as long as she lives, no matter how old we are. I suspect the same is true of dogs, which gives one pause when you consider that we separate puppies from their mothers so young, often far too young. I had no doubt that this might have been part of Calamity's behavior problems and could keep her from ever being a well-adjusted member of anyone's household. Whenever I wore my Puppy Breath out on the town for any occasion, I would really be wearing a mother's enduring love for her offspring. It's the same way I feel about my own offspring, so perhaps I'd just have to come up with a uniquely lovely fragrance of my own creation one day and call it Nona.

With Skip coming over later for supper, I didn't want to overwhelm him with my current essence of D.O. (Doggy Odor), so I decided I'd better shower and tidy up. This particular aroma, mixed with my spicy chili and garlic bread, would probably take anyone's appetite, even that die-hard bean eater, Skip's.

CHAPTER 25

Anytime I served my chili, Skip had a standing invitation to join me for dinner. He was late arriving tonight, which wasn't like him. Skip is never late for a free meal if he can help it. When I saw him, I understood why he was tardy this time.

"Gosh, Skip. You look whipped. Been working double shifts or something?"

"Something like that. How'd you know?"

"From the dark circles under your eyes."

"I haven't been sleeping much at night."

"You look like you've been dipped in gunpowder."

"That would be Cannon fodder."

"Oh, you mean your partner, Rusty?"

"Yes, her."

"Problems with the new recruit?"

"And how! Say, you got any beer in the fridge?"

"Sure. I'll go get you one."

"One'll do for starters."

Our conversation had aroused Cruiser and Calamity from their slumbers. Cruiser waddled over and greeted Skip with his usual basset hound version of enthusiasm, and Calamity followed suit. I could tell that some comforting canine attention was just what my friend needed. I knew from personal experience that it's all anyone needs when life is getting you down. That and chocolate.

Calamity nudged Skip's hand, and he stroked her head. "Did

you take in another rescue?"

"No, it's the same one."

"Really? I'd never have guessed. She certainly seems a lot calmer than the last time I saw her. I had to practically pry her off me before."

"You and everyone else."

"Those dog trainers are miracle workers."

"Doc Heaton is the miracle worker, but it's only a temporary miracle, I'm afraid. She's still sedated from her emergency visit at the vet's."

"Uh-oh. What happened?"

"We had a little mishap with some chocolate. She's fine now, though."

"That's good. Whatever he gave her sure made a different dog out of her."

"Yeah, Nona asked me if she was a Calamity clone."

Skip laughed and took a swig of his brew. I could see him starting to loosen up. Beer was apparently a good sedative, too.

"I doubt that the effects will last, unfortunately. I expect we'll have the same old troublesome girl back soon."

The mention of trouble swept the smile off Skip's face. Something was wrong. I hoped he felt he could confide in me. After all, what are friends for besides killer chili and cold beer, and occasionally saving your life?

"I can tell something's bothering you, Skip. Feel like talking about it?"

He took another long slug of cold draft before answering. "Rusty has accused me and others in the department of discrimination."

"That's not good."

"No, it's not. It gets worse, though."

"How so?"

"She also threatened to slap us with a sexual harassment lawsuit."

"You're right. That's a lot worse."

"She may have to go on administrative leave until this is resolved. I should never have hired her in the first place. Even Cruiser could have smelled she was trouble from the get-go. Note to self: Never hire a centerfold."

"You don't know whether there might be extenuating circumstances that forced her to earn extra cash. Maybe she has a sick mother to support or something."

"It doesn't matter. She's an officer of the law, and it's inappropriate for her to be moonlighting in the sex industry. If she wants to do that kind of work, she can get a job at Mustang Ranch. She'd probably earn more there, anyway, than she does at the sheriff's office."

"Come on now, Skip. Why is she making these accusations? You didn't hang that pin-up of her in your locker after all, did you?" I was trying to lighten him up, but it wasn't working tonight.

"No, I didn't, but some of the other guys got another one and did. She claims they've been hitting on her, too."

"Not too surprising. She's an attractive gal, and that uniform of hers is pretty form-fitting, but she wasn't wearing it in her *Playboy* spread. Anyway, I'm sure it's not the first time she's been hit on."

"Maybe not, but she's an officer too, and they should know better."

"What did you do to her, though?"

"She thinks I'm holding her back professionally because she's a female and . . . well, you know."

"A former stripper?"

"Yeah. I don't think I've treated her any different than I would any other officer on the force."

"She's a female in a traditionally male profession. That automatically puts her at a disadvantage."

"I think it's mostly her inexperience that's holding her back, not anything she claims I've done."

"What did she say to you?"

"She said her only regret was that she didn't do it sooner. She's made a bundle from her exposure, so to speak. She's even had a couple of movie offers, but she didn't say what kind of roles she's been offered."

"Being beautiful can be a blessing or a curse for a woman. Just ask Nona. She's had to deal with some of the same issues in her profession. That glass ceiling may have some cracks, but it's still not broken. Nice girls finish last, and sometimes we have to break a few rules to get where we're going. A woman nearly made it to the White House, but we still have a long way to go before we're Queen of the Hill."

"Where is Nona tonight, anyway?"

"She went to the Washoe Health Center."

"What for?"

"She's getting a second opinion from them."

"Opinion about what?"

"She probably would be furious at me for talking about this to you behind her back, but Nona has had a suspicious mammogram."

"Oh."

"Her grandmother died of breast cancer, and those things often skip a generation, so it's got me plenty worried."

"I'm sure."

"I try not to show it for her sake, though."

"Probably for the best."

I could see Skip was uncomfortable talking about breasts, unless they were bared on a pin-up girl. Most men have trouble expressing themselves about personal problems, particularly if they have to do with "womany stuff." I did us both a favor and changed the subject back to helping him solve his problems, which suited him just fine.

"What are you going to do about the trouble you're having with Rusty?"

"I'm not sure. I've gone out of my way to be nice to her and make things as easy as possible for her."

"Maybe that's the trouble. She didn't seem like the kind of gal who would appreciate preferential treatment, especially from a man. She probably finds it condescending. If she joined the force, that means she wants to play hardball with the boys, not be handled with kid gloves."

"You may be right. Anyway, it's out of my hands now. This is one for internal affairs. I'm glad because I have problems of my own with this Marx murder case still unsolved. We really don't have much to go on thus far. The only prints we lifted from the crime scene were canine."

"What else would you expect to find at a dog pound?"

We laughed, but we both knew it was no laughing matter. There was a killer on the loose, and until he or she was collared, no one could rest easy, except maybe for those lazy bassets, Cruiser and Calamity, who had gone back to whatever bad guys they chased in their dog dreams. If only it were that easy chasing bad guys for real.

CHAPTER 26

Skip didn't stay long after he downed his chili and beer. Ordinarily, he wouldn't eat and run, but I knew he had a lot more on his plate than my chili. Not long after he left, Nona got home. Calamity's head popped up. She already recognized the sound of Nona's car engine, like Cruiser knows the sound of mine. She got up and moseyed toward the front door, apparently still a bit loopy from her visit to the vet. Cruiser looked up briefly and resumed his nap. He figured Calamity had the doorbell covered this time. There were some advantages to having another dog in the household. That meant he didn't have to jump up every time the door needed answering.

"Hey, Calamity. How're you feeling, girl?" Nona knelt down to greet the young dog, something she never would have done before, especially if any drool were involved. She didn't seem to mind the saliva from Calamity's lip folds that smeared on her forearm. "She still looks a bit doped, doesn't she, Mom?"

"Yeah, with eyes as bloodshot as hers, I'm surprised Skip didn't throw her in the drunk tank for the night to sleep it off."

"I saw him leaving as I drove up. From the aroma in here, I'm guessing he came over for some chili, huh?"

"What else?"

"He didn't stay very long."

"I know. He has a lot going on at the office. How was your visit at the health center?"

"Fine. It was a little different than I was expecting."

"What were you expecting?"

"I don't know. I guess because it's tribal I thought it was going to be all primitive and everything, but it's really more of a blend of old and new medicine, from a Native perspective. I like that."

"Good, honey. I'm glad you'll be comfortable with the treatment you'll receive there."

"They suggested I visit a Native American Church, but I don't even know what that is. You know I've never been very 'churchy.' "

"I never liked the White Man's churches."

"I know. The only time I've been in a church was for Dad's funeral. Would you come along with me?"

"Of course."

I knew Nona would get some good medicine in our people's church. So would I. She wasn't the only one who needed to chase away some evil spirits, especially with all this murder on my mind.

I never brought Nona up in any kind of church and was never much of a churchgoer myself, even though Tom was Presbyterian and would have liked me to join him on Sundays. I felt out of place in the White Man's church. Still do. My church doesn't have four walls. It is out in nature. Why would I want to be inside a stuffy building when I can be under the wide-open sky inhaling the scent of pines and listening to the wind talk among the branches? No sermon can move me like that, nor can any pipe organ chords compare with the chorus of birds and woodland creatures and water burbling over stones in mountain streams. The light from candles cannot match the light of the sun reflected on the surface of the lake or stars strewn like rare diamonds across a black velvet night.

No, the White Man's religion never had much appeal for our

people, even though Whites have spent a lot of time and spilled a lot of blood trying to convert Native Americans to their beliefs. Whites still don't like us practicing our Indian ways, and they sure don't like the Native American Church, where many of our tribe worships. They even passed laws to keep us from going to our church to practice our own religion. So far, the local law had turned a blind eye to our sacred ceremonies, thanks mostly to my friend who is also the county sheriff.

Religion's a personal thing, in my way of thinking, and it's not right to impose your own beliefs on anyone else. Who's to say that one person's way of connecting to God or Spirit or whatever you want to call it is any more right than another? Like up here in the mountains, there are many trails a man can follow to reach the same summit. So I chose not to push religion of any kind on my daughter while she was growing up, leaving her to choose her own, or not.

This wasn't my first time in the Native American Church, but it would be Nona's. Like a lot of the young people in her generation, she isn't much interested in learning the old ways. Whether it was hope or mere curiosity on her part, she wanted to join the ceremony. In fact, she was the main reason for this meeting. The people were coming together not just to sit in the circle and sing. There was work to do. We had come here to pray in a healing ceremony for my daughter, and she was open to that.

We decided to meet in a secluded area where there would be no likelihood of intruders. As Sonseah requested, I hadn't told anyone outside the tribe about our assembly. She didn't want to attract the wrong attention. I didn't even tell Skip about it. Some locals might decide to take an exception to our prayer meetings because of the medicine we use in the ceremony, so I didn't want to put Skip in a tight spot with the sheriff's department. He had enough troubles to deal with right now. Washoe have the legal right to use the medicine in the practice of their religion, but anyone else might end up in jail for using it. That's kind of funny to us Indians since God created the medicine for us, and we've been using it for all kinds of purposes for thousands of years, long before the Whites ever set foot on our land.

It was nightfall when we gathered for the ceremony. The deerskin of the tipi glowed ghostly white in the light of the full moon that crested the eastern ridge of the Sierra. One could almost believe that the spirit of the animal that gave up its hide for the tipi still inhabited it. Most Native American Churches have only canvas instead of deer or buffalo skins, but our chief, Dan Silvernail, has the real thing.

My grandfather was also a tribal chief in his time. He'd had a tipi that was made from an animal that lived many generations ago, and it was passed down to him from his grandfather. That was in the days when our animal brethren were much more abundant in Tahoe, and there weren't so many rules telling the Washoe that they couldn't freely hunt them. The Indians were never greedy and cruel like the Whites, though, killing animals merely for sport or profit. We never stacked up heaps of carcasses like they did the plains buffalo, wolves, and other animals for the price of their pelts while Indians starved and froze. When we killed an animal, it was for a good reason, for food or clothing or shelter or to survive. Or for use in the practice of our religion. We always honored the animal that gave up its life to keep us alive. No animal ever died in vain.

Dan and his helpers had made sure everything was prepared for the meeting. First they raised the four big poles of the tipi and bound them together. North, south, east and west poles symbolize the unity of all the races on Earth and that we'll someday be reunited in heaven. The tipi always faces east, but every direction has its own special meaning for the tribe.

Dan and his helpers swept the ground clean inside and outside the tipi before the meeting began. They cut enough wood to last through the night and keep the fire burning. The fire must never go out during the ceremony. The inside of the tipi smelled of juniper, which was brought in to burn on the fire to make some aromatic smoke. That is for healing any sickness. Sometimes sage is used to make good smoke.

The chief fanned the fire with his ceremonial fan made of magpie feathers, like the Washoe used in the old days. Feathers have special powers, depending on the bird they came from, but eagle feathers are the most potent. The magpie feathers, darker than the deepest waters of the lake, shimmered in the firelight. The old Washoe often used the feathers from those birds because they're tough and aggressive. They chase predators away from their nests and fearlessly protect what's theirs. That's why warriors liked to put a lone magpie feather in their hair before they went to war.

When everything was ready, Chief Dan said a prayer for the meeting, and we all followed him into the tipi. He sat on the west side of the tipi, and the rest of us went around on the left side and took a seat. The men sat up front near the fire. Women and new members sat at the back, as is the tribal custom, which sometimes rankled this old women's libber, but I deferred to tribal custom. Dan was flanked by the drummer on his right and the cedar helper on his left. The fire keeper sat beside the door of the tipi so he could get more wood when it was needed. Sonseah was our water girl tonight, in place of Dan's wife, who usually carried the water. Her job was to bring cleansing water in at midnight and some food at daybreak, so she had to be at the ready to do her part when the time came. It was an important job that made Sonseah feel important, as she was accustomed to whenever the occasion arose. But all was good tonight. I didn't feel jealous of her as I usually did. She had shown me a softer, kinder side to her personality. Though I didn't know if we would ever really be good friends, we were on the same team and had roles to play for the good of all. It was important that everyone be in a positive frame of mind and that the rules be followed during the meeting so that we could focus on praying and the real reason for this meeting, my daughter's healing.

The drumming and singing began, low and slow at first, like the true Washoe way. My heart beat in steady rhythm with the music. It was good being among my own kind and practicing our ways for the good of those present in the circle, especially Nona. I spent too much time in the White Man's world. I needed this connection with my own people sometimes to remind me who I really am.

The drum had been assembled especially for this meeting with newly washed skin, cinched up so it would stay together and make the best tone. Even the rhythm of Cruiser's and Calamity's tails I'd heard drumming in unison on the pine floor of my cabin was never as soothing to me as the sound of the drummer's steady beating.

CHAPTER 27

"What is this?" Nona asked.

"It's a special kind of herbal tea. Drink up."

Nona sniffed the liquid, took a sip, and made a face. "Eww, if this is tea, it sure isn't Earl Grey. It tastes terrible."

Nona was right. It wasn't Earl Grey, and this wasn't any tea party. "It's part of the ceremony, Nona. You have to take some of the medicine for it to work its magic. Try to drink a little more, if you can."

Nona steeled herself and took a few more sips of the bitter tea. Then she passed the bowl to me, and I did the same, though I managed to swallow more of it than she did. Everyone in the circle did the same.

Dan beat the drum and sang his songs along with the other men. Each used his own special drumstick to get a different tone. One of the men played a whistle carved from the leg bone of an elk. The music of their voices blending with the rhythmic drumbeats, rattles, and whistles filled every part of the tipi, drifting out into the night and reaching everyone in the whole world. It was like an electrical conduit connecting all our people everywhere. I had my own gourd that my grandfather used, which was passed down to his only child, my mother, after he died. She had still believed like the old Washoe, though, and didn't want to keep anything that belonged to the dead because she thought an angry spirit might be trapped inside it. But the instrument was too old and fine to simply cast aside. To me it was a part of Grandfather, so I changed the rocks and beads inside the gourd and adorned it with my own special feathers from mountain birds to make it mine alone. I played it at every meeting, rattling it gently in rhythm with the thundering drums, and the sound was like hearing rain on the lake in a storm.

The moon rose high above the mountains to illuminate the forest floor, as it had for many generations of my ancestors, but the only light we saw inside the tipi was from the flames of the fire. Dan's drumming never wavered throughout the night, and the songs rose up high and strong like an eagle soaring on great wings spread above the deep blue lake. As I gazed into the fire, I saw figures dancing in the flames keeping time with the drumbeats. Then I beheld images of my mother and my grandfather, who had joined our circle. They seemed so real, I felt as though I could reach out and touch them. I felt the gentle caress of my mother's hand upon my cheek.

Grandfather's pipe smoke rose toward the apex of the tipi and the smoke morphed into the shapes of a bear, eagle, and coyote. Then the smoke transformed into a rainbow of brilliant colors. I could not describe these colors to you because I have never seen anything like them before in nature. Soon I felt something rising up in me along with the white curls of smoke. I had become the smoke.

I had left my body. From high above, I could see Nona inside the tipi and all the other people gathered there in the meeting. Higher and higher I flew until I could see Lake Tahoe from shore to shore and the surrounding Sierra mountain range for many miles. I heard the sounds of thunder rolling across the heavens as I was carried upward on eagle wings through a great wall of white clouds into the blackness of the night.

Traveling higher still, I saw California, the entire North American continent, the blue marble of Mother Earth, onward beyond the moon and even the Milky Way. Floating, sailing into another realm, I was far beyond the rainbow now, in the spirit world, traveling on a road illuminated by countless stars, to I knew not where. From a distance, I could hear the sound of howling, but it was not the howling of a coyote or a wolf. It was a hound baying.

I didn't know where I was, but I understood it was not a place I had ever been before. I certainly wasn't at Lakeside Shelter, but from all the dogs and other animals I saw, it could have been, except for the fact that this place was beautiful and peaceful, unlike anywhere else I had ever been before. Ahead I saw a bridge of a thousand different colors. The colors vibrated, and a sound like a choir of angels emanated from beyond the bridge. I approached, but I understood that I must not cross over this brilliant span of many colors. Not yet. Though I could see what lay beyond the bridge.

Before me lay a miraculous Eden of endless fields drenched in glorious golden sunshine. The light was almost too bright to look at, but before long my weak human eyes could see clearly into another realm most believe does not exist. Now I knew without any doubt that it did.

Running through endless green pastures, cavorting on the gentle leas, frolicking among sibilant grasses were dogs of every breed, size, and color. Like stars in the heavens, there were so many it was impossible to count them all. Every animal appeared young, happy, and healthy. Among their numbers I saw Dusty and Sandy, my grandparents' mongrel dogs I knew when I was a child. I always loved coming to visit them because I couldn't have dogs in the big city where I lived. I'd spend every summer playing with Dusty and Sandy, and I credit them with my enduring love for dogs. Both dogs were now playful youngsters again, not old and arthritic with grizzled muzzles like the last time I saw them.

I ventured partway across the magical bridge, stopping at its crest so that I could better see what miracles lay beyond. I gazed upon the idyllic scene before me, feeling more at peace than I ever had in my life. At that moment, a basset hound waddled out from among the other dogs and approached the end of the bridge. That explained the distinctive howling I had heard before. The dog was a beautiful white color, like the perfect clouds tumbling above the scene beyond the bridge where I stood. She had the longest snow-white ears with distinctive flecks of gold on their tips. I instantly recognized her from the photos that had appeared in the *Tattler*. This was the ill-fated Gilda.

I summoned Gilda to me. True to her nature, she did not respond to my command to come. Apparently, bassets in the afterlife are as stubborn as Cruiser and Calamity. That is their true hound essence, after all, but of course she didn't know me. I was not her mistress. I tried calling her again, but she only lifted her muzzle to a tangerine sky and bayed mournfully. It was the saddest sound I had ever heard. She was here in a safe, happy place, but her world was still incomplete. I was not the person upon whose arrival she awaited. She waited here for Bertie, not me. Yet I understood that she had summoned me to travel on this incredible journey for some special purpose. I knew I had not been transported all this way for no good reason. Gilda had brought an important message for the one she left behind so tragically and prematurely, and I was chosen to be her courier.

I walked back to my side of the bridge. It was time to return to my earthbound plane. When I turned to look back at beautiful Gilda one last time, she was no longer there. She had waddled off to join her new pack mates. Joining in a basset chorus, Gilda and the other young hounds scampered down a flower-strewn path of a million delightful scents a heavenly hound like her could track with basset tenacity.

In less than a single beat of a hummingbird's wing, I was back beside Nona inside the tipi. When I saw the light streaming in the doorway of our native tent, I thought at first I was still at Rainbow Bridge, so incredibly brilliant was the light, but I realized it was only the breaking dawn. I was back in my earthbound plane. The drumming had stopped, and the meeting was over.

Sonseah brought a traditional breakfast of fish, pine nut soup, and acorn biscuits and blessed it before we partook. The sunlight was bright, but not as bright as that I had seen on my unforgettable vision during my night journey. I glanced at Nona. She had never appeared so serene to me. She seemed to be glowing from within, and there was an expression of peace and contentment I had never seen before on my daughter's beautiful face. I hadn't felt this close to my only child since the day I held my tiny papoose in my arms for the first time. I hugged her, and hand-in-hand we left the meeting of our Native American Church, feeling more purified than if we'd been baptized a hundred times in the White Man's church. Our peace of mind and spirit wasn't destined to last long, though.

CHAPTER 28

When we stepped out into the new day, we also stepped right into a pack of trouble. Blinding bright lights of another kind were flashing in our eyes, but they were those spinning atop the patrol cars. The law lay in wait for our meeting to adjourn, ready to pounce upon us the moment we exited the tipi. It looked like the whole Tahoe police force was on the scene and ready for a showdown. At least they'd demonstrated enough respect for our tribal customs not to break in on the ceremony before it was over.

"My goodness. All this fuss just for drinking a little herbal tea?"

"Why are the police here, Mom?"

"I think we're about to find out, Nona."

Rusty Cannon approached us, her weapon drawn. Two other officers flanked her.

Who did she think she was, anyway, Annie Oakley? Was she planning to stage her own Wild West Show right here with the tribe outside our tipi? She must have spotted Dan Silvernail's Bowie knife he always carries with him, and that was reason enough reason for her to cock her six-shooter. This pin-up girl turned policewoman was apparently hell-bent on making her mark in the force, and she was planning on doing it at our expense.

"Put down your weapon," Rusty ordered Dan. He complied.

"What's the trouble, officers?" I asked.

"We're here to take you into custody."

"All of us?" Dan said. "What for?"

"For using an illegal substance."

"We Washoe use our medicine for religious and healing ceremonies. That's what we were doing here. You have no business messing with our religious practices."

"Doesn't matter. It's against the law."

"Do you also arrest Catholics for drinking wine in communion at church?"

"That's not the same thing."

"It is to us, and the cops around here understand that. They don't interfere with our tribal meetings or religion, and you should have been aware of that before the troops were called out on us. You are the one who is breaking the law of the Washoe people."

"Well, let's leave that to the court to decide," Rusty insisted. "All right, officers. Do your duty!"

Rusty and her boys began cuffing everyone who'd attended the meeting, including Nona and me.

We were herded into our rides to the county jail. Nona and I shared the back seat of a cruiser. When I glanced over at her, I saw a tear trail down her cheek. This healing ceremony certainly hadn't turned out as I had hoped it would. Being booked and thrown into the jail was yet more stress my daughter didn't need in her current state. I was worried about her and also about Cruiser and Calamity, who'd been left all alone at my cabin. No one knew how long we would be gone, and I hadn't left any food out for the dogs to eat while we were away. This was one time I wouldn't mind if Calamity raided the pantry. At least she and Cruiser would have something to eat while Nona and I were sharing a cell in our own version of Lakeside Animal Shelter.

★ ★ ★ ★ ★

This day certainly hadn't ended up as I'd planned. I sure hadn't expected to be peering through the wrong side of the bars of a cell at the county jail when I took Nona along to one of our tribal meetings for a healing ceremony. Thanks to Skip's overzealous new deputy, half the Washoe tribe had been rounded up and thrown in the clink, including our water girl, Sonseah, who had not taken their interference in native affairs lightly. I rightly guessed that Tahoe law enforcement had not heard the last of this from her. She wasn't one to take such affronts to our tribal traditions lying down.

In fact, when one of the officers tried to put another kind of silver bracelets on her wrists, she didn't hesitate to pick up the ceremonial water bucket and upend it over his head, which he didn't take lightly, either. He completely lost it, but when he started getting a little rough with his dunker, Chief Dan stepped in front of her to block his assault. The officer, who was no pee-wee himself, surveyed from toes to nose the towering Dan, who tops six foot four, not including his Stetson hat. The cop backed off and decided to continue his cuffing with someone less intimidating.

Sonseah had taken part in lots of demonstrations of one kind or another, which was bound to cause a person to run afoul of the law now and then. She was always protesting about some social issue, particularly if it had anything to do with Washoe affairs, as in the case of Cave Rock. I would gladly pound the pavement for Native American affairs too, but it was mainly anything associated with animal welfare that was sure to get me on the warpath.

However, this was the first time either of us had ended up behind bars for walking a different trail than others did. It appeared that we might be in here for a while. I was getting more concerned by the minute about Cruiser and Calamity. I should have hired a dog sitter or told someone, anyone, where Nona and I were going. Someone had evidently learned about the meeting that was planned last night, or we wouldn't be in our current predicament.

Looking out through the cold steel bars, I finally understood exactly how the animal inmates at the shelter must feel, waiting and waiting for liberation that too often never came. This was the same thing dogs must feel every single time a person walked past their cage at the shelter. I had seen it too often when I toured animal shelters. The hopeful, searching canine eyes looking up whenever someone entered the kennel. *Is it you? Have you come to take me home, at last?* Those eyes always say the same thing, but the answer to their unspoken query is usually the same. Soon, unflagging hope is followed by disappointment and eventually despair when the person they long for never arrives.

Fortunately for us, our freedom was to be quickly restored. When I saw Skip coming down the corridor toward our cell, a flood of relief washed over me as palpably as the contents of Sonseah's upended water bucket had washed over that surprised deputy.

"Beanie, I never expected to see you and Nona in here."

"Neither did we, but here we are, thanks to Deputy Cannon. She's the one responsible for this travesty."

"I already had a talk with her about it. She admitted she was being a little overzealous in executing her duties. You're both free to go."

"Hooray!" Nona said. "Let's blow this joint!'

"What about the rest of us?" Sonseah demanded.

"You, too."

"Thanks, Skip. I owe you one."

"Forget it. If you'd only given me a heads-up about your little tea party, I'd have made sure Rusty had something else to keep her busy for the night. She's new blood, so she doesn't know about all the tribal stuff around Tahoe. I'll see it doesn't happen again."

"Let's hope so," Sonseah piped in.

Dan slipped his big blade into its sheath and strode out of the jail. The rest of the tribe trailed behind him, including my daughter and me. This was one trail of tears we both hoped never to travel again.

CHAPTER 29

The sun dipped low on the western ridge by the time we finally headed for home. A gusting evening wind had come up, and the tips of the pines that surround my property swept the blushing sky like an artist's paintbrush.

For a second time I thought I heard the distant sound of hounds baying, but I discovered it was coming from inside my own house. Nona and I heard the commotion as we pulled into the driveway. Calamity's hysterical yelps drowned out Cruiser's melodious howls.

"That crazy Calamity!" I said. "Who will ever adopt a dog like her with such severe separation anxiety?"

"She seemed all right when we left. Maybe something is wrong with her."

"Something's wrong with her, all right. The dog's a total nut job. I'll never be able to re-home her, and I'll be stuck with her forever. It's no wonder she was dumped at the shelter."

"Gosh, Mom. Cut the poor girl a little slack. We've been gone all night and most of the day."

"True. We've never left her alone so long before, but I assumed that Cruiser's presence would be enough to keep her from going berserk while we were away. I may have to resort to drugging her next time we have to leave her for any period of time. I have some of her remedy on hand from when I first brought her home from the shelter. I should have dosed her with it last night before we left."

As we neared the front door and I heard Cruiser's familiar alarm, I instinctively knew that something more than our long absence had upset the dogs. Calamity was absolved for her bad behavior, at least this time.

"What on earth has gotten into those dogs?" Nona said as we approached the front door.

"I don't know, but something's amiss or Cruiser wouldn't be carrying on so." I knew every subtle nuance of Cruiser's vocalizations and immediately understood that this was certainly no case of separation anxiety on Calamity's part. She was joining in on helping Cruiser guard the home front in our absence. Perhaps she was a better watchdog than I gave her credit for. What were they protecting the house from, though?

When I aimed my key for the lock, I felt the hairs on my neck bristle like the ruff of Cruiser's neck when he spots a cat. It was obvious that someone had tried to break in while we were gone. The door was still shut; only the lock had been damaged. Had the dogs frightened the intruder away, or was he hiding inside the house, waiting to ambush the owner? If that wasn't the case, why were they raising such a ruckus? This wasn't a "Happy to see you; where have you been so long?" greeting.

"You wait out here, Nona."

"Do you think you should go in there alone? What if a burglar is still in the house?"

She was right. It was always wiser to call the police in the case of a break-in, but at the moment, I was more concerned about the dogs' safety than I was my own. Besides, with budget cutbacks and layoffs in the ranks of law enforcement, who knew how long I'd be standing out there waiting for an officer to arrive? Of course, they still had plenty of manpower (and womanpower) to arrest the whole Washoe tribe. This wouldn't be the first crime I'd been first on the scene to investigate.

"Don't worry, I'll be careful. Why don't you see if you can contact Skip on your cell while I check things out?"

"Please be careful, Mom. Here, take my pepper spray with you, just in case. If you see anyone in there, give 'em a shot right in the kisser."

"Gotcha, Dead-eye." There were times like this when I wondered if packing heat might not be a good idea, but pepper spray was about as hot as it was going to get for now.

I nudged the front door open a couple of inches and cringed when the door hinges squealed like a trapped mouse. So much for stealth. I needed a canister of WD40 to go with my pepper spray. The howling basset chorus abruptly ceased, and a black nose popped out the aperture to sniff the air. When Cruiser caught my scent, he whined softly. Immediately, another nose shoved its way through the open door. When Calamity recognized not only my scent but Nona's, she began barking in her usual frenzied manner. I tried shushing her, to no avail. She didn't stop barking until Nona followed me inside.

"I thought I told you to wait outside."

"Sorry. I couldn't stand idly by when you might be in mortal danger. I figured if there was going to be any trouble, two of us are better than one."

Nona had a valid point. It was the same with bassets. A brace of hounds tracks prey more efficiently than a single dog. Apparently, this twosome trait had worked for Cruiser and Calamity. The thing about bassets is that they have a great big bark to match that big dog's body on short legs. They might be funny-looking to most people, but a formidable voice belies their clownish demeanor. Hearing a basset barking inside a house without actually seeing who's doing the barking, an intruder would assume the dog is much larger than it really is. If a burglar heard two bassets barking in unison, he would no doubt be "braced" for trouble, even though he'd probably only get a good licking if he dared to enter the premises. That was, if he didn't die laughing at the sight of those two silly hound dogs.

CHAPTER 30

Nona and I relaxed a bit when everything appeared to be in order upon entering the house. Nothing seemed out of place other than the overturned garbage can in the kitchen and the shoe Calamity had been gnawing on. Compared to what we could have found upon our arrival, a chewed loafer seemed inconsequential. Nothing had been stolen. The coast seemed clear.

"Evidently, the dogs scared our would-be thief away before he could enter the house," Nona said.

"It certainly looks that way. He managed to break the door lock, but the noise he made doing that interrupted Cruiser's and Calamity's beauty sleep and put them on high alert. Their barking must have scared him away."

At least that's what I thought until I discovered the back door swinging open and shut in the breeze. Apparently this break-in wasn't an open and shut case, though. The hounds had scared someone off, all right, but whoever it was had been inside the house, awaiting my return. Perhaps we had averted an ambush, after all. So much for the two attack bassets on duty. I could only conclude they'd been bribed with treats to gain entry into their territory. Hand over a few Snausages or Bacon Beggin' Strips and these fearsome watchdogs would probably roll out the Welcome Home Invaders mat. Either that, or the interloper was someone they recognized.

Rusty Cannon strode from Skip's patrol car, ready to add more notches to her Sam Browne with another arrest. Not Nona and me again, I hoped. I'd seen as much as I ever cared to see of the El Dorado County jail.

"What are *you* doing here?" I said. "We were expecting Sheriff Cassidy."

"He couldn't respond to a burglary. He has bigger fish to fry."

Officer Shapely must have known fisherman Skip a lot better than I first thought she did. Just how well, I didn't know. Maybe the Skipper had even taken her out in his new speedboat for a moonlight cruise. I was merely the first mate on the good ship *Trout Scout.*

"What seems to be the problem?"

"Someone broke into my house."

Rusty immediately spotted the jimmied lock on the front door. "So I see. Did you go inside before calling us?"

"Yes."

"You should have waited for the police to arrive, ma'am."

Smile when you say that, Sister. Words like that used to grind my gears, but as I grow older, I am beginning to find *ma'am* preferable to *sweetie, honey,* or *dear.* Worst of all is *young lady,* especially if being delivered by a young man in the guise of courtesy.

Of course, I imagine women like Rusty have their own special crosses to bear. It seems that no matter what a woman's age, respect is something we must constantly fight hard to earn in our society, and I guessed that was what Rusty was all about. She was fighting to gain respect in her profession and earn a decent living, all the while bumping her head on the ceiling that was still impenetrable for all but the most ambitious females. While you might expect Rusty's good looks to work in her favor, they could turn out to be her Waterloo with the sheriff's office, especially now that she'd been officially outed as a centerfold.

"That might have been too long. Besides, whoever was here is gone now, Officer. He probably broke in while my daughter and I were locked up in jail." I hoped my intended sarcasm wasn't lost on her, but if it wasn't, she probably didn't care. In her estimation, she had just been doing her duty when she set up the ambush at our prayer meeting. If there was one thing positive you could say about Officer Cannon, it was that she was tenacious in the execution of her duties. Once on the trail, you couldn't distract her from her quarry for anything. In fact, if she were a dog, she'd be a basset hound.

Even though I'd said the intruder was gone, Rusty followed standard procedure, just in case I was wrong about that assumption. It was decidedly preferable to have Officer Rusty on your side than not.

"You both had better wait out here while I take a look inside, just to be sure it's all clear."

"Cruiser! Calamity!" I didn't want the dogs to get caught in the crossfire, in case there was about to be a shootout at the OK-9 Corral. Cruiser responded right away, but no Calamity appeared, even when I summoned her again. Nothing unusual about that.

For the second time that day, Rusty drew her weapon. She entered my home cautiously, making her way slowly but steadily through each room. I heard her yelling "Clear!" as she finished scanning each room of my house for a possible burglary suspect. I guessed she was following that procedure mostly to assure herself, since no other officers were present who would have needed to know the coast was clear.

Everything was going fine until she made her way into my kitchen, the last room on her search. Then, I heard Rusty shout out the command, "Freeze!" Had she found someone hiding in the house after all? How could I have missed that? I'm not exactly an amateur when it comes to sniffing out criminals, but I'm sure no pistol-packin' momma. For the first time since I'd met her, I was glad that Officer Cannon was on the scene and ready for action. When I heard a single shot fired inside the house, I couldn't wait out on the front porch any longer. I charged in the door, with Nona and Cruiser close behind, despite my insistence that they stay out. I couldn't argue with Nona right now. Officer Cannon could be in trouble. And where was that naughty Calamity?

"Is everything all right, Officer?"

"Yes."

From the bullet hole in my kitchen ceiling, I wasn't so sure.

"If everything's all right, what were you firing at?"

"I almost shot your dog!"

Frantic, Nona cried out. "Calamity! Calamity! Where are you?"

A nose popped out of the pantry and sniffed the traces of Cannon shot in the air.

Nona coaxed the frightened dog. "Come on out, girl. It's okay."

"What happened?"

"I was just checking to make sure no one was hiding in your pantry. I must have surprised her. She leapt out at me. I thought I was being attacked and fired off a round. I wasn't expecting to be ambushed by a hound dog."

One ambush deserves another, Officer Nasty. "I guess she wasn't expecting you, either. She was probably already spooked by the intruder."

Of course, Nona and I knew that the pantry was where you'd usually find Calamity, but she was hiding there now for good reason. She was afraid of thunder, so the sound of gunfire at close range should have sent her right through the roof along with that stray bullet. I was just glad the rookie's aim was off and that no harm had been done. At least that's what I thought until I noticed the drops of blood staining the linoleum on my kitchen floor.

"Whose blood is this on the floor? Are you sure you didn't shoot the dog?" I said, suddenly concerned about Calamity. Perhaps she was hurt, and that's why she had been hiding in the pantry. She might have been injured by the intruder and that's why she reacted as she did to the officer when she opened the pantry door.

Nona examined Calamity from the tip of her nose to the last hair on her tail for any wound. "There's no mark on her. She isn't hurt, Mom."

Well, that was welcome news in more than one way. No more vet visits were in our immediate future.

"Did Calamity bite you, Officer?"

"No, although I wouldn't have taken any bets on it when she came hurtling out of there at me. She meant business. She was growling and seemed very aggressive, which is why I fired off a shot."

"We've had some behavioral issues with her since I rescued her from Lakeside Shelter, and I saw some fear aggression from her at a shelter worker, but she has never bitten anyone that I know of."

"So far, you mean."

"To be perfectly honest with you, I wouldn't take any bets on that, either. I'm glad she didn't bite you, though." Was I ever! I didn't need this gal to file a lawsuit against me too, like she was threatening to do to the whole sheriff's office.

"Perhaps it was the uniform she's wearing, Mom. Lots of dogs don't like them. You, know how dogs react to postal carriers."

Yep, Calamity definitely didn't like uniforms, or veterinary lab coats, either. I remembered how she had reacted to Rex at the shelter whenever he approached her. He wore a uniform, too. This could have been no more than a post-traumatic shelter disorder flashback for Calamity. Or could it have been Rex who had paid us a visit and bled on my kitchen floor after Calamity finally gave him a well-deserved retaliatory bite?

Sleep eluded me that night, but it had nothing to do with my occasional insomnia episodes. Pine branches clawed the outer cabin walls in the windstorm that had increased to gale force. Rain pelted the roof in a relentless downpour. Every time I heard the house creaking against the storm's power, my neck hair spiked. Was it only the storm, or had our intruder returned?

We'd managed to blockade the front door since the lock was broken, but once your home has been invaded, you never feel truly safe again. Having a home alarm system of two barking dogs helped make me feel a bit more secure, but the knowledge that the hounds were here wasn't putting me at ease tonight, especially with Cruiser snoring away at the foot of the bed, drooling blissfully on his quilt. It was hard to stretch out enough to relax with a seventy-pound hound taking up half the bed. His presence was always a comfort, though. Still, I suspected that if Jack the Ripper were lurking outside my bedroom door, Cruiser would never be the wiser. That dog could really count his Zs.

As for me, counting sheep, or bassets, has never worked to induce slumber. It's hard to quiet my mind at times like this, so the only thing that helps me is to do a little novel plotting in my head until I finally drift off. That worked fine under normal circumstances, but right now all I could think of was who might have had a reason to break into my home and what that reason could be.

Instead of the usual cast of literary characters, a list of possible suspects roiled in my brain like the black storm clouds blustering their way over the peaks of majestic Mount Tallac. I doubt even Charles Dickens himself could have imagined the likes of Victoria Thatcher for a character in one of his novels. But people in Dickens's day never wore their hair dyed purple, and the only multiple piercings, chains, or spikes were to be found deep in the dungeons of the Tower of London's bloody history.

I had such a painful assortment of body aches from the physical and emotional strain of this case, not to mention chasing that crazy Calamity from one end of Lake Tahoe to the other, I felt like I was being pierced and poked with spikes. As though thoughts of Tori weren't enough to chase the Sandman away and hit him on the head with his own sandbags, there was always the executioner, Rex, who was probably the scariest-looking fellow I'd seen inside or outside an animal shelter. Now there was a bedtime bogeyman that could make anyone want to pull the covers over her head or hide under the bed. His sheer size was enough to make me suspect he could easily have killed Rhoda. I already knew he was certainly capable of efficiently administering death to any living thing, but whether meting out a death sentence at the shelter also included his boss, I still didn't know. It seemed as if he had more in common with her temperamentally than anyone else I'd yet encountered while investigating this case, so what would be his motive to kill her? Perhaps he just detested her as much as every other employee at Lakeside and every pet lover in Tahoe did.

There was also Bertie Finch, whose dear Gilda had tragically died at Rhoda's command. Perhaps of all the possible motives for Rhoda's death, I could understand Bertie's the best. I know if it were Cruiser instead of Gilda, and I had been in Bertie's shoes, that would be more than enough motive to make Rhoda suffer the same fate.

I still had a large collection of possible suspects to consider as the perpetrator of Rhoda's killing. From what I'd heard about the victim and seen of her myself when visiting the shelter, I could easily understand why she was so vehemently disliked by all who knew her. As Sally had said when asked who would want Rhoda Marx dead, her answer was the same as mine. Who wouldn't?

CHAPTER 31

Nona was up long before me, which was unusual. I'm normally an early riser, but even Cruiser was up before me that morning. The same thing lured me as lured him from the comfort of the bed—the smell of food. I could never resist the aroma of warm cinnamon buns. Like a hungry hound, I tracked the scent and found the hot buns and also Cruiser. He was exactly where I would expect to find him hanging out, in the kitchen. He and Calamity flanked Nona at the dinette table, waiting for handouts or accidental droppage.

"Hey, lazybones. You're finally up. Even Cruiser was awake before you today."

"I had trouble getting to sleep last night. I didn't even feel him get off the bed. I guess I was out cold."

"Did the storm keep you awake, too?"

"That and worrying about what happened last night."

"It's enough to make you worry. You keep putting yourself and Cruiser at risk, getting involved in all these crazy cases up here. When are you going to retire and enjoy life a little?"

"I'm only fifty. That's not exactly retirement age. Fifty is the new forty, haven't you heard? Besides, I do enjoy my life."

"You know what I mean. I wish you'd do something that doesn't involve putting yourself in danger all the time. Like your writing."

"When I become a rich and famous author, I can rest on my laurels, or on my front porch knitting Afghans."

"With you, that would be Afghan hounds, wouldn't it, Mom?"

"Hounds of some kind or other, I suppose."

Nona knew I craved the excitement of crime-solving, but sometimes it got a little too exciting, even for me. When danger crawled right up on my front porch and invaded my inner sanctum, that was cause for real alarm, so I understood her concern. I knew she was looking out for me—and my best buddy, of course.

"Do you have any ideas about who our intruder might have been?"

"I was counting possibilities like sheep last night, which is why I didn't get much sleep."

"I had a little trouble myself with all that rain pounding on the roof."

"I know. You'd have thought we did a rain dance last night in the tipi."

"What exactly did we do last night in the tipi, Mom?"

"It was a healing ceremony, in the true Washoe tradition."

"Have you told Skip about it?"

"No. He's my best friend, but he's as white as Wonder Bread and doesn't really understand the ways of our people. It's better for us both if it stays that way."

"I think you're probably right. That whole experience was pretty intense, but I'm glad you took me there with you."

"Me, too."

"Did you ever get hold of Skip?"

"No. I left a message on his phone, but he hasn't gotten back to me yet."

"You really should report the break-in. Others in the community might be in jeopardy."

"You're right, honey. I think I'll go over after I finish my breakfast and pay the sheriff a little visit."

Nona was right that any crime should be reported, but I had

the uncomfortable feeling that I was the only one who should be worried about more trouble.

It was nearing ten A.M. by the time I drove over to Skip's place. His patrol car was still parked in the driveway, which seemed unusual, considering it wasn't his day off and there were crimes that needed solving; namely, the Marx murder and now a home invasion. Had he taken the day off sick? That could explain why he hadn't responded to my message.

I rang the bell. No response. I knocked once. Twice. Finally, I heard the sound of footsteps. The door opened to reveal a disheveled Skip still cloaked in his bathrobe. Skip's skinny legs reminded me of those on the seagulls I used to see hanging around Fisherman's Wharf. His hair looked like a haystack on his head, and sprigs of straw-colored chest hair poking out the top of his robe made me think this scarecrow needed re-stuffing.

"Beanie, what are you doing here?"

"You haven't answered any of my phone messages. I thought something might be wrong, so I came over to check on you. Are you sick or something?"

"Uh, er, yeah. Something."

"You took the day off?"

"Yes, I did. Do I need a doctor's note?"

"No, of course not." Where was this defensive attitude coming from? My question was quickly answered when I heard a female voice beckon from inside.

"Who's that, Skippy?"

I'd heard that voice somewhere before, but it wasn't the nasal twang of Rita Ramirez.

"I can't talk now. I'll give you a call later, okay?"

"Sure. Okay. Later."

The door clicked shut. I didn't need a farmhouse to drop on me to deduce what was going on. Skip was taking the day off, but it wasn't because he was sick. Far from it. Skippy got lucky. If his hair looked like hay, it was because he'd had a roll in it. I didn't have to be Sherlock Holmes to figure out who his lucky charm was.

As I drove away, puzzling over Skip's odd behavior, I realized I forgot why I had come over to talk to him in the first place. I didn't even get a chance to tell him about the intruder at my house last night. Apparently, if any sleuthing was to be done on this crime, it would be up to me and my only witnesses—the drooling duo, Cruiser and Calamity.

I was dying to share this juicy tidbit about Skip with Nona, but I didn't want to gossip about my friend behind his back. I had the feeling that news of this collaboration was going to make the rounds in the community and his department without any help from me, like a "Cannon" shot heard 'round the lake.

CHAPTER 32

I made sure I was the first person on the scene at the town hall meeting. I intended to make sure I had the best vantage point and would have a basset's-eye view of every attendee—that would be from the knees up, of course. I would observe everyone as intently as Calamity and Cruiser watch my every movement in the kitchen and around the house. In the same way they patiently await the incidental dropping of any tidbit that might fall within easy reach, I would be watching everyone's actions for any suspicious behavior and listening for revealing statements that might incriminate a killer who could be lurking among the crowd. I had brought my mini tape recorder along with me to record the meeting secretly from within my shirt pocket, so I didn't have to rely much on my memory, which seemed to fail me every now and then.

While I had aced Mr. Walker's typing class in high school, I found shorthand in Mr. Dudley's class a far more difficult subject to learn. All those odd squiggles and swirls looked like Egyptian hieroglyphs to me. I never knew what any of them meant, and I got a D in Dudley's class to prove it. Besides typing, my best class was English. The fact that I had a crush on handsome Mr. Curran, who had a thick Welsh accent and large hairy hands, didn't hurt. Whenever he helped me with an essay and his furry arm accidentally brushed against mine, I had to stifle a giggle because it tickled me like fuzz on a caterpillar. I was always getting crushes on my teachers, most recently Professor Blayne, which ended rather disastrously. But I never had a crush on Mr. Dudley, mainly because he could crush any student in his class. He must have weighed at least 500 pounds. His car was fitted with a special steering wheel that adjusted so he could get into it.

Too bad about the shorthand; fortunately, some genius invented tape recorders for people like me, so as it turns out, I didn't need to know shorthand after all. Nyah, nyah, Mr. Fuddy Duddy Dudley. Using my mini-tape, I was free to focus more on observing the goings-on at the meeting than trying to scribble every word down on paper. I could also refer to the tape for reference material when it came time to write my article. Nothing like a taped conversation for assuring the accuracy of quotations.

However, I find it's not always what people say but how they say it that reveals their true nature and underlying intentions. Do they blink a lot or avert their eyes from yours whenever they talk? Or do they gaze at you unblinkingly, as some skilled liars can do with the greatest of ease? Does a gesture or barely perceptible facial tic betray a false statement? Body language is truly the universal language. People don't even need have to open their mouths to tell you what you need to know about them. All you had to do was watch George W. Bush blink and smirk his way through a press conference to know he was lying like Barney on the Oval Office rug. Perhaps Barney perceived something about his commander-in-chief that most people couldn't, and that's why he didn't seem to like ol' George very much. Dogs are great judges of character.

I have learned how to observe, but mastering the art of listening is equally important. I don't have an ear for music, but I have two ears for crime-busting, like Cruiser does. Liars betray themselves with their voice inflections and variations in speech cadence, which often speeds up when someone tells a lie. If you listen to the police questioning of Lee Harvey Oswald when he was apprehended after the assassination of President John Kennedy, you know he's not telling the truth. All I had to do was rewind and play my tape over and over as many times as necessary to pick up on anything I might have missed the first time around. If only life worked the same way. There are certainly one or two things in my life I'd love to rewind, not the least of them the untimely loss of my husband. I suspected that Roberta Finch felt much the same about the loss of her dog, Gilda.

Half an hour before the meeting was scheduled to begin, the room was filled to capacity with people from the community who were either for or against the building of a new shelter. Mostly they were for it, which boded well for our camp, but we had to convince the council members to take a stand for the animals. When it comes to money versus mutts, money usually prevails.

All the Found Hounds volunteers were present, including Bertie Finch and Jenna Fairbanks. Amanda Peabody and other shelter employees were also there, although it wasn't so easy to determine which side of the kennel fence they were on with regard to this issue. Whether they would argue for or against a new shelter seemed to hinge on budgetary concerns. Even if they got their new shelter, they had to be able to sustain its operation, and the money for that had to come from someplace. While most of the employees cared just as much about animal welfare as Found Hounds or TAILS did, no one wanted to sacrifice his or her job in the bargain. Paychecks are too hard to come by these days.

I might have guessed that the last one to arrive at the meeting would be none other than the Princess of Piercings, Tori Thatcher. Her late entrance was no doubt staged for maximum drama. She wanted everyone in the community to know that she was a force to be reckoned with in this issue. When Tori entered the room, all heads snapped in her direction, and it wasn't because of her purple spiked hair and tattoos. Maybe the crowd's reaction had a little bit to do with her unusual appearance, but it probably had more to do with the fact that the whole TAILS organization trailed after Tori carrying bold placards protesting the abuses that had gone on for too long at Lakeside Shelter: Lakeside, the Animals' Abu Graib! Shut Down the Pound! I probably wasn't the only one in the room who had the uncomfortable feeling that a demonstration of another type was imminent.

CHAPTER 33

Members of the city council were doubtlessly hoping for a quick and easy resolution to the shelter quagmire, but by no stretch of the imagination would this be quick and or easy. Tori the Terrible would make certain of that. Her presence at any public gathering was like shaking a bottle of Coca Cola before popping the cap. It was obvious after a few minutes that the lid was about to blow off this meeting over what should be done about Lakeside Shelter. Once the floor was open to public comment, the dogs of dissent were definitely let out.

"Shut down the pound!" Tori blasted like a diesel truck horn. She sure didn't need a microphone to get her message heard. Everyone was a bit taken aback by the sheer volume of her androgynous voice, which matched her demeanor and appearance. But that was nothing compared to the sound of the whole group of demonstrators howling in chorus like so many basset hounds.

"Down with the Pound! Down with the Pound!" If only Cruiser and Calamity had been there, they could have joined in, too. "Roo-roo, Aarooo!"

Only the pounding of a gavel managed to quell the growling of the "down with the pound" pack. Once the room had quieted down, Mayor Thor Petersen spoke up. "I think we are probably all in agreement that the past management of Lakeside Shelter has left much to be desired."

"That's the understatement of the century," Roberta Finch snipped.

"A new manager will take over the operation of the shelter as soon as we've found the best person for the job," the mayor said. "We've already begun to . . ."

Bertie cut Thor off mid-sentence, which annoyed him, but she obviously didn't care. After I had shared with her Gilda's message from beyond Rainbow Bridge, she seemed even more resolute in her intention to see the dismantling of the shelter where Gilda had met her untimely end. "I'm in total agreement that Lakeside Shelter should be shut down for good. No one who loves animals and knows the history of the place would ever want to set foot in it. It's high time Tahoe had a new shelter."

"I think we all would like to see Tahoe have a state-of-the-art shelter, Ms. Finch, but building a new shelter presents some challenges. The first of those, of course, is budgetary. The other is finding adequate space to accommodate a building project of this scope. Undeveloped land that is not National Forest is somewhat limited at Lake Tahoe. I do agree that we need a larger facility to meet the demand, but funding concerns may not make that possible. We're looking, instead, into updating the existing structure to handle more animals."

"Codswallop!" Bertie barked. "You seem to find ample funds for other pet projects in the community that having nothing to do with the welfare of people's pets."

Amanda Peabody piped in. "While you're at it, how about funding a program to educate the public on how to better care for their companion animals? If people were more responsible for their pets' welfare and spayed and neutered their animals, perhaps we wouldn't need a bigger shelter."

"Amanda's right," Jenna Fairbanks said. "What we need is a state-of-the-art spay/neuter clinic with veterinarians on our staff to do the surgeries. A similar facility in Sacramento does ten thousand such surgeries a year! We also need behaviorists and trainers who can rehabilitate adoptable pets. The more of them we can re-home, the fewer need be destroyed. That's a job none of us wants to do . . . well, almost none."

No one had to guess who Jenna was referring to, and my guess was that no one in the room would shed any tears for Rhoda Marx, least of all Tori. She didn't seem the type to shed tears for anyone or anything. What good did tears ever do for the animals' plight, anyway? Even she understood that action is what brings about change in our increasingly complacent, self-centered world. And more often than not, it takes extreme action to occupy the public's attention. If the pen is mightier than the sword, Tori's tongue was mightier still. I had the feeling there was absolutely nothing she and her cohorts wouldn't do to accomplish their goal of raising public awareness about animal welfare. They probably would think nothing of splashing red paint on anyone wearing a fur coat or of marching naked down Lake Tahoe Boulevard to promote their cause. But had they gone as far as committing murder for the animals?

Sometimes it's not who is present but who is not that provides me with a needed clue, and there was one person who was conspicuously absent from this meeting. Conspicuous, because he would be impossible to miss if he were present. The only staff member from the shelter who had not joined the town hall meeting was Rex, the kennel attendant I'd met at Lakeside Shelter. And, of course, Rhoda Marx couldn't make it either because, like the animals entrusted to Rex's care, she was another one to "bite the dust," as he sang when leading the next victim of pet overpopulation down the gray mile. Had Rhoda been forced to walk the mile with Rex, too? She would have had a hard time fending off someone his size.

When Mayor Peterson and the council focused their attention on finding a new shelter manager, I could only hope that Rex's name wasn't on a short list for the position. In my way of thinking, he wouldn't be an improvement over his former boss, Rhoda. Of all the personnel I had met at Lakeside Shelter, he was the only one, besides Rhoda, who really seemed to be "into" his line of work.

I know that animal police and shelter staff try their best to assume an air of detachment as a way of distancing themselves from the emotionally charged environment in which they work daily. It is too easy for most to become attached to the dogs and cats they take into their care, but with Rex you could sense that there was no danger of his becoming attached to any of the animals he attended to. This was clearly only a job to him, and that wasn't the ideal employee to have working at a shelter. Too often with people like him in such a setting abuses can occur, as Calamity's response to Rex suggested might have been the case before she was released from Lakeside into my care. A compassionate heart should be a prerequisite for working with animals in any setting, as anyone who'd had dealings with Lakeside Shelter under "euthanasia expert" Marx's management would agree.

CHAPTER 34

Reporting on the meeting about the shelter would be a challenge. There wasn't much to report because no agreement had been reached about building a new shelter. Regardless of public sentiment, it would be business as usual at Lakeside Shelter, but some changes were implemented to help keep the peace.

Besides putting the shelter under new management, the council made a few concessions to improve pound policy. They decided to update their scanning system to a universal scanner that could detect any brand of chip and made it mandatory for staff to scan all incoming strays for a microchip and make every effort to contact the owner. The holding period was increased from only three days to one week, and longer in the case of more easily adoptable dogs and purebreds, which would improve the odds of survival in the future for dogs like Gilda. They also made it easier for local animal rescue groups to try to re-home adoptable dogs and cats.

The changes helped to quell some, but not all, of the public rancor over the shelter. Animal activists and welfare groups would not be completely satisfied until the outdated Lakeside Shelter was history and a new shelter was constructed to take its place. We had a long way to go before that would become a reality. It became sort of a double-dog dare to do everything in our power to make our dream a reality, and we all vowed to redouble our efforts to raise money and solicit donors for a new shelter. There's a lot of money in Tahoe, if you know where to look for it. Fortunately, there are a lot of animal lovers with money to throw at a worthy cause like a new animal shelter.

The word about our upcoming Bassetille Day event had spread far and wide, thanks to articles and announcements I'd submitted to national pet magazines and newspapers throughout California and beyond. The number of expected attendees was rising so fast, we were going to have to find a venue large enough to accommodate them all. Where else would that be but Alpine Paws Park, Tahoe's new dog park right on the lake? Although the off-leash park might be a bit more crowded with dogs than usual, the increase in the number of attendees was great news for the homeless hounds. We'd be taking in more money, but the best part was that dogs like Calamity stood a better chance of being adopted.

However, she wouldn't find a new home without some basic training, and that was how I ended up at an evening dog training class at Petropolis. Nona had flaked out on me, which surprised me since she seemed so enamored with Calamity. It wasn't because she had a date, which was her usual excuse to me about anything she didn't want to do. She said she had a headache, so I didn't press her. I've had enough cranium crushers myself. Perhaps she'd inherited a tendency for migraines from me. Whatever the reason, I understood that she wanted to be alone.

I left Cruiser behind to comfort Nona. Handling two strong-willed basset hounds at once is a two-person job. Just keeping Calamity from sampling the treats at Petropolis would be daunting. Tonight's training session would be no different.

Getting her in the front door of the pet store was the first challenge. Being in a mall the size of Petropolis was sensory overload for humans, let alone dogs. I feared that this excursion with Calamity wasn't going to go much better than our experience at the vet had.

The whoosh of the electric doors gave her such a fright, she nearly became airborne. Once we were inside the store, she did a kind of canine crab walk down the aisle, hunkering as close to the floor as she possibly could. Pulling me along, she kept peering up at everything and everyone as though she was about to be eaten by some alien life form. The rawhide chews and other yummy treats stored in basset-level bins didn't slow her down one bit. All she wanted was out the nearest exit as quickly as possible. Only when she spotted the other dogs inside the training arena did she appear to relax any. Her stance was more erect, and I even discerned a slight tail wag. Being around my gregarious Cruiser for a while had socialized her some, evidently.

I had less trouble guiding her into the training ring. A young woman wearing a blue coat with a Petropolis logo greeted us. Thank goodness it wasn't a white coat, or Calamity would have thought I was taking her to the vet again.

"Welcome. I'm Trixie. I'll be your trainer tonight. We'll be starting class in a few minutes, so go ahead and find a place over there with the other students." I thought it a bit odd that Trixie didn't even acknowledge her new four-legged student. Did this woman even like dogs? Perhaps she recognized trouble when she saw it. I just hoped that Trixie could teach this dog some new tricks.

I didn't have to find my place. Calamity found one for us right away. She dragged me straight over to where the other owners were trying to keep their dogs in check while waiting impatiently for the training class to begin. At least Calamity was social with the other dogs. She wanted to make friends with all of them. And she hadn't bitten anyone. Yet.

There were the usual assortment of small dogs, mostly terriers, a hyper cocker spaniel, and a couple of large breeds, including a goofy old English sheepdog and another basset hound. When Calamity spotted him, she tried to make friends. He was obviously a show dog, which the owner was quick to point out in case there was any confusion about that on my part.

His owner shifted uncomfortably in her seat when Calamity approached her dog. She wanted to stay as far away as possible from my lowly shelter hound so that Champion Milford of Mandeville Acres would not catch anything from her, including poor breeding and bad manners. The blue-blood basset seemed to have the same haughty attitude as his owner. The basset's demeanor is typically blasé, but even Cruiser hadn't given poor Calamity such a cold shoulder upon their first meeting.

Milford sniffed at her briefly and then scratched at his ear. Perhaps it was an infection brewing inside the ear canal, a constant problem for dogs bred for long ears like his and Calamity's. After Milford finished scratching, he gave a shake of his exceptionally pendulous flews, showering everyone within range in slobber. Believe it or not, show dogs can transform any gathering into a total slobberfest, but not even Cruiser could produce that much spit. Even His Highness Milford didn't pass the first lesson of tonight's training class, along with Calamity. Evidently, Trainer Trixie was not familiar with the rather unique qualities of the basset hound, not the least of them being a stubborn streak a mile wide and twice as long. Getting a basset to do anything on command is a tall order. Treats are a plus to achieve results, but even treats were no help here.

"All right, everyone. Command your dog to sit." Trixie instructed. Most of the dogs did a perfect sit on command the first time, except for the sheepdog, who would rather have been off herding sheep somewhere, though there aren't any sheep herds in Tahoe. *Sit* is a pretty basic command, and some dogs had obviously already learned it before coming to the class. When a couple of dogs didn't get the idea right off, their owners had to help them learn the command. "Don't push on the dog's rear. Draw his attention to your face, then lift up on his leash," Trixie said. "He'll just naturally sit down."

After a few tries, all the dogs were sitting on command with no problem. Both of the bassets responded to the command too, but instead of squatting on their haunches like the other dogs, they lounged on one hip. That wouldn't pass muster for this trainer.

"No, no!" Trixie said. "That's not a proper sit." She tried every way possible to induce the bassets to lift up their assets and get into a proper sit, as her other students had done.

"You silly woman, that *is* how a basset hound sits," Milford's owner declared.

"It is not a correct sit on command," Trixie insisted.

"She's right, you know." I hated to agree with Ch. Milford's snooty mistress, but facts were facts. "Basset hounds have a long spine, which makes it impossible for them to sit upright like other breeds do. You'd no doubt have the same problem if one of your students was a dachshund or a corgi."

"Well, I'm afraid it won't do in my class."

"Come along, Milford." Milford's owner led him out of the training ring. He followed behind her as she marched to the manager to insist on a refund. I wanted to show Miss Trixie a few tricks of my own. I would have led Calamity out right behind Milford, but I wasn't about to do anything that would prevent my foster hound from getting the training that might help her find a permanent home. Even if she flunked the class, at least she'd get some much-needed instruction and socialization in the bargain. For this dog, even a little training was better than none at all. She was bound to acquire some improvement in her behavior by osmosis. At least I hoped so, for her sake . . . and mine! One way or another, I was determined to find this dog another home when it came time for the Basset Waddle.

CHAPTER 35

By the time our training class was over, I don't know who was more exhausted from the experience, Calamity or me. I wasn't sure whether to attribute her not tugging at the end of her leash to fatigue or to having actually learned some leash manners in the class. Either way, I was grateful that she wasn't dragging me out of Petropolis. Our exit was certainly an improvement over our entrance. When I put her back in her travel carrier, she instantly curled up and fell asleep. This dog needed training classes every night to wear her out. It worked even better than Doc Heaton's miracle drug.

When we got home, Nona was dozing in Tom's old chair with Cruiser at her side. I don't know how many times I had come home to find Tom doing the same thing. Cruiser stirred from his slumber when he heard us come in. Nona woke up, too. Cruiser got up and came to greet me. He gave Calamity the onceover, reading the various scents on her coat that revealed to him where she'd been all evening. His attentiveness to her made me think he may have missed his crazy little houseguest. Were they starting to bond and become pack mates, despite my best-laid plans?

"Hi, Mom. Back already?"

"What do you mean, already? That was the longest two hours of my life."

"Sorry I couldn't go with you."

"Did your headache get any better?"

"Yes. I took a couple of your pills."

"I'd better take a couple myself. I have a headache now, too."

"How did Calamity do?"

"She learned to sit, heel, and stay. I didn't think she had it in her. I was proud of her."

"What a good girl you are!" Calamity plodded over to Nona and flopped down atop her slippers. I could tell that she was glad to be in familiar territory again, but I knew it was also her way of claiming Nona. I hoped she wasn't going to become too attached before we could find another home for her. It would be hard placing her in yet another unfamiliar environment if she became too comfortable here.

Like any other shelter dog, what this dog needed more than anything was some stability in her life. How can you ever have any kind of normal life when you can never depend on anyone to consistently love and care for you? How can you feel secure while being bounced from shelter to shelter or from home to home? The damage done to the psyche is no different for these sensitive creatures than it is for a human being. Too often the emotional trauma is irreversible.

I also feared it might be just as hard for Nona to let Calamity go. Calamity eased her way onto the ottoman Cruiser-style. I knew I probably shouldn't let her climb up on the furniture, at least until she knew who was top dog in the pack, but I was too tired to make a fuss. Watching Nona stroke the dog's silky soft ears, I knew she was becoming attached to her in spite of herself. But I also knew she couldn't house a dog that size in her high-rise San Francisco apartment. At some level Nona knew it, too. Perhaps that was the real reason she had opted not to take Calamity to her first training class, because she was hesitant to bond any further with a dog she would ultimately have to part with. I suppose that's why there are so many foster flunkies who grow too attached to their fostered fur children and can't part with them. If Calamity wasn't such a problem child, I'm sure I'd end up the same way.

"I think I'm going to turn in."

"So early?"

"I'd love to sit up with you a while, dear, but I'm really beat tonight. You should go to bed, too. You don't want that headache coming back."

"I think I'll sit out here with the dogs and read for a while."

"Good. I can have some time alone in my bed before Cruiser makes his move. Don't stay up too late now."

"I won't. Oh, I almost forgot to tell you that Amanda Peabody from Lakeside Shelter called. She says they've had more trouble down at the shelter."

"Trouble? What kind of trouble? It's not another . . ."

"No, it's nothing like that. She didn't say exactly what, but she asked if you could come over to the shelter tomorrow and see her."

"Okay. Thanks for letting me know." Frankly, I wish Nona had waited until morning to tell me about Amanda's phone call. Quality sleep was hard enough to come by lately. All I needed was something else weighing on my mind for a good nocturnal toss-and-turn session.

I find I sometimes have better luck drifting off to sleep when I am using the creative part of my mind trying to craft an article opening or plot a chapter of a book rather than fretting about a problem, although I have often arrived at solutions to problems in my sleep. Tonight it was thinking about the upcoming Bassetille Day that finally brought the Sand Basset waddling along to sprinkle me with magic drool to help me off to dreamland. The last thing I remember was Cruiser climbing up on his usual spot at the foot of the bed and settling down on his Raining Cats and Dogs quilt for a long night's slumber.

Cruiser and I were at the Basset Waddle. He was winning all the contests with ease. Calamity was there too, running amok and creating havoc at every opportunity. She ran away from me, and I took off running after her, hollering at the top of my lungs. She completely ignored me, of course. Finally, I caught up with her and led her back to where I'd left Cruiser. He was gone! After searching for him everywhere, in desperation I found myself at Lakeside Shelter. The place was deserted, except for all the animals barking, howling, and meowing their lament. I searched every kennel, but Cruiser was nowhere to be found. Desperate, I began to cry. Where was my boy?

Suddenly, I found myself standing in front of Kennel 9. There was a basset hound inside, but it wasn't Cruiser. It was a female basset. At first I thought it must be Calamity, but it wasn't. This dog was a lemon and white variety of the breed, almost a golden color. The light shone on the dog's brass nametag. The name on the tag said Gilda.

All at once, the door to the kennel flew open with a bang that echoed through the shelter. Gilda waddled out. Looking sadder than any basset I'd ever seen (and that's saying a lot), she headed down the gray mile very slowly. She stopped once and turned to look back at me sorrowfully. I understood that she wanted me to follow her, so I did. We came to the door of the euthanasia room. Gilda walked right through it!

I opened the door and followed the phantom dog to the euthanasia chamber. I looked through the viewing panel. Cruiser was inside! I screamed and opened up the chamber. When I opened it, he stood up and walked into my arms. I hugged him with all my might, but he pulled away and followed Gilda through the door. I realized that Cruiser was dead.

Next thing I knew I was the one trapped inside the chamber,

which was filling with deadly gas. I gasped for air. My life was slipping away as I felt a sensation of being smothered slowly, slowly . . .

Gasping for breath, I yanked the pillow from off my head. Cruiser had apparently nudged my down-filled pillow onto my face when he wormed his way up to the head of the bed. I had probably been thrashing around so much in my nightmare that even he couldn't sleep. I didn't make him resume his place at the foot of the bed but let him snuggle under the covers with me. I fell back into a deep, restful sleep with my arms wrapped about Cruiser, who was soon snoring along with his adoring mom.

CHAPTER 36

The following afternoon, I was back at Lakeside Shelter, but this time I wasn't dreaming. Amanda Peabody was at the front desk doing some paperwork on a stray dog that had been brought in. At least it would have a fighting chance for a new home now that Rhoda Marx was gone. A volunteer took over while Amanda and I went into her office.

"My daughter gave me your message."

"Thanks for coming by. I thought you'd be the best person to talk to about this."

"What's going on?"

"There's been some weird stuff going on here."

"Is TAILS up to their old tricks again?"

"Could be. I really don't know. If so, these are some pretty clever tricks."

"What do you mean?"

"Dogs are disappearing."

"Disappearing? You mean someone is letting them out like before?"

"No, I mean I put them in the kennel, and when I go back to the kennel, it's empty. The dog has vanished."

"Dogs don't vanish into thin air. Someone had to have come and let the dog out. Who usually has the keys to the kennels?"

"Rex does. But he's been on vacation, so I keep them in my desk drawer."

"Someone must know where you keep them and is just jerking your choke chain."

"I don't think so. I keep the drawer locked at all times. I'm especially vigilant about it because of what happened before."

"You mean when someone let the dogs out?"

"Someone . . . or something."

"What are you getting at?"

Amanda paused a moment before answering. She knew how what she was going to say would sound to someone else.

"Bertie Finch was right about this place. It should be torn down."

"I tend to agree with her, but why do *you* say that?"

"Because it's haunted, that's why."

"Haunted? By what?" I didn't really have to ask. I think I already knew the answer to that question.

"Gilda's ghost!"

I was naturally skeptical of what Amanda had told me about the strange goings-on at the shelter. It seemed more likely that these manifestations were being caused by a two-legged phantom named Tori than a four-legged one named Gilda. But I was intrigued, nevertheless. If dogs were disappearing from the shelter, I felt compelled to find out why.

There was only one way to prove whether or not it was Gilda's ghost that had been causing all the havoc lately at Lakeside Shelter. I'd stay overnight at the shelter and do watchdog duty. Of all the odd jobs I'd done over the years, this had to be one of the oddest. When I told Nona about it, she thought I had flipped my ever-loving Beanie. She should know her nutty mother by now—the same one who sees monsters floating in the lake and creatures lurking outside her kitchen window. I couldn't help wondering what I might witness tonight at the haunted animal shelter. Since I wasn't sleeping much lately anyway, there was no reason not to spend the night at Lakeside with Gilda's ghost.

CHAPTER 37

When I drove into the empty parking lot at Lakeside Shelter, a full moon lit my way to the entrance. I decided to take my crime-busting hound along with me to the shelter, partly as protection but also for his keen CSP (canine sensory perception). Dogs can sense things long before we can, and that was a skill I might need tonight. If anything was amiss or if I was in any danger, he would alert me.

No one but my daughter and Amanda Peabody knew that I would be staying in the shelter overnight. Amanda had given me a key to let myself in. I hadn't worked a graveyard shift since I was in my teens and lasted all of four nights waitressing at a Denny's. I'm no Rita Ramirez, that's for sure. Suffering from sleep deprivation, I dumped a plateload of food in a patron's lap, and that was the end of my brief career as a waitress. I wasn't much of a night owl in those days, but I can hoot with the best of them now.

Cruiser and I entered the shelter, walked past the front office and into the kennel area. Unfortunately, it had quickly filled to capacity again. Most of the escapees had been captured and there were others that had been surrendered since then. Moonbeams spilled through a window at the end of the shelter corridor. I had brought along a flashlight, but the bright moonlight made it unnecessary. I didn't want to announce my presence to anyone.

The inmates were all sound asleep, but when we entered, a

dog barked at Cruiser, then another and another. Soon the whole place echoed with the din of barking dogs. Either they were voicing their displeasure that Cruiser was outside and they were on the inside, or they thought I was there to liberate them and were pleading for me to release them from their cages. I hoped they would settle down in a while and go back to sleep. That ghastly noise would be intolerable if it lasted all night long. It might also tip off any would-be intruder that someone was here. Dogs don't bark to hear themselves bark; well, most don't. Calamity was an exception.

Cruiser followed along at my heels as I passed the kennels, noting the number of dogs contained in each cage so I would know if any were to suddenly go missing while I was there. We came to the kennel that Amanda claimed was haunted. This was formerly Gilda's kennel, from which she said dogs had been mysteriously disappearing. Apparently, she planned on putting her theory to the test since a lone beagle mix was impounded inside the "haunted" kennel.

The cage door was locked to prevent the dog's escape or removal. I thought it rather strange that this was the only dog in the entire place that was not barking its head off. It was huddled in a corner, shivering the same way Calamity had when I found her here. She could be sick, but I didn't think so. The dog's coat was glossy and her eyes clear and bright. She appeared healthy and showed no obvious signs of illness. I recognized a terrified dog when I saw one. As we approached the cage, Cruiser froze in his tracks.

"Come on, Cruiser."

He began to shiver and shake, too.

"Cruiser, come!"

He didn't budge an inch when I commanded him to come to me, which isn't all that unusual, but something else besides stubbornness was causing him to disobey me.

"What is it, boy? What's wrong?"

Cruiser raised his nose to the ceiling and bayed mournfully. Several of the other dogs responded in kind, probably the ones with a bit of hound blood flowing in their veins. That included the beagle mix in K-9. Their eerie vocalizations reminded me of the coyotes I hear in the forest near my cabin on moonlit nights like this one. It always sent a little chill zipping up my spine and caused the hair on my neck to prickle, the same way it was now. Perhaps I was sensing the same thing Cruiser was, for I noticed the ruff of his neck was as spiked as Tori Thatcher's hair.

The din in the shelter was becoming too much to bear. I was starting to get a throbbing headache. With all this uproar, no one was going to make an appearance at the shelter tonight—at least no one living. I decided I'd have to leave Cruiser enclosed in the front office for now. He could do sentry duty there and sound the alarm for me if anyone were to enter the shelter. With his loud, resonant bellow, I'd be certain to hear it clear from the other end of the compound.

I led Cruiser back to the front office and got him settled down in the dog bed that used to belong to Spirit, the magnificent white shepherd Nona and I had encountered out in the woods. Evidently, the dogcatcher had not recaptured him. He was smart enough to evade capture and by now had probably joined up with some other rogue pack in the woods, assuming he hadn't been hit by a car or come to other harm, as many strays do.

As soon as I took Cruiser out of the kennel area, he stopped his shivering and seemed fine again. The other dogs stopped their barking, too. But suddenly I heard a startling noise. A loud, metallic crash reverberated from somewhere inside the shelter.

"Stay here, Cruiser."

Once more I approached the kennel area, now with some

trepidation. I wasn't sure what had caused the noise, but I knew it wasn't one of the dogs. This time I flipped on the lights so I could see what was wrong or surprise whoever might be there. I expected that I might find a certain troublemaker with purple spiked hair making another misguided attempt to focus public attention on the animals' plight on behalf of TAILS. I hurried past the kennels until I came to number 9 again. This time it was I who froze in my tracks. The cage door was thrown wide open and the padlock lay unlocked on the corridor floor. When I peered inside the cage, it was empty. The beagle had vanished into thin air, just as Amanda had described. I looked up and down the corridor for some sign of the missing beagle, and searched every other area of the shelter. There was no sign of her anywhere or any sign of anyone having entered the shelter from outside. Something strange was definitely going on at Lakeside Shelter, and I was more determined than ever to find out what it was.

I was ready to give up the ghost and leave the shelter with Cruiser when I heard a door slam at the farthest end of the building. Cruiser heard it, too. He let out a baritone bark, and when I opened the office door to the kennels he took off tracking at full speed. Tracking what, I had no clue. At least not yet.

Cruiser's alarm was all it took for the Lakeside inmates to be roused from their fitful slumbers and join the barkfest. I had never heard so much noise. How did people work in these places day in and day out and remain sane? If dogs can go kennel crazy after being penned up for so long in shelters with no hope of release from their torment, perhaps people can, too. Is that what had really happened here at Lakeside Shelter? Had one of the shelter workers decided he or she had finally had enough of this stressful job and a hard-nosed boss? Perhaps the Marx woman was the victim of a crazed kennel worker, and she just happened to be in the wrong place at the wrong time. It could also have been a volunteer who might be even more prone to such a psychosis. Volunteers are there because they choose to be. It's not hard to imagine they might be even more inclined to take revenge on someone like her who represented a roadblock to happy endings for the pets at the shelter. From the people I'd spoken to thus far who knew Rhoda, I suspected revenge against her was something that was on the minds of many. The question still remaining was who? Perhaps Cruiser and I were hot on the trail of the killer right now.

I covered my ears to drown out the barking and yelping of the dogs as we passed the kennel rows on our way to the rear of the shelter. Hearing their desperate cries was as distressful to me as hearing a child wailing for its mother. I think it was upsetting Cruiser, too. He understood their language far better than I. What I did understand was why someone had released all the dogs at the shelter, ill advised though it may have been. Part of me wanted to break open every cell door in the place and liberate the dogs from their prison. No one who loves dogs wants to see them end up in a place like this. But there are far worse places to end up besides a shelter. At least in shelters, the animals have a safe place to rest, food and water, medical care, and protection from danger and the elements . . . for a time.

Just as we came to the back door of the shelter, I heard a car engine start up in the rear lot where the animal control vans were parked. I bolted through the door in time to see one of the vehicles backing out of its space. I tried to wave down the person inside the cab, but when he saw me, the van shifted into high gear and sped off. The screeching tires laid a zipper of rubber marks on the pavement. As the van zoomed past me, under the flood of security lights I was able to discern the identity of the driver. It was none other than "Another One Bites the Dust" Rex.

What was he doing skulking around here this late at night? From the looks of things inside the shelter, he hadn't been working overtime cleaning the place. When I heard the distinctive yelps of a hysterical beagle coming from inside the van, I suspected I knew who our mysterious shelter ghost was. What I didn't know was why he was secretly taking animals out of the shelter. And where was he taking them? I decided I had better report this theft to the police immediately. For all I knew, Rex might return, and I wouldn't want him to find me here alone snooping around. I'd already seen how he dealt with animals in the shelter. Right now, I was the one biting Rex's dust from a speeding dogcatcher's van.

CHAPTER 38

Last-minute preparations for the Bassetille Day event were exactly what I needed to take my mind off of murder and mayhem for a little while. The big day was only a couple of days away, and the Waddle countdown was officially on. There was still plenty to do before the fundraiser, including getting potential adoptees ready to put their best paw forward. In the hope of finding her a new home, Calamity had a date at the groomer to get prettied up, which turned out to be a good thing. For when I got home I discovered that she'd been excavating in my backyard to uncover Cruiser's private reserve, his buried treats, which he liked to age thoroughly before sampling.

Nona had abdicated her pet-sitting duties for the afternoon, so that meant Calamity had enjoyed free reign of the place. She had put her freedom to ample use, indoors and outdoors, as I was about to discover. Fortunately, this pup perp had left plenty of evidence to link her to the crime. All I had to do was follow the muddy paw prints through the house from one end to the other to see what devilment she'd been up to in our absence.

"Cruiser, why didn't you keep her out of trouble while I was gone?" He gave me a sheepish look, which I at first interpreted as being a response to my angry tone of voice until I ascertained that he'd been an accomplice in the caper. I needed look no further for proof than my kitchen. The sight of emptied bags and boxes of treats strewn helter-skelter on the kitchen floor was enough to wrap up this case in short order. Skip might trace his perps with bloodstains, but slobber stains were the trace evidence at this canine crime scene. It was hard to imagine how two short-legged dogs could get into so much mischief in such a short time. But being short dogs did not exclude either Calamity or her cohort, Cruiser, from being prime suspects. Aside from the demolition in my kitchen, this did demonstrate one thing to me: Cruiser and Calamity were definitely beginning to bond with each other, at least long enough to join forces in a pantry raid.

I had begun cleaning up the mess when I heard Nona pull into the driveway.

Calamity began barking hysterically and ran to the front door to greet her. I wasn't sure whether she was really that happy to see Nona or if she sensed my displeasure with her and was seeking asylum with the one person she had shown any real connection with since coming here. Nona, of course, was completely taken in by that craven little thief.

"Hey, girl, whatcha been up to?" Evidently, she didn't notice the mud on Calamity's paws. If she'd jumped up on her like usual, Nona would have known right off what that naughty dog had been up to.

"Plenty!"

Nona's jaw dropped when she saw the demolition. "Gosh, Mom! What happened in here?"

"What do you think?"

"Calamity did all this?"

"I think she had a little help from her long-eared partner in crime."

"I'm really sorry. I was only gone for a little while. I thought she could be trusted for a few minutes."

"Evidently not. She'll have to be crated from now on if one of us can't be here with her."

"What a naughty girl you are, Calamity!"

Calamity cowered at the sharp tone of Nona's voice. I'm sure it wasn't the first time she'd been yelled at, or worse, for bad behavior.

"It's no good scolding her now, Nona. She doesn't know what you're punishing her for. You'd have to catch her in the act for her to make the connection."

"You're right, but even then I'm not sure it would do any good. This dog is a real hard case."

"Fortunately, she already has a date with the groomer to get prettied up for the Waddle. She'll need to look her best if she's going to get adopted this weekend."

An odd expression clouded Nona's face that I couldn't quite interpret, except that it was similar to the looks she'd given me in the past when I didn't approve of her choice of boyfriends. "Looks like Cruiser could use a little clean-up, too. Why don't you take them both with you while I finish cleaning up the mess here?"

"Thanks, honey. I appreciate that."

I was relieved when Nona agreed to clean up the mess Calamity and Cruiser had made in the house while I took them both to Rub-a-Dub-Dog at Petropolis for a good cleansing. Cruiser hadn't gotten as down and dirty in the yard as Calamity had, so he didn't really need a full bath, but cleanliness is next to doGliness. Even though he wasn't in the market for a new home like Calamity was, I also wanted him to look his best for the Waddle.

I could have tried bathing both the dogs in my bathtub at home, but I knew it would make a worse mess in my house than there already was. I love having dogs, but there are times I wouldn't mind living in a dog-free zone. Tom's mother kept their home so clean, you could have given it the white-glove test at any time. It must have been quite an adjustment for him living with me. I guess I always believed that there were more important things in life than having your house look perfect, and for me a house without a dog is no home. Fortunately, after Cruiser came to live with us, Tom came to share my feelings about that. Keeping Cruiser happy and healthy became paramount at the MacBean abode.

I was starting to think that Nona was taking after her dad in that respect. She was becoming a pretty good sport about all the dog duties she was being asked to perform. Was this the same fussy glamour girl who never let a lock of hair fall out of place and had a hissy fit if she broke a fingernail? These days she didn't seem to mind getting down and dirty for Cruiser, and especially for Calamity. Was my daughter finally going to the dogs like her mother? I could only hope so. The transformation I was seeing in Nona went much deeper than that, though.

CHAPTER 39

I had actually managed to lead Calamity through the mall to Petropolis and through the door of the pet salon. The fact that Cruiser went along with us was reassuring to her. Despite her errant behavior, the newcomer to the household clearly perceived Cruiser as the alpha of the pack, and his presence had a calming effect upon her. A dog that is confused as to who is leader of the pack is not a well-adjusted dog, and Calamity was undoubtedly the least well-adjusted dog I'd ever encountered.

I even managed to get her into the tub and get her sudsed and partially rinsed without incident. We were doing fine until she heard a blow dryer start up in the next cubicle. She yelped an alarm, snapped her restraint, and bolted out the door of Rub-a-Dub-Dog with me in hot pursuit. I chased after that crazy dog, my hysterical and futile commands echoing all through Petropolis. I worried that she might make it into the main mall and out the front door right into traffic.

Shoppers pointed and laughed at the berserk basset racing through Petropolis covered in foam as though she were rabid. As I ran after her, cursing under my breath, I thought that whoever had named this impossible dog Calamity certainly knew what they were doing. Why no one had ever named a hurricane after her was beyond me.

The soap scum coating Calamity made her as slippery as a greased pig. Twice I nearly nabbed her, but she evaded my grasp each time. My breath came in ragged gasps and I was about to give up the chase when a bystander managed to lasso her with a black leather belt. When I finally caught up with my wayward hound, I realized that the purple-haired basset wrangler was none other than Tori Thatcher. She was there with some of her other rabble-rousers, which made me wonder what trouble they were stirring up at the mall.

"This slippery girl gave you a run for your money, eh?" Tori said, a wry smile lighting her usually stormy countenance.

"No kidding! Thanks for catching her for me." Good thing for Calamity and me that Tori always wore an assortment of leather belts and accessories, including the spiked collar she sported around her neck like a pit bull, only this pit bull wore lipstick.

"Isn't this your latest foster dog from Lakeside?" she said.

"Yes. Her name is Calamity, and that she is."

"Poor girl probably went through a lot before she ended up with you."

"No doubt of that. She definitely has some issues from her past. I wish I knew more about her background, but one rarely knows much about the history of these rescued dogs. Judging from her lack of socialization, I'm fairly certain she was a puppy mill dog."

"And probably a pet shop girl, too," Tori said, stroking one of Calamity's long ears. She gave herself a good shake, showering us both in sudsy water.

"Yep, that's where they usually end up, assuming they survive their deprived puppyhood."

"From the mill to the mall."

"And then to the local shelter after behavior issues surface and the novelty of dog ownership wears off. Discarded like yesterday's newspaper."

"That's part of why we're here today," Tori said, pausing to hand a flyer to a passing shopper. She gave one to me, too. I was right about TAILS being at the mall to stir up trouble, but it was mainly trouble for Lakeside Animal Shelter. They were planning to stage a demonstration to close the facility down for good.

I noticed one detail of the flyer in particular. It so happened that the rally was scheduled on the same day as our Waddle. Was it purely coincidence or had Tori planned it that way? Whether their protest was intended to work in concert with our adoption efforts or to steal our thunder and divert attention to their cause was open to interpretation.

Although Tori claimed to be an advocate for animal rights, her methods always seemed to work at cross purposes to their best interests. She seemed to attract more enemies than allies. I'd seen it happen all too often in other organizations when people's egos are unleashed. The message somehow gets lost before the messenger can deliver it. Whatever Tori did, good or bad, I had come to understand one thing about her. She believed that the ends justified the means if it somehow served the cause of animal welfare. Whether those means had also included murder I had yet to discover.

CHAPTER 40

The weather was perfect on the day of our first annual Basset Waddle. Tahoe's temperate seventies and a cool breeze would keep the hounds from overheating in their Waddle Wear, which ranged from silly to bizarre. Calamity and other homeless bassets sported green jackets with yellow lettering that read, ADOPT ME! Bassetille Day would go down in Heavenly Valley history as an earmark gathering of basset hounds from hither and yon. Two attendees were real French hounds that had been flown all the way from Paris. *Vive les Bassets!* In all, they were nearly 1,000 strong, long, and ready to waddle.

By the time Nona and I arrived with Cruiser and Calamity in tow, legions of bassets and their owners were already milling about the lakefront dog park getting acquainted.

"I don't know whether it was such a good idea to bring Calamity along with us, Mom. I'm not sure she's ready for the big time yet."

"There's only one way to find out."

"But she'll probably freak out in the crowd. This dog is still not very well socialized."

"If she isn't socialized after today, then I guess there's no hope for her. Besides, this is her best chance to be placed in a permanent home." I didn't want to say it might also be her last chance, but I didn't have to say it. Nona read between the lines. We both knew the truth was that Calamity had already proved she wasn't a good fit at the MacBean house. A psychotic, destructive dog was more trouble than I could handle in my already complicated life. I could only hope that for this important occasion she'd be on her best behavior, for her sake and mine.

"What do you think the chances are that someone will adopt her today?" Nona said.

"It's hard to say. She's a beautiful dog, and there'll be plenty of hard-core basset lovers here who might be willing to take her on. She may get lucky."

"And what if no one adopts her? What will become of her then?"

"Let's wait and see what happens before we start worrying about that, okay? Try to think positively. The chances are good that she could find her forever home with someone."

"Perhaps you're right." Nona didn't know it, but I was pretty good at reading between the lines. I knew that she had taken a liking to Calamity from the beginning and that the dog had bonded with her, too. I suspected that Nona was secretly hoping no one would adopt her because she wanted to keep Calamity for herself. There was only one problem with that. Nona lived in a small apartment in San Francisco that didn't allow dogs, at least not dogs her size.

As we entered the dog park, Cruiser took an immediate interest in all the activity. This was an off-leash event, so I unsnapped his lead and let him go his merry way, which he proceeded to do without delay. He lifted his head to the air to sample the buffet of scents wafting past his sensitive nose, then headed off in the direction where hot dogs and hamburgers were being grilled. Calamity had picked up the same delectable scents Cruiser had, but I didn't dare let her off the leash in a crowd this large. I didn't need a repeat of our Petropolis episode. Besides, it was Nona's job to lead her around and make sure everyone knew that she was available for adoption.

"It looks like you have things in hand here with Calamity. Walk her around the park and let's hope someone takes a shine to her. Maybe you can enter her in some of the contests to showcase her a bit. She'd be a shoo-in for the longest ears competition."

"Great idea! Sounds like fun."

"I have to take my shift now in the Found Hounds booth. Keep an eye on Cruiser for me, will you? He's waddling around here somewhere."

"Sure." I watched as Nona led Calamity off among the crowd. Almost immediately an elderly couple took interest in her. Calamity seemed a bit hesitant at first about all the attention she was getting, but Nona's presence was reassuring to her. A couple of treats didn't hurt, either. The surest way to a basset's heart is through its stomach, as the assortment of belly draggers at this event proved without a doubt. The more attention Calamity could get here, the better. Even if she didn't leave the Waddle with a new family, she would come away with some new experiences, and that was good for an unsocialized dog like her.

Found Hounds had set up their booth in the dog park along with an assortment of vendors selling sundry basset-a-bilia and everything from leashes and collars to doggy designer duds and snoods for keeping long ears from dipping in food bowls. Calamity's ears could sure use one of those. It would probably be helpful for the infections that are inherent with the extreme breeding practices that continue to produce exaggerated features like those ridiculously lengthy ears of hers. Whoever adopted Calamity would have their work cut out for them with her, in more ways than that. Luckily, the kinds of people this type of function attracts are already familiar with the breed and its inherent challenges, but they love them anyway.

At the Found Hounds booth I handed out flyers, brochures, and other materials to educate folks about the organization.

Our booth was located in the animal health and welfare section, right next to TAILS! I felt it was poor event organization to set up a booth for them right next to us, but I tried to make the best of the situation. Their volunteers were so aggressive with their animal rights spiel that I was beginning to feel like a sideshow barker, if you'll forgive the pun. But the one barking the loudest was Tori the Terrible, who had arrived on the scene. Even if I didn't approve of her methods, I had to admit that she was a force to be reckoned with on behalf of the animals. She certainly put her all into anything she did.

"Tori, I didn't expect to see your group at this event."

"We couldn't pass up a crowd of this size to get the word out."

"Who signed you up for the Waddle?"

"Jenna Fairbanks, why?"

"Your organization is probably too radical for a breed-specific fun event like this."

"I was under the impression you're also trying to place some homeless dogs here in adoptive homes."

"Yes, we are."

"Then I think our message is certainly *à propos*."

Now she was hurling fancy French words at me, which I guess was *à propos* at an event for French dogs. I just hoped that Tori, whose middle name is trouble, wasn't here to stir up some.

CHAPTER 41

It was time for some grub when my stomach roared louder than Tori Thatcher. That woman's voice was like the sound of broken glass in a cement mixer. She sure didn't need a megaphone to make her point. Tori had missed her true calling as a carnival barker, but I had to admit she was good at getting people fired up for her cause.

She was busy talking with so many other people she didn't have much time to spend talking to me, but there are other ways besides that to gather valuable information about someone. As any dog would tell you if he had the power of speech, people communicate their intentions far more accurately without words. A dog can tell you what you're feeling even before you're aware of it yourself. Body language and other forms of nonverbal communication speak volumes about humans. Tori's alpha essence emanated from every pore of her stocky body. Even I sensed that. Clearly, there was much more to her than met the eye of the casual observer, but you could say that about most anyone if you studied the person carefully enough. People can be a bit like assorted candies. A hard shell can encase a gooey soft center, or sometimes there's a tough nut buried inside a deceptively smooth, creamy coating.

Jenna Fairbanks approached my booth toting an armload of leaflets.

"Here to replenish my stock?"

"Yes. How are things going?" She brushed away a stray flaxen lock of hair.

"All right. I think I'm about ready for a break, though. Can you cover for me while I eat a bite?"

"Actually, I was about to relieve you. They want you over in the ring to help judge some of the contests."

"What kind of contests?"

"Oh, they have several categories: longest ears, lowest ground clearance, best trick, best treat catch, to name a few."

"That should be a hoot!"

I spotted Nona heading for my booth with Calamity hot on her heels. I figured I could send her for provisions, but she was way ahead of me.

"I thought you must have been getting hungry by now, Mom. All they had were hot dogs and hamburgers."

"No veggie burgers, huh?"

"Nope, sorry. I brought you a regular burger, though."

"If that's all they have, I guess I'll have to bend my dietary rules for the occasion. I'm starving!"

Apparently, I wasn't the only one. If I were a flea on Calamity's back, I might have noticed that her doggy radar was tracking Nona's every move with that burger. There's nothing quite as keen as the nose of a basset hound, and hers was certainly no exception, as I had already discovered on several occasions.

I have Calamity to thank for keeping me vegetarian in spite of myself. I was so hungry I would have gladly gobbled down every bit of that burger if she hadn't beat me to it. As I chatted with Jenna, she saw her chance and took advantage of the distraction. The hamburger, on a paper plate near my elbow and a little too near the edge of the table, disappeared in one gulp. She'd devoured half the paper plate too, before I realized what had happened. Even David Copperfield couldn't make anything vanish into thin air as quickly as Calamity snatched that burger right from under my nose. The paw is quicker than the eye.

"Bad girl!" It was no good protesting. My burger had already disappeared down the biscuit hole. I tugged at the paper plate to retrieve it before the rest of it was gone, but she fought me with every ounce of her will. Finally, rather than lose a digit, I gave in and let her have what was left of my white plate special. A little paper pulp was nothing compared to what else she'd ingested so far since joining my household, and she'd survived that with no trouble.

"She's a little food guarder, isn't she?" Jenna said.

"I'm afraid so. She's never nipped me, but it's probably because the hand's been quicker than the tooth thus far. I'm not sure I'd trust this dog around small children. She might not be able to discern the difference between baby fingers and Snausages."

"That's too bad. A behavior fault like that may limit her chances for adoption."

"You're probably right. This one slipped through the screening process, or I wouldn't even have her."

"Rhoda Marx would never have let that happen. I saw her fail perfectly adoptable dogs for much less than food-guarding."

"That must have bothered you."

"Yes, but not as much as it bothered Bertie, who lost Gilda to Rhoda's inflexible policies. No one hated that woman as much as she did."

"I guess it's fortunate for Calamity that Rhoda wasn't at the shelter the day I came for her. She would probably have ended up the same way Gilda did. I guess no one misses Rhoda Marx much, but I'm not sure she deserved to die like a dog."

"I'm sorry about what happened to Rhoda, but the truth is things have been better for the shelter since she's been gone. In fact, most of the dogs up for adoption at this event wouldn't be here today if she were still around. She saw euthanizing pets as the quickest, least costly solution to overpopulation. She actually seemed to relish her reputation for efficiency in carrying out those distasteful duties."

"In her way, she may have thought she was doing the right thing."

"Are you defending her?"

"Of course not, but the fact remains that she was responsible for running a small, overcrowded shelter with a limited budget in a community overrun with strays. As Rex said, there's only so much space for homeless pets in the shelter. I'm sure her decisions weren't easy ones."

"They weren't, but she never seemed to have any trouble making them. Rhoda would have made a good prison matron, but she was ill-suited to her job as shelter manager and should have been replaced a long time ago."

"Seems to be the consensus. Obviously, someone wanted her out of there, by whatever method."

"Murder is a pretty drastic method, though, even for someone like Rhoda."

"Who do you think killed her?"

A maelstrom swirled in Jenna's sea green eyes as she pondered my question. I think its bluntness caught her off guard. I'm usually good at reading people, especially when I look into their eyes, which truly are the windows of the soul, but I could not quite determine the emotion I was seeing within hers. She had worked with Rhoda and expressed regret for her fate. Whether that regret was genuine was hard to determine. If anyone who'd had any dealings with Rhoda felt sad about her demise, I had not seen any evidence of it yet. At length, Jenna spoke, and her answer surprised me. "I think we are all responsible for what happened to Rhoda."

"Really? How so?"

"Because we allowed her to remain in control of the shelter and let her polices go unchallenged, even though we knew she was all wrong for the shelter, the community and especially the animals in her care. Everyone despised her. It was only a matter of time before someone took matters into their own hands."

Jenna was right. Anyone who knew Rhoda's reputation at the shelter and remained silent was as guilty as the one who put her inside that chamber and turned on the gas. Only one question remained: Who actually killed the dog killer?

CHAPTER 42

I hadn't been having much fun thus far at the Waddle, so I was grateful to be relieved from booth duty to help judge the talent contest. Having such a contest for basset hounds would probably not be much of a competition, I figured, since the main talents I've seen in bassets are sleeping and eating. Well, a little sleuthing too, in Cruiser's case.

I was selected to judge the Best Howl and Best Trick competitions. The dog that won the prize for Best Trick was the only one that actually performed a trick on command, and I had to admit it was a good one. Sonny's owner had taught him how to paint. With a tennis player's terrycloth wristband placed on the dog's paw, he dipped the terry "brush" in paint, then held up a blank sheet of paper for his dog. Of course, there was a treat involved in the performing of this trick. Upon hearing the repeated command, "Paint!" Vincent van Basset did his artistic stuff. What he painted was up for interpretation, but it looked about as good as some modern art I've seen exhibited in galleries. Regardless, it was a clever trick, and he was the paws-down winner of the contest.

Other categories were the Best Treat Catch and Counter Surfing competitions. Calamity had already unofficially claimed the counter surfing title with her Houdini disappearing hamburger act. Anyone who had happened to witness her agility on the table where I was momentarily distracted from my lunch couldn't argue that this was the fastest-moving basset they'd seen at the Waddle, or anywhere else. There were also competitions for longest body; lowest ground clearance, measured tummy to turf; and longest wingspan, where long ears were measured tip-to-tip while extending them like Dumbo the flying elephant's.

This was Calamity's big moment in the ring. Nona led the contestant into the competition circle to join a group of other bassets with very long ears. Now, anyone who knows this breed is aware of the original purpose of those low-hanging ears, and it has nothing to do with dog shows or competitions of any kind. If you were to watch a basset hound running in slow motion, which is poetry for any basset lover, you'd see the gentle flapping of the ears as the dog runs, nose to the ground. That flapping motion stirs up scents, which are trapped in folds inside that ultra-sensitive nose of his. Of course, the one scent that would hold particular interest for a basset is rabbit, which is what he was especially bred to track for the hunter following him on foot. It's easy to see that ears so long the dog trips on them while running are pretty useless for hunting purposes, but they are perfect for contests like the one being held at the Waddle.

One contestant for the longest ears contest wore a snood, which is customary at Westminster and other conformation dog shows for keeping ears clean and tidy before entering the judging ring. They help prevent ears from dragging on the ground and keep bacteria from collecting in ears that are already the perfect breeding grounds for infection since not much air gets into the dog's ear canals. Cruiser's ears had never been much of a problem because they are not exceptionally long or heavy, but Calamity's were the opposite and would always be troublesome for whoever adopted her. I was hoping that she might win the longest ears contest, not for any award she might win but because being showcased in the winner's circle was sure to grab the attention of a potential adopter.

"Come on, girls, do your stuff," I cheered as Nona and Calamity entered the arena of long-eared contestants.

Nona looked rather proud as she extended Calamity's ears to their full breadth as the judge wielded his tape across her "wingspan" for the official measurement. Since pairs of ears can vary in length, each ear was measured individually and the numbers combined.

"We have a total of 27.25 inches for Calamity. That matches the world record holder."

"Woo, hoo!" Nona yelled. Calamity leapt for joy because she understood from Nona's reaction that she had pleased the one who was clearly becoming the object of affection for a dog that had not had much of the same in her short life.

"Hooray for Calamity!" All the spectators were cheering and applauding for her, and she was eating it all up with more enthusiasm than she'd earlier exhibited for an unguarded hamburger. Could this be the key to Calamity that I'd been missing all along? Perhaps all she really needed was to be the center of attention for a change. Who knew what she had experienced before she ended up at Lakeside Shelter or what positive reinforcement she had been denied in her young life? Certainly, there had been a lack of love. She had much in common with many humans who seek attention because they never had enough of it in their early lives. They derive that attention through acting out in negative ways or becoming the clown. This dog used both to get the attention she craved. But her moment of adulation was over, at least for now. The longest ears competition wasn't quite over. There was still one more competitor remaining who might measure up to Calamity, and his name was Longfellow.

When the un-neutered male basset waddled into the ring, it was immediately evident how Longfellow may have acquired his name. You wanted to believe it was because of the length of his body or his ears . . . until you got the view of his undercarriage. Fortunately, no one would be measuring anything else on the dogs today, but I was guessing that Longfellow must have already prevailed in the Lowest Ground Clearance contest.

You could almost have heard the familiar strains of Strauss's "Also Sprach Zarathustra" rising to its Odysseyan crescendo when Longfellow's snood finally came off and the dog's prodigious ears unfurled in all their glory. The dog was already so low in stature that his ears dragged the ground when he walked, causing him to trip and stumble. Everyone laughed, but I felt a strong urge to track down the insane breeder who was responsible for these mutant ears and strangle him or her with them. What on earth do you do with ears like those except keep them folded up in a silly snood until the next longest ears contest? We were all about to find out the answer to that question. A dramatic hush fell over the crowd as Longfellow's voluminous ears were extended horizontally to their full breadth. No one had ever seen ears that long on a basset before, except perhaps in a Berkley Breathed cartoon. One good gust of wind and the dog would have taxied down the dog park for take-off.

The judge measured first one ear and then the other. He was taking so long to confirm the measurement that at first I thought it was only for dramatic effect, but it was really only to recheck his numbers for accuracy. He gaped in amazement. Evidently, even he couldn't believe what he was seeing on the tape measure. At long last he spoke to the crowd, who clearly couldn't believe what they were seeing, either.

"Fellow Waddlers, the official winner of the Longest Ears contest is Longfellow." And this time he did pause for dramatic effect before making his next announcement. "At a total length of 30.5 inches, we have an entry for the *Guinness Book of World*

Records. Mr. Jeffries the basset hound and Tigger the blood-
hound have been bested for the world's longest ears. Congratu-
lations, Longfellow!"

The crowd went wild, but the victor seemed unimpressed by
all the attention he was getting. Perhaps there was good reason
for his *laissez faire.* After all, he was the one who had to live
with those bothersome ears day in and day out, tripping over
them, having them stepped on, dragging them in his food and
water bowls. The truth was, Longfellow was far more interested
in sniffing the nearest tree trunk, where he left a message for
the contestants in the next competition and grand finale to the
Waddle . . . Best Howl. This would be Cruiser's moment to
shine, because everyone knew that there was no better howler in
all of Lake Tahoe than my crooning Caruso, Cruiser.

CHAPTER 43

The commotion from the howling competition finally subsided, and Cruiser was polishing off the remaining crumbs of his victory biscuit. His reigning title as Best Howler had prevailed despite some truly impressive vocalizing, including the people, who were hoarse from coaxing their dogs to howl loudest and longest. If South Tahoe residents didn't know there was a Basset Hound Waddle under way from all that caterwauling, they soon would.

It was time to waddle down Lake Tahoe Boulevard, not only to show off our dogs dressed in their best Waddle Wear but also to raise the public's awareness of the plight of homeless pets and the need for a modern, no-kill shelter in the community. Along the way, other people with their dogs of all breeds joined the march until our numbers were truly formidable.

Tori and her placard-toting gang, who had infiltrated our parade, joined in the procession despite a few protests from Found Hounds members. Some people didn't like the fact that their posters were such in-your-face, graphic statements about the evils of animal neglect and cruelty. This wasn't exactly the image we wanted to project to the public for our first annual Bassetille Day Waddle. We naturally wished to garner support for our cause, but this day was meant for fun and celebration of the dogs, and of course, to find good homes for some of them. There wasn't much we could really do to keep Tori and her storm troopers from joining in our Thousand Hound March.

Last time I checked, it was still a free country, and freedom of speech is an inalienable right for TAILS as much as it is for Found Hounds.

Leading the march through town was the Jowl-flappers Float with a banner proclaiming the hoards of waddling hounds to follow. The float carried the two dogs that had been crowned as Waddle King and Queen. Those honors were reserved for dogs that had survived despite all odds against them to be adopted into permanent homes and live out their remaining years happily with people who understood them and showered them with all the love and attention every dog deserves.

The Waddle King, named Subway, still bore deep facial scars from the barbed wire his former owner had used to wire his mouth shut to keep him from howling. The scars looked like tears on his muzzle. It had taken him a long time to rediscover his loud and beautiful voice, and he was using it today with gusto. He seemed to understand that this was a special celebration of him and his fellow hounds.

Sharing the float with Subway were the winners of the various contests, including Longfellow, Cruiser, and also the winner of the costume contest, a Basset Boeing 747, wearing a body stocking with Styrofoam wings glued to the airplane fuselage. The float also served as a Saggin' Wagon for a couple of senior hounds with health issues who couldn't keep pace with the pack. The other thousand or so dogs followed the float, at varying rates of speed, or lack thereof, led by their proud owners, some of whom deserved prizes of their own for silliest costume.

Other doggy attire consisted of goofy hats or ready-made costumes purchased at Petropolis or the Haute Hydrant. With the exception of several dogs that shook off their chapeaux quicker than a basset does anything except eat, most of the dogs were good sports about being dressed up for the amusement of others and didn't seem to mind being the focus of all the cheering, jeering spectators lined up along the Waddle route.

As we made our way at snail's pace down Lake Tahoe Boulevard, leaving a slime trail of basset drool in our wake, people spilled out of the tourist shops at Heavenly Village to gape at the spectacle and laugh at the funny dogs in dress-up. We didn't mind the ridicule, as long as we got a new shelter and more adoptive homes for dogs like these. Reno might have its low-riders on Hot August Nights, but South Tahoe had its own version of low-riders on Bassetille Day.

Everything was going smoothly enough with our pup parade and our colorful banners about building a new shelter in Tahoe. Then spectators got an eyeful of the graphic placards. No one really wants reminding of the result of puppy mills and people's failure to spay and neuter their pets, and certainly not in the way TAILS chose to get the message across. Mothers shielded their children's eyes, and others averted their gaze. One guy actually threw up, but it wasn't clear whether the cause was the offensive signage or one too many drinks in the casinos.

Tori's troops already had earned a reputation in the community as troublemakers, having been blamed for various acts of vandalism and even a fire that broke out at a pet store accused of selling puppies from Midwest puppy mills. Whether or not TAILS was really responsible for everything they got blamed for hadn't yet been proved, but they were guilty by association. As their group passed by, some people in the crowd turned and walked away, disgusted. Others shouted and hurled insults at those carrying signs, particularly at Tori, who was an irresistible target with her Goth attire and purple spiked hair. You had to wonder if she liked the attention she got with that hair and all the rest of what made Tori Thatcher who she was, even if it was mostly negative.

We had nearly made it through the entire Waddle route down Lake Tahoe Boulevard when a spectator stepped out from among the crowd and ripped the placard Tori carried from her hand.

"Someone should euthanize you, you freak!" he shouted.

Tori snatched at the sign, but the spectator struck her over the head with it. Another member leapt to her defense, and the aggressor's buddy leapt to his. Others in the parade joined in the fray, and the dogs began baying in discordant chorus their excitement and distress over their humans behaving badly. Despite my own negative attitude about Tori and company, their demonstration had been peaceful. I couldn't stand idly by and watch them be harmed in a preemptive attack. I soon found myself right in the middle of an all-out dogfight.

Dogs waddled at will as leashes were released in the midst of the mêlée. Several dogs broke out in fights. Never in the history of Lake Tahoe had anyone witnessed anything like the grand finale of the first annual Bassetille Day Waddle. Not since the French Revolution had there been a protest march to rival this one, at least one with a pack of unruly French dogs. No one from the casinos was making any bets on who would win the battle for the boulevard, but all bets were off when the police arrived, wielding their batons. With their sensitive noses, the hounds were no doubt grateful that the cops didn't use pepper spray, too!

CHAPTER 44

It didn't take long for the law to subdue the crowd run amok. The sight of uniforms and riot gear quickly took the fight out of them, and no one got the business end of the baton, except for the guy who had whacked Tori with her own protest sign. He was taken into custody, and the officer doing the cuffing was none other than Skip's protégé, Rusty Cannon. She might have been small in stature, but there was nothing small about her attitude, as I'd already discovered on more than one occasion. Meanwhile, other officers took the opportunity to round up several drunks for a ride in the paddy wagon.

Once the Waddle attendees and lookie-loos began to disperse, the event was officially concluded. Those who had participated in the parade turned to the business of collecting their wayward hounds. With nose-blind bassets, that might be even more of a challenge than gaining public support for a new shelter was turning out to be. I spotted another familiar face among the officers who were busy restoring peace in the Valley of the Dogs.

"Skip, am I glad to see you!"

"Beanie, what the heck are you doing in the middle of this fracas?"

"It wasn't by choice, I assure you. We were just trying to have a fun day out at our first Tahoe Basset Waddle, and we would have if it hadn't turned into a mob scene."

"It may be your last Basset Waddle if they all end up like this one."

"If Tori Thatcher has anything to do with it, you mean. She never misses an opportunity for advancing her TAILS agenda."

"She and that bunch of wackos are starting to make such a bad name for themselves in this community, I'll have to keep a closer eye on their activities from now on."

Speaking of keeping an eye on things, I'd completely lost track of my own dog in all the confusion. The Jowl Flappers float was now devoid of dogs, except for a couple of senior hounds who were too old or blind to find their way around without assistance. I saw no sign of Cruiser there, though, or anywhere among the other hounds that had waddled in the parade. Where, oh where, had my basset hound gone?

"Skip, have you seen Cruiser?"

"No, but he must be wandering around here somewhere. He can't have gone far."

"That's what you think. You know that dog has the wander-lust. How do you think I ended up with him in the first place?"

"I'd like to help you look for him, but as you can see I've got my hands full right now. Isn't Nona here with you?"

"I've lost track of her too, in all the confusion."

"Well, go find her. Maybe she has him."

"I hope so. They'll be letting the traffic through on the boulevard soon. Bassets have no road sense whatsoever."

"Don't worry, Beanie. You'll find him. Think like Cruiser. Where would he be most likely to go?"

I pondered that question only a moment when the answer became obvious. Where does a basset go? Where there's food, of course. "Thanks, Skip. I know just where to look for him."

I headed for the spot I felt sure I'd find Cruiser. Fortunately, I remembered passing a hot dog stand earlier along the parade route. Where else would you expect to find a hungry hound dog? Cruiser had been hanging around the barbecue at the Waddle earlier where hamburgers and hot dogs were being cooked. I'd caught him nabbing wieners from unwary tots, leaving them bawling while holding empty hot dog buns. That is, when he wasn't being offered treats from folks who couldn't resist that artful beggar basset of mine. At a Basset Waddle, soft touches for treats are always in abundance.

I found the hot dog stand, all right, but no Cruiser. The dog mom in me was beginning to panic, especially after a steady stream of traffic had resumed its busy course along Lake Tahoe Boulevard. He is pretty smart, but he's still a basset, and no basset's keen nose is immune to leading him straight into trouble. I was glad that Tom wasn't around to witness this disaster. He would have been very upset with me for letting Cruiser out of my sight, even for a second. Nona wasn't too happy with me either, when she finally appeared with Calamity, safely tethered on her leash. I was proud of Nona for taking good care of her charge. I, however, had broken the first commandment of dog safety: Love 'em and leash 'em. Calamity would have been long gone if she'd been let off her leash, but I'd trusted Cruiser. He'd been with me a long time, but it was trust apparently undeserved.

"Dad would be furious with you for losing his dog."

"No need to remind me of that. I should never have let him off his leash, but the Waddle was an off-leash event. I thought he'd be safe on the float with the other dogs and people, but I didn't expect all hell to break loose. After all this time, I thought I could rely on Cruiser not to wander away from me."

"Now you know better."

"We have to keep looking for him. He can't have gotten that far in such a short time. That inquisitive sniffer of his is bound to slow him down some, especially if he encounters any tasty tidbits along the way."

"Maybe Calamity can help us track him down. She has a keen sniffer, too."

217

I wasn't placing any bets on Calamity to provide any assistance in our search for Cruiser, but it was worth a try. "I
guess we can use all the help we can get. The sooner we find
Cruiser, the better the chance he won't get into trouble."

"Come on, girl. Let's go find Cruiser!"

In response to Nona's command, Calamity dropped her nose
to the ground as though it was magnetized. She shifted into
warp waddle and bayed so loudly it surprised even her. Had she
picked up his scent so quickly? She seemed to understand that
this was a bona fide hound dog emergency. Even in the short
time she had lived with us, she had bonded with Cruiser well
enough to recognize what constituted a full pack in my home. It
was evident even to crazy Calamity that an important member
of the MacBean pack was missing and must be located without
delay.

CHAPTER 45

Calamity tugged at her tether like a team of huskies in the Iditarod, with Nona and me following her lead in our frantic search for Cruiser. We queried everyone we passed along the way as to the whereabouts of my wayward hound but got no leads. No one had seen a dog matching his description or any bassets at all since the parade had ended. All hounds were accounted for, except mine.

We searched for him until nightfall made it impossible to continue. I didn't want to give up, but it was no use with dark coming on. When we were just about to rein in Calamity's search and rescue effort, she froze at the entrance to a Pay & Park lot. She read the pavement with her nose like it was basset Braille, then let out a howl and dragged us into the lot. She led us right to a vacant parking space, flopped down on her haunches and bayed at the rising moon. I already knew she was a strong contender in the best howl competition, but I'd never heard her carry on like this before. It was clear that she had brought us to the end of the scent trail, or at least as far as she was able to follow it. There was no sign of Cruiser in the parking lot, but I had a strong sense that this was the last place he'd been. So did Calamity. What no one knew was where he'd gone from here.

My distress over not having found Cruiser was matched by that of Nona and Calamity. As we loaded the young dog into her crate and reluctantly headed for home, even she seemed aware that something was wrong because Cruiser wasn't coming home with us, too. I brushed away tears as I thought about Cruiser wandering the streets of South Lake Tahoe, the same as when Tom discovered him one summer's end wandering starved and lost. I hoped he hadn't survived that trauma and more only to end up under the wheels of a car on Lake Tahoe Boulevard or some other busy road before I could rescue him all over again. Calamity heard me crying, and her anguished cries of distress echoed mine from the back of the car.

"Don't worry, Mom. Cruiser's a pretty street-wise dog. He knows how to avoid traffic. He did before, didn't he?"

"True."

"I'm sure he'll be okay. Someone may have already picked him up."

"Could be. If that's the case, I hope it was the right kind of person who'll attend to his welfare until I can reclaim him." It seemed like a strong possibility Cruiser had caught a ride with someone, especially since Calamity had tracked him to a parking lot. The only thing that worried me was who might have picked up my long-eared hitchhiker. Was it another basset lover or had the dogcatcher found him first?

At least I knew it couldn't be Round 'em Up Rhoda. Of course, there was the possibility it could be her protégé, Rex. Fortunately, Doc Heaton had microchipped Cruiser, so his identification could be easily traced if someone did find him. That and his ID tag were his best insurance of being returned safely to his home.

"He's got to be somewhere in Tahoe. He can't have gotten too far on those stubby legs of his. We'll post some signs tomorrow and place an ad in the paper. Someone is bound to have seen a handsome fellow like him wandering around town."

I knew Nona was trying to keep things light for my benefit, but she was right about one thing. A comical-looking basset hound doesn't usually go unnoticed for long. Surely, someone would find Cruiser before any harm could befall him. But I also worried about all the dogs that had been disappearing from the shelter. The night I saw someone abscond with the beagle, I knew that something sinister was afoot. The possibility that Cruiser might end up in a research lab or as bully bait was too horrid a prospect to consider.

When we arrived home, Calamity explored every room in the house, but for once she wasn't interested in looking for mischief to get into. She was clearly intent on searching for her pack mate, Cruiser. Once she'd made her rounds of the cabin and discovered that there was no other dog on the premises, she slunk to her snuggly bed in the living room, where she curled up, giving me the sagging, mournful look that only a basset hound can. Such a countenance surely must have inspired Shakespeare to write his tragedies. After all, Will did pen verse about bassets. "Ears that sweep away the morning dew; slow in pursuit, but matched in mouth like bells"—what else could the bard have been describing but a basset hound? Calamity's Hershey's kiss eyes, accented with prominent whites and cherry red haws for effect, spoke the same sad query we all were thinking that night: Where is Cruiser?

I felt a glimmer of hope when, upon arriving home, I noticed the blinking red light on my phone indicating that someone had left a message. Nona was right. Someone had found Cruiser and mercifully had wasted no time dialing the number engraved on his trusty dog tag, the first line of defense in insuring the quick return of a lost dog. There was also a better chance of reclaiming an older dog like Cruiser than a puppy. People were not so inclined to part with a pup, especially a purebred, but finding a large senior dog that could eat you out of house and home and cost you a bundle in vet bills was usually a guaranteed return ticket for the dog's swift trip home. In this respect,

Cruiser's age was in his favor. At least he hadn't gone missing in the dead of winter. Even the coyotes found it hard surviving snowbound Tahoe winters.

I wasted no time in playing back the phone message. It was about Cruiser, all right. I was crestfallen to learn that it was only Skip checking to see if we'd found him, but the second part of his message was even more disturbing. He told me Roberta Finch had been found dead at the Basset Waddle.

CHAPTER 46

In his message, Skip had neglected to mention the cause of Bertie's death. Theoretically, this unexpected turn of events should have narrowed my field of suspects in the ongoing Marx murder investigation. Who hated Rhoda worse than Bertie had or wanted as badly to get even with her? Just about everyone who hated Rhoda Marx would have been at the Waddle. Was Bertie now also a victim of the killer? Why? I called Skip right back but got no answer and had to leave a message for him, too.

"Skip, it's Beanie. I got your message. Thanks for calling to check on Cruiser. We haven't found him yet. I was hoping you were someone calling to say they had. Nona and I will resume our search first thing tomorrow. Keep an eye out for my boy, okay? I'm worried sick about him. Terrible news about Bertie Finch. I need to talk to you about that as soon as possible."

When I hung up the phone, I noticed that the red light was still on. Someone had left a new message while I was returning Skip's call. This time I hoped it was the call I was waiting for, that someone had found Cruiser and he was safe in their keeping until I could bring him home again. I played it back.

"Elsie, it's Jenna. We found Cruiser. He's here at the shelter, and it's about to close. Better hurry!"

I didn't call her back. No time to waste. I passed Nona and Calamity on my way out the door. Nona sensed the urgency. So did Calamity, but she probably just thought it was time for her walk.

"Someone has found Cruiser, Mom?"

"Yes. That was Jenna Fairbanks. He's turned up at Lakeside Shelter. Thank goodness he's safe!"

"Want us to come along?"

"No, it's okay. It might upset Calamity to be around the shelter again. You stay here and keep your dog company."

I anticipated a retort at my suggestion that Calamity was Nona's dog, but the only response I got was, "Okey-dokey." I think all three of us understood now whose dog Calamity was, especially Calamity herself.

I snatched my sweater from the hall tree as I left. Summer evenings at Tahoe often turn chilly. Excused from having to join the search for lost dogs, Nona curled up with a book in her father's old easy chair as Calamity made herself comfy on the ottoman. "All right, you two. I'll be back in a jiffy from the pound with my found hound."

When I drove up to Lakeside's entrance, the shelter was pitch dark except for a streetlight in the lot. I expected that Jenna would be waiting for me with Cruiser up front, but the lights were out in the office, too. Perhaps she'd had to leave before I arrived, but she'd left the door unlocked, so I let myself in.

Light spilled down the hallway from the rear of the shelter, so I followed it, assuming she must be attending to something back in the kennel area. When I got there, though, I saw no sign of Jenna or my dog. I was beginning to get a funny feeling about this. Something didn't seem quite right to me, and that feeling was affirmed when I heard Cruiser let out a mournful howl.

I had lived with my dog long enough to recognize every nuance of his canine language, and this was without any doubt a howl of distress. Like a mother responding to the cry of her child, I bolted through the shelter, all the way down the gray mile to the place from where the sound seemed to originate. I hoped I wasn't going to find Jenna in the same condition as I'd found her boss, Rhoda, but my main concern right now was to locate my dog as quickly as possible. As I drew closer, I noticed that Cruiser's cries sounded distant or muffled, as though he was barking from inside a box. My anxiety grew tenfold when my frantic search for Cruiser led me right to the door of the euthanasia room.

When I thrust open the door, I was horrified to discover Cruiser trapped inside the death chamber. Now I understood why his vocalizations had sounded so strangely distant. When he saw me enter the room, his loud howls for help subsided to a pitiful whimper.

"Cruiser! What on earth are you doing in there, boy?"

Thank goodness I had arrived in time. Unlike in my nightmare, he was still alive. I had no idea why he was locked inside the deadly contraption, or who would have put him in it, but I wasted no time in getting him out. Fortunately, no one had turned the thing on while he was in there. I unlatched the death chamber door to free my dog, but as I did, Cruiser grumbled a warning. I instinctively knew he wasn't growling at me but at something else. By the time I realized the peril I was in, it was too late to defend myself. I felt a sudden jerk and something tightening sharply around my neck until I was gasping for breath. My last thought before my world went black was what the kennel attendant Rex had said about "choking out" cats with the catchpole.

CHAPTER 47

When I regained consciousness, the first thing I became aware of was the sound of Cruiser barking his head off. My throat was sore from the constriction with the choke pole that had been used to subdue me.

I was still so dazed that at first I didn't know exactly where I was, but I knew it wasn't where I should be, at home safe and sound with Nona and my Cruiser. When I saw Jenna Fairbanks peering in at me through the viewing panel of the CO chamber, I realized I was in a tight spot, in more than one way. She had lured me here to Lakeside Shelter with my own dog! Was he only bait for this trap, or had she really meant to kill Cruiser? Why would she do that?

It appeared she had the same fate in mind for me. If it had been Tori Thatcher out there instead of Jenna, I wouldn't have been so befuddled by my desperate situation. I could more easily have believed Tori capable of such a dastardly deed, but Jenna was on our team, wasn't she? My earlier inklings about her had been correct, after all, because it was becoming uncomfortably clear that Jenna meant me grave harm. Exactly why was still unclear, but not for long. She was about to do me the favor of enlightening me of her motives before flipping the switch. I suppose she figured I wouldn't be telling anyone what she was about to tell me.

At least I was the only one inside here now. There was some comfort in knowing that Cruiser was safe in a holding cell across the room. He was barking hysterically because he knew I wasn't safe and he was powerless to come to my aid. Neither could Skip. He couldn't know the danger I was in. Neither of my crime-fighting comrades would be dashing to my rescue this time.

"I'm sorry to have to do this, Elsie, but you really leave me no alternative."

"You don't have to do this, Jenna."

"Yes, I do. I have no choice now. You were getting too close to the truth about what happened to Rhoda Marx, and I can't go to prison. What would happen to my dogs? They're my responsibility, you see. There aren't enough good homes for all of them."

When she talked of her dogs, I understood that she was referring to all the Found Hounds she rescued that were still in need of adoptive homes. But I also understood that the Milkbones had finally spilled out of Jenna's biscuit jar. The woman was clearly seriously disturbed.

I tried to remain as calm as I could under the circumstances. I was going to have to do my best to talk my way out of this situation. Fortunately, I'd learned a few tricks from Skip about calming a potentially violent suspect and defusing difficult situations. This one definitely qualified.

"I understand exactly how you feel about the dogs, Jenna. I feel the same way."

"I didn't mean to kill Rhoda, but you just couldn't reason with that woman. She threatened to euthanize Gilda because she was old and her owner couldn't come to claim her immediately. She could have waited one more day and spared Gilda, but her attitude was that senior dogs can never be placed, so you'd best save the county money and dispatch them as quickly as possible."

No wonder they called her Mengele Marx and Lakeside was

considered a canine concentration camp. As a devoted dog lover, I understood Jenna's, and everyone else's, feelings about Rhoda, but that still didn't justify murder.

I was starting to feel like I was a priest inside a confessional listening to a sinner seeking absolution, but no priest ever heard a confession from inside a chamber like this one!

"Gilda had a home and someone who loved her," Jenna continued, "but Rhoda killed her just to be her usual nasty self and assert her power over all of us like the miserable control freak she was. She tried to block every adoption, so we had to get fake adopters to come in and rescue all the pets they could. It nearly killed poor Bertie, losing her dear pet like that, and it ultimately did."

"I just heard about Bertie's death. I'm so sorry about your friend, Jenna."

"It was her heart."

"She had a heart attack?" Well, that was one less murder in Tahoe that needed to be solved.

"They'll call it that, but poor Bertie really died of a broken heart, thanks to that horrid Marx woman. I tried to work around her to rescue the dogs, but it was already too late for Gilda. When I found out what Rhoda had done, I confronted her and threatened to get her fired. We got into a shoving match, and when I pushed her back she fell and hit her head hard. When I realized she was dead, I panicked."

Panic was certainly an emotion I could appreciate at the moment.

Jenna wrung her hands as she talked, not really to me at all, but to herself, purging her guilty conscience as though that made everything she'd done all right. "I didn't know what to do, so I tried to cover up her death by making it look like TAILS did it. They already have such a bad reputation in the community, I figured the police would automatically pin the crime on them."

Who wouldn't suspect TAILS of foul play? I did, too. Tori made such a convenient target with her purple hair and posturing.

"So I dragged Rhoda's body into the chamber and turned on the gas. I confess it gave me immense pleasure to do the same thing to her as she'd done to poor Gilda and all those other helpless pets." Jenna placed her hand over the switch as she spoke, which made me increasingly nervous.

"If her death was accidental, Jenna, then the courts will show leniency, but if you kill me, you'll get murder one for sure. I know you're confused right now, but please stop and think about what you're doing."

"There's no way out of this for me. It's too late. Too late."

"You do have a way out of this. Listen to me, Jenna. You do!"

Clearly I didn't, however. I watched in horror as Jenna prepared to depress the switch to start the flow of deadly gas into the chamber. "Jenna, stop! You know you wouldn't do it to a dog. Please don't do it to me. Let me out of here!"

I heard a hissing sound. Jenna had turned on the gas! I couldn't smell anything, but you can't smell carbon monoxide. It's odorless.

"Help! Help me!" I pounded on the panel and screamed as loud as I could, but I realized that I was inside a device that was designed to muffle the desperate cries of the dying. Who would ever be able to hear me inside this doggone chamber of death?

Chapter 48

Cruiser was baying his dear old heart out from within the holding cell, where dogs were contained briefly before it was their turn to take the Big Sleep. What must it be like to watch your brethren being dragged to their deaths but be powerless to save them or yourself? Like them, Cruiser couldn't get free from his prison. He had come to my rescue so many times before, but it looked like it was my turn to find out whether or not euthanasia really was a "good death," as the Greeks say.

I heard the steady hiss of gas leaking into the chamber. Soon my lungs would be robbed of life-giving oxygen and within seconds I would be dead. I imagined I heard the sound of a basset duo howling in chorus. Was it the sound of Cruiser's distressed cries I heard echoing through the halls of the shelter? Or was I back at the Basset Waddle again judging the Best Howl contest? I feared that, like Gilda, I might be headed for the last Waddle across the Bridge.

As I pounded on the chamber walls in the hope of being freed, I was vaguely aware of the percussive sound of a door banging open. Then I heard a familiar bark, but it wasn't Cruiser's. Even through my terror, I recognized the sound as that of a certain crazy dog named Calamity.

Jenna turned to see what all the commotion was about, but her reaction was too slow for Calamity, who was younger and speedier than her pack mate, Cruiser. Faster than a basset can flick a dollop of drool on a divan, she reared up on my assailant, boxing at her like a kangaroo with her paws, knocking Jenna right off her feet. I heard a loud thud as her head connected hard with the concrete. Jenna lay stretched on the floor like an old hound dog on the hearth, out cold and not stirring a muscle.

Calamity reared up on the chamber and scratched at the viewing panel to get to me. Now I understood how the paw prints Skip and his team had lifted from this contraption had gotten there. I guessed that Rhoda's pal, Spirit, had known she was trapped in here and had done the same thing Calamity was doing now. Perhaps that was why he had looked so downcast the day I first saw him at the shelter lying beside Rhoda's desk. Heck, even Adolf Hitler's German shepherd dog, Blondie, was devoted to her fuehrer. Only a dog could love someone like him or Rhoda Marx. The next face I saw peering at me through the panel of the chamber was a welcomed one that I loved more than anyone else's on earth besides Cruiser's, of course. It was Nona's sweet countenance, which appeared to me as an angel of mercy.

"Mom! Hold on. I'm getting you out of there right now."

Nona turned off the flow of gas, flipped the latches, and opened the chamber door, freeing me. She helped me to my feet, which I could barely feel after being cramped up inside there. My legs wobbled like two elastic bands beneath me. Nona went over to Cruiser's cell and opened the door to free him, too.

"I've never been so glad to see anyone in my life. Thank heavens you arrived when you did."

"I got worried when you didn't come back right away with Cruiser. I knew something must be wrong. Are you all right?"

"I will be."

"Looks like we arrived just in time."

"I'll say! What a good girl you are, Calamity!"

Now that was something Calamity hadn't heard too often in

her life, but this time she had rightly earned her accolades and was deserving of the title of Good Dog. She waddled over to me for a pet and gave me a thorough sniffing as I stroked her silky brown coat. At first I thought she was checking me over to make sure I was all right, and that may have been the case. But I realized I might have also borne the pungent scent of fear and death from all the animals that had met their fate in that chamber, as I too nearly had.

Calamity's hindquarters were aquiver, but her puzzling reaction had nothing to do with the scent of my clothing. Something else was causing this strange behavior, and it was evidently something only a dog could detect with its keen senses, for when I glanced over at Cruiser I saw that he was also exhibiting the same strange reaction as Calamity's to something unseen in our midst.

Nona had alerted Skip on her cell phone on her way over to the shelter. This was one time I could forgive her for breaking the law about dialing and driving. The sheriff and his ravishing Rusty were quick to arrive on the scene. I was glad to learn she had decided not to pursue her harassment case against the department, and they didn't take any punitive action against her. Either Skip was more persuasive than I gave him credit for, or she had proved to them she could do her job and keep her privates private. Whatever their reasons, the sheriff's department let sleeping dogs lie and kept her on the force. She and Skip were a team again, not to mention an item, and they weren't about to let this sleeping dog lie. It was time to round up the pup perp and officially close this doggone case. Rusty smacked the cheeks of the unconscious woman to bring her around.

Jenna moaned in pain and began to stir. Now fully conscious, she sat up and rubbed the back of her head where a goose egg formed. Rusty did the cuffing while Skip read Jenna her rights before taking her into custody. Jenna had sealed her fate when she turned on the gas while I was inside the gas chamber. The only reason I was still alive to see justice done was because the CO tank was empty. The fact that she had not made sure to check the tank first carried no weight in the eyes of the law, however. Her sentence might have been lighter for Rhoda's accidental death, but her attempted murder of yours truly carried a stiffer penalty for which she would be punished to the full extent of the law. What sympathy I might have felt for her motives on behalf of homeless pets had dissipated when she entrapped Cruiser and then me inside a chamber of death.

CHAPTER 49

I was the last living thing ever to see the inside of the euthanasia chamber because its use was forthwith banned at the newly renovated no-kill Lakeside Animal Shelter Cruiser and I were touring today with its new manager, Amanda Peabody.

Two kittens batted playfully at each other inside a new state-of-the art cat colony with clear Plexiglas cages. Others climbed on a kitty condo. A husky and a lab cavorted with each other while an old coonhound lounged on a comfy sofa inside a large windowed play area strewn with toys. Volunteers chatted with shelter visitors, answering their questions and holding relaxed meet-and-greets in ambient private rooms where potential adopters could interact with the animals in peaceful surroundings. Hold times for all pets, licensed or not, had been increased from three days to three weeks, giving owners plenty of time to reclaim their pet before putting it up for adoption or fostering with Found Hounds or other rescue groups until placed in a loving home. What had happened to Gilda would never happen again. In fact, they had renamed the adoption branch of the shelter Gilda's Adoption Center.

"They've done wonders with this place, Amanda. It looks nothing like the old shelter."

"Lakeside Shelter has been transformed inside and out."

"So I can see."

"How did you get the money for all these wonderful improvements? I thought that they would be a long time coming with the current budget constraints."

"Thanks to fundraisers and a generous bequest from the Abigail Haversham Tahoe Trust she provided for in her estate, we were able to buy up some adjacent property to expand the size of the shelter. We've increased the quantity and dimensions of kennels and added a state-of-the art spay/neuter clinic, but as you can see, we have also improved on what was already here. The cages are now visitor friendly. Pets can be easily viewed by prospective adopters through one-way glass without even having to enter the kennel area, so it's not so stressful for the animals."

Lakeside now looked less like a lockdown and more like an alpine pet resort worthy of Lake Tahoe. I was pleased to see that everything possible had been done to make the animals' hopefully brief stay there more pleasant.

"We have hired new staff who are well qualified and better suited to their jobs, unlike some who worked here before."

"Yes, I know." Amanda didn't have to say their names aloud. I was just as glad as she was that they were no longer here.

"With plenty of staff on hand to do adoptions, deal with people bringing in animals, and other customer services duties, we're better able to focus on feeding and caring for the animals and maintaining the shelter. All the kennels are sanitized every day, and we make sure that all water and chemicals are cleaned up and safely stored before customers arrive."

"I noticed the difference the moment I entered the shelter."

"Smells a lot better now, huh? I'm sure Cruiser agrees, don't you, boy?"

"Roo, roo!" The only doggy scent his sensitive nose detected now was that of the treats stashed in a jar on the counter. Amanda offered Cruiser a biscuit, which he accepted without a moment's hesitation.

Noticeably absent from the new shelter was Calamity's old nemesis, Rex. He'd not only been fired from his job, but was jailed and heavily fined after it was discovered he'd been selling animals from the shelter to pet shops and research labs, though he denied ever having unleashed any strays on the community. The judge decreed that he account for every cent of the money he had made from the sale of the animals and donate it to Tahoe's new animal shelter.

At least I knew it wasn't TAILS activists who were responsible for the shelter break-ins. They had thankfully redirected their attention to protesting at research labs to liberate the animals there. Though I still wasn't too fond of Tori or her troublemakers, I hoped they would eventually succeed in their goal of ending animal experimentation once and for all.

The shelter had hired new animal care officers, whose attention to animal welfare in the community could continue. Updated transport vehicles made the ride to the shelter more comfortable and less stressful for strays. The objective now wasn't to catch 'em and kill 'em, as Rhoda's had been, but to rescue animals from deplorable living conditions, cite and prosecute cruel or neglectful owners, attend to sick and injured animals, and protect them from further injury and distress. Humane officers were specially trained to assess a stray animal's condition in the field and provide preliminary medical assistance to sick or injured dogs and cats until the animal could be transported to a veterinarian for treatment. A team of humane educators now made regular rounds in Tahoe, including at schools where children were taught early lessons in kindness to animals and the responsible care of pets.

"We have a large exercise yard and several homey get-acquainted rooms," Amanda added. "We also have raised beds for the dogs, better security, and surveillance cameras installed inside and out. We've hired more vets and animal behaviorists to rehabilitate the pets we take in so they're more adoptable. We even pipe in music to help calm the animals."

"A little mutt music, eh?"

She laughed. "It's recorded especially for dogs, but the cats seem to like enjoy it, too."

"I have to admit the place is a lot more peaceful than it was when Calamity was kenneled here. I'll have to try some of that music at home."

"How is your latest foster doing, by the way? Have you found an adopter for her yet?"

"Why, yes. I believe I have."

"That's great! Who took her?"

"My daughter did. Nona fell in love with Calamity from the get-go, and the feeling was mutual. They bonded almost instantly. Calamity has a new home with her in San Francisco."

"How is Nona doing, anyway? I heard she had a health scare."

"She did, but she's fine now. Fortunately, the tumor was benign and has completely disappeared without her having to undergo any surgery."

"That's wonderful, Beanie! They have so many new ways in medicine."

"True, but sometimes it's the old ways that work best."

Nona probably wasn't as likely as I was to claim that Native American medicine had any part in her healing, but I was glad my daughter was learning a new respect for traditional Indian ways. If more of our youngsters in the tribe can do the same, things may finally improve for the Washoe in Tahoe. Of course, I couldn't discount the healing power of a pet. Calamity deserved some credit, too. There's just no better medicine than the love of a devoted dog.

"I'm glad she's going to be okay, Elsie."

"Yep, Nona has a new lease on life and also on a larger apartment near Golden Gate Park, so Calamity will get lots of exercise. Maybe she won't be so crazy now that she's settled in a permanent home with Nona."

"That will be good for her, I'm sure. How is Cruiser handling his pack mate's absence?"

"He's fine with it. He likes being king of his own castle, you know. He tolerates other dogs in his territory for a little while, but he really prefers being an only dog. He likes being the center of attention. Of course, Nona will bring Calamity along with her whenever she visits, so he isn't completely rid of her."

Nor was I. I didn't say it out loud, but I knew what we were both thinking. Amanda had met Calamity too, so she knew what she was like. An occasional Calamity at the house was better than having that crazy hound around all the time. Cruiser's yum-yum nook was all his for the raiding again, at least for the time being.

CHAPTER 50

Dog-shaped clouds chased a yellow ball sun along the western horizon as Lakeside Shelter's grand opening celebration was winding down. Most of the other visitors had already left, and many went home with a new canine or feline friend.

There had been many adoptions on the opening day of Lake Tahoe's new shelter. Seeing the animals looking happier and healthier in their shelter surroundings made them more appealing to prospective adopters. Everyone who remembered what our community's animal shelter had once been like under Rhoda Marx felt confident that there would be many more happy endings for the homeless pets that came to stay here in comfort and safety for a little while before finding their forever homes with people who would give them the full measure of love that should be every pet's birthright. Calamity was one of the lucky ones that had been re-homed, thanks to the efforts of Amanda Peabody and others who went to great lengths to ensure their survival against all odds.

As Cruiser and I made our way down a quiet corridor of the new shelter, we had no choice but to walk past the same kennel that had once briefly held the ill-fated basset hound named Gilda. The cage was now assigned a different number and was presently unoccupied, or so I thought until we approached it. Cruiser froze in his tracks, his attention trained on something inside the haunted kennel. Had someone left some stray crumbs of kibble or a biscuit behind? No, that wasn't it. I couldn't see anything that would elicit such a reaction in him.

"Come on, boy. It's time for us to go home now."

No matter how much I coaxed him to follow me, Cruiser wouldn't budge an inch from the spot. His tail began to helicopter in a friendly greeting. He let out a friendly bark and kept barking insistently at something inside the vacant kennel.

Roo, roo! I was puzzled by his odd reaction. What did he see in there that I couldn't? His focus was now trained on the hallway. I tried tugging on his leash to lead him away from the spot, but he resisted, standing his ground doggedly, as only a basset can. Something was definitely there, all right.

"What is it, Cruiser?"

Through a window, the late afternoon sun illuminated the corridor. Then I saw it, too! Cruiser lifted his nose and bayed at the vaporous apparition that waddled slowly away from us. With white-tipped tail carried gaily aloft in true hound fashion, the phantom of Lakeside Animal Shelter dissolved in golden beams of light. Gilda had gone home at last.

ABOUT THE AUTHOR

Sue Owens Wright is an award-winning writer of both fiction and nonfiction about dogs. She is a fancier and rescuer of basset hounds, which are frequently featured in her books and essays. She is a nine-time nominee for the Maxwell, awarded annually by the Dog Writers Association of America to the best writer on the subject of dogs. She has twice won the Maxwell Award and also earned special recognition from the Humane Society of the United States for her writing on animal welfare issues. She lives in Northern California with her husband and bassets.

CHILTON'S
REPAIR & TUNE-UP GUIDE

ASPEN VOLARÉ 1976-80

Dodge Aspen 1976-80 • Plymouth Volaré 1976-80

Vice President and General Manager JOHN P. KUSHNERICK
Managing Editor KERRY A. FREEMAN, S.A.E.
Senior Editor RICHARD J. RIVELE, S.A.E.
Editor RON WEBB

CHILTON BOOK COMPANY
Radnor, Pennsylvania
19089

SAFETY NOTICE

Proper service and repair procedures are vital to the safe, reliable operation of all motor vehicles, as well as the personal safety of those performing repairs. This book outlines procedures for servicing and repairing vehicles using safe, effective methods. The procedures contain many NOTES, CAUTIONS and WARNINGS which should be followed along with standard safety procedures to eliminate the possibility of personal injury or improper service which could damage the vehicle or compromise its safety.

It is important to note that repair procedures and techniques, tools and parts for servicing motor vehicles, as well as the skill and experience of the individual performing the work vary widely. It is not possible to anticipate all of the conceivable ways or conditions under which vehicles may be serviced, or to provide cautions as to all of the possible hazards that may result. Standard and accepted safety precautions and equipment should be used when handling toxic or flammable fluids, and safety goggles or other protection should be used during cutting, grinding, chiseling, prying, or any other process that can cause material removal or projectiles.

Some procedures require the use of tools specially designed for a specific purpose. Before substituting another tool or procedure, you must be completely satisfied that neither your personal safety, nor the performance of the vehicle will be endangered.

Although information in this guide is based on industry sources and is as complete as possible at the time of publication, the possibility exists that the manufacturer made later changes which could not be included here. While striving for total accuracy, Chilton Book Company cannot assume responsibility for any errors, changes, or omissions that may occur in the compilation of this data.

PART NUMBERS

Part numbers listed in this reference are not recommendations by Chilton for any product by brand name. They are references that can be used with interchange manuals and aftermarket supplier catalogs to locate each brand supplier's discrete part number.

ACKNOWLEDGMENTS

The Chilton Book Company expresses its appreciation to the Chrysler Corporation for technical information and illustrations contained herein.

Chilton's Repair & Tune-Up Guide: Aspen/Volaré 1976–80
ISBN 0-8019-7193-4 pbk.
Library of Congress Catalog Card No. 81-70240

CONTENTS

Quick Reference Specifications For Your Vehicle

Fill in this chart with the most commonly used specifications for your vehicle. Specifications can be found in Chapters 1 through 3 or on the tune-up decal under the hood of the vehicle.

Tune-Up

Firing Order_____

Spark Plugs:

    Type_____

    Gap (in.)_____

Point Gap (in.)_____

Dwell Angle (°)_____

Ignition Timing (°)_____

    Vacuum (Connected/Disconnected)_____

Valve Clearance (in.)

    Intake_____   Exhaust_____

Capacities

Engine Oil (qts)

    With Filter Change_____

    Without Filter Change_____

Cooling System (qts)_____

Manual Transmission (pts)_____

    Type_____

Automatic Transmission (pts)_____

    Type_____

Front Differential (pts)_____

    Type_____

Rear Differential (pts)_____

    Type_____

Transfer Case (pts)_____

    Type_____

FREQUENTLY REPLACED PARTS

Use these spaces to record the part numbers of frequently replaced parts.

PCV VALVE

Manufacturer_____

Part No._____

OIL FILTER

Manufacturer_____

Part No._____

AIR FILTER

Manufacturer_____

Part No._____

General Information and Maintenance

HOW TO USE THIS BOOK

Chilton's Repair and Tune-Up Guide for the Aspen/Volaré is intended to give you a basic idea of how your car works and how to save money and time by servicing it yourself. The first two chapters will be the most frequently used, since they contain maintenance and tune-up information and procedures. The following 9 chapters provide information and service techniques for the more complex systems of the car. Operating systems from engine through brakes are included to the extent that the average do-it-yourselfer should get involved. This book won't explain rebuilding the automatic transmission for the simple reason that the expertise required and the investment in special tools make this task uneconomical. We will tell you how to change your own brake pads and shoes, replace distributor cap and rotor, and many more jobs that will save you money, give you personal satisfaction, and help you avoid problems.

Before starting to loosen any bolts, please read through the entire section and the specific procedure. This will give you the overall view of what will be required as far as tools, supplies, and you. There is nothing more frustrating than having to walk to the bus stop on Monday morning because you were short one gasket during your Sunday afternoon repair work. So read ahead and plan ahead. Have all the necessary tools, parts, and materials assembled before you start.

The sections begin with a discussion of the system and what it involves. Adjustments and/or maintenance are then discussed, followed by removal and installation procedures and then repair or overhaul procedures where they are feasible. When repair or overhaul procedures are considered to be slightly more difficult, we tell you how to remove the part and then how to install the new or rebuilt replacement part; you at least save the labor costs of installation. Backyard repair of such components as the alternator aren't usually practical.

Two basic mechanic's rules are observed throughout. One, whenever the left side of the car is referred to, it is meant to specify the driver's side of the car. Conversely, the right side of the car means the passenger side of the car. Second, most screws and bolts are removed by turning counterclockwise and tightened by turning clockwise. Always keep safety uppermost in your mind. Stay aware of the hazards involved in working on an automobile and take the proper precautions. Use sturdy jackstands when working under a raised vehicle. Don't smoke or allow an exposed flame to come near the battery or any part of the fuel system. Use the correct tool for the job at hand. Take your time and be patient, as you gain experience you'll be able to work more quickly.

TOOLS AND EQUIPMENT

The following list is the basic tool requirement to perform most of the procedures described in this guide. Consider tools as an investment that will more than repay their initial cost several times over.

1. A ⅜ in. drive socket set and a spark plug socket. If your car is equipped with a six cylinder engine, you'll need a ⅝ in. spark plug socket. V8 engines will require ¹³/₁₆ in. spark plug socket. Both of these are available just about anywhere that automotive parts are sold.

2. A set of combination wrenches (one end open and one end box) in sizes ranging from ⅜ in. to ¾ in.

3. A spark plug wire gauge.

4. Slot and phillips head screwdrivers.

5. Timing light, preferably a DC battery hook-up type.

6. Tachometer.

7. Torque wrench. This assures proper tightening of important fasteners and avoids costly stripping (too tight) or leaks (too loose).

8. Oil can filler spout.

9. Oil filter strap wrench. This tool makes removal of a tight filter much easier. Never use it to install a filter.

10. A pair of channel lock pliers.

11. Two sturdy jackstands are necessary if you plan to work under the car. Cinder blocks, bricks, and other makeshift supports are not safe.

Special Tools

Normally, the use of special factory tools is avoided for repair procedures, since these are not readily available for the do-it-yourself mechanic. When it is possible to perform the job with more commonly available tools, it will be pointed out, but occasionally, a special tool was designed to perform a specific function and should be used. Before substituting another tool, you should be convinced that neither your safety nor the performance of the vehicle will be compromised.

SERVICING YOUR VEHICLE SAFELY

It is virtually impossible to anticipate all of the hazards involved with automotive maintenance and service but care and common sense will prevent most accidents.

The rules of safety for mechanics range from "don't smoke around gasoline," to "use the proper tool for the job." The trick to avoiding injuries is to develop safe work habits and take every possible precaution.

Do's

• Do keep a fire extinguisher and first aid kit within easy reach.

• Do wear safety glasses or goggles when cutting, drilling, grinding or prying. If you wear glasses for the sake of vision, then they should be made of hardened glass that can serve also as safety glasses, or wear safety goggles over your regular glasses.

• Do shield your eyes whenever you work around the battery. Batteries contain sulphuric acid; in case of contact with the eyes or skin, flush the area with water or a mixture of water and baking soda and get medical attention immediately.

• Do use safety stands for any under-car service. Jacks are for raising vehicles; safety stands are for making sure the vehicle stays raised until you want it to come down. Whenever the vehicle is raised, block the wheels remaining on the ground and set the parking brake.

• Do use adequate ventilation when working with any chemicals. Asbestos dust resulting from brake lining wear can cause cancer.

• Do disconnect the negative battery cable when working on the electrical system. The primary ignition system can contain up to 40,000 volts.

• Do follow manufacturer's directions whenever working with potentially hazardous materials. Both brake fluid and antifreeze are poisonous if taken internally.

• Do properly maintain your tools. Loose hammerheads, mushroomed punches and chisels, frayed or poorly grounded electrical cords, excessively worn screwdrivers, spread wrenches (open end), cracked sockets, slipping ratchets, or faulty droplight sockets can cause accidents.

• Do use the proper size and type of tool for the job being done.

• Do when possible, pull on a wrench handle rather than push on it, and adjust your stance to prevent a fall.

• Do be sure that adjustable wrenches are tightly adjusted on the nut or bolt and pulled so that the face is on the side of the fixed jaw.

• Do select a wrench or socket that fits the nut or bolt. The wrench or socket should sit straight, not cocked.

• Do strike squarely with a hammer; avoid glancing blows.

• Do set the parking brake and block the drive wheels if the work requires that the engine be running.

Dont's

• Don't run an engine in a garage or anywhere else without proper ventilation—EVER! Carbon monoxide is poisonous; it is absorbed by the body 400 times faster than oxygen; it takes a long time to leave the human body and you can build up a deadly supply of it in your system by simply breathing in a little every day. You may not realize you are slowly poisoning yourself. Always use power vents, windows, fans or open the garage doors.

• Don't work around moving parts while wearing a necktie or other loose clothing. Short sleeves are much safer than long, loose sleeves. Hard-toed shoes with neoprene soles protect your toes and give a better grip on slippery surfaces. Jewelry such as watches, fancy belt buckles, beads or body adornment of any kind is not safe working around a car. Long hair should be hidden under a hat or cap.

• Don't use pockets for toolboxes. A fall or bump can drive a screwdriver deep into your body. Even a wiping cloth hanging from the back pocket can wrap around a spinning shaft or fan.

• Don't smoke when working around gasoline, cleaning solvent or other flammable material.

• Don't smoke when working around the battery. When the battery is being charged, it gives off explosive hydrogen gas.

• Don't use gasoline to wash your hands; there are excellent soaps available. Gasoline may contain lead, and lead can enter the body through a cut, accumulating in the body until you are very ill. Gasoline also removes all the natural oils from the skin so that bone dry hands will suck up oil and grease.

• Don't service the air conditioning system unless you are equipped with the necessary tools and training. The refrigerant, R-12, is extremely cold and when exposed to the air, will instantly freeze any surface it comes in contact with, including your eyes. Although the refrigerant is normally non-toxic, R-12 becomes a deadly poisonous gas in the presence of an open flame. One good whiff of the vapors from burning refrigerant can be fatal.

HISTORY

The Aspen and Volaré model lines were introduced by the Chrysler Corporation in 1976 as an alternative between full or intermediate size cars and sub-compact cars. The two-door coupe is built on a 108.5 inch wheelbase, while the four-door sedan and four-door station wagon models are both built on 112.5 inch wheelbases. The station wagon model is the first compact sized wagon available from an American manufacturer since 1967 and the first from Chrysler Corporation since 1966.

SERIAL NUMBER IDENTIFICATION

Vehicle

The vehicle identification number is stamped on a metal plate attached to the upper left of the instrument panel. The VIN plate can easily be seen by looking through the windshield. The VIN is made up of thirteen digits. The first digit identifies the car line, the second the price class, and the third and fourth digits body style. Engine displacement is identified by the fifth digit. Model year and assembly plant are shown by the sixth and seventh digits. The last six digits are the sequential serial number.

Vehicle identification number plate

Engine

The engine number can contain as many as fifteen characters and digits. The first character on 225 engines designates the model year, the next three numerals are 225 (the displacement), the next one or two letters designate the model, the following four numerals the date the engine was built, and the last number the shift during which the engine was built.

On 318 and 360 engines, the first number designates model year, the next letter manufacturing plant, the next three numbers give the displacement, the next one or two designate model, the next four numbers denote the build date, and the last four the engine sequence number.

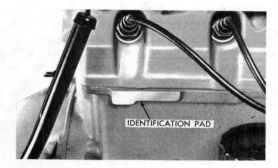

Six cylinder engine number location

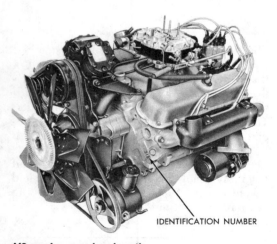

V8 engine number location

Special information identifying an undersized crankshaft, oversized tappets, low compression, oversized cylinder bores, engine build date, and the shift is stamped on the locations shown in the illustrations.

Engine Codes

6 Cylinder			
225		1 bbl.	C
225		2 bbl.	D
V8			
318		2 bbl.	G
318		4 bbl.	H
360		2 bbl.	K
360		4 bbl.	J

Transmission

Manual transmission numbers are stamped on a pad located on the right side of the case. TorqueFlite transmission numbers are stamped on a pad on the left side of the oil pan flange.

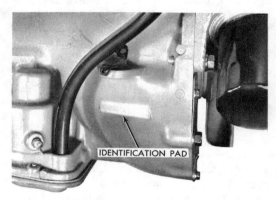

TorqueFlite identification number location

Manual transmission identification number location

ROUTINE MAINTENANCE

Air Cleaner

All models are equipped with a replaceable paper element in the air cleaner housing. Chrysler recommends that the filter be replaced every 30,000 miles. It should be checked more often than this, however, as a restrictive filter element will reduce fuel mileage and increase exhaust emissions. To

The wing nut comes off counterclockwise

If the filter is clean, leave it alone

Wipe the housing clean before installing a new filter

Positive Crankcase Ventilation

The positive crankcase ventilation system routes crankcase vapors to the carburetor to be burned with the air/fuel mixture. A clogged PCV system will cause poor idle and rough running. It can also create oil leaks due to increased crankcase pressure. So it pays to keep the system clear and free flowing. Once a year or every 15,000 miles (sooner if the car is only used for short trips) the system should be tested. The PCV valve should be replaced every 30,000 miles.

TESTING

1. With engine running at normal idle speed, remove the PCV valve from the rocker arm cover. If the valve isn't clogged, you should hear a loud hiss and feel a strong suction when you place your finger over the valve intake.

2. Replace the PCV valve and remove the crankcase inlet air cleaner from the rocker arm cover. This is the large can located at the rear of the rocker cover on six cylinder engines and the opposite rocker arm cover

Six-cylinder PCV valve location

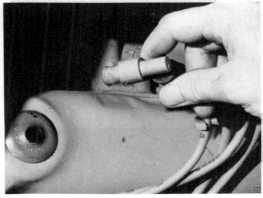

V8 PCV valve location

check the filter element, unscrew the wing nut at the top of the air cleaner and lift off the lid. The filter element lifts out. If it's completely gray or black, replace it. If it's badly contaminated with oil, replace it. Before installing the new filter element, wipe out the air cleaner housing with a clean rag.

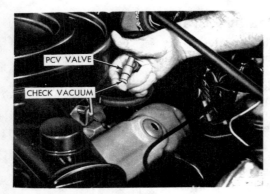

Checking PCV valve vacuum

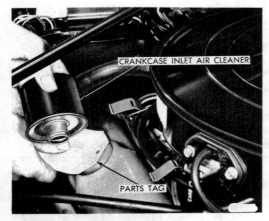

Checking crankcase inlet vacuum

from the PCV valve on V8s. Hold a stiff piece of paper loosely over the hole in the rocker arm cover. After waiting a moment, you should feel the paper sucked tightly against the opening.

3. With the engine off, remove the PCV valve from the rocker arm cover and give it a good shake. If the valve is okay, you'll hear a clicking noise.

If the PCV system meets the tests, everything is okay. If not replace the PCV valve. Repeat the paper test in step 2. If the results are negative, it will be necessary to clean the PCV valve hose and the passage in the bottom of the carburetor will have to be cleaned.

1. Spray carburetor solvent into the PCV valve hose and blow it dry. Don't allow the hose to remain in solvent for more than a half hour.

2. Remove the carburetor as outlined in Chapter 4. Use a ¼ in. drill rod to clean the passages in the base of the carburetor.

3. Remove the crankcase inlet air cleaner from the rocker arm cover and disconnect the hose. Clean the hose in the same manner as the PCV valve hose. Wash the crankcase inlet air cleaner in solvent. Dry it. Wet the filter by pouring a small amount of SAE 30 motor oil into it until the oil runs from the small inlet vent. Be sure that all excess oil is drained off.

PCV VALVE REPLACEMENT

Be sure that you purchase the correct valve for your car. Different engines have different rates of PCV valve flow.

1. Locate the PCV valve in the rubber grommet in the rocker arm cover.

2. Pull the valve free from the rocker cover.

3. Pull the valve out of the rubber hose connected to the other end.

4. Insert the replacement valve into the hose and then push the other end into the rubber grommet on the rocker cover.

Evaporative Canister

This plastic canister, located in the engine compartment, stores carburetor and fuel tank vapors while the engine is off, holding them

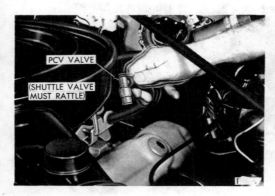

Shaking PCV valve

Evaporative canister

to be drawn into the engine and turned when the engine is started. The filter mounted on the bottom of the canister requires replacement every 30,000 miles (15,000 miles on 1976 models).

FILTER REPLACEMENT

1. Loosen the screw retaining the canister in its bracket.
2. Lift the canister out of its bracket. It's not necessary to detach the hoses from the top of the canister.

Evaporative canister filter

3. Remove the old filter from the bottom of the canister.
4. Install the replacement filter by working it into the retainers on the bottom of the canister.

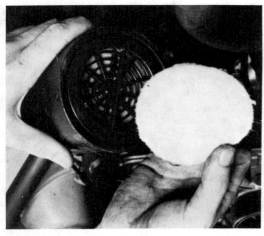

You'll have to work the new filter into place

5. Lower the canister back into its bracket and tighten the screw.
6. Check all connecting hoses and replace any that are suspect.

Drive Belts

Make it a habit to check the drive belts that run the water pump, alternator, power steering pump, air pump, and air conditioning compressor. Examine the belts for cracks which can cause the belt to break without warning. Belts which are soaked with oil or grease should also be discarded. Beside the danger of slippage, such belts will wear out quickly and can snap. Glazed belts may slip and cause an undercharged battery and/or engine overheating. After checking drive belt condition, test belt tension at the midpoint of each belt. No belt should deflect more than ⅜ in.–½ in. Adjust any belt on which deflection is greater than ½ in.

Check the belt tension about midway between the two pulleys

BELT ADJUSTMENT AND REPLACEMENT

1. Loosen all retaining nuts on the accessory bracket.

Alternator adjusting bolt (arrow)

HOW TO SPOT WORN V-BELTS

V-Belts are vital to efficient engine operation—they drive the fan, water pump and other accessories. They require little maintenance (occasional tightening) but they will not last forever. Slipping or failure of the V-belt will lead to overheating. If your V-belt looks like any of these, it should be replaced.

Cracking or weathering

This belt has deep cracks, which cause it to flex. Too much flexing leads to heat build-up and premature failure. These cracks can be caused by using the belt on a pulley that is too small. Notched belts are available for small diameter pulleys.

Softening (grease and oil)

Oil and grease on a belt can cause the belt's rubber compounds to soften and separate from the reinforcing cords that hold the belt together. The belt will first slip, then finally fail altogether.

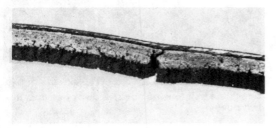

Glazing

Glazing is caused by a belt that is slipping. A slipping belt can cause a run-down battery, erratic power steering, overheating or poor accessory performance. The more the belt slips, the more glazing will be built up on the surface of the belt. The more the belt is glazed, the more it will slip. If the glazing is light, tighten the belt.

Worn cover

The cover of this belt is worn off and is peeling away. The reinforcing cords will begin to wear and the belt will shortly break. When the belt cover wears in spots or has a rough jagged appearance, check the pulley grooves for roughness.

Separation

This belt is on the verge of breaking and leaving you stranded. The layers of the belt are separating and the reinforcing cords are exposed. It's just a matter of time before it breaks completely.

HOW TO SPOT BAD HOSES

Both the upper and lower radiator hoses are called upon to perform difficult jobs in an inhospitable environment. They are subject to nearly 18 psi at under hood temperatures often over 280°F., and must circulate nearly 7500 gallons of coolant an hour—3 good reasons to have good hoses.

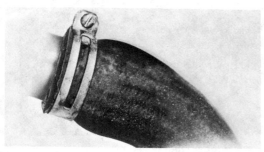

Swollen hose

A good test for any hose is to feel it for soft or spongy spots. Frequently these will appear as swollen areas of the hose. The most likely cause is oil soaking. This hose could burst at any time, when hot or under pressure.

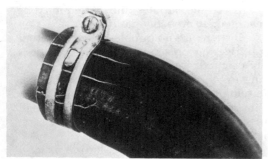

Cracked hose

Cracked hoses can usually be seen but feel the hoses to be sure they have not hardened; a prime cause of cracking. This hose has cracked down to the reinforcing cords and could split at any of the cracks.

Frayed hose end (due to weak clamp)

Weakened clamps frequently are the cause of hose and cooling system failure. The connection between the pipe and hose has deteriorated enough to allow coolant to escape when the engine is hot.

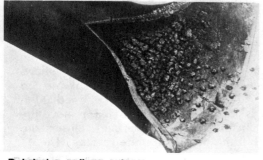

Debris in cooling system

Debris, rust and scale in the cooling system can cause the inside of a hose to weaken. This can usually be felt on the outside of the hose as soft or thinner areas.

2. When replacing a belt, pry the accessory toward the engine and slip the belt from the pulleys.

3. Carefully pry the accessory out with a bar, such as a ratchet handle or broom handle, and then tighten the bracket nuts.

CAUTION: *Do not exert too much pressure on accessories such as the alternator; it's easy to damage an aluminum housing. Use just enough force to hold the accessory in place while you tighten the bracket nuts.*

4. Recheck the tension. It may be necessary to do this a few times before you get it right.

It's a good idea to carry spare belts in the trunk.

Air Conditioning

No air conditioning repair or maintenance procedures except sight glass check are given; all repair work on the air conditioning system should be left to expert repairmen in that field. They are well aware of the hazards and have the proper equipment.

CAUTION: *Never open or disconnect any part of the air conditioning system. The compressed refrigerant used in the air conditioning system expands and evaporates into the atmosphere at a temperature of −21.7°F or lower. This will freeze any surface, including your eyes, that it contacts. Air conditioning refrigerant also decomposes into a poisonous gas in the presence of a flame.*

SIGHT GLASS CHECK

This is the only check that should be performed by anyone not specially trained to work on an air conditioning system. The following is a completely safe method for determining if your air conditioner requires service. The tests work best at normal temperatures (70–8°F), if the temperature is above 100°F there may be bubbles or foam in the sight glass as a part of normal operation.

1. Place the automatic transmission in Park or the manual transmission in Neutral. Put the parking brake ON.

2. Run the engine at a fast idle.

3. Set the controls for maximum cold with the blower on high position.

4. Locate the sight glass on top of the receiver-drier. This is a tall black cylinder located at the front of the engine compartment. Wipe the sight glass in the top of the receiver-drier clean with a soft rag.

Air-conditioner sight glass

5. If you see bubbles, the system must be recharged. It probably has a leak.

6. If there are no bubbles, there is either no refrigerant present in the system or it is fully charged. To check, feel the two hoses going to the compressor. If they are both at the same temperature, the system will have to be recharged. If one hose is warm (high pressure) and the other cool (low pressure), then the system is okay.

7. If the system is leaking, have it fixed as soon as possible. Leaks will eventually allow moisture to enter the system causing rust and the replacement of expensive components.

NOTE: *It's a good practice to run the air conditioner for a few minutes every so often during the cold months. This prevents the seals from drying out and the compressor possibly becoming stuck from disuse.*

Fluid Level Checks
ENGINE OIL

Since the lubricating oil in the engine is the life blood of your motor, it's a good practice to keep a close watch on engine oil level. Check it at least everytime you refuel. The best time to check the engine oil level is before operating the engine or after it has been sitting for at least a few minutes in order to get an accurate reading. This allows the oil to drain back into the crankcase. To check the engine oil level, make sure that the car is resting on a level surface, remove the oil dipstick, wipe it clean and reinsert the stick firmly for an accurate reading. The oil dipstick has two marks to indicate high and

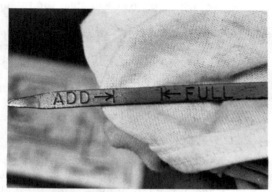

Add oil only to the full line

Manual transmission filler plug

Sometimes it's a little difficult to reach the oil filler cap through all the paraphernalia

low oil level. If the oil level is at or below the "add" mark on the dipstick, oil should be added as necessary to bring it up to the "full" line. The oil should be maintained in the safety margin, neither going above the "full" mark or below the "add" mark. Be sure that the dipstick is in the tube tight after checking the oil to prevent dirt from entering the oil pan.

TRANSMISSION

Manual

The manual transmission level should be checked twice a year, but hard use such as trailering requires more frequent checks. All manual transmissions have two square headed pipe plugs, the upper for filling and the lower for draining. Both are located on the right side of the transmission on 3-speeds. The drain plug is located on the lower left side of the 4-speed and the fill plug on the right side.

Unscrew the top plug and insert your finger to feel if the lubricant is at the level of

the filler hole. If it's not, top it up with the recommended fluid discussed in fluid changes later in this chapter.

Automatic

Check the automatic transmission fluid level whenever you check the engine oil. It is even more important to check the fluid level when you are pulling a trailer or subjecting the car to any other type of hard use.

Check the fluid level with the car parked on a level spot, engine warm, and the transmission lever in Neutral. The parking brake should be on.

1. Slowly move the selector lever through all the gear positions, pausing momentarily in each one. Place the lever in Neutral.

2. Open the hood and locate the automatic transmission dipstick on the right side of the car near the firewall.

3. Wipe off the top of the dipstick and around the tube to prevent dirt from falling into transmission.

Automatic transmission dipstick

4. Remove the dipstick. Fluid should be at the "Full" mark or slightly below. It should never be over the "Full" mark.

5. Add or drain fluid as necessary to bring the level to the "Full" mark. Use only automatic transmission fluid marked Dextron®. Add fluid sparingly, the difference between the "Add" and "Full" lines is only one pint. Chrysler does not recommend using any fluid additives.

BRAKE MASTER CYLINDER

The master cylinder is in the left rear side of the engine compartment, on the firewall. To check the fluid level as recommended at each engine oil change interval:

1. Clean off the area around the cap. Very small particles of dirt can cause serious problems in the braking system.

2. Pry off the wire retaining clip to one side with a screwdriver. Remove the cover.

3. The proper level in each of the two reservoirs is ¼ in. from the edge. Add fluid as necessary.

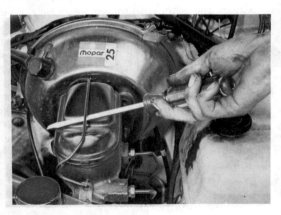

Prying off the retaining clip

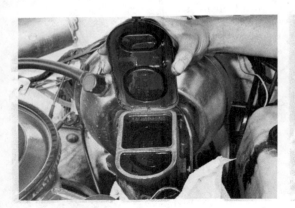

Correct fluid level

4. Replace the cover and snap the retaining wire back in place.

NOTE: *Use fluid marked DOT 3 or 4 only. Buy only as much fluid as you need and keep the cap closed tightly on the brake fluid can. The fluid attracts moisture and if water contaminated brake fluid is used in the hydraulic system it can cause real problems.*

ENGINE COOLANT

All models are equipped with a plastic expansion tank located near the radiator as part of the coolant reserve system. This prevents losing coolant when the engine is hot and the coolant expands.

Check coolant when the engine is warm and running. Observe the level in the expansion tank. It should be between the one and two quart marks. The radiator normally remains completely full, so it is not necessary to remove the radiator cap. If the system is low, add a 50% water/50% anti-freeze solution to the expansion tank.

Every two years or 30,000 miles, the coolant should be drained and the system refilled with a fresh water/anti-freeze solution. Refer to the Capacities chart for the amount of coolant you'll need and to the Anti-Freeze Chart in the Appendix for the proper solution for your average temperature.

To drain the system:

1. Open the radiator drain petcock located on the bottom of the radiator on the left side.

2. Remove the drain plugs in the sides of the cylinder block. You may have to poke a screwdriver into these if they are clogged with sediment.

3. Remove the radiator cap after the cool-

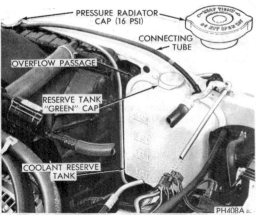

Coolant expansion tank

ant expansion tank is empty. Flush the system with a garden hose. If the old coolant is rusty and/or full of sediment, use a cooling system cleaning solution.

4. Close the petcock and replace the drain plugs when the system is emptied.

5. Add coolant solution to the radiator until it is completely filled. Replace the radiator cap.

6. Start the engine and run it until the top radiator hose feels warm to the touch.

7. Shut the engine off and add more coolant to the radiator if necessary.

8. Fill the expansion tank to the one quart level.

REAR AXLE

It is recommended that the rear axle lubricant level be checked at each engine oil change interval. The proper lubricant is called out in the Rear Axle Lubricant Chart. The rear axle filler plug is located on the rear face of the axle on all models except the 1976

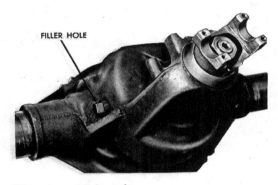

FILLER HOLE

Filler plug—8¼ in. axle

8¼ in. axle, where it is located on the right front of the housing. Plugs on 1976 models are pipe plugs and you'll need a wrench to remove them. 1977 and later models use a new rubber press-in type plug, which you can remove with your fingers. Remove the plug and insert your finger into the filler hole to feel the fluid level. It should be at the level given in the chart for that particular axle. Add lubricant as necessary to bring the level up to the correct height.

STEERING GEAR

The steering gear on all models is lubricated at the factory and sealed. There are no periodic services necessary on the steering gear.

POWER STEERING RESERVOIR

The power steering pump is located under the front of the engine. Check the fluid level in the reservoir at every oil change.

1. Clean off the cap and around the reservoir to prevent dirt from falling in. Foreign matter in the power steering system can cause the same problems as dirt in the brake hydraulic system.

2. Remove the cap. All models are equipped with an integral cap/dipstick.

3. Wipe the dipstick with a clean cloth and reinsert it into the reservoir. Be sure that it is firmly seated.

4. Remove the cap and check the fluid level on the dipstick. If the engine has been running, the fluid should be at the "hot" level, if not it should be at the "cold" level.

5. If it is necessary to add fluid, add only power steering fluid. Do not add automatic

Rear Axle Identification and Lubrication Chart

Year	Axle Size (ring gear dia)	Filler Location	Cover Bolts	Capacity (pts)	Lubricant Level
1976	7¼	Rear Cover	9	2.1	Bottom of filler hole to ⅝ in. below
	8¼	Front Right Side	10	4.4	From ⅛ in.–¼ in. below filler hole ①
1977–80	7¼	Cover	9	2.1	Bottom of filler hole to ⅜ in. below
	8¼	Cover	10	4.4	Bottom of filler hole to ½ in. below

① Do not raise oil to bottom of filler hole as this will result in an overfill condition.
Lube required: (API) GL-5 (add Friction Modifier if equipped with Sure-Grip).

Checking the power steering fluid level

transmission fluid to the power steering system. Do not overfill the reservoir.

BATTERY (NON-SEALED)

Check the electrolyte level in the battery every two months. Chrysler states that the Long Life battery need only be checked every year or 10,000 miles. Remove the cap (if equipped) and check that the electrolyte is at the bottom of the filler well (about ⅜ in. above the plates). Use distilled water to top up the battery.

Checking the battery electrolyte level

Tires and Wheels

Buy a tire pressure gauge and keep it in the glove compartment of your car. Service station air pressure gauges are generally not working or inaccurate and should not be relied upon. The decal on the door post on the driver's side gives the recommended air pressures for the standard tires. If you are driving on replacement tires of a different type, follow the inflation recommendations of the manufacturer and never exceed the maximum pressure given on the sidewall. Always check tire pressure when the tires are cool because air pressure increases with heat and readings will go 4–6 psi higher after the tire has been run a few miles. For continued expressway driving, increase the tire pressure by a few pounds in each tire. Never mix tires of different construction on your car.

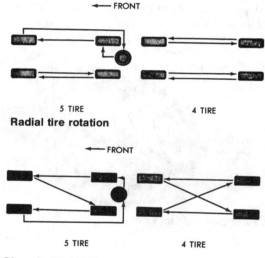

Radial tire rotation

Bias-ply tire rotation

Capacities

Year	Engine No. Cyl Displacement (Cu In.)	Engine Crankcase Add 1 Qt For New Filter	Transmission Pts To Refill After Draining			Drive Axle (pts)	Gasoline Tank (gals)	Cooling System (qts)	
			Manual		Automatic			With Heater	With A/C
			3-Speed	4-Speed					
'76–'80	6-225	4	3.5	7.0	17 ⑤	①	18	13 ②	17.5 ②
	8-318	4	4.75	7.0	17 ⑤	①	18	16 ③	17.5 ③
	8-360	4	—	—	17 ⑤	①	18	16 ④	16 ④

—Not Applicable
① 7¼" axle—2.1 pts: 8¼" axle—4.4 pts: 9¼" axle—4.5 pts
② 1979–80; 11.5/12.5
③ 1979–80; 15/16.5
④ 1979–80; 15/16.5
⑤ 1979–80; 16.3

When replacing tires, ensure that the new tire(s) are the same size and type as those which will be remaining on the car. Intermixing bias ply tires with radial or bias belted tires can result in treacherous and unpredictable handling.

Rotate the tires every 10,000 miles. The rotation pattern shown will result in all tires wearing out at about the same time. If you plan on replacing the original equipment tires with duplicate types, don't use the spare and rotate only the four road wheels in the correct pattern according to the tire type. When you buy new tires, you'll only require three—the spare will be fresh and you can use a worn tire as the spare.

When removing studded snow tires in the Spring, mark them left or right with chalk so that they can be returned to the same position next Winter. Studded snow tires take a "set" and noise and wear will increase if they are installed on the opposite side from which they were removed, in addition to the possibility of losing studs. Always tighten the wheel nuts in a criss-cross pattern. Tighten them to 85 ft. lbs. The accompanying chart shows the available range of tire sizes and appropriate wheel sizes for Aspen and Volare models.

Fuel Filter

All models are equipped with an in-line fuel filter. The filter on six cylinder engines is located near the carburetor. The V8 fuel filter is mounted lower, closer to the fuel pump.

REPLACEMENT

Replace the fuel filter every 15,000 miles on 1976 models and every 30,000 on 1977 and later models. You'll need hose clamp pliers to

Fuel filter (arrow)

remove the fuel line corbin clamps. Be sure the engine is cool when changing filters to prevent an accidental fire.

1. Place a rag under the filter to catch any fuel that leaks from the line.

2. Squeeze and remove the hose clamps. Remove and discard the old filter.

3. Install the replacement filter in the same manner using the new rubber hose supplied with the filter.

4. Remove the rag, start the engine, and check for leaks.

Battery
OPERATION

Many people are unaware of exactly how a battery functions and, as a result, have battery problems. There are many ways of abusing a battery and, hopefully, these will be more obvious and better understood after reading this section.

The automotive battery is essentially a hard rubber or plastic case containing a number of positive and negative lead plates immersed in a solution of sulfuric acid and water (electrolyte). The negative plates are made of sponge lead and the positive plates are largely lead dioxide. The acid reacts with these chemicals and produces electrical current. A 12 volt (V) battery consists of six 2V batteries (individual cells) separated from each other by case partitions. These partitions prevent the mixing of electrolyte from cell to cell; therefore, each cell has its own electrolyte supply. Contained in each cell is an assembly of positive and negative lead plates. To prevent electrical contact between the two plates, each positive plate is isolated from the negative by a plastic separator. The number of plates within each cell depends upon the ampere hour rating of the particular battery. The more plates that a battery has, the higher its rating. A more expensive battery, having a 70 ampere hour rating, contains six positive plates per cell while a less expensive battery, rated at 48 ampere hours, has only four positive plates per cell. The battery with a high rating can do more work before discharging than one with a lower rating. A car with many electrical accessories (air conditioning, radio, electric windows, etc.) requires a high ampere-hour battery. The cells are electrically connected in series (they are interdependent—if one cell goes bad, the battery will not work) by connections going through the cell partitions. The

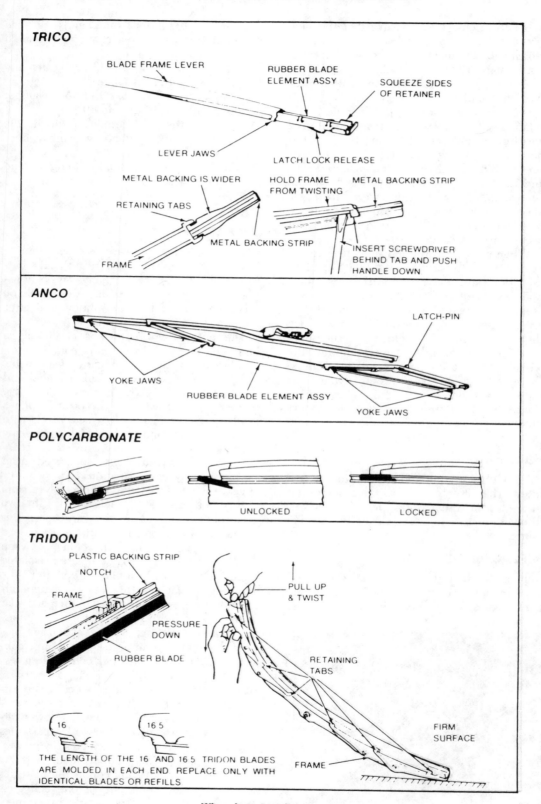

TRICO

BLADE FRAME LEVER

RUBBER BLADE ELEMENT ASSY

SQUEEZE SIDES OF RETAINER

LEVER JAWS

LATCH LOCK RELEASE

METAL BACKING IS WIDER

HOLD FRAME FROM TWISTING

METAL BACKING STRIP

RETAINING TABS

METAL BACKING STRIP

FRAME

INSERT SCREWDRIVER BEHIND TAB AND PUSH HANDLE DOWN

ANCO

LATCH-PIN

YOKE JAWS

RUBBER BLADE ELEMENT ASSY

YOKE JAWS

POLYCARBONATE

UNLOCKED

LOCKED

TRIDON

PLASTIC BACKING STRIP

NOTCH

FRAME

PULL UP & TWIST

PRESSURE DOWN

RUBBER BLADE

RETAINING TABS

16

16 5

FIRM SURFACE

THE LENGTH OF THE 16 AND 16 5 TRIDON BLADES ARE MOLDED IN EACH END. REPLACE ONLY WITH IDENTICAL BLADES OR REFILLS

FRAME

Wiper insert replacement

positive terminal of the first cell and the negative of the last are actually the posts to which the battery cables are attached.

The battery produces (it does not store) electrical energy within its case and uses this electrical energy to perform three functions: start the car; provide current for electrical components; and act as a voltage stabilizer for the system. To perform these functions, the lead plates, in effect, absorb acid and, if the battery is not recharged by the alternator, absorb all of the acid and the battery is completely discharged. Current supplied to the battery by the alternator, a charger, or another battery, reverses the chemical reaction and forces acid off the plates and returns it to the electrolyte. Returning the acid to the electrolyte restores the battery's ability to produce current. The alternator sends current into the battery and recharges it by maintaining the acid content of the electrolyte. When the acid content is low, the battery performs poorly and, so, the voltage regulator increases the alternator output in order to recharge the battery.

MAINTENANCE

In addition to routinely checking the electrolyte level of the battery, some other minor maintenance will keep your battery in peak starting condition. Two inexpensive battery tools, a hydrometer and a post and cable cleaner, are available in most auto or hardware stores for about a dollar and more than earn back that small outlay. Besides checking the level of electrolyte, you should occasionally take a specific gravity reading to

Clean battery cable clamps with a wire brush

see what's going on inside the battery cells. Using your hydrometer, insert the tip into each cell and withdraw enough electrolyte to make the float ride freely. While holding the hydrometer straight up, take a reading. The specific gravity of a fully charged battery (at 80°F) is 1.270. Most commercially available hydrometers also have colored sections to save you reading the scale and these will clearly tell you your battery cell is (a) charged, (b) borderline—should be recharged, or (c) dead. Repeat the specific gravity for each cell.

NOTE: *Battery electrolyte or "acid" is very caustic and will dissolve skin and paintwork with equal relish, so be careful. Readings should be taken in as normal a room temperature atmosphere as possible. If the temperature varies from the 80°F standard above, add or subtract four (0.004) points for every 10° above (+) or below (−) the standard.*

The most completely charged battery will do you no good on a cold, rainy evening if the cables and posts are caked with corrosion. This is where your little wire brush cleaner comes in. Loosen and remove the cable clamps from the battery posts. Using the pointed end of the brush, give the inside surface of the clamp a good cleaning until it

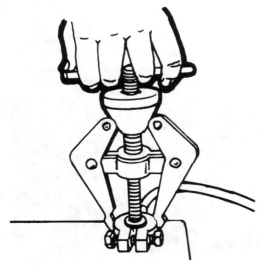

Use a puller to remove the battery cable

shines. Next take the other end and place it over the post. Clean the post with a rotating motion until you achieve a shiny post. This done, install the clamps and retighten.

Keep the top of the battery clean, as a film of dirt can sometimes completely discharge a battery. A solution of baking soda and water may be used to clean the top surface, but be careful to flush this off with clear water and that none of the solution enters the filler holes.

LUBRICATION

Fuel and Oil Recommendations

Unleaded gasoline should be used in all Aspens and Volares except for 1976 models equipped with the 318 cu. in. V8, Torqueflite transmission, and air pump which were ordered without the catalytic converter system. All other cars must use unleaded fuel. Using leaded gasoline in a converter equipped car will render the system inoperative. Cars with the converter system will have unleaded fuel markings on the instrument panel and near the gas cap. Most importantly, converter cars have the narrow filler tube which permits only the smaller unleaded nozzles to be used.

The fuel used must have a minimum anti-knock rating of 87, gasoline classification number of 2, or a 91 Research Octane Number. The anti-knock rating is marked on most gas pumps throughout the country and is obtained by adding the Motor Octane and the Research Octane numbers and then dividing by two. Look for the 87 anti-knock rating.

Cars which are equipped with the catalytic converter system should not use any gasoline additives, such as fuel system cleaners. Fuel system additives may have a detrimental effect on the converter.

Engine oil should be selected with regard to the anticipated temperatures during the period before the next oil change. Using the chart, select the oil viscosity for the lowest expected temperature and you will be assured of easy cold starting and adequate engine protection. The oil you pour into your engine should have the designation SE/SF marked on the top or side of its container.

Lubricant Changes
ENGINE OIL AND FILTER

In order to maintain adequate engine protection and performance, the oil should be changed at least every 6 months or 7500 miles (5000 miles for 1976 models). The manufacturer recommends that the oil filter be changed at the first oil change and every other one after that. It may be a better idea to change the filter every time you drain the oil. The filter holds one quart of dirty oil and the expense of a new filter is more than outweighed by increased engine protection.

The recommended oil change interval is only for cars driven normally. If your automobile is being used under extremely dusty conditions, change the oil and filter sooner. The same thing goes for cars which are constantly driven in stop and go city traffic; extended idling can cause an acid and sludge buildup problem. Always drain the oil after the engine has been run long enough to bring it to normal operating temperature. Hot oil will flow more easily and more contaminants will be removed with the oil than if it were drained cold. A large capacity drain pan (5 or 6 quarts), oil filter, strap wrench, oil can spout, and a wrench to fit the oil pan drain plug are the only necessary tools. These are readily available at any automotive parts store or most large discount stores. These tools will more than pay for themselves after a few do-it-yourself oil changes. One other necessity is containers for the used

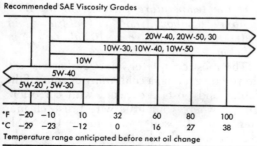

Recommended SAE Viscosity Grades

		20W-40, 20W-50, 30				
		10W-30, 10W-40, 10W-50				
	10W					
5W-40						
5W-20*, 5W-30						

°F	−20	−10	10	32	60	80	100
°C	−29	−23	−12	0	16	27	38

Temperature range anticipated before next oil change

*SAE 5W-20 Not recommended for sustained high speed vehicle operation.

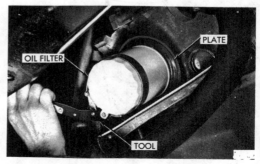

Oil filter removal

oil. You will find that plastic bleach containers make excellent storage bottles. Two ecologically desirable solutions to the used oil problem are to take it to a service station and ask permission to dump it into their sump tank or keep it and use it around the yard as a preservative for exposed wood such as fence posts.

To change your oil and filter:

1. Run the engine until it reaches normal operating temperature. Jack up the front of the car and support it on jackstands or use drive-on ramps.

2. Slide a drain pan under the oil pan drain plug. Be sure that it holds at least 5 quarts.

3. Loosen the drain plug with a wrench and then turn it out by hand. If you maintain a slight pressure on it with your hand, you can prevent hot oil from squirting onto your fingers.

4. Remove the plug and allow the oil to drain into the pan.

5. When all oil has drained from the engine, clean the plug and install it in the pan. Don't overtighten it.

6. Move the drain pan under the oil filter. The filter is located on the lower right side of six cylinder engines, almost in the center. The V8 oil filter is located at the right rear of the engine.

7. Install the oil filter strap wrench on the filter and turn it slowly off, allowing the oil to drain into the pan. This can be done from the top on six cylinder engines.

8. Completely remove and discard the old oil filter. Use a clean rag to wipe off the filter mounting base on the engine.

9. Wipe a small amount of fresh oil onto the rubber gasket of the replacement filter.

10. Spin the filter into place by hand. When the gasket is flush with the mounting

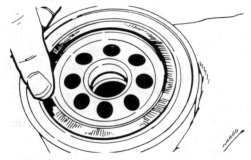

Lubricate the gasket on the new filter with clean engine oil. A dry gasket may not make a good seal and will allow the filter to leak

on the engine, give it another ½ to ¾ of a turn. If you overtighten the filter, it will probably leak and will surely be difficult to remove for the next oil change.

NOTE: *If you cannot remove an old filter that someone has overtightened, drive a punch or screwdriver through the filter and use it to turn the filter off.*

11. Clean up the area around the filter. Oil invariably drips onto the V8 exhaust pipe and the side of the six cylinder engine.

12. Remove the oil filler cap and add five quarts of fresh oil (only four if you didn't change the filter). An oil can spout is handy for this, but you can use a can opener and a funnel if you don't have one.

13. Check the oil level with the dipstick, it should be at "full." Replace the oil filler cap.

14. Start the engine. The oil pressure warning light should go out in a few seconds. If it doesn't, stop the engine and check for the problem. Perhaps you forgot to replace the drain plug and lost your oil.

15. With the engine running and the oil light out, check for leaks at the filter and drain plug.

16. Stop the engine, wait a few minutes, and then check the oil level again.

TRANSMISSION

Manual

Chrysler doesn't specifically recommend manual transmission lubricant changes, but it is suggested that it be changed at regular intervals on cars which see heavy duty use such as trailer towing. It might be a good idea to change the manual transmission lube if you have just purchased the car from a previous owner.

To drain the lubricant, remove the plug from the transmission (right side on 3-speeds, left side on 4-speeds) and allow the lube to drain into a pan. Replace the drain plug. Remove the filler plug and fill the transmission with Dexron® automatic transmission fluid up to the level of the filler hole. Transmission capacity is given in the Capacities Chart.

NOTE: *If gear rattle at idle speeds or under light acceleration has been a problem, fill the transmission with SAE 90 gear lubricant. This should eliminate any objectionable noise.*

Occasional greasing of the shift linkage will ease gear shifting. On column shift models, lubricate the linkage at the lower end of the steering column with multi-purpose chassis grease. On 3-speed floor shift models, the shift mechanism has a grease nipple which can be reached from under the car. With the shifter in neutral, grease the nipple until lubricant appears on the operating levers which are covered with a rubber boot. On 4-speed transmissions, remove the shift boot bezel and pull the boot up to expose the shifter. Apply grease to the sliding surfaces of the mechanism, while moving the shifter back and forth through the gears.

Automatic

Chrysler recommends that the automatic transmission fluid and filter be changed at 24,000 mile intervals on cars used for trailer towing. It doesn't specifically recommend fluid and filter changes for vehicles in normal use, but it might not be a bad idea to do it if you purchased the car used. 1976 models and 1977 models built before January 10, 1977 have a torque converter drain plug which allows draining the complete transmission. Models manufactured after that date do not have the drain plug, so that only the transmission pan can be drained. To change the transmission fluid and filter you'll need a new filter, pan gasket, and sufficient fluid to refill the transmission. Four quarts are enough for the later models, 9 quarts will be needed if you're draining the complete transmission on earlier models with the torque converter drain plug. All models use Dexron® fluid.

1. Run the engine until it reaches normal operating temperature.

2. Jack up the front of the car and support it on jackstands or use drive-on ramps. Be sure to block the rear wheels.

3. Place a large container under the transmission oil pan. If you are draining the torque converter, it will have to hold 9 quarts.

4. Loosen the rear pan bolts first to allow the fluid to drain into the pan without making a mess on the garage floor. Remove the pan and discard the gasket.

5. If you're draining the converter, remove the access plate at the front of the torque converter housing. If you can't see the drain plug, turn the engine clockwise with a wrench on the crankshaft pulley until you can. Remove the drain plug and allow the fluid to empty into the pan.

6. Install the drain plug. Tightening torque is 90 in. lbs. Don't overtighten it. Install the access plate.

7. Unscrew and discard the old transmission filter.

8. Install a new filter. Don't overtighten the retaining screws.

9. Clean the oil pan in solvent and allow it to dry. Make sure that you don't leave any lint in the pan.

10. Install the oil pan using a new gasket. Tighten the bolts in a criss-cross pattern. Tightening torque on the bolts is only 150 in. lbs. (about 12 ft. lbs.), so don't overtighten them. The transmission case is aluminum.

11. If the torque converter has been drained, pour six quarts of Dexron® automatic transmission fluid down the dipstick tube. If only the pan has been drained, add two quarts of transmission fluid. A long neck funnel is handy for this job.

12. Start the engine and let it idle for about two minutes.

13. With the parking brake on, move the transmission selector through each of the gear positions. Stop in Neutral.

14. Add enough fluid to bring the level up to the "add one pint" line. Check the fluid as described earlier in this chapter. Add only enough fluid to bring the level up to "Full." Never overfill the automatic transmission; this can cause foaming and leakage.

REAR AXLE

Chrysler recommends that the rear axle lubricant need not be changed except for cars used in severe service. Trailer towing is in that category, and if you frequently pull a trailer the rear axle lubricant should be changed at 36,000 mile intervals. If the car has been purchased used or the rear axle submerged on a boat ramp, it is also a good idea to change the lubricant. You'll need sufficient lubricant of the viscosity called for in the Rear Axle Lubricant Chart and a suction gun, since there's no drain plug.

In lieu of a suction gun to drain the rear axle lubricant, the cover can also be removed.

Converter drain plug

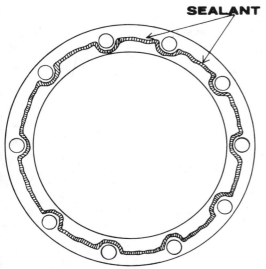

SEALANT

Rear axle sealant application

To drain the lube by removing the cover:

1. Jack the rear of the car and support the axle housing with jackstands. Position a drain pan.

2. Gradually loosen the cover bolts until lubricant begins to seep out past the gasket. It may be necessary to pry the cover loose from the housing.

3. When all the lubricant has drained, scrape away all traces of the old gasket and thoroughly clean the surface.

4. Apply a $^1/_{16}$ in. bead of MOPAR Silicone Rubber Sealant (Part No. 3683829) or an equivalent gasket forming substitute, along the bolt circle of the cover.

5. Allow the sealant to cure while you clean the housing cover and dry it.

6. Install the cover. Install the ratio identification tag beneath one of the bolts.

NOTE: *If for any reason, the cover is not installed within 20 minutes of applying the sealant, the old sealant should be removed and a new bead installed.*

7. Fill the rear axle with the proper type and quantity of lubricant, selected from the Rear Axle Lubricant Chart.

To remove the lubricant by suction gun:

1. Jack up the rear of the car and support the axle housing with jackstands.

2. Remove the filler plug and siphon the lubricant out with a suction gun.

3. Fill the rear axle to the level specified in the Rear Axle Lubricant Chart.

4. Replace the filler plug and lower the car.

Chassis Greasing

Upper and lower ball joints (four in all) the pitman arm, and the tie-rod ends (four) require greasing every three years or 30,000 miles. Halve that interval for cars driven regularly over unpaved back roads or used for other severe service. You'll need a cartridge of #2 chassis lubricant rated EP and a hand grease gun.

1. Jack up the front of the car and support it at the lower control arms with jack stands.

2. Locate the grease fittings and wipe them clean.

3. Push the grease gun over the grease fitting and pump the lubricant in until grease flows freely from the bottom of the seal or when the seal begins to balloon.

4. Wipe off any excess grease and lower the car.

Heat Riser

Every 30,000 miles, the heat riser valve should be checked for free operation and lubricated with penetrating oil. The valve is located on the exhaust manifold near the point that the exhaust pipe attaches to the manifold. Try to turn the valve counterweight by hand. If it's stuck, tap the end of the shaft a few times with a hammer. Apply penetrating oil to the shaft ends and work the valve back and forth a few times. If the valve is still stuck and can't be loosened with oil and/or heat, it will have to be replaced.

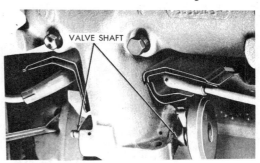

VALVE SHAFT

V8 heat riser

Body Lubrication

An occasional cleaning and lubrication of body parts will keep them operating smoothly and quietly and prevent rusting.

HOOD LOCK, RELEASE MECHANISM, AND SAFETY CATCH

Use chassis grease on these parts. Sparingly apply grease to all the sliding contact areas of

Maintenance Interval Chart

		Mileage Intervals Mileage in Thousands			
		7.5	15	22.5	30	37.5
Automatic choke	Check and adjust as required				•	
Carburetor choke shaft	Apply solvent every six months	•	•	•	•	•
Carburetor air filter	Replace			•		
Cooling system	Check and service as required every 12 months		•		•	
Crankcase inlet air cleaner	Clean				•	
Engine oil	Change every six months	•	•	•	•	•
Engine oil filter	Replace at initial oil change and every 2nd oil change thereafter					
Fast idle cam and pivot pin	Apply solvent every six months	•	•	•	•	•
Fuel filter	Replace		•		•	
Idle speed and air-fuel mixture	Check and adjust as required				•	
Ignition cables	Check and replace as required at time of spark plug replacement					
Manifold heat control valve	Apply solvent				•	
Positive crankcase vent valve	Check operation and replace if necessary			•		
Positive crankcase vent valve	Replace				•	
Spark plugs (without cat. conv.)	Replace		•		•	
Spark plugs (with cat. conv.)	Replace					•

Maintenance Interval Chart (cont.)

	Mileage Intervals Mileage in Thousands	7.5	15	22.5	30	37.5
Tappet adjustment 6 cyl. eng.	Check and adjust as required			•		•
Underhood rubber and plastic components (emission hoses)	Inspect and replace if necessary			•		•
Vapor storage canister filter element	Replace					•
Power steering	Check fluid level	Every oil change				
Exhaust system	Check for leaks, missing or damaged parts	Every 6 months				
Brake master cylinder	Inspect fluid level	Every 6 months				
Transmission	Inspect fluid level	Every 6 months				
Brake & power steering hoses	Check for deterioration or leaks	Every 6 months				
Air conditioned cars	Check belts, sight glass & operation of controls	Every 6 months				
Ball joints, steering linkage, and universal joints	Inspect seals	Every 6 months				
Hood lock, rel. mech. & safety catch	Lubricate	Every 6 months				
Drive belts	Check condition & tension	Every oil change				
Upper and lower control arm bushings	Inspect	Every oil change				

Maintenance Interval Chart (cont.)

Cooling system	Drain, flush & refill	At 24 months or 30,000 miles and every 12 months or 15,000 miles thereafter
Brake linings	Inspect	Every 15,000 miles
Front wheel bearings * ①	Inspect	Every 22,500 miles
Automatic transmission—severe usage only	Change fluid & filter, adjust bands	Every 24,000 miles
Ball joints & tie rod ends	Lubricate	Every 3 years of 30,000 miles

NOTE: *Local driving conditions, or special equipment such as high performance or heavy duty options may require special service recommendations.*

* Inspect the front wheel bearings whenever the brake drums or rotors are removed to inspect or service the brake system.
① Severe usage such as police or taxi service involving frequent or continuous brake application: Lubricate every 9,000 miles.

the latch and release lever and to the ends of the hood lock release links (on models with an inside hood release). Work lubricant into the lock mechanism until all rubbing surfaces are coated. Apply a film of grease to the pivot contact areas of the safety catch.

HOOD HINGES AND DOOR HINGES

Use engine oil on all link or hinge pivots and Lubriplate® to the gear teeth and sliding contact areas. Use engine oil on the door hinges. Apply oil to the lower hinge spring ends and contact areas.

LOCKS

Apply a thin film of Lubriplate® on the key and insert it into the lock. Operate the key in the lock cylinder several times and then remove the key and wipe off any excess lubricant. Apply engine oil to the door lock ratchet and striker bolt.

STATION WAGON LIFTGATE

Sparingly apply engine oil to the liftgate hinge pivot pins. Do not lubricate the hydraulic lift props. Use a stainless wax lubricant on the liftgate latch striker plate and bolt.

Front Wheel Bearings

The front wheel bearings should be checked when replacing brake pads or removing the brake disc for any service. They should be repacked every 22,500 miles regardless of any other required service. Rear wheel bearings require no attention. The front wheel bearings should be removed, cleaned, and packed with a grease recommended for disc brake service. Wheel bearing packing and adjustment are covered in Chapter 9.

Pushing and Towing

Cars with automatic transmission may not be started by pushing or towing. Manual transmission cars may be started by pushing. The car need not be pushed very fast to start.

To push start a manual transmission car:

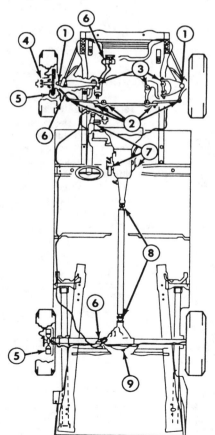

1. Suspension ball joints—every 6 months, inspect seals—replace if damaged or leaking
2. Steering linkage joints—every 3 years or 30,000 miles relubricate with P/N 2525035 or equivalent
3. Upper and lower control arm bushings—inspect for deterioration every oil change
4. Front wheel bearings—inspect, clean, relubricate with P/N 3837794 or equivalent AT LEAST every 22,500 miles or whenever brakes are serviced
5. Brake linings—inspect every 15,000 miles and/or during wheel bearing service
6. Brake and power steering hoses—every 6 months inspect for deterioration and leaks
7. Transmission—Manual—every 6 months check fluid level. Maintain fluid level at bottom of filler plug hole with DEXRON automatic transmission fluid
   Shift mechanisms—lubricate with P/N 2932524 or equivalent. Column (3 speed) as required. Floor, 3 speed (through fitting) every 7,500 miles, 4 speed (pack) every 10,000 miles or 6 months
8. Universal joint seals—every 6 months inspect for leakage, replace joint if leakage is evident
9. Rear axle—lubricant, no periodic level check required. Examine for leakage during engine oil change, use P/N 3744994 or equivalent, if required

Lubrication points

Jump Starting a Dead Battery

The chemical reaction in a battery produces explosive hydrogen gas. This is the safe way to jump start a dead battery, reducing the chances of an accidental spark that could cause an explosion.

Jump Starting Precautions

1. Be sure both batteries are of the same voltage.
2. Be sure both batteries are of the same polarity (have the same grounded terminal).
3. Be sure the vehicles are not touching.
4. Be sure the vent cap holes are not obstructed.
5. Do not smoke or allow sparks around the battery.
6. In cold weather, check for frozen electrolyte in the battery.
7. Do not allow electrolyte on your skin or clothing.
8. Be sure the electrolyte is not frozen.

Jump Starting Procedure

1. Determine voltages of the two batteries; they must be the same.
2. Bring the starting vehicle close (they must not touch) so that the batteries can be reached easily.
3. Turn off all accessories and both engines. Put both cars in Neutral or Park and set the handbrake.
4. Cover the cell caps with a rag—do not cover terminals.
5. If the terminals on the run-down battery are heavily corroded, clean them.
6. Identify the positive and negative posts on both batteries and connect the cables in the order shown.
7. Start the engine of the starting vehicle and run it at fast idle. Try to start the car with the dead battery. Crank it for no more than 10 seconds at a time and let it cool off for 20 seconds in between tries.
8. If it doesn't start in 3 tries, there is something else wrong.
9. Disconnect the cables in the reverse order.
10. Replace the cell covers and dispose of the rags.

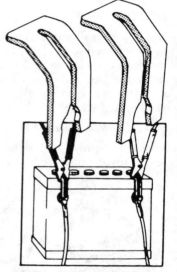

Side terminal batteries occasionally pose a problem when connecting jumper cables. There frequently isn't enough room to clamp the cables without touching sheet metal. Side terminal adaptors are available to alleviate this problem and should be removed after use.

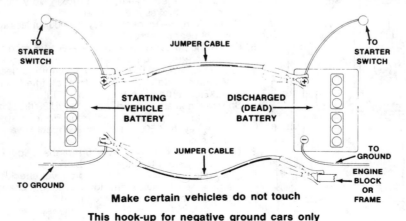

TO STARTER SWITCH

JUMPER CABLE

TO STARTER SWITCH

STARTING VEHICLE BATTERY

DISCHARGED (DEAD) BATTERY

JUMPER CABLE

TO GROUND

ENGINE BLOCK OR FRAME

TO GROUND

Make certain vehicles do not touch

This hook-up for negative ground cars only

1. Make sure that the bumpers of the two cars align so as not to damage either one. It might be a good idea to put an old tire between the two bumpers.

2. Turn on the ignition switch in the pushed car. Place the transmission in Second or Third gear and hold down the clutch pedal.

3. Have the car pushed to a speed of 10–15 mph.

4. Ease up on the clutch and press down on the accelerator slightly at the same time. If the clutch is engaged abruptly, damage to the push vehicle may result.

The car should not be towed to start, since there is a chance of the towed vehicle ramming the tow car.

These cars should not be towed farther than 15 miles or faster than 30 mph. If these limits must be exceeded, remove the driveshaft to prevent transmission damage.

JACKING AND HOISTING

The jack supplied with the car should never be used for any service operation other than tire changing. NEVER get under the car while it is supported only by the jack. They often slip or topple over. Always block the wheels when changing tires.

Some of the service operations in this book require that one or both ends of the car be raised and supported safely. It is understood that hydraulic lifts are not often found in the home garage, but there are reasonable and safe substitutes. Small hydraulic, screw, or scissors jacks are satisfactory for raising the car.

Heavy wooden blocks or adjustable jack-stands should be used to support the car while it is being worked on. Drive-on trestles, or ramps, are also a handy and safe way to raise the car. These can be bought or constructed from suitable heavy timbers or steel.

In any case, it is always best to spend a little extra time to make sure that the car is lifted and supported safely.

CAUTION: *Concrete blocks are not recommended. They may break if the load is not evenly distributed. Boxes and milk crates of any description should not be used.*

Tune-Up

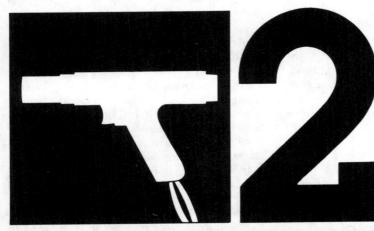

TUNE-UP PROCEDURES

An automotive tune-up is an orderly process of inspection, diagnosis, testing, and adjustment that may be needed to maintain peak engine performance or restore the engine to original operating efficiency.

Tests by the Champion Spark Plug Company showed that an average 11.36% improvement in gas economy could be expected after a tune-up. A change to new spark plugs alone provided a 3.44% decrease in fuel use. As for emissions, significantly lower emissions were recorded at idle after a complete tune-up on a car needing service. An average 45.37% reduction of CO emissions was recorded at idle after a complete tune-up, HC emissions were cut 55.5%.

The tune-up is also a good opportunity to perform a general preventive maintenance check-out on everything in the engine compartment. Look for failed or about to fail components such as loose or damaged wiring, leaking fuel lines, cracked coolant hoses, and frayed fan belts.

Chrysler recommends replacing spark plugs at 30,000 mile intervals on cars equipped with catalytic converters and 15,000 mile intervals on non-converter cars. It would be a good idea to check the spark plugs and ignition system before those mileage readings as a preventive maintenance measure. If you are experiencing starting problems or below average fuel economy you will, of course, want to tune the car before those intervals. Each step of the tune-up should be followed in the order given. If any of the specifications on the emission control sticker under your hood differ from those given in the "Tune-Up Specifications" chart, use the figures from the sticker. Running changes made by the manufacturer are often incorporated into the sticker. When you decide on a tune-up schedule for your car, follow it religiously. A regular tune-up will head off winter no-starts and summer stalling. A small investment in time and parts pays off in improved gas mileage and engine performance. The procedures given here are tailored specifically for your Volare or Aspen.

Spark Plugs

A typical spark plug consists of a metal shell surrounding a ceramic insulator. A metal electrode extends downward through the center of the insulator and protrudes a small distance. Located at the end of the plug and attached to the side of the outer metal shell is the side electrode. The side electrode bends in at 90° so its tip is even with, and parallel to, the tip of the center electrode. The distance between these two electrodes (measured in thousandths of an inch) is called the spark plug gap. The spark plug in no way produces a spark but merely provides a gap across which the current can arc. The coil produces over 30,000 volts, which travels to the distributor where it is distributed through the spark plug wires to the plugs. The current passes along the center electrode and jumps the gap to the side electrode and, in so doing, ignites the air/fuel mixture in the combustion chamber. All plugs have a resistor built into the center electrode to reduce interference to any nearby radio and television receivers. The resistor also cuts down on the erosion of plug electrodes caused by excessively long sparking. Resistor spark plug wiring is original equipment on all models.

Spark plug life and efficiency depend upon the condition of the engine and the temperatures to which the plug is exposed. Combustion chamber temperatures are affected by many factors such as compression ratio of the engine, fuel/air mixtures, exhaust emission equipment, and the type of driving you do. Spark plugs are designed and classified by number according to the heat range at which they will operate most efficiently. The amount of heat that the plug absorbs is determined by the length of the lower insulator. The longer the insulator (it extends farther into the engine), the hotter the plug will operate; the shorter it is, the cooler it will operate. A plug that absorbs little heat and remains too cool will quickly accumulate deposits of oil and carbon since it is not hot enough to burn them off. This leads to plug fouling and consequently to misfiring. A plug that absorbs too much heat will have no deposits but, due to the excessive heat, the electrodes will burn away quickly and, in some instances, pre-ignition may result. Pre-ignition takes place when plug tips get so hot that they glow sufficiently to ignite the fuel/air mixture before the spark does. This early ignition will usually cause a pinging (sounding much like castanets) during low speeds and heavy loads. In severe cases, the heat may become high enough to start the fuel/air mixture burning throughout the combustion chamber rather than just to the front of the plug as in normal operation. At this time, the piston is rising in the cylinder making its compression stroke. The burning mass is compressed and an explosion results forcing the piston and rod assembly down in the

cylinder while it is still trying to go up. Something has to give, and it does-pistons are often damaged. Obviously, this detonation (explosion) is a destructive condition that can be avoided by installing a spark plug designed and specified for your particular engine.

A set of spark plugs usually requires replacement after 15,000 to 20,000 miles depending on the type of driving. The electrode on a new spark plug has a sharp edge but, with use, this edge becomes rounded by erosion causing the plug gap to increase. In normal operation, plug gap increases about 0.001 in. for every 1,000–2,000 miles. As the gap increases, the plug's voltage requirement also increases. It requires a greater voltage to jump the wider gap and about two to three times as much voltage to fire a plug at high speeds and acceleration than at idle.

The higher voltage produced by the electronic ignition is one of the primary reasons for the prolonged replacement interval for spark plugs in later cars. A consistently hotter spark prevents the fouling of plugs for much longer than could normally be expected; this spark is also able to jump across a larger gap more efficiently than a spark from a conventional system. However, even plugs used with the electronic ignition system wear after time in the engine.

In addition to performing their primary function of igniting the air/fuel mixture, spark plugs can also serve as very useful diagnostic tools. Once removed, compare your spark plugs with the samples in the "Troubleshooting" chapter at the end of this book. Typical plug conditions are illustrated along with their causes and remedies. Pugs which exhibit only normal wear and deposits can be cleaned, gapped, and reinstalled. However, it is a good practice to replace the spark plugs at each tune-up.

SPARK PLUG REPLACEMENT

Tools needed for spark plug replacement include a ratchet handle, short extension, spark plug socket ($^{13}/_{16}$ in. for V8s, $^{5}/_{8}$ in. for sixes), combination spark plug gap gauge and bending tool, and a can of penetrating oil. A torque wrench makes for more accurate spark plug tightening, but is not absolutely necessary. Check the "Tune-Up Specifications" chart for the correct spark plugs for your engine before rushing out to the parts store.

When you're removing spark plugs, you

Tune-Up Specifications

When analyzing compression test results, look for uniformity among cylinders rather than specific pressures.

Year	Engine No. Cyl Displacement (cu in.)	hp	Spark Plugs Orig. Type◆	Gap (in.)	Distributor Point Dwell (deg)	Point Gap (in.)	Ignition Timing (deg)▲ Man Trans●	Auto Trans	Valves Intake Opens ■(deg)	Fuel Pump Pressure (psi)	Idle Speed (rpm)▲ Man Trans●	Auto Trans
'76	6-225	100	RBL-13Y	.035	Electronic		6B(4B)	2B	16	3½–5	750(800)	750
	8-318	150	RN-12Y	.035	Electronic		2B	2B(TDC)	10	5–7	750	750
	8-318①	150	RN-12Y	.035	Electronic		—	2A	10	5–7	—	900
	8-360	170	RN-12Y	.035	Electronic		—	2B	18	5–7	—	850
'77	6-225	100	RBL-15Y	.035	Electronic		12B	12B(8B)	16	3½–5	700(750)	700(750)
	6-225	110	RBL-15Y	.035	Electronic		12B	12B	16	3½–5	700(750)	700(750)
	8-318	145	RN-12Y	.035	Electronic		8B	8B	10	5–7	700	700(850)
	8-360	155	RN-12Y	.035	Electronic		—	10B	18	5–7	—	700
'78	6-225	90	RBL-16Y	.035	Electronic		12B(8B)	12B(8B)	16	3½–5	700(750)	700(750)
	6-225	110	RBL-16Y	.035	Electronic		12B(10B)	12B(10B)	16	3½–5	700(750)	700(750)
	8-318	140	RN-12Y	.035	Electronic		16B	16B	10	5¾–7¼	700(750)	700(750)

8-318	155	RN-12Y	.035	Electronic	—	10B	10	5¾–7¼	700(750)	700(750)
8-360	155	RN-12Y	.035	Electronic	—	20B	18	5¾–7¼	—	750
'79 6-225	90	RBL-16Y	.035	Electronic	12B(8B)	12B(8B)	16	3½–5	700(750)	700(750)
6-225	110	RBL-16Y	.035	Electronic	12B	12B	16	3½–5	700(750)	700(750)
8-318	All	RN-12Y	.035	Electronic	—	16B	10	5–7	—	750
8-360	All	RN-12Y	.035	Electronic	—	16B	18	5–7	—	750
'80 6-225	90	560 PR	.035	Electronic	12B	12B	16	3½–5	725	725(750)
6-225	110	560 PR	.035	Electronic	—	12B	16	3½–5	725	725②
8-318	120	65 PR	.035	Electronic	—	12B	10	5–7	—	700
8-318	155	65 PR	.035	Electronic	—	10B②(16B)	10	5–7	—	750②(700)
8-360	185	65 PR	.035	Electronic	—	16B	18	5–7	—	750

① with air pump, no converter
② Canada
▲ See text for procedure
■ All figures Before Top Dead Center
● Figure in parentheses indicates California Engine
NOTE: The underhood specifications sticker often reflects specification changes made in production. Sticker figures must be used if they disagree with those in this chart.

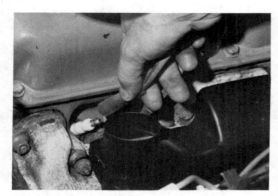

Twist the boot to remove the plug wire

Keep the socket straight on the plug to avoid breaking it

Checking spark plug gap

should work on one at a time. Don't start by removing the plug wires all at once, because unless you number them, they may become mixed up. Take a minute before you begin and number the wires with tape. The best location for numbering is near where the wires come out of the distributor cap.

1. Twist the spark plug boot and remove the boot and wire from the plug. Do not pull on the wire itself.

2. Once the wire is removed, use a brush or rag to clean the area around the spark plug. Make sure that all dirt is removed so that none will enter the cylinder after the plug is removed.

3. Remove the spark plug using the proper size socket. V8s require a $13/16$ in. socket. Six cylinder engines use tapered seat spark plugs and require the smaller ⅝ in. socket. Turn the socket counterclockwise to remove the plug. On six cylinder engines, the spark plug tube will sometimes also come out. Wipe it clean before replacing it.

4. If the spark plug is stubborn, squirt some penetrating oil onto the plug threads.

Give the oil a minute to work and then remove the plug. Be sure to hold the socket straight on the spark plug. This is sometimes difficult, but you can crack the insulator or round off the hex on the plug if the socket isn't held straight.

5. Once the plug is out, check it against those shown in the "Color" section of chapter four.

6. Most new spark plugs come pre-gapped, but the factory setting sometimes changes in shipping and should be checked. Use a wire feeler gauge. Flat feeler gauges are not accurate when used on spark plugs. The correct size feeler gauge should pass through the electrode gap with a slight drag. If you're in doubt, try one size smaller and one larger. The smaller gauge should go through easily, while the larger one shouldn't fit at all. If the gap is incorrect, use the electrode bending tool on the end of the gauge to adjust the gap. When adjusting the gap, always bend the side electrode. Never bend or try to adjust the center electrode.

7. Squirt a drop of penetrating oil on the threads of the new plug and install it. Don't heavily oil the threads. Turn the plug in clockwise by hand.

8. When the spark plug is finger tight, tighten it with a wrench. If a torque wrench is available, tighten the spark plug to 30 ft. lbs. (V8) or 10 ft. lbs. (six). If you don't have a torque wrench, give the plug about ⅛ of turn with the wrench after its finger tight. Don't overtighten the spark plug.

9. Install the spark plug boot firmly over

the plug. Proceed to remove the remaining plugs in the same manner. Should the wires become mixed up, refer to the firing order illustration in the beginning of Chapter 3.

CHECKING AND REPLACING SPARK PLUG CABLES

Visually inspect the spark plug cables for burns, cuts, or breaks in the insulation. Check the spark plug boots and the nipples on the distributor cap and the coil. Replace any damaged wiring. If no physical damage is obvious, the wires can be checked with an ohmmeter for excessive resistance. Remove the distributor cap and leave the wires connected to the cap. Connect one lead of the ohmmeter to the corresponding electrode inside the cap and the other lead to the spark plug terminal (remove it from the spark plug for the test). Replace any wire which shows over 50,000 ohms. Test the coil wire by connecting the ohmmeter between the center contact in the cap and either of the primary terminals at the coil. If the total resistance of the coil and cable is more than 25,000 ohms, remove the cable from the coil and check the resistance of the cable. If the resistance is higher than 15,000 ohms, replace the cable. If resistance is less, check the coil for a loose connection or for a bad coil. Check the top of the coil for cracks or carbon tracking.

Replace spark plug cables one at a time when installing a new set, this way there can be no mix-ups. Refer to the firing order illustration in Chapter 3 if you do become confused. Start by replacing the longest cable first. Install the boot firmly over the spark plug. Route the wire exactly the same as the original. Insert the nipple firmly into the tower on the distributor cap. Repeat the process for each cable.

Electronic Ignition System

Chrysler Corporation has been using this system on all of its cars since 1973. The system consists of a magnetic pulse distributor, electronic control unit, dual element ballast resistor, and special ignition coil. The distributor outwardly resembles a standard breaker point unit, but is internally quite different. The usual breaker points, cam, and condenser are replaced with a reluctor and pickup unit.

The ignition primary circuit is connected from the battery, through the ignition switch, through the primary side of the igni-

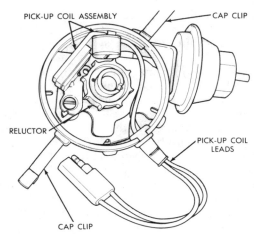

PICK-UP COIL ASSEMBLY   CAP CLIP

RELUCTOR

PICK-UP COIL LEADS

CAP CLIP

Electronic single pickup distributor

tion coil, to the control unit where it is grounded. The secondary circuit is the same as in a conventional ignition system: the secondary side of the coil, the coil wire to the distributor, the rotor, the spark plug wires, and the spark plugs.

The magnetic pulse distributor is also connected to the control unit. As the distributor shaft turns, the reluctor rotates past the pickup unit. As the reluctor turns by the pick-up unit, each of the six or eight teeth on the reluctor pass near the pick-up unit once during each distributor revolution (two crankshaft revolutions since the distributor turns at one half crankshaft speed). As the reluctor teeth move close to the pick-up unit, the rotating reluctor induces voltage into the magnetic pick-up unit. When the pulse enters the control unit, it signals the control unit to interrupt the ignition primary circuit. This causes the primary circuit to collapse and begins the induction of the magnetic lines of force from the primary side of the coil into the secondary side of the coil. This induction

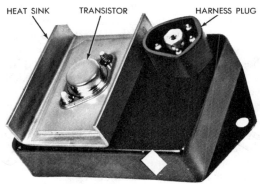

HEAT SINK   TRANSISTOR   HARNESS PLUG

Electronic control unit

provides the required voltage to fire the spark plugs.

The advantages of this system are that the transistors in the control unit can make or break the primary ignition circuit much faster than the conventional ignition points can, and higher primary voltage can be utilized, since this system can be made to handle higher voltage without adverse effects, where standard breaker points would quickly burn. The quicker switching time of this system allows longer coil primary circuit saturation time and longer induction time when the primary circuit collapses. This increased time allows the primary circuit to build up more current and the secondary circuit to discharge more current.

INSPECTION

The electronic ignition system is practically maintenance free and should require very little attention, but an inspection at tune-up intervals is advised to prevent problems.

Check the ignition wires as previously discussed. Ignition wire condition is more critical on electronic ignition systems than on conventional breaker point systems. Using either your finger or a screwdriver, pry the two retaining clips from the distributor cap. Lift the cap off the distributor and check the outside of the cap for cracks or other damage. Examine the inside of the cap for carbon tracking. Check each of the contacts for erosion or chipping. Replace the cap if damage or excessive erosion of the contacts is present. Pull straight up on the rotor to remove it. Check the tip of the rotor for pitting or erosion, replace if necessary. For detailed troubleshooting, see Chapter 11.

Ignition Timing

Timing should be checked at each tune-up. The timing marks consist of a notch on the rim of the crankshaft pulley or vibration damper and a graduated scale attached to the engine front (timing) cover. A stroboscopic flash (dynamic) timing light must be used, as a static light is too inaccurate for emission controlled engines.

There are three basic types of timing light available. The first is a simple neon bulb with two wire connections. One wire connects to the spark plug terminal and the other plugs into the end of the spark plug wire for the No. 1 cylinder, thus connecting the light in series with the spark plug. This type of light

V8 timing marks

is pretty dim and must be held very closely to the timing marks to be seen. Sometimes a dark corner has to be sought out to see the flash at all. This type of light is very inexpensive. The second type operates from the car battery—two alligator clips connect to the battery terminals, while an adapter enables a third clip to be connected to the No. 1 spark plug and wire. This type is a bit more expensive, but it provides a nice bright flash that you can see even in bright sunlight. It is the type most often seen in professional shops. The third type replaces the battery power source with 110 volt current.

To check and adjust the timing:

1. Warm up the engine to normal operating temperature. Stop the engine and connect the timing light to the No. 1 (left front on V8, front on six) spark plug wire. Clean off the timing marks and mark the pulley or damper notch and timing scale with white chalk.

2. Disconnect and plug the vacuum line(s)

Six-cylinder timing marks

at the distributor. This is done to prevent any distributor vacuum advance.

3. Start the engine and adjust the idle speed to that specified in the "Tune-Up Specifications" chart.

4. Aim the timing light at the point marks. Be careful not to touch the fan, because it may appear to be standing still. If the pulley or damper notch isn't aligned with the proper timing mark (see the "Tune-Up Specifications" chart), the timing will have to be adjusted.

> NOTE: *TDC or Top Dead Center corresponds to 0 degrees. B, or BTDC, or Before Top Dead Center may be shown as BEFORE. A, or ATDC, or After Top Dead Center may be shown as AFTER.*

5. Loosen the distributor base clamp locknut. You can buy trick wrenches which make this task a lot easier. Turn the distributor slowly to adjust the timing, holding it by the body and not the cap. Turn the distributor in the direction of rotor rotation (found in the "firing Order" illustration in Chapter 3) to retard, and against the direction of rotation to advance.

6. Tighten the locknut. Check the timing again, in case the distributor moved slightly as you tightened it.

7. Replace the distributor vacuum line. Correct the idle speed if it changed.

8. Stop the engine and disconnect the timing light.

Valve Lash

This adjustment is required only on the six-cylinder; it should be done at every tune-up or whenever there is excessive noise from the valve mechanism.

> NOTE: *Do not set the valve lash closer than specified in an attempt to quiet the valve mechanism. This will result in burned valves.*

The valves can be adjusted with the engine running, but the amateur will have better luck with the following procedure.

1. The engine must be at normal operating temperature. Mark the crankshaft pulley into three equal 120° segments, starting at the timing mark.

2. Remove the valve (rocker) cover and the distributor cap.

3. Set the engine at TDC on the No. 1 cylinder by aligning the mark on the crankshaft pulley with the 0° mark on the timing cover pointer. The distributor rotor should

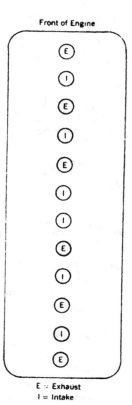

Front of Engine

E = Exhaust
I = Intake

Valve location—slant six

point at the position of the No. 1 spark plug wire in the distributor cap. Both rocker arms on the No. 1 cylinder should be free to move slightly. If all this isn't the case, you have No. 6 cylinder at TDC and will have to turn the engine 360° in the normal direction of rotation.

4. The cylinders are numbered from front to rear. The intake and exhaust valves are in the following sequence, starting at the front: E-I, E-I, E-I, I-E, I-E, I-E. Note that intake and exhaust valves have different settings.

5. The lash is measured between the rocker arm and the end of the valve.

6. To check the lash, insert the correct size feeler gauge between the rocker arm and the valve. Press down lightly on the other end of the rocker arm. If the gauge cannot be inserted, loosen the self-locking adjustment nut on top of the rocker arm. Tighten the nut until the gauge can just be inserted and withdrawn without buckling.

7. After both valves for the No. 1 cylinder are adjusted, turn the engine so that the pulley turns 120° in the normal direction of rotation (clockwise). The distributor rotor

will turn 60°, since it turns at half engine speed.

8. Check that the rocker arms are free and adjust the valves for the next cylinder in the firing order, 5. The firing order is 1–5–3–6–2–4.

9. Turn the engine 120° to adjust each of the remaining cylinders in the firing order. When you are done the engine will have made two complete revolutions (720°) and the rotor one complete revolution (360°).

10. Replace the rocker cover with a new gasket. Replace the distributor cap. Start the engine and check for leaks.

Carburetor Adjustments

The following are basic carburetor adjustments which are performed as part of the engine tune-up procedure, for more complete adjustment procedures, see Chapter 4, "Emission Controls and Fuel System."

IDLE SPEED/MIXTURE

To adjust the idle speed and mixture, it is best to use an exhaust gas analyzer. This will insure that the proper level of emissions is maintained. However, if you do not have an exhaust gas analyzer, use the following procedure and eliminate those steps which pertain to the exhaust gas analyzer. When you have adjusted the carburetor it would be wise to have it checked with an exhaust gas analyzer.

1. Leave the air cleaner installed.

2. Run the engine at fast idle speed to stabilize the entire temperature.

3. Make sure the choke plate is fully released.

Curb idle speed adjustment screw

Idle mixture screw (arrow). The one on the other side is hidden

4. Connect a tachometer to the engine, following the manufacturer's instructions.

5. Connect an exhaust gas analyzer and insert the probe as far into the tailpipe as possible.

6. Check the ignition timing and set it to specification if necessary.

7. If equipped with air conditioning, turn the air conditioner off.

8. Put the transmission in Neutral. Make sure the hot idle compensator valve is fully seated.

9. If equipped with a distributor vacuum control valve, place a clamp on the line between the valve and the intake manifold.

10. Turn the engine idle speed adjusting screw in or out to adjust the idle speed to specification. If the carburetor is equipped with an electric solenoid throttle positioner, turn the solenoid adjusting screw in or out to obtain the specified rpm.

CAUTION: *On engines equipped with catalytic converters, be careful not to adjust the idle speed with the catalyst protection system solenoid; a dangerous engine overspeed condition could result. See Chapter 4 for a description of this system.*

11. Adjust the curb idle speed screw until it just touches the stop on the carburetor body. Back the curb idle speed screw out 1 full turn.

12. Turn each idle mixture adjustment screw $1/16$ turn richer (counterclockwise). Wait 10 seconds and observe the reading on the exhaust gas analyzer. Continue this procedure until the meter indicates a definite increase in the richness of the mixture.

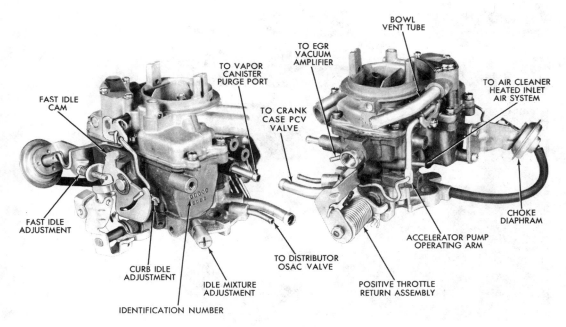

Holley one-bbl carburetor adjustment points

NOTE: *This step is very important when using an exhaust gas analyzer. A carburetor that is set too lean will cause a false reading from the analyzer, indicating a rich mixture. Because of this, the carburetor must first be known to have a rich mixture to verify the reading on the analyzer.*

13. After verifying the reading on the meter, adjust the mixture screws to obtain an air-fuel ratio of 14.2. Turn the mixture screws clockwise (leaner) to raise the meter reading or counterclockwise (richer) to lower the meter reading.

14. If the idle speed changes as the mixture screws are adjusted, adjust the speed to specification (see Step 10) and readjust the mixture so that the specified air/fuel ratio is maintained at the specified idle speed.

If the idle is rough, the screws may be adjusted independently provided that the 14.2 air/fuel ratio is maintained.

15. Remove the analyzer, the tachometer, and the clamp on the vacuum line.

Engine and Engine Rebuilding

ENGINE ELECTRICAL
Distributor
REMOVAL

1. Disconnect the vacuum advance line(s) at the distributor.

2. Disconnect the primary wire at the coil. On electronic ignition, disconnect the lead wire at the harness connector.

3. Unfasten the distributor cap retaining clips and lift off the cap.

4. Mark the distributor body and the engine block to indicate the position of the body in the block. Scribe a mark on the edge of the distributor housing to indicate the position of the rotor on the distributor. These marks can be used as guides when installing the distributor.

5. Remove the distributor hold-down clamp screw and clamp.

6. Carefully lift the distributor out of the block. Note the slight rotation of the distributor shaft on a six as the distributor is removed. When installing the distributor the rotor must be in this position as the distributor is inserted into the block.

INSTALLATION (ENGINE HAS NOT BEEN ROTATED)

1. Install a new seal in the groove of the distributor shaft and carefully lower the distributor into the distributor bore.

2. With the rotor positioned slightly to the side of the mark on the distributor body, engage the distributor drive gear with the camshaft drive gear on a six. As the distributor slides into place the rotor will rotate slightly and align with the mark on the body. On a V8, engage the distributor shaft tongue with the oil pump drive gear slot.

3. Install the distributor hold-down clamp and bolt. Do not tighten.

4. Install the distributor cap and coil primary wire or lead wire.

5. Set the point gap where necessary and time the engine.

6. Tighten the distributor hold-down clamp and install the vacuum advance hose.

INSTALLATION (ENGINE HAS BEEN ROTATED)

If the crankshaft has been rotated or otherwise disturbed (as during engine rebuilding) after the distributor was removed, proceed as follows to install the distributor.

1. Bring the No. 1 piston to TDC by removing the No. 1 spark plug and inserting a finger over the hole while rotating the crankshaft. The compression pressure can be felt as the No. 1 piston approaches TDC on the compression stroke. The TDC timing mark on the crankshaft vibration damper should now be opposite the indicator on the timing chain case.

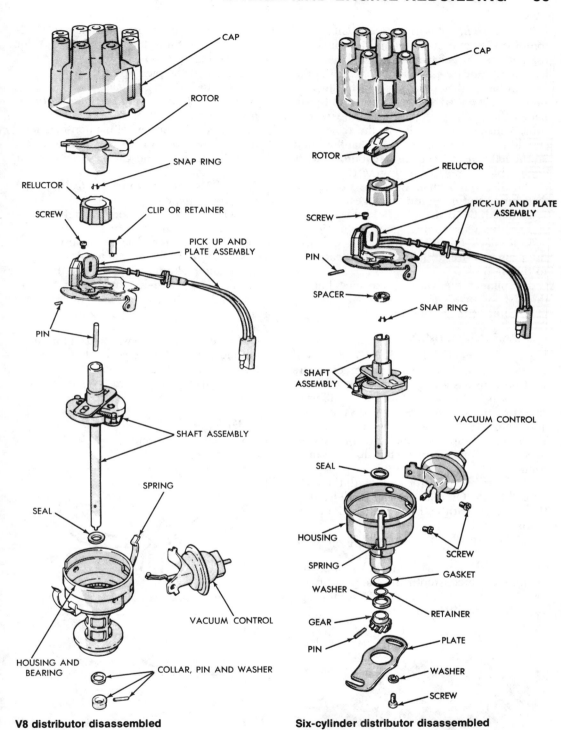

CAP

ROTOR

SNAP RING

RELUCTOR

SCREW

CLIP OR RETAINER

PICK UP AND PLATE ASSEMBLY

PIN

SHAFT ASSEMBLY

SPRING

SEAL

VACUUM CONTROL

HOUSING AND BEARING

COLLAR, PIN AND WASHER

V8 distributor disassembled

CAP

ROTOR

RELUCTOR

SCREW

PICK-UP AND PLATE ASSEMBLY

PIN

SPACER

SNAP RING

SHAFT ASSEMBLY

VACUUM CONTROL

SEAL

HOUSING

SPRING

SCREW

GASKET

WASHER

RETAINER

GEAR

PLATE

PIN

WASHER

SCREW

Six-cylinder distributor disassembled

2. *For six-cylinder engines:* Align the distributor so that the rotor will be in position *just ahead* of the distributor cap terminal for the No. 1 spark plug when the distributor is installed. Now lower the distributor into its engine block opening, engaging the distributor gear with the camshaft drive gear. Be sure that the rubber O-ring seal is in the groove in the distributor shank. When the distributor is properly seated, the rotor should be under the No. 1 distributor cap terminal. Proceed with step 4.

3. *For eight-cylinder engines:* Clean the top of the engine block around the distributor opening to ensure a good seal between the distributor base and the block. Align the distributor so that the rotor will be in position *directly under* the distributor cap terminal for the No. 1 spark plug when the distributor is installed. The slot in the drive gear should point to the first intake manifold bolt on the left side. Lower the distributor into its engine block opening, engaging the tongue of the distributor shaft with the slot in the distributor and oil pump drive gear.

4. Install the distributor hold-down clamp and tighten its retaining screw finger tight.

5. Replace the distributor cap. Connect the primary wire to the coil or the lead wire to the harness.

6. Connect the vacuum advance line to the distributor.

7. Check the ignition timing.

AIR GAP ADJUSTMENT

Lean Burn engines through 1977 (first generation system) have two pick-up coils. The start pick-up has a larger connector than the run pick-up. The two pick-ups have different air gaps, but are adjusted in the same manner. Some 1980 models have two pick-ups. The start pick-up has a dual prong male connector; the run pick-up has a male and female connector.

1. Align one reluctor tooth with the pick-up coil tooth. On dual pick-up models, align the reluctor tooth with the start pick-up coil tooth.

2. Loosen the pick-up coil hold-down screw.

3. Insert a non-magnetic feeler gauge between the reluctor tooth and the pick-up coil tooth. The gauge should be 0.008 in. through 1976, 0.006 in. 1977 and later.

4. Adjust the air gap so that contact is made between the reluctor tooth, the feeler gauge, and the pick-up coil tooth.

5. Tighten the pick-up coil screw.

6. Remove the feeler gauge.

NOTE: *No force should be required to remove the gauge.*

7. Check the air gap with a non-magnetic feeler gauge: 0.010 in. through 1976, 0.008 in. 1977 and later. The gauge should not fit into the air gap.

CAUTION: *Do not force the feeler gauge into the air gap.*

8. On dual pick-up models, align one reluctor tooth with the run pick-up coil tooth. Loosen the pick-up coil screw. Insert a 0.012 in. non-magnetic feeler gauge between the reluctor and pick-up coil, and move the pick-up coil against the feeler gauge, as in Step 4.

9. Tighten the screw and remove the gauge. No force should be required to remove the gauge.

10. Check the air gap with a 0.014 in. non-magnetic gauge. The gauge should not fit into the air gap.

CAUTION: *Do not force the feeler gauge into the air gap.*

Firing Order

To avoid confusion, replace spark plug wires one at a time.

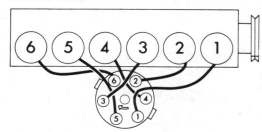

Six cylinder firing order

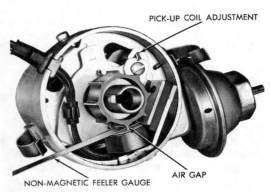

PICK-UP COIL ADJUSTMENT

NON-MAGNETIC FEELER GAUGE

AIR GAP

Air gap adjustment

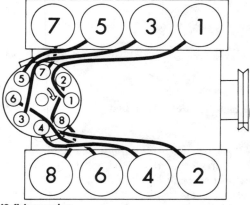

V8 firing order

Troubleshooting Chrysler Electronic Ignition

Condition	Possible Cause	Correction
ENGINE WILL NOT START (Fuel and carburetion known to be OK)	a) Dual Ballast	Check resistance of each section: Compensating resistance: .50–.60 ohms @ 70°–80°F Auxiliary Ballast: 4.75–5.75 ohms Replace if faulty. Check wire positions.
	b) Faulty Ignition Coil	Check for carbonized tower. Check primary and secondary resistances: Primary: 1.41–1.79 ohms @ 70°–80°F Secondary: 9,200–11,700 ohms @ 70°–80°F Check in coil tester.
	c) Faulty Pickup or Improper Pickup Air Gap	Check pickup coil resistance: 400–600 ohms Check pickup gap: .010 in. feeler gauge should not slip between pickup coil core and an aligned reluctor blade. No evidence of pickup core striking reluctor blades should be visible. To reset gap, tighten pickup adjustment screw with a .008 in. feeler gauge held between pickup core and an aligned reluctor blade. After resetting gap, run distributor on test stand and apply vacuum advance, making sure that the pickup core does not strike the reluctor blades.
	d) Faulty Wiring	Visually inspect wiring for brittle insulation. Inspect connectors. Molded connectors should be inspected for rubber inside female terminals.
	e) Faulty Control Unit	Replace if all of the above checks are negative. Whenever the control unit or dual ballast is replaced, make sure the dual ballast wires are correctly inserted in the keyed molded connector.
ENGINE SURGES	a) Wiring	Inspect for loose connection and/or broken conductors in harness.
SEVERELY (Not Lean	b) Faulty Pickup Leads	Disconnect vacuum advance. If surging stops, replace pickup.
Carburetor)	c) Ignition Coil	Check for intermittent primary.
ENGINE MISSES (Carburetion OK)	a) Spark Plugs	Check plugs. Clean and regap if necessary.
	b) Secondary Cable	Check cables with an ohmmeter, or observe secondary circuit performance with an oscilloscope.
	c) Ignition Coil	Check for carbonized tower. Check in coil tester.
	d) Wiring	Check for loose or dirty connections.
	e) Faulty Pickup Lead	Disconnect vacuum advance. If miss stops, replace pickup.
	f) Control Unit	Replace if the above checks are negative.

Alternator

The alternator is basically an alternating current (AC) generator with solid state rectifiers which convert AC current to DC current (direct current) for charging the battery.

Be sure to read and follow the "Alternator Service Precautions" before servicing the vehicle charging system.

ALTERNATOR SERVICE PRECAUTIONS

Because alternator (AC) systems differ from generator (DC) systems, special care must be taken when servicing the charging system.

1. Battery polarity should be checked before any connections, such as jumper cables or battery charger leads, are made. Reversed battery connections will damage the rectifiers. It is recommended that the battery cables be disconnected before connecting a battery charger.

2. The battery must *never* be disconnected while the alternator is running.

3. Always disconnect the battery ground lead before replacing the alternator.

4. Do not attempt to polarize an alternator, or the regulator of an alternator equipped car.

5. Do not short across or ground any alternator terminals.

6. Always disconnect the battery ground lead before removing the alternator output cable, whether the engine is running or not.

7. If electric arc welding has to be done on the car, first disconnect the battery and alternator cables. Never start the car with the welding unit attached.

REMOVAL AND INSTALLATION

1. Disconnect both battery cables at the battery terminals.

2. Disconnect the alternator output (BAT) and field (FLD) leads, and disconnect the ground wire.

3. Remove the alternator mounting bracket bolts and remove the alternator.

4. Installation is the reverse of the above. Adjust the alternator drive belt tension. Details are given in Chapter 1.

Voltage Regulator

The function of the voltage regulator is to limit the output voltage by controlling the flow of current in the alternator rotor field coil which, in effect, controls the strength of the rotor magnetic field.

All models have a solid-state (silicon transistor) voltage regulator which is not adjustable. The regulator is in the engine compartment and clearly labeled.

REMOVAL AND INSTALLATION

1. Release the spring clips and pull off the regulator wiring plug.

2. Unbolt and remove the regulator.

3. Installation is the reverse of removal. Be sure that the spring clips engage the wiring plug.

VOLTAGE REGULATOR TEST

1. Clean the battery terminals and check the specific gravity of the battery electrolyte. If the specific gravity is below 1.200, charge the battery before performing the voltage regulator test as it must be above 1.200 to allow a prompt, regulated voltage check.

2. Connect the positive lead of the test voltmeter to the positive lead to the positive battery terminal.

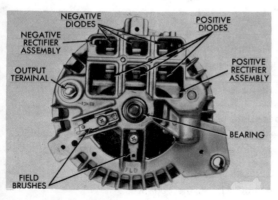

Alternator rear view

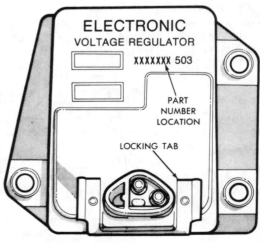

Typical voltage regulator

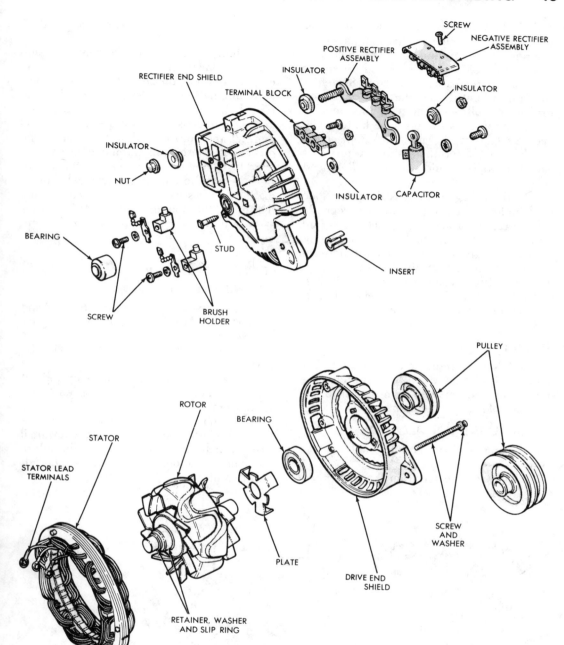

Alternator—exploded view

3. Connect the voltmeter negative lead to a good body ground.

4. Start and operate the engine at 1,250 rpm with all lights and accessories switched off. Observe the voltmeter reading. The regulator is working properly if the voltage readings are as follows:

Ambient Temp Near Regulator	Voltage Range
Below 20° F	14.9–15.9
80° F	13.9–14.6
140° F	13.3–13.9
Above 140° F	Less than 13.6

5. If the voltage reading is below the specified limits or fluctuates, check for a bad voltage regulator or ground. If the reading is still low, switch off the ignition and disconnect the voltage regulator connector. Switch on the ignition but do not start the car. Check for battery voltage at the wiring harness terminal. Both leads should have battery voltage. Switch off the ignition. Replace the regulator if the terminals show battery voltage. The trouble could also be the field-loads relay.

6. If the voltage reading is above the specified limits, check the ground between the voltage regulator and the vehicle body, and between the vehicle body and the engine. Check the ignition switch circuit between the switch battery terminal and the voltage regulator. If the voltage reading is still high (more than ½ V above the specified limits), replace the voltage regulator.

Starter

All models use a reduction gear starter. The solenoid is mounted on the starter. The starter must be removed from the car to service the solenoid and motor brushes.

REMOVAL AND INSTALLATION

1. Disconnect the ground cable at the battery.
2. Remove the cable from the starter.

3. Disconnect the solenoid leads at their solenoid terminals.

4. Remove the starter securing bolt and stud nut and remove the starter from the engine flywheel housing. On some models with automatic transmissions, the oil cooler tube bracket will interfere with starter removal. In this case, remove the starter securing bolt and stud nut, slide the cooler tube bracket off the stud, then remove the starter.

5. Installation is the reverse of the above. Be sure that the starter and flywheel housing mating surfaces are free of dirt and oil. When tightening the bolt and nut, hold the starter away from the engine to ensure proper alignment.

STARTER OVERHAUL

Solenoid and Brush Service

1. Remove the starter from the car and support the starter gear housing in a vise with soft jaws.

2. Remove the two thru-bolts and the starter end assembly.

3. Carefully pull the armature up and out of the gear housing and the starter frame and field assembly.

4. Carefully pull the frame and field assembly up just enough to expose the terminal screw (which connects the series field coils to one pair of motor brushes) and support it with two blocks.

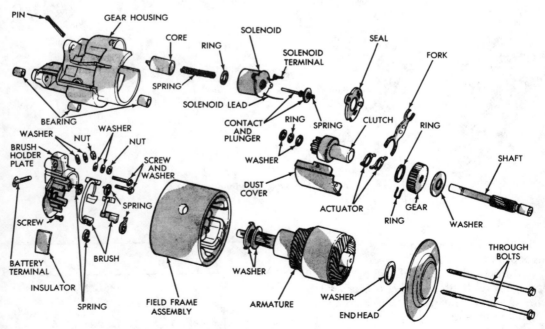

Exploded view—reduction gear starter

Removing the starter terminal screw

Unwinding the solenoid lead wire

5. Support the terminal by placing a finger behind the terminal and remove the terminal screw.

6. Unwrap the shunt field coil lead from the other starter brush terminal. Unwrap the solenoid lead wire from the brush terminals.

7. Remove the steel and fiber thrust washer.

8. Remove the nut, steel washer, and insulating washer from the solenoid terminal.

9. Straighten the solenoid wire and remove the brush holder plate with the brushes and solenoid as an assembly.

10. Inspect the starter brushes. Brushes that are worn more than one-half the length of new brushes or are oil-soaked, should be replaced.

11. Assemble the starter using the reverse of the above procedure. When resoldering the shunt field and solenoid leads, make a strong, low-resistance connection using a high-temperature solder and resin flux. CAUTION: *Do not break the shunt field*

wire units when removing and installing the brushes.

Battery

Refer to Chapter 1 for details on the battery.

REMOVAL AND INSTALLATION

1. Disconnect the negative (ground) cable terminal and then the positive cable terminal. Special pullers are available to remove battery terminals. Remove the heat shield.
NOTE: *Always disconnect the battery ground cable first, and connect it last.*
2. Remove the hold-down clamp.
3. Remove the battery, being careful not to spill the acid.
NOTE: *Spilled acid can be neutralized with a baking soda/water solution. If you somehow get acid into your eyes, flush with lots of water and visit a doctor.*
4. Clean the cable terminals of any corrosion, using a wire brush or an old jackknife inside and out.
5. Install the battery. Replace the hold-down clamp. Replace the heat shield.
6. Connect the positive and then the negative cable terminal. Do not hammer them in place. The terminals should be coated lightly (externally) with grease to prevent corrosion.
CAUTION: *Make absolutely sure that the battery is connected properly before you start the engine. Reversed polarity can destroy your alternator and regulator in a matter of seconds.*

ENGINE MECHANICAL

Design

The standard equipment engine in most models is the 225 cu in. slant-six. Although this engine has a long stroke by modern standards, it presents a low profile because the block is canted 30° to the right.

The 318 and 360 cu in. engines belong to Chrysler's A block series of V8s. The 318 cu in. engine answers the need for a small, reliable, economy power-plant, while the 360 offers more power.

REMOVAL AND INSTALLATION

There are two methods of engine removal. The first is to remove the transmission from the car, then take out the engine. The second

General Engine Specifications

Year	Engine No. Cyl. Displacement (Cu. In.)	Carburetor Type	Horsepower @ rpm	Torque @ rpm (ft. lbs.)	Bore x Stroke (in.)	Compression Ratio	Oil Pressure @ 2000 rpm
'76	6-225	1 bbl	100 @ 3600	170 @ 1600	3.406 x 4.125	8.4 : 1	55
	6-225 Calif.	1 bbl	90 @ 3600	165 @ 1600	3.406 x 4.125	8.4 : 1	55
	8-318	2 bbl	150 @ 4000	255 @ 1600	3.910 x 3.310	8.5 : 1	55
	8-318 Calif.	2 bbl	140 @ 3600	250 @ 2000	3.910 x 3.310	8.5 : 1	55
	8-360	2 bbl	170 @ 4000	280 @ 2400	4.000 x 3.580	8.4 : 1	55
	8-360 HP	4 bbl	220 @ 4000	280 @ 3200	4.000 x 3.580	8.4 : 1	55
'77	6-225	1 bbl	100 @ 3600	170 @ 1600	3.406 x 4.125	8.4 : 1	55
	6-225 Calif.	1 bbl	90 @ 3600	170 @ 1600	3.406 x 4.125	8.4 : 1	55
	6-225	2 bbl	110 @ 3600	180 @ 2000	3.406 x 4.125	8.4 : 1	55
	8-318	2 bbl	145 @ 4000 '	245 @ 1600	3.910 x 3.310	8.5 : 1	55
	8-318 Calif.	2 bbl	135 @ 3600	235 @ 1600	3.910 x 3.310	8.5 : 1	55
	8-360	2 bbl	155 @ 3600	275 @ 2000	4.000 x 3.580	8.4 : 1	55
'78	6-225	1 bbl	90 @ 3600	160 @ 1600	3.406 x 4.125	8.4 : 1	55
	6-225	2 bbl	110 @ 3600	180 @ 2000	3.406 x 4.125	8.4 : 1	55
	8-318	2 bbl	140 @ 4000	245 @ 1600	3.910 x 3.310	8.5 : 1	55
	8-318 Calif.	4 bbl	155 @ 4000	245 @ 1600	3.910 x 3.310	8.5 : 1	55
	8-360	2 bbl	155 @ 3600	270 @ 2400	4.000 x 3.580	8.4 : 1	55
	8-360	4 bbl	160 @ 3600	265 @ 1600	4.000 x 3.580	8.0 : 1	55
'79	6-225	1 bbl	90 @ 3600	160 @ 1600	3.406 x 4.125	8.4 : 1	55
	6-225 ESC Calif.	1 bbl	90 @ 3600	160 @ 1600	3.406 x 4.125	8.4 : 1	55
	6-225	2 bbl	110 @ 3600	180 @ 2000	3.406 x 4.125	8.4 : 1	55
	8-318 ESC	2 bbl	140 @ 4000	245 @ 1600	3.910 x 3.310	8.5 : 1	55
	8-318 ESC Calif.	4 bbl	155 @ 4000	245 @ 1600	3.910 x 3.310	8.5 : 1	55

General Engine Specifications (cont.)

Year	Engine No. Cyl. Displacement (Cu. In.)	Carburetor Type	Horsepower @ rpm	Torque @ rpm (ft. lbs.)	Bore x Stroke (in.)	Compression Ratio	Oil Pressure @ 2000 rpm
	8-360 ESC	2 bbl	155 @ 3600	270 @ 2400	4.000 x 3.580	8.4 : 1	55
	8-360 ESC Calif.	4 bbl	160 @ 3600	265 @ 1600	4.000 x 3.580	8.4 : 1	55
'80	6-225	1 bbl	90 @ 3600	160 @ 1600	3.406 x 4.125	8.4 : 1	55
	8-318	2 bbl	120 @ 3600	245 @ 2000	3.910 x 3.310	8.5 : 1	55
	8-318	4 bbl	155 @ 4000	240 @ 2000	3.910 x 3.310	8.5 : 1	55
	8-360 ESC	4 bbl	185 @ 4000	275 @ 2000	4.000 x 3.580	8.0 : 1	55

Valve Specifications

Year	Engine No. Cyl. Displacement (cu in.)	Seat Angle (deg)	Face Angle (deg)	Spring Test Pressure (lbs. @ in.)	Spring Installed Height (in.)	Stem to Guide Clearance (in.) Intake	Exhaust	Stem Diameter (in.) Intake	Exhaust
'76	6-225	45	45	143 @ 1.31	$1^{21}/_{32}$	.0010 – .0030	.0020 – .0040	.3725	.3715
	8-318	45	①	177 @ 1.31	$1^{21}/_{32}$	.0010 – .0030	.0020 – .0040	.3725	.3715
	8-360	45	①	182 @ 1.31	$1^{21}/_{32}$	.0010 – .0030	.0020 – .0040	.3725	.3715
'77	6-225	45	①	143 @ 1.31	$1^{21}/_{32}$	.0010 – .0030	.0020 – .0040	.3725	.3715
	8-318	45	①	177 @ 1.31	$1^{21}/_{32}$	.0010 – .0030	.0020 – .0040	.3725	.3715
	8-360	45	①	193 @ 1.25	$1^{21}/_{32}$	.0010 – .0030	.0020 – .0040	.3725	.3715
'78	6-225	45	①	143 @ 1.31	$1^{21}/_{32}$	.0010 – .0030	.0020 – .0040	.3725	.3715
	8-318	45	①	177 @ 1.31	$1^{21}/_{32}$	.0010 – .0030	.0020 – .0040	.3725	.3715
	8-360	45	①	177 @ 1.31	$1^{21}/_{32}$	.0010 – .0030	.0020 – .0040	.3725	.3715
'79 – '80	6-225	45	①	143 @ 1.31	$1^{21}/_{32}$	.0010 – .0030	.0020 – .0040	.3725	.3715
	8-318	45	45	177 @ 1.31	$1^{21}/_{32}$	.0010 – .0030	.0020 – .0040	.3725	.3715
	8-360	45	45	177 @ 1.31	$1^{21}/_{32}$	.0010 – .0030	.0020 – .0040	.3725	.3715

① Intake 45°, Exhaust 43°
EFM Electronic Fuel Metering

Crankshaft and Connecting Rod Specifications

All measurements are given in inches

Year	Engine No. Cyl. Displacement (cu in.)	Crankshaft				Connecting Rod		
		Main Brg. Journal Dia	Main Brg. Oil Clearance	Shaft End-Play	Thrust on No.	Journal Diameter	Oil Clearance	Side ③ Clearance
'76	6-225	2.7495–2.7505	.0005–.0020	.002–.007	3	2.1865–2.1875	.0005–.0025	.006–.012
'77–'80	6-225	2.7495–2.7505	.0005–.0020	.002–.009	3	2.1865–2.1875	.0005–.0025	.006–.025
'75–'80	8-318	2.4995–2.5005	.0005–.0020 ②	.002–.009 ①	3	2.1240–2.1250	.0005–.0025	.006–.014
'75–'76	8-360	2.8095–2.8105	.0005–.0020	.002–.007	3	2.1240–2.1250	.0005–.0025	.006–.014
'77–'80	8-360	2.8095–2.8105	.0005–.0020 ②	.002–.009	3	2.1240–2.1250	.0005–.0025	.006–.014

① .002–.007 —'75–'76
② 1980 #1—.0005–.0015; #2, #3, #4, #5—.0005–.0020
③ Total for two rods on V8s

Torque Specifications
All readings in ft. lbs.

Year	Engine No. Cyl. Displacement (cu. in.)	Cylinder Head Bolts	Rod Bearing Bolts	Main Bearing Bolts	Crankshaft Damper Bolt	Flywheel to Crankshaft Bolts	Manifold	
							Intake	Exhaust
'76	6-All	70	45	85	Press fit	55	①	10
'77–'82	6-225	70	45	85	Press fit	55	②	10
'75–'76	8-318, 360	95	45	85	100	55	40	15/20 ③
'77–'80	8-318, 360	105 ④	45	85	100	55	45 ⑤	15/20 ③

① Intake to exhaust manifold bolts—20 ft. lbs., studs—30 ft. lbs.
② Intake to exhaust manifold bolts—17 ft. lbs., studs—20 ft. lbs.
③ Nuts/screws
④ 95— 1977
⑤ 40— 1980

Ring Gap
All measurements are given in inches

Year	Engine No. Cyl. Displacement (cu. in.)	Top Compression	Bottom Compression	Year	Engine No. Cyl. Displacement (cu. in.)	Oil Control
'76–'80	6-198, 225 8-318, 360	.010–.020	.010–.020	'76–'80	All	.015–.055

Ring Side Clearance
All measurements are given in inches

Year	Engine No. Cyl. Displacement (cu. in)	Top Compression	Bottom Compression	Year	Engine No. Cyl. Displacement (cu. in.)	Oil Control
'76–'80	6-198, 225	.0015–.0030	.0015–.0030	'76–'80	6-198, 225, 8-318, 340, 360	.0002–.0050
'76–'78	8-318, 360	.0015–.0030	.0015–.0030			
'79–'80	8-318, 360	.0015–.0040	.0015–.0040			

Piston Clearance
All measurements are given in inches

Year	Engine No. Cyl. Displacement (cu. in.)	Piston-to-Bore Clearance (in.)*
'77–80	6-225	0.0005–0.0015
'76–'80	8-318	0.0005–0.0015
'76–'80	8-360 2 bbl.	0.0005–0.0015
'76–'80	8-360 4 bbl.	0.0010–0.0020

*At top of skirt

is to remove only the engine, leaving the transmission in place.

CAUTION: *If the car has air conditioning, detach the compressor from the engine and set it aside. Do not disconnect any refrigerant lines–refer to the air conditioning "Caution" in Chapter 1. Keep the compressor upright. On reinstallation, turn the compressor pulley by hand a few turns to make sure that all the compressor oil is in the sump.*

REMOVAL OF TRANSMISSION AND ENGINE

1. Scribe the outline of the hood hinge brackets on the bottom of the hood and remove the hood.
2. Drain the cooling system. Remove the radiator.
3. Remove and plug the fuel lines from the pump. Remove the air cleaner.
4. Being sure to take note of their positions, remove all wires and hoses which at-

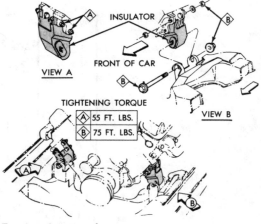

Front motor mounts

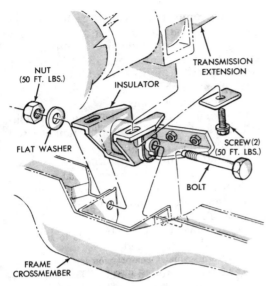

NUT
(50 FT. LBS.)

INSULATOR

TRANSMISSION
EXTENSION

FLAT WASHER

SCREW (2)
(50 FT. LBS.)

BOLT

FRAME
CROSSMEMBER

Rear engine mounts

tach to the engine (except air conditioning hoses). Remove all emission control equipment which may be damaged by the engine removal procedure. Remove the emission canister, coolant reservoir, and any other interfering items.

5. If the vehicle is equipped with air conditionning and/or power steering, remove the unit from the engine and position it out of the way without disconnecting the lines.

6. On six-cylinder models, attach a lifting sling to the engine cylinder head. On V8 models remove the carburetor and attach the engine lifting fixture to the carburetor flange studs on the intake manifold.

7. Raise the vehicle support the rear of the engine with a jack.

8. On automatic transmission models, drain the transmission and torque converter. On standard transmission models, disconnect the clutch torque shaft from the engine.

9. Disconnect the exhaust pipe/s from the exhaust manifold/s.

10. Remove the driveshaft.

11. Disconnect the transmission linkage and any wiring or cables which attach to the transmission.

12. Remove the engine rear support crossmember and remove the transmission.

13. Remove the bolts which attach the motor mounts to the chassis.

14. Lower the vehicle and attach a chain hoist or other lifting device to the engine.

15. Raise the engine and carefully remove it from the vehicle.

16. Reverse above procedure to install.

REMOVAL OF ENGINE ALONE

It is possible to remove the engine without removing the transmission. If this is to be done, care must be taken not to allow the weight of the engine to rest on the torque converter hub (automatic transmission) or transmission input shaft (standard transmission).

Perform Steps 1–7 and 10 of the "Removal of Transmission and Engine" operation. If the car has an automatic transmission, attach a remote starter switch to the engine, remove the inspection plate from the bellhousing, crank the engine to gain access to the torque converter-to-drive-plate attaching nuts and remove the nuts. Remove the starter. If the car has a manual transmission, disconnect the clutch torque shaft from the engine block and the clutch linkage from the adjustment rod. Remove the bolt which attaches the transmission filler tube to the engine (automatic transmission). Support the transmission and remove the bolts which attach the transmission to the engine or clutch bellhousing. When removing the engine, place a block of wood on the lifting point of a floor jack and position the jack under the transmission. As the engine is removed from the vehicle, raise and lower the jack as required so that the angle of the transmission duplicates as nearly as possible the angle of the engine. Use a clamp so that the torque converter doesn't fall out of the transmission.

When installing the engine into a vehicle with an automatic transmission, keep in mind that the crankshaft flange bolt circle, the inner and outer circle of holes in the driveplate, and the four tapped holes in the front face of the converter all have one hole offset.

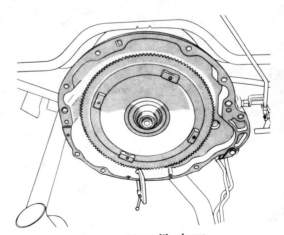

Holding torque converter with clamp

To ensure proper engine-torque converter balance, the torque converter must be mounted to the driveplate in the same location in which it was originally installed.

When installing the engine into a vehicle with a manual transmission, it may be necessary to disconnect the driveshaft, and turn the transmission output shaft, with the transmission in gear, to get the transmission input shaft splines to mesh with the inner hub on the clutch disc.

Cylinder Head
REMOVAL AND INSTALLATION

CAUTION: *Don't loosen the head bolts until the engine is thoroughly cool, to prevent warping.*

Six-Cylinder

1. Disconnect the battery.
2. The entire cooling system must be drained by opening the drain cock in the radiator and removing the drain plug on the right-side of the engine block.
3. Remove the vacuum line at the carburetor and distributor. Remove the air cleaner and fuel line.
4. Disconnect the accelerator linkage.
5. Remove the spark plug wires at the plugs.
6. Disconnect the heater hoses.
7. Disconnect the temperature sending wire.

8. Disconnect the exhaust pipe at the exhaust manifold flange.
9. Disconnect the diverter valve vacuum line at the intake manifold and take the air tube assembly from the cylinder head.
10. Remove the PCV and evaporative control system connections.
11. Remove the intake/exhaust manifold and carburetor as an assembly. Remove the valve cover.
12. Remove the rocker arm and shaft assembly.
13. Remove the pushrods, being sure to mark them so they may be installed in their original location.
14. Remove the head bolts and the cylinder head. If the head sticks, operate the starter to loosen it by compression or rap it upward with a soft hammer. Do not force anything between the head and block.
15. Clean the gasket surfaces of both the head and the block. Remove the carbon deposits from the top of each piston and from the combustion chambers.
16. Check the head for warpage as detailed in the "Engine Rebuilding" section.

Installation of the cylinder head is as follows:

17. Use a new head gasket and coat both of its sides with sealer.
18. Tighten the head bolts in three stages and the sequence illustrated to the proper torque specification.

The bolts should be retorqued after the

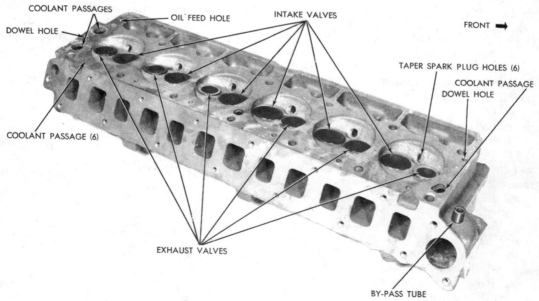

COOLANT PASSAGES — OIL FEED HOLE — INTAKE VALVES — FRONT ➡

DOWEL HOLE

TAPER SPARK PLUG HOLES (6)

COOLANT PASSAGE DOWEL HOLE

COOLANT PASSAGE (6)

EXHAUST VALVES

BY-PASS TUBE

Cylinder head—slant six engine

first 500 miles or so, unless a special gasket is used.

19. The rest of installation is the reverse of removal. Refill the cooling system when completed.

V8s

1. Drain the cooling system and disconnect the battery ground cable.

2. Remove the alternator, air cleaner, and fuel line.

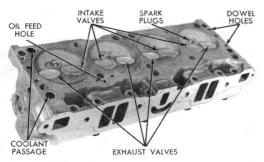

V8 cylinder head

3. Disconnect the accelerator linkage.

4. Remove the vacuum advance line from between the carburetor and the distributor.

5. Remove the distributor cap and wires as an assembly.

6. Disconnect the coil wires, water temperature sending unit, heater hoses, and by-pass hose.

7. Remove the closed ventilation system, the evaporative control system (if so equipped), and the valve covers.

8. Remove the intake manifold, ignition coil, and carburetor as an assembly. Remove the tappet chamber cover.

9. Remove the exhaust manifolds.

10. Remove the rocker and shaft assemblies.

11. Remove the pushrods and keep them in order to ensure installation in their original location.

12. Remove the head bolts from each cylinder head and remove the cylinder heads. If the head sticks, operate the starter to loosen it by compression or rap it upward with a soft hammer. Do not force anything between the head and the block.

Head torque sequence—6 cylinder engine

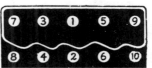

Head torque sequence—V8 engine

To install the cylinder heads, proceed as follows:

13. Clean all the gasket surfaces of the engine block and the cylinder heads. Remove the carbon deposits from the top of each piston and from the combustion chambers.

14. Check the head for warpage as detailed in the "Engine Rebuilding" section.

15. Coat new cylinder head gaskets with sealer, install the gaskets, and replace the cylinder heads.

16. Tighten the head bolts in the sequence shown in three stages until the specified torque is reached. The bolts should be retorqued after the first 500 miles or so unless special gaskets are used. The special gaskets don't require retorquing.

17. The rest of the installation procedure is the reverse of removal. The last step is to refill the cooling system.

Valve Guides

These engines do not have removable valve guides. 0.005, 0.015, and 0.030 in. oversize valves (stem diameter) are available. To use these, ream the worn guides to the smallest oversize which will clean up wear. Always start with the smallest reamer and proceed in steps to the largest, as this maintains the concentricity of the guide with the valve seat.

As an alternate procedure, some automotive machine shops bore out the stock guides and replace them with bronze or cast iron guides which are of stock internal dimensions.

OVERHAUL

See the "Engine Rebuilding" section at the end of this chapter for details on a valve job or cylinder head overhaul. This section should be consulted for checking head warpage, even if no other work is to be done on the head.

Rocker Shafts

REMOVAL AND INSTALLATION

Six-Cylinder

1. Remove the closed ventilation system.

2. Remove the evaporative control system (if so equipped).

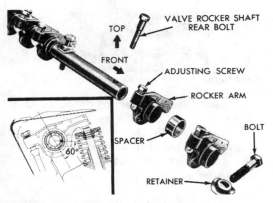

Six-cylinder rocker arm and shaft assembly

3. Remove the valve cover with its gasket.

4. Take out the rocker arm and shaft assembly securing bolts and remove the rocker arm and shaft.

5. Reverse the above for installation. The oil hole on the end of the shaft must be on the top and point toward the front of the engine to provide proper lubrication to the rocker arms. The special bolt goes to the rear. Torque the rocker arm bolts to 25 ft. lbs. and be sure to adjust the valves.

V8s

The stamped steel rocker arms are arranged on one rocker arm shaft per cylinder head. To remove the rocker arms and shaft:

1. Disconnect the spark plug wires.

2. Disconnect the closed ventilation and evaporative control system (if so equipped).

3. Remove the valve covers with their gaskets.

4. Remove the rocker shaft bolts and retainers, and lift off the rocker arm assembly.

5. Reverse the above procedure to install.

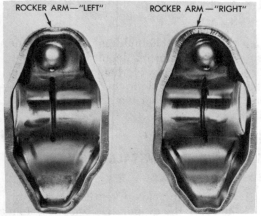

V8 rocker arm identification

The notch on the end of both rocker shafts should point to the engine centerline and toward the front of the engine on the left cylinder head, or toward the rear on the right cylinder head. Torque the rocker shaft bolts to 17 ft. lbs.

Intake Manifold

REMOVAL AND INSTALLATION

Six-Cylinder Combination Manifold

1. Remove the air cleaner and the fuel line from the carburetor.

2. Disconnect the accelerator linkage. Detach the vacuum lines, crankcase vent hose, carburetor vent line, carburetor air heater, and automatic choke rod.

3. Disconnect the exhaust pipe at the exhaust manifold flange. Remove the carburetor.

4. Remove the manifold assembly-to-cylinder head nuts and washers and remove the intake and exhaust manifolds as a single unit. The manifolds may be separated by removing the three bolts which hold them together.

5. Installation is the reverse of the removal procedure. When installing the manifold assembly, use new gaskets and a good commercial sealer. Loosen the three bolts which secure the intake manifold to the exhaust manifold to maintain proper alignment in relation to each other and the block. Torque these three bolts to 20 ft. lbs. in this sequence: inner bolts first, then the outer two bolts. Torque the manifold assembly to cylinder head nuts to 10 ft. lbs.

V8s

1. Drain the cooling system and disconnect the battery.

2. Remove the air cleaner and fuel line

V8 intake manifold—torque sequence

from the carburetor. Disconnect any interfering air pump system components.

3. Disconnect the accelerator linkage.

4. Remove the vacuum control line between the carburetor and distributor.

5. Remove the distributor cap and wires.

6. Disconnect the coil wires, temperature sending unit wires, and heater and by-pass hoses.

7. Remove the intake manifold securing bolts and remove the manifold and carburetor as an assembly.

8. To install the manifold, reverse the removal procedure. Be sure to torque the manifold in three steps and remember to use a good commercial sealer on new manifold gaskets.

Exhaust Manifold

REMOVAL AND INSTALLATION

Six-Cylinder

The intake and exhaust manifolds are combined in one unit on this engine. Refer to the intake manifold removal procedure.

V8

1. Disconnect the exhaust manifold at the flange where it mates to the exhaust pipe.

2. If the vehicle is equipped with air injection and/or a carburetor-heated air stove, remove them.

3. Remove the exhaust manifold by removing the securing bolts and washers. To reach these bolts, it may be necessary to jack the engine slightly off its front mounts. When the exhaust manifold is removed, sometimes the securing studs will screw out with the nuts. If this occurs, the studs must be replaced with the aid of sealing compound on the coarse thread ends. If this is not done, water leaks may develop at the studs. To install the exhaust manifold, reverse the removal procedure. No conical washers are used on the center branch.

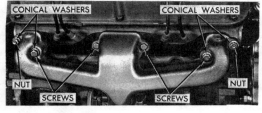

V8 exhaust manifold

Timing Cover and Chain

NOTE: *Check the slack in the chain after installation.*

REMOVAL AND INSTALLATION

Six-Cylinder

1. Drain the cooling system and disconnect the battery.

2. Remove the radiator and fan.

3. With a puller, remove the vibration damper.

4. Loosen the oil pan bolts to allow clearance, and remove the timing case cover and gasket.

5. Slide the crankshaft oil slinger off the front of the crankshaft.

6. Remove the camshaft sprocket bolt.

7. Remove the timing chain with the camshaft sprocket.

8. On installation: Turn the crankshaft to line up the timing mark on the crankshaft sprocket with the centerline of the camshaft (without the chain).

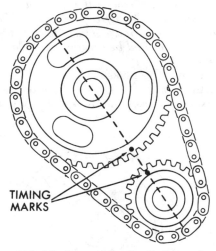

Alignment of timing marks—6 cylinder engine

9. Install the camshaft sprocket and chain Align the timing marks.

10. Torque the camshaft sprocket bolt to 35 ft. lbs.

11. Replace the oil slinger.

12. Reinstall the timing case cover with a new gasket and torque the bolts to 17 ft. lbs. Retighten the engine oil pan to 17 ft. lbs.

13. Press the vibration damper back on.

14. Replace the radiator and hoses.

15. Refill the cooling system.

V8

1. Disconnect the battery and drain the cooling system.

2. Remove the vibration damper pulley. Unbolt and remove the vibration damper with a puller. Remove the fuel lines and fuel pump, then loosen the oil pan bolts and remove the front bolt on each side.

3. Remove the timing gear cover and the crankshaft oil slinger.

4. Remove the camshaft sprocket lockbolt, securing cup washer, and fuel pump eccentric. Remove the timing chain with both sprockets.

5. To begin the installation procedure, place the camshaft and crankshaft sprockets on a flat surface with the timing indicators on an imaginary centerline through both sprocket bores. Place the timing chain around both sprockets. Be sure that the timing marks are in alignment.

CAUTION: *When installing the timing chain, have an assistant support the camshaft with a screwdriver to prevent it from contacting the freeze plug in the rear of the engine block. Remove the distributor and the oil pump/distributor drive gear. Position the screwdriver against the rear side of the cam gear and be careful not to damage the cam lobes.*

6. Turn the crankshaft and camshaft to align them with the keyway location in the crankshaft sprocket and the keyway or dowel hole in the camshaft sprocket.

7. Lift the sprockets and timing chain while keeping the sprockets tight against the chain in the correct position. Slide both sprockets evenly onto their respective shafts.

8. Use a straightedge to measure the alignment of the sprocket timing marks. They must be perfectly aligned.

9. Install the fuel pump eccentric, cup washer, and camshaft sprocket lockbolt, and torque to 35 ft. lbs. If camshaft end play exceeds 0.010 in., install a new thrust plate. It should be 0.002–0.006 in. with the new plate.

CHECKING TIMING CHAIN SLACK

1. Position a scale next to the timing chain to detect any movement in the chain.

2. Place a torque wrench and socket on the camshaft sprocket attaching bolt. Apply either 30 ft. lbs. (if the cylinder heads are installed on the engine) or 15 ft. lbs. (cylinder heads removed) of force to the bolt and rotate the bolt in the direction of crankshaft rotation in order to remove all slack from the chain.

3. While applying torque to the camshaft

Checking timing chain slack—six cylinder

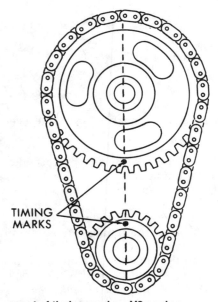

Alignment of timing marks—V8 engine

Checking timing chain slack—V8

sprocket bolt, the crankshaft should not be allowed to rotate. It may be necessary to block the crankshaft to prevent rotation.

4. Position the scale over the edge of a timing chain link and apply an equal amount of torque in the opposite direction. If the movement of the chain exceeds ⅛ in., replace the chain.

TIMING GEAR COVER SEAL REPLACEMENT

NOTE: *A seal remover and installer tool is required to prevent seal damage.*

1. Using a seal puller, separate the seal from the retainer.
2. Pull the seal from the case.
3. To install the seal place it face down in the case with the seal lips downward.
4. Seat the seal tightly against the cover face. There should be a maximum clearance of .0014 in. between the seal and the cover. Be careful not to overcompress the seal.

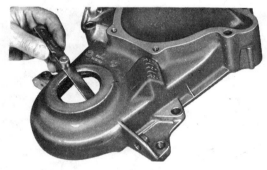

Inspecting seal for proper seating

Camshaft
REMOVAL AND INSTALLATION
Six-Cylinder

1. Remove the cylinder head, timing gear cover, camshaft sprocket, and timing chain.
2. Remove the valve tappets, keeping them in order to ensure installation in their original locations.
3. Remove the crankshaft sprocket.
4. Remove the distributor and oil pump.
5. Remove the fuel pump.
6. Install a long bolt into the front of the camshaft to facilitate its removal.
7. Remove the camshaft, being careful not to damage the cam bearings with the cam lobes.
8. Lubricate the camshaft lobes and bearing journals. It is recommended that 1 pt of

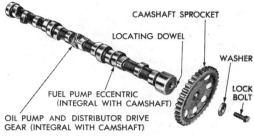

Six-cylinder camshaft

Camshaft removal

Chrysler Crankcase Conditioner be added to the initial crankcase oil fill.

9. Install the camshaft in the engine block. From this point, reverse the removal procedure.

V8

1. Remove the cylinder heads. Remove the timing gear cover, the camshaft and crankshaft sprocket, and the timing chain.
2. Remove the valve tappets, keeping them in order to ensure installation in their original location.
3. Remove the distributor and lift out the oil pump and distributor driveshaft.
4. Remove the camshaft thrust plate.
5. Install a long bolt into the front of the camshaft and remove the camshaft, being careful not to damage the cam bearings with the cam lobes.
6. Lubricate the camshaft lobes and bearing journals. It is recommended that 1 pt. of Chrysler Crankcase Conditioner be added to the initial crankcase oil fill. Insert the camshaft into the engine block within 2 in. of its final position in the block.

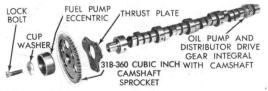

V8 camshaft

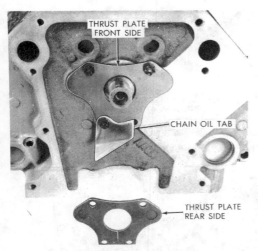

V8 timing chain oil tab installation

Positioning the distributor drive gear

7. Have an assistant support the camshaft with a screwdriver to prevent the camshaft from contacting the freeze plug in the rear of the engine block. Remove the distributor and the oil pump/distributor drive gear. Position the screwdriver against the rear side of the cam gear and be careful not to damage the cam lobes.

8. Replace the camshaft thrust plate. If camshaft end play exceeds 0.010 in., install a new thrust plate. It should be 0.002–0.006 in. with the new plate.

9. Install the oil pump and distributor driveshaft. Install the distributor.

10. Inspect the crown of all the tappet faces with a straightedge. Replace any tappets which have dished or worn surfaces. Install the tappets.

11. Install the timing gear, gear cover, and the cylinder heads.

Piston and Connecting Rods

The following are specific instructions for all Aspen/Volare engines. For more detailed instructions, see the "Engine Rebuilding" section at the end of this chapter.

The notch on the top of each piston must face the front of the engine.

To position the connecting rod correctly, the oil squirt hole should point to the right-side on all six-cylinder engines. On all V8 engines, the larger chamber of the lower connecting rod bore must face toward the crankpin journal fillet.

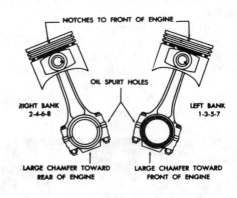

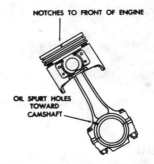

Piston and connecting rod positioning

ENGINE LUBRICATION

Oil Pan

REMOVAL AND INSTALLATION
Six-Cylinder

1. Drain the radiator, disconnect the radiator hoses, disconnect the battery, and remove the oil dipstick. Remove the fan shroud attaching screws, and loop the shroud rearward over the engine. Jack up the vehicle and drain the oil.

2. Remove the steering arm center link. Disconnect the idler arm ball joints.

3. Disconnect the exhaust pipe from the manifold and secure it out of the way.

4. Support the block with a jack and wooden block. Remove the front engine mounts and raise the engine 1½ to 2 inches. Take out the oil pan attaching bolts. Rotate the engine crankshaft in order to clear the counterweights. Remove the oil pan.

5. To install the pan, reverse the removal procedure. Torque the pan bolts to 200 in. lbs. Use a new gasket.

V8

1. Disconnect the battery and remove the dipstick.

2. Jack up the vehicle and drain the oil. Remove the torque converter-to-engine left housing strut.

3. Remove the idler arms and steering linkage ball joints from the center link.

4. Disconnect the exhaust pipe(s) from the manifold and move it out of the way.

5. Place a jack under the transmission and remove transmission-to-rear engine mount bolts. Raise the transmission to clear the oil pan. Remove the oil pan bolts and the oil pan.

6. To install the pan, be sure that the oil strainer will touch the bottom of the pan.

7. Using a new gasket, install the oil pan. Torque the bolts to 200 in. lbs. On 360 engines, be certain that the notches on the side gaskets overlap the rear seal.

8. Install the engine-to-converter housing strut.

9. From this point, reverse the removal procedure.

Rear Main Bearing Oil Seal

Replacement oil seals are the split rubber type. Both halves of the seal must be replaced at the same time.

1. Remove the oil pan. On V8 engines, remove the oil pump.

2. Remove the rear main bearing cap and seal retainer.

3. Remove the lower half rope seal from the bearing cap. Remove the upper half by driving on either exposed end with a short piece of ³/₁₆ in. brazing wire. As the end of the seal becomes exposed, grasp it with a pair of pliers and pull it gently from the block.

4. Loosen the crankshaft main bearing caps just enough to allow the crankshaft to drop ¹/₁₆ in. Do not allow the crankshaft to

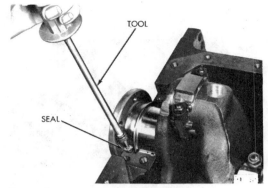
Removing upper seal—six cylinder

Trimming oil seal

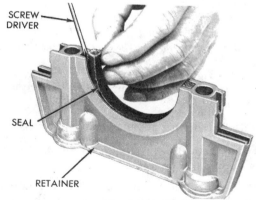
Removing lower seal—six cylinder

drop enough to permit the main bearings to become displaced.

5. Wipe the crankshaft clean and lightly oil the crankshaft and new seal before installation.

6. Hold the seal tightly against the crank-

Removing upper seal—V8

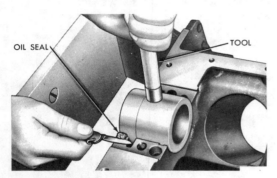

Trimming V8 rear main seal

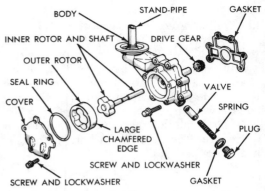

Oil pump—6 cylinder engine

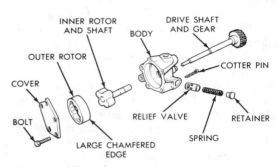

Oil pump—V8 engine

shaft (with the paint stripe to the rear) and install the upper seal half into its groove. If necessary, rotate the crankshaft as the seal is pushed in place.

7. Install the lower seal half into the rear main bearing cap, with the paint stripe to the rear.

8. Install the rear main bearing cap.

CAUTION: *Make sure that all main bearings are properly located before tightening the rest of the bearing caps.*

9. Tighten the rest of the bearing caps.

10. Install the oil pump, if removed, and oil pan.

Oil Pump

REMOVAL AND INSTALLATION

Six-Cylinder

1. Drain the radiator, disconnect its upper and lower hoses, and remove the fan shroud.

2. Raise the vehicle and remove the front engine mounting bolts. Jack the engine up 2 in. under the right front corner of the oil pan.

3. Remove the oil filter, oil pump attaching bolts, and pump assembly.

4. Installation is the reverse of the removal procedures. Always us a new O-ring and gaskets. Torque the bolts to 200 in. lbs.

V8s

1. Remove the oil pan.

2. Remove the oil pump from the rear main bearing cap.

3. Reverse the above steps to install. Torque the bolts to 30 ft. lbs.

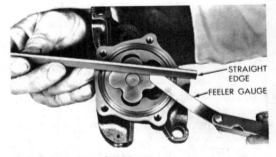

Measuring rotor clearance

ENGINE COOLING

Refer to Chapter 1 for the coolant level checking procedure and to the Appendix for "Antifreeze" charts. The coolant should periodically be drained and the system flushed with clean water, at the intervals specified in

Chapter 1. Service stations have reverse flushing equipment available; there are also permanently-installed do-it-yourself reverse flushing attachments available at a reasonable price.

There is a coolant drain cock at the bottom of the radiator. Six-cylinder engines have a coolant drain plug on the right side of the engine block; V8s have one on each side.

The coolant should always be maintained at a minimum of −20°F freezing protection, regardless of the prevailing temperature. This concentration assures rust protection and the highest possible boiling point. It also prevents the heater core from freezing on air-conditioned cars.

Certain simple modifications can be made to the cooling system for improved performance under severe conditions. The fan can be replaced with either a high-output unit or a clutch type designed for air conditioned cars or a flextype. The flex unit flattens out at high rpm, moving less air and reducing the horsepower required to drive it.

Radiator

REMOVAL AND INSTALLATION

1. Drain the cooling system. Detach and plug the oil cooling lines for the automatic transmission.

2. Disconnect the hose clamps and remove the upper and lower radiator hoses from the radiator.

3. Remove the fan shroud. Slide the shroud rearward over the fan and rest it on the engine.

4. Remove the radiator attaching bolts and lift the radiator out of the car.

5. Reverse the above steps to install. On automatic transmission cars, check the fluid level. Fill the cooling system with the proper misture of anti-freeze and water. Run the engine with the heater on and the radiator cap off for about 10 minutes, checking the level frequently.

Water Pump

REMOVAL AND INSTALLATION

Six-Cylinder Without Air Conditioning And/Or Air Pump

1. Drain the cooling system. Remove the battery. If the engine has a fan shroud, remove and swing it back over the engine.

2. Remove the power steering and alternator belts.

3. Take off the fan, spacer, pulley, and bolts as a unit.

4. Move the lower by-pass hose clamp to the center of the hose. Disconnect the heater hose and the lower hose of the water pump.

5. Remove the water pump bolts and the pump.

6. Reverse the procedure for installation.

Six-Cylinder With Air Conditioning And/Or Air Pump

1. Remove the battery and drain the cooling system. Remove the fan shroud and swing it back over the engine.

2. Disconnect the transmission oil cooler lines (if automatic transmission) and remove the lower radiator hoses. Cap the openings to prevent the entry of dirt and excessive fluid loss.

3. Remove the radiator.

4. Loosen the alternator, power steering pump, idler pulley, and air pump.

5. Take off the fan, spacer, pulley, and bolts as an assembly. Remove all the belts.

6. Remove the compressor and/or air pump bracket and secure it out of way.

7. Move the lower by-pass hose clamp to the center of the hose. Disconnect the heater hose.

8. Remove the water pump bolts and the pump.

9. Reverse the procedure for installation.

V8

1. Drain the cooling system and move the fan shroud out of the way.

2. Disconnect the transmission oil cooler lines (automatic) and all radiator hoses. Cap the openings to prevent the entry of dirt or excessive fluid loss.

3. Remove the radiator, if necessary.

4. Loosen the alternator adjusting strap bolts. Remove the belts.

5. On engines with no air conditioning, remove the alternator bracket bolts from the water pump. Swing the alternator out of the way and tighten the pivot bolt. On engines with air conditioning, remove the idler pulley assembly and alternator with the adjusting bracket.

6. Remove the fan, spacer/fluid drive, pulley, and bolts as an assembly.

CAUTION: *Do not let fluid drain into the fan-drive bearing.*

7. Disconnect the heater and all by-pass hoses.

8. Remove the compressor-to-front mounting bracket bolts.

9. Remove the water pump attaching bolts and the water pump.

10. Carefully lift the compressor out of the way.

On installation:

11. Install the by-pass hose and position the clamp in the center of the hose.

12. Install the pump with a new gasket and torque it to 30 ft. lbs. Be sure that the pump turns freely.

13. Install the heater hose and route it near the by-pass hose clamps.

14. On V8s with air conditioning, install the front bracket on the compressor. Torque the bracket bolts to 50 ft. lbs. Torque the pump bolts to 30 ft. lbs.

15. Replace the alternator, bracket, and idler pulley assembly. Torque to 30 ft. lbs.

16. Install the compressor clutch assembly (if applicable).

17. Install the fan assembly. Check and adjust all belts.

18. Install the radiator, hoses, and transmission cooling lines.

19. Install the fan shroud and fill the cooling system. Check the fluid level in the transmission.

Thermostat

The thermostat is located in the engine water outlet housing at the front of the engine, connected to the upper radiator hose. Poor heater output is often caused by a thermostat stuck in the open position; occasionally a thermostat sticks shut causing overheating.

CAUTION: *Do not attempt to correct an overheating condition by permanently removing the thermostat. This will result in the coolant flowing through the radiator too fast to be cooled properly or in coolant loss. Thermostat flow restriction is designed into the system.*

V8 thermostat housing

REMOVAL AND INSTALLATION

1. Partially drain the cooling system to a level slightly below the thermostat. The thermostat is at the engine end of the upper radiator hose.

2. Remove the upper radiator hose from the thermostat housing.

3. Remove the thermostat housing bolts. Remove the housing.

4. Remove the thermostat from the block.

5. To install, reverse the above steps. Use a new gasket and gasket sealer. Always place the thermostat with the temperature sensing end facing into the block. On the six, the vent hole must be up.

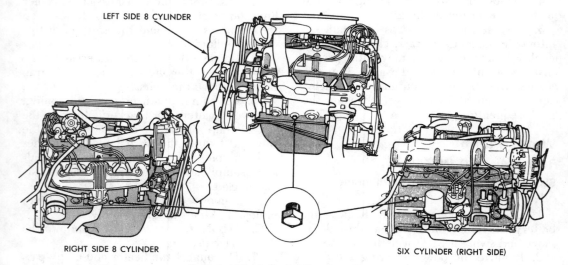

LEFT SIDE 8 CYLINDER

RIGHT SIDE 8 CYLINDER

SIX CYLINDER (RIGHT SIDE)

Cylinder Block Drain Plug Locations

ENGINE REBUILDING

Most procedures involved in rebuilding an engine are fairly standard, regardless of the type of engine involved. This section is a guide accepted rebuilding procedures. Examples of standard rebuilding practices are illustrated and should be used along with specific details concerning your particular engine, found earlier in this chapter.

The procedures given here are those used by any competent rebuilder. Obviously some of the procedures cannot be performed by the do-it-yourself mechanic, but are provided so that you will be familiar with the services that should be offered by rebuilding or machine shops. As an example, in most instances, it is more profitable for the home mechanic to remove the cylinder heads, buy the necessary parts (new valves, seals, keepers, keys, etc.) and deliver these to a machine shop for the necessary work. In this way you will save the money to remove and install the cylinder head and the mark-up on parts.

On the other hand, most of the work involved in rebuilding the lower end is well within the scope of the do-it-yourself mechanic. Only work such as hot-tanking, actually boring the block or Magnafluxing (invisible crack detection) need be sent to a machine shop.

Tools

The tools required for basic engine rebuilding should, with a few exceptions, be those included in a mechanic's tool kit. An accurate torque wrench, and a dial indicator (reading in thousandths) mounted on a universal base should be available. Special tools, where required, are available from the major tool suppliers. The services of a competent automotive machine shop must also be readily available.

Precautions

Aluminum has become increasingly popular for use in engines, due to its low weight and excellent heat transfer characteristics. The following precautions must be observed when handling aluminum (or any other) engine parts:
—Never hot-tank aluminum parts.
—Remove all aluminum parts (identification tags, etc.) from engine parts before hot-tanking (otherwise they will be removed during the process).
—Always coat threads lightly with engine oil or anti-seize compounds before installation, to prevent seizure.
—Never over-torque bolts or spark plugs in aluminum threads. Should stripping occur, threads can be restored using any of a number of thread repair kits available (see next section).

Inspection Techniques

Magnaflux and Zyglo are inspection techniques used to locate material flaws, such as stress cracks. Magnaflux is a magnetic process, applicable only to ferrous materials. The Zyglo process coats the matrial with a fluorescent dye penetrant, and any material may be tested using Zyglo. Specific checks of suspected surface cracks may be made at lower cost and more readily using spot check dye. The dye is sprayed onto the suspected area, wiped off, and the area is then sprayed with a developer. Cracks then will show up brightly.

Overhaul

The section is divided into two parts. The first, Cylinder Head Reconditioning, assumes that the cylinder head is removed from the engine, all manifolds are removed, and the cylinder head is on a workbench. The camshaft should be removed from overhead cam cylinder heads. The second section, Cylinder Block Reconditioning, covers the block, pistons, connecting rods and crankshaft. It is assumed that the engine is mounted on a work stand, and the cylinder head and all accessories are removed.

Procedures are identified as follows:
Unmarked—Basic procedures that must be performed in order to successfully complete the rebuilding process.
Starred (*)—Procedures that should be performed to ensure maximum performance and engine life.
Double starred (**)—Procedures that may be performed to increase engine performance and reliability.

When assembling the engine, any parts that will be in frictional contact must be pre-lubricated, to provide protection on initial start-up. Any product specifically formulated for this purpose may be used. NOTE: *Do not use engine oil.* Where semi-permanent (locked but removable) installation of bolts or nuts is desired, threads should be cleaned and located with Loctite® or a similar product (non-hardening).

Repairing Damaged Threads

Several methods of repairing damaged threads are available. Heli-Coil® (shown here), Keenserts® and Microdot® are among the most widely used. All involve basically the same principle—drilling out stripped threads, tapping the hole and installing a pre-wound insert—making welding, plugging and oversize fasteners unnecessary.

Two types of thread repair inserts are usually supplied—a standard type for most Inch Coarse, Inch Fine, Metric Coarse and Metric Fine thread sizes and a spark plug type to fit most spark plug port sizes. Consult the individual manufacturer's catalog to determine exact applications. Typical thread repair kits will contain a selection of pre-wound threaded inserts, a tap (corresponding to the outside diameter threads of the insert) and an installation tool. Spark plug inserts usually differ because they require a tap equipped with pilot threads and a combined reamer/tap section. Most manufacturers also supply blister-packed thread repair inserts separately in addition to a master kit containing a variety of taps and inserts plus installation tools.

Before effecting a repair to a threaded hole, remove any snapped, broken or damaged bolts or studs. Penetrating oil can be used to free frozen threads; the offending item can be removed with locking pliers or with a screw or stud extractor. After the hole is clear, the thread can be repaired, as follows:

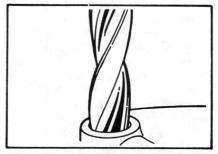

Drill out the damaged threads with specified drill. Drill completely through the hole or to the bottom of a blind hole

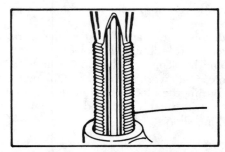

With the tap supplied, tap the hole to receive the thread insert. Keep the tap well oiled and back it out frequently to avoid clogging the threads

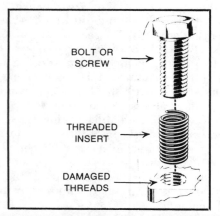

Damaged bolt holes can be repaired with thread repair inserts

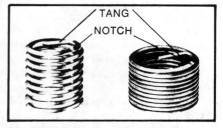

Standard thread repair insert (left) and spark plug thread insert (right)

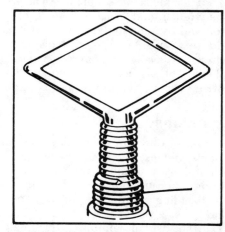

Screw the threaded insert onto the installation tool until the tang engages the slot. Screw the insert into the tapped hole until it is ¼–½ turn below the top surface. After installation break off the tang with a hammer and punch

Standard Torque Specifications and Fastener Markings

The Newton-metre has been designated the world standard for measuring torque and will gradually replace the foot-pound and kilogram-meter. In the absence of specific torques, the following chart can be used as a guide to the maximum safe torque of a particular size/grade of fastener.

- There is no torque difference for fine or coarse threads.
- Torque values are based on clean, dry threads. Reduce the value by 10% if threads are oiled prior to assembly.
- The torque required for aluminum components or fasteners is considerably less.

U. S. BOLTS

SAE Grade Number				1 or 2			5			6 or 7	
Bolt Markings											
Manufacturer's marks may vary—number of lines always 2 less than the grade number.											
Usage			*Frequent*			*Frequent*			*Infrequent*		
Bolt Size (inches)—(Thread)			*Maximum Torque*			*Maximum Torque*			*Maximum Torque*		
	Ft-Lb	*kgm*	*Nm*	*Ft-Lb*	*kgm*	*Nm*	*Ft-Lb*	*kgm*	*Nm*		
¼—20	5	0.7	6.8	8	1.1	10.8	10	1.4	13.5		
—28	6	0.8	8.1	10	1.4	13.6					
⁵⁄₁₆—18	11	1.5	14.9	17	2.3	23.0	19	2.6	25.8		
—24	13	1.8	17.6	19	2.6	25.7					
⅜—16	18	2.5	24.4	31	4.3	42.0	34	4.7	46.0		
—24	20	2.75	27.1	35	4.8	47.5					
⁷⁄₁₆—14	28	3.8	37.0	49	6.8	66.4	55	7.6	74.5		
—20	30	4.2	40.7	55	7.6	74.5					
½—13	39	5.4	52.8	75	10.4	101.7	85	11.75	115.2		
—20	41	5.7	55.6	85	11.7	115.2					
⁹⁄₁₆—12	51	7.0	69.2	110	15.2	149.1	120	16.6	162.7		
—18	55	7.6	74.5	120	16.6	162.7					
⅝—11	83	11.5	112.5	150	20.7	203.3	167	23.0	226.5		
—18	95	13.1	128.8	170	23.5	230.5					
¾—10	105	14.5	142.3	270	37.3	366.0	280	38.7	379.6		
—16	115	15.9	155.9	295	40.8	400.0					
⅞— 9	160	22.1	216.9	395	54.6	535.5	440	60.9	596.5		
—14	175	24.2	237.2	435	60.1	589.7					
1— 8	236	32.5	318.6	590	81.6	799.9	660	91.3	894.8		
—14	250	34.6	338.9	660	91.3	849.8					

METRIC BOLTS

NOTE: *Metric bolts are marked with a number indicating the relative strength of the bolt. These numbers have nothing to do with size.*

Description	Torque ft-lbs (Nm)			
Thread size x pitch (mm)	Head mark—4		Head mark—7	
6 x 1.0	2.2–2.9	(3.0–3.9)	3.6–5.8	(4.9–7.8)
8 x 1.25	5.8–8.7	(7.9–12)	9.4–14	(13–19)
10 x 1.25	12–17	(16–23)	20–29	(27–39)
12 x 1.25	21–32	(29–43)	35–53	(47–72)
14 x 1.5	35–52	(48–70)	57–85	(77–110)
16 x 1.5	51–77	(67–100)	90–120	(130–160)
18 x 1.5	74–110	(100–150)	130–170	(180–230)
20 x 1.5	110–140	(150–190)	190–240	(160–320)
22 x 1.5	150–190	(200–260)	250–320	(340–430)
24 x 1.5	190–240	(260–320)	310–410	(420–550)

NOTE: *This engine rebuilding section is a guide to accepted rebuilding procedures. Typical examples of standard rebuilding procedures are illustrated. Use these procedures along with the detailed instructions earlier in this chapter, concerning your particular engine.*

Cylinder Head Reconditioning

Procedure	Method
Remove the cylinder head:	See the engine service procedures earlier in this chapter for details concerning specific engines.
Identify the valves:	Invert the cylinder head, and number the valve faces front to rear, using a permanent felt-tip marker.
Remove the rocker arms:	Remove the rocker arms with shaft(s) or balls and nuts. Wire the sets of rockers, balls and nuts together, and identify according to the corresponding valve.
Remove the valves and springs:	Using an appropriate valve spring compressor (depending on the configuration of the cylinder head), compress the valve springs. Lift out the keepers with needlenose pliers, release the compressor, and remove the valve, spring, and spring retainer. See the engine service procedures earlier in this chapter for details concerning specific engines.
Check the valve stem-to-guide clearance: 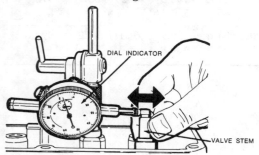 Check the valve stem-to-guide clearance	Clean the valve stem with lacquer thinner or a similar solvent to remove all gum and varnish. Clean the valve guides using solvent and an expanding wire-type valve guide cleaner. Mount a dial indicator so that the stem is at 90° to the valve stem, as close to the valve guide as possible. Move the valve off its seat, and measure the valve guide-to-stem clearance by rocking the stem back and forth to actuate the dial indicator. Measure the valve stems using a micrometer, and compare to specifications, to determine whether stem or guide wear is responsible for excessive clearance. NOTE: *Consult the Specifications tables earlier in this chapter.*

Cylinder Head Reconditioning

Procedure	Method
De-carbon the cylinder head and valves: 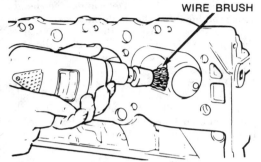 WIRE BRUSH **Remove the carbon from the cylinder head with a wire brush and electric drill**	Chip carbon away from the valve heads, combustion chambers, and ports, using a chisel made of hardwood. Remove the remaining deposits with a stiff wire brush. NOTE: *Be sure that the deposits are actually removed, rather than burnished.*
Hot-tank the cylinder head (cast iron heads only): CAUTION: *Do not hot-tank aluminum parts.*	Have the cylinder head hot-tanked to remove grease, corrosion, and scale from the water passages. NOTE: *In the case of overhead cam cylinder heads, consult the operator to determine whether the camshaft bearings will be damaged by the caustic solution.*
Degrease the remaining cylinder head parts:	Clean the remaining cylinder head parts in an engine cleaning solvent. Do not remove the protective coating from the springs.
Check the cylinder head for warpage: 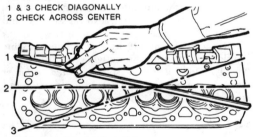 1 & 3 CHECK DIAGONALLY 2 CHECK ACROSS CENTER **Check the cylinder head for warpage**	Place a straight-edge across the gasket surface of the cylinder head. Using feeler gauges, determine the clearance at the center of the straight-edge. If warpage exceeds .003″ in a 6″ span, or .006″ over the total length, the cylinder head must be resurfaced. NOTE: *If warpage exceeds the manufacturer's maximum tolerance for material removal, the cylinder head must be replaced.* When milling the cylinder heads of V-type engines, the intake manifold mounting position is altered, and must be corrected by milling the manifold flange a proportionate amount.
*Knurl the valve guides: 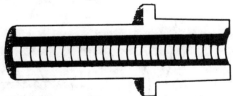 **Cut-away view of a knurled valve guide**	*Valve guides which are not excessively worn or distorted may, in some cases, be knurled rather than replaced. Knurling is a process in which metal is displaced and raised, thereby reducing clearance. Knurling also provides excellent oil control. The possibility of knurling rather than replacing valve guides should be discussed with a machinist.
Replace the valve guides: NOTE: *Valve guides should only be replaced if damaged or if an oversize valve stem is not available.*	See the engine service procedures earlier in this chapter for details concerning specific engines. Depending on the type of cylinder head, valve guides may be pressed, hammered, or shrunk in. In cases where the guides are shrunk into the head, replacement should be left to an equipped machine shop. In other

Cylinder Head Reconditioning

Procedure	Method

A—VALVE GUIDE I.D.   B—LARGER THAN THE VALVE GUIDE O.D.

WASHERS

A—VALVE GUIDE I.D.   B—LARGER THAN THE VALVE GUIDE O.D.

Valve guide installation tool using washers for installation

cases, the guides are replaced using a stepped drift (see illustration). Determine the height above the boss that the guide must extend, and obtain a stack of washers, their I.D. similar to the guide's O.D., of that height. Place the stack of washers on the guide, and insert the guide into the boss.

NOTE: *Valve guides are often tapered or beveled for installation.* Using the stepped installation tool (see illustration), press or tap the guides into position. Ream the guides according to the size of the valve stem.

Replace valve seat inserts:

Replacement of valve seat inserts which are worn beyond resurfacing or broken, if feasible, must be done by a machine shop.

Resurface (grind) the valve face:

FOR DIMENSIONS, REFER TO SPECIFICATIONS

CHECK FOR BENT STEM

DIAMETER

VALVE FACE ANGLE

1/32″ MINIMUM

THIS LINE PARALLEL WITH VALVE HEAD

Critical valve dimensions

Using a valve grinder, resurface the valves according to specifications given earlier in this chapter.

CAUTION: *Valve face angle is not always identical to valve seat angle.* A minimum margin of $1/32''$ should remain after grinding the valve. The valve stem top should also be squared and resurfaced, by placing the stem in the V-block of the grinder, and turning it while pressing lightly against the grinding wheel.

NOTE: *Do not grind sodium filled exhaust valves on a machine. These should be hand lapped.*

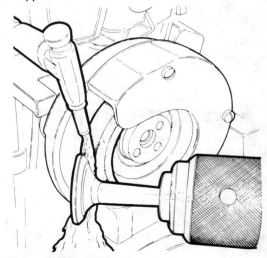

Valve grinding by machine

Cylinder Head Reconditioning

Procedure	Method

Resurface the valve seats using reamers of grinder:

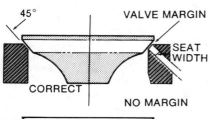

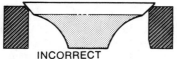

Valve seat width and centering

Reaming the valve seat with a hand reamer

Select a reamer of the correct seat angle, slightly larger than the diameter of the valve seat, and assemble it with a pilot of the correct size. Install the pilot into the valve guide, and using steady pressure, turn the reamer clockwise.

CAUTION: *Do not turn the reamer counterclockwise.* Remove only as much material as necessary to clean the seat. Check the concentricity of the seat (following). If the dye method is not used, coat the valve face with Prussian blue dye, install and rotate it on the valve seat. Using the dye marked area as a centering guide, center and narrow the valve seat to specifications with correction cutters.

NOTE: *When no specifications are available, minimum seat width for exhaust valves should be* $5/64''$*, intake valves* $1/16''$*.*

After making correction cuts, check the position of the valve seat on the valve face using Prussian blue dye.

To resurface the seat with a power grinder, select a pilot of the correct size and coarse stone of the proper angle. Lubricate the pilot and move the stone on and off the valve seat at 2 cycles per second, until all flaws are gone. Finish the seat with a fine stone. If necessary the seat can be corrected or narrowed using correction stones.

Check the valve seat concentricity:

Check the valve seat concentricity with a dial gauge

Coat the valve face with Prussian blue dye, install the valve, and rotate it on the valve seat. If the entire seat becomes coated, and the valve is known to be concentric, the seat is concentric.

*Install the dial gauge pilot into the guide, and rest of the arm on the valve seat. Zero the gauge, and rotate the arm around the seat. Run-out should not exceed .002".

Cylinder Head Reconditioning

Procedure	Method

*Lap the valves:
NOTE: *Valve lapping is done to ensure efficient sealing of resurfaced valves and seats.*

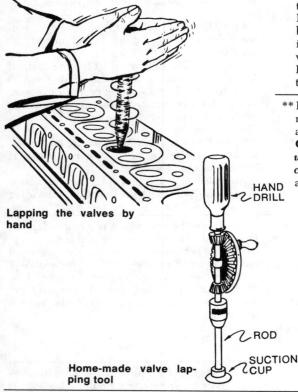

Lapping the valves by hand

HAND DRILL

ROD

SUCTION CUP

Home-made valve lapping tool

Invert the cylinder head, lightly lubricate the valve stems, and install the valves in the head as numbered. Coat valve seats with fine grinding compound, and attach the lapping tool suction cup to a valve head.
NOTE: *Moisten the suction cup.* Rotate the tool between the palms, changing position and lifting the tool often to prevent grooving. Lap the valve until a smooth, polished seat is evident. Remove the valve and tool, and rinse away all traces of grinding compound.

** Fasten a suction cup to a piece of drill rod, and mount the rod in a hand drill. Proceed as above, using the hand drill as a lapping tool.
CAUTION: *Due to the higher speeds involved when using the hand drill, care must be exercised to avoid grooving the seat.* Lift the tool and change direction of rotation often.

Check the valve springs:

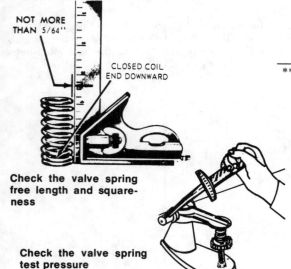

NOT MORE THAN 5/64"

CLOSED COIL END DOWNWARD

Check the valve spring free length and squareness

Check the valve spring test pressure

Place the spring on a flat surface next to a square. Measure the height of the spring, and rotate it against the edge of the square to measure distortion. If spring height varies (by comparison) by more than $1/16''$ or if distortion exceeds $1/16''$, replace the spring.

** In addition to evaluating the spring as above, test the spring pressure at the installed and compressed (installed height minus valve lift) height using a valve spring tester. Springs used on small displacement engines (up to 3 liters) should be ∓ 1 lb of all other springs in either position. A tolerance of ∓ 5 lbs is permissible on larger engines.

Cylinder Head Reconditioning

Procedure	Method
*Install valve stem seals: 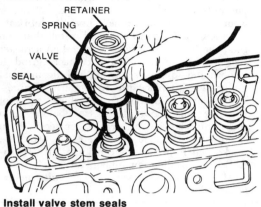 **Install valve stem seals**	*Due to the pressure differential that exists at the ends of the intake valve guides (atmospheric pressure above, manifold vacuum below), oil is drawn through the valve guides into the intake port. This has been alleviated somewhat since the addition of positive crankcase ventilation, which lowers the pressure above the guides. Several types of valve stem seals are available to reduce blow-by. Certain seals simply slip over the stem and guide boss, while others require that the boss be machined. Recently, Teflon guide seals have become popular. Consult a parts supplier or machinist concerning availability and suggested usages. **NOTE:** *When installing seals, ensure that a small amount of oil is able to pass the seal to lubricate the valve guides; otherwise, excessive wear may result.*
Install the valves:	See the engine service procedures earlier in this chapter for details concerning specific engines. Lubricate the valve stems, and install the valves in the cylinder head as numbered. Lubricate and position the seals (if used) and the valve springs. Install the spring retainers, compress the springs, and insert the keys using needlenose pliers or a tool designed for this purpose. **NOTE:** *Retain the keys with wheel bearing grease during installation.*
Check valve spring installed height: 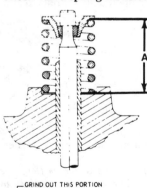 **Valve spring installed height (A)** 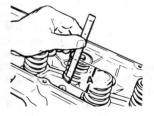 **Measure the valve spring installed height (A) with a modified steel rule**	Measure the distance between the spring pad the lower edge of the spring retainer, and compare to specifications. If the installed height is incorrect, add shim washers between the spring pad and the spring. **CAUTION:** *Use only washers designed for this purpose.*

Cylinder Head Reconditioning

Procedure	Method
Inspect the rocker arms, balls, studs, and nuts: 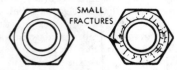 **Stress cracks in the rocker nuts**	Visually inspect the rocker arms, balls, studs, and nuts for cracks, galling, burning, scoring, or wear. If all parts are intact, liberally lubricate the rocker arms and balls, and install them on the cylinder head. If wear is noted on a rocker arm at the point of valve contact, grind it smooth and square, removing as little material as possible. Replace the rocker arm if excessively worn. If a rocker stud shows signs of wear, it must be replaced (see below). If a rocker nut shows stress cracks, replace it. If an exhaust ball is galled or burned, substitute the intake ball from the same cylinder (if it is intact), and install a new intake ball. **NOTE:** *Avoid using new rocker balls on exhaust valves.*
Replace rocker studs: 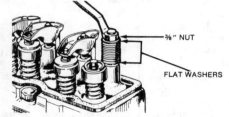 **Extracting a pressed-in rocker stud** 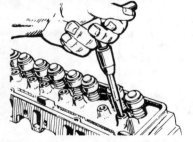 **Ream the stud bore for oversize rocker studs**	In order to remove a threaded stud, lock two nuts on the stud, and unscrew the stud using the lower nut. Coat the lower threads of the new stud with Loctite, and install. Two alternative methods are available for replacing pressed in studs. Remove the damaged stud using a stack of washers and a nut (see ilustration). In the first, the boss is reamed .005–.006″ oversize, and an oversize stud pressed in. Control the stud extension over the boss using washers, in the same manner as valve guides. Before installing the stud, coat it with white lead and grease. To retain the stud more positively drill a hole through the stud and boss, and install a roll pin. In the second method, the boss is tapped, and a threaded stud installed.
Inspect the rocker shaft(s) and rocker arms: 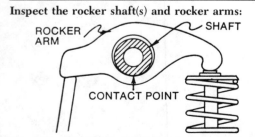 **Check the rocker arm-to-rocker shaft contact area**	Remove the rocker arms, springs and washers from rocker shaft. **NOTE:** *Lay out parts in the order as they are removed.* Inspect rocker arms for pitting or wear on the valve contact point, or excessive bushing wear. Bushings need only be replaced if wear is excessive, because the rocker arm normally contacts the shaft at one point only. Grind the valve contact point of rocker arm smooth if necessary, removing as little material as possible. If excessive material must be removed to smooth and square the arm, it should be replaced. Clean out all oil holes and passages in rocker shaft. If shaft is grooved or worn, replace it. Lubricate and assemble the rocker shaft.

Cylinder Head Reconditioning

Procedure	Method
Inspect the pushrods:	Remove the pushrods, and, if hollow, clean out the oil passages using fine wire. Roll each pushrod over a piece of clean glass. If a distinct clicking sound is heard as the pushrod rolls, the rod is bent, and must be replaced.
	*The length of all pushrods must be equal. Measure the length of the pushrods, compare to specifications, and replace as necessary.
*Inspect the valve lifters: 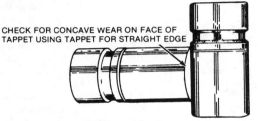 CHECK FOR CONCAVE WEAR ON FACE OF TAPPET USING TAPPET FOR STRAIGHT EDGE **Check the lifter face for squareness**	Remove lifters from their bores, and remove gum and varnish, using solvent. Clean walls of lifter bores. Check lifters for concave wear as illustrated. If face is worn concave, replace lifter, and carefully inspect the camshaft. Lightly lubricate lifter and insert it into its bore. If play is excessive, an oversize lifter must be installed (where possible). Consult a machinist concerning feasibility. If play is satisfactory, remove, lubricate, and reinstall the lifter.
*Testing hydraulic lifter leak down:	Submerge lifter in a container of kerosene. Chuck a used pushrod or its equivalent into a drill press. Position container of kerosene so pushrod acts on the lifter plunger. Pump lifter with the drill press, until resistance increases. Pump several more times to bleed any air out of lifter. Apply very firm, constant pressure to the lifter, and observe rate at which fluid bleeds out of lifter. If the fluid bleeds very quickly (less than 15 seconds), lifter is defective. If the time exceeds 60 seconds, lifter is sticking. In either case, recondition or replace lifter. If lifter is operating properly (leak down time 15–60 seconds), lubricate and install it.

Cylinder Block Reconditioning

Procedure	Method
Checking the main bearing clearance: 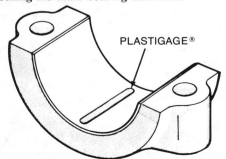 PLASTIGAGE® **Plastigage® installed on the lower bearing shell**	Invert engine, and remove cap from the bearing to be checked. Using a clean, dry rag, thoroughly clean all oil from crankshaft journal and bearing insert. NOTE: *Plastigage® is soluble in oil; therefore, oil on the journal or bearing could result in erroneous readings.* Place a piece of Plastigage along the full length of journal, reinstall cap, and torque to specifications. NOTE: **Specifications are given in the engine specifications earlier in this chapter.** Remove bearing cap, and determine bearing clearance by comparing width of Plastigage to the scale on Plastigage envelope. Journal taper is determined by comparing width of the Plas-

Cylinder Block Reconditioning

Procedure	Method

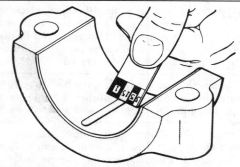

Measure Plastigage® to determine main bearing clearance

tigage strip near its ends. Rotate crankshaft 90° and retest, to determine journal eccentricity. **NOTE:** *Do not rotate crankshaft with Plastigage installed.* If bearing insert and journal appear intact, and are within tolerances, no further main bearing service is required. If bearing or journal appear defective, cause of failure should be determined before replacement.

*Remove crankshaft from block (see below). Measure the main bearing journals at each end twice (90° apart) using a micrometer, to determine diameter, journal taper and eccentricity. If journals are within tolerances, reinstall bearing caps at their specified torque. Using a telescope gauge and micrometer, measure bearing I.D. parallel to piston axis and at 30° on each side of piston axis. Subtract journal O.D. for bearing I.D. to determine oil clearance. If crankshaft journals appear defective, or do not meet tolerances, there is no need to measure bearings; for the crankshaft will require grinding and/or undersize bearings will be required. If bearing appears defective, cause for failure should be determined prior to replacement.

Check the connecting rod bearing clearance:

Connecting rod bearing clearance is checked in the same manner as main bearing clearance, using Plastigage. Before removing the crankshaft, connecting rod side clearance also should be measured and recorded.

*Checking connecting rod bearing clearance, using a micrometer, is identical to checking main bearing clearance. If no other service is required, the piston and rod assemblies need not be removed.

Remove the crankshaft:

Using a punch, mark the corresponding main bearing caps and saddles according to position (i.e., one punch on the front main cap and saddle, two on the second, three on the third, etc.). Using number stamps, identify the corresponding connecting rods and caps, according to cylinder (if no numbers are present). Remove the main and connecting rod caps, and place

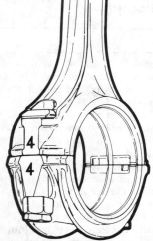

Match the connecting rod to the cylinder with a number stamp

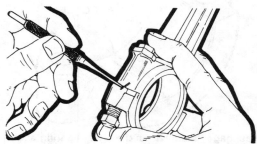

Match the connecting rod and cap with scribe marks

Cylinder Block Reconditioning

Procedure	Method
	sleeves of plastic tubing or vacuum hose over the connecting rod bolts, to protect the journals as the crankshaft is removed. Lift the crankshaft out of the block.
Remove the ridge from the top of the cylinder: RIDGE CAUSED BY CYLINDER WEAR CYLINDER WALL TOP OF PISTON **Cylinder bore ridge**	In order to facilitate removal of the piston and connecting rod, the ridge at the top of the cylinder (unworn area; see illustration) must be removed. Place the piston at the bottom of the bore, and cover it with a rag. Cut the ridge away using a ridge reamer, exercising extreme care to avoid cutting too deeply. Remove the rag, and remove cuttings that remain on the piston. **CAUTION:** *If the ridge is not removed, and new rings are installed, damage to rings will result.*
Remove the piston and connecting rod: **Push the piston out with a hammer handle**	Invert the engine, and push the pistons and connecting rods out of the cylinders. If necessary, tap the connecting rod boss with a wooden hammer handle, to force the piston out. **CAUTION:** *Do not attempt to force the piston past the cylinder ridge* (see above).
Service the crankshaft:	Ensure that all oil holes and passages in the crankshaft are open and free of sludge. If necessary, have the crankshaft ground to the largest possible undersize.
	** Have the crankshaft Magnafluxed, to locate stress cracks. Consult a machinist concerning additional service procedures, such as surface hardening (e.g., nitriding, Tuftriding) to improve wear characteristics, cross drilling and chamfering the oil holes to improve lubrication, and balancing.
Removing freeze plugs:	Drill a small hole in the middle of the freeze plugs. Thread a large sheet metal screw into the hole and remove the plug with a slide hammer.
Remove the oil gallery plugs:	Threaded plugs should be removed using an appropriate (usually square) wrench. To remove soft, pressed in plugs, drill a hole in the plug, and thread in a sheet metal screw. Pull the plug out by the screw using pliers.

Cylinder Block Reconditioning

Procedure	Method
Hot-tank the block: NOTE: *Do not hot-tank aluminum parts.*	Have the block hot-tanked to remove grease, corrosion, and scale from the water jackets. NOTE: *Consult the operator to determine whether the camshaft bearings will be damaged during the hot-tank process.*

Check the block for cracks:	Visually inspect the block for cracks or chips. The most common locations are as follows:
	    Adjacent to freeze plugs.
	    Between the cylinders and water jackets.
	    Adjacent to the main bearing saddles.
	    At the extreme bottom of the cylinders.
	Check only suspected cracks using spot check dye (see introduction). If a crack is located, consult a machinist concerning possible repairs.

	** Magnaflux the block to locate hidden cracks. If cracks are located, consult a machinist about feasibility of repair.
Install the oil gallery plugs and freeze plugs:	Coat freeze plugs with sealer and tap into position using a piece of pipe, slightly smaller than the plug, as a driver. To ensure retention, stake the edges of the plugs. Coat threaded oil gallery plugs with sealer and install. Drive replacement soft plugs into block using a large drift as a driver.
	* Rather than reinstalling lead plugs, drill and tap the holes, and install threaded plugs.
Check the bore diameter and surface: 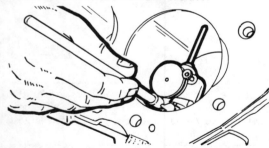 **Measure the cylinder bore with a dial gauge**	Visually inspect the cylinder bores for roughness, scoring, or scuffing. If evident, the cylinder bore must be bored or honed oversize to eliminate imperfections, and the smallest possible oversize piston used. The new pistons should be given to the machinist with the block, so that the cylinders can be bored or honed exactly to the piston size (plus clearance). If no flaws are evident, measure the bore diameter using a telescope gauge and micrometer, or dial gauge, parallel and perpendicular to the engine centerline, at the top (below the ridge) and bottom of the bore. Subtract the bottom measurements from the top to determine taper, and the parallel to

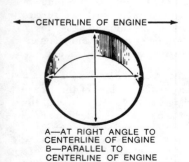

A—AT RIGHT ANGLE TO CENTERLINE OF ENGINE
B—PARALLEL TO CENTERLINE OF ENGINE

Cylinder bore measuring points

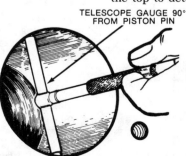

Measure the cylinder bore with a telescope gauge

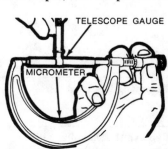

Measure the telescope gauge with a micrometer to determine the cylinder bore

Cylinder Block Reconditioning

Procedure	Method
	the centerline measurements from the perpendicular measurements to determine eccentricity. If the measurements are not within specifications, the cylinder must be bored or honed, and an oversize piston installed. If the measurements are within specifications the cylinder may be used as is, with only finish honing (see below). NOTE: *Prior to submitting the block for boring, perform the following operation(s).*
Check the cylinder block bearing alignment:  **Check the main bearing saddle alignment**	Remove the upper bearing inserts. Place a straightedge in the bearing saddles along the centerline of the crankshaft. If clearance exists between the straightedge and the center saddle, the block must be alignbored.
*Check the deck height:	The deck height is the distance from the crankshaft centerline to the block deck. To measure, invert the engine, and install the crankshaft, retaining it with the center main cap. Measure the distance from the crankshaft journal to the block deck, parallel to the cylinder centerline. Measure the diameter of the end (front and rear) main journals, parallel to the centerline of the cylinders, divide the diameter in half, and subtract it from the previous measurement. The results of the front and rear measurements should be identical. If the difference exceeds .005″, the deck height should be corrected. NOTE: *Block deck height and warpage should be corrected at the same time.*
Check the block deck for warpage:	Using a straightedge and feeler gauges, check the block deck for warpage in the same manner that the cylinder head is checked (see Cylinder Head Reconditioning). If warpage exceeds specifications, have the deck resurfaced. NOTE: *In certain cases a specification for total material removal (cylinder head and block deck) is provided. This specification must not be exceeded.*
Clean and inspect the pistons and connecting rods: 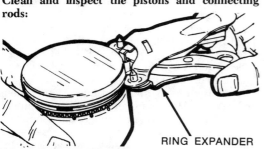 RING EXPANDER **Remove the piston rings**	Using a ring expander, remove the rings from the piston. Remove the retaining rings (if so equipped) and remove piston pin. NOTE: *If the piston pin must be pressed out, determine the proper method and use the proper tools; otherwise the piston will distort.* Clean the ring grooves using an appropriate tool, exercising care to avoid cutting too deeply. Thoroughly clean all carbon and varnish from the piston with solvent. CAUTION: *Do not use a wire brush or caustic solvent on pistons.* Inspect the pistons for scuffing, scoring, cracks, pitting, or excessive ring

Cylinder Block Reconditioning

Procedure	Method

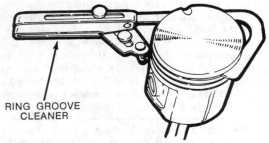

RING GROOVE
CLEANER

Clean the piston ring grooves

groove wear. If wear is evident, the piston must be replaced. Check the connecting rod length by measuring the rod from the inside of the large end to the inside of the small end using calipers (see illustration). All connecting rods should be equal length. Replace any rod that differs from the others in the engine.

* Have the connecting rod alignment checked in an alignment fixture by a machinist. Replace any twisted or bent rods.

* Magnaflux the connecting rods to locate stress cracks. If cracks are found, replace the connecting rod.

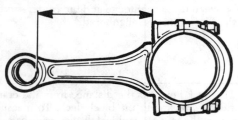

Check the connecting rod length (arrow)

Fit the pistons to the cylinders:

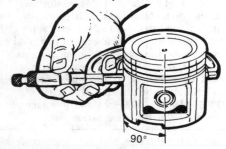

90°

Measure the piston prior to fitting

Using a telescope gauge and micrometer, or a dial gauge, measure the cylinder bore diameter perpendicular to the piston pin, 2½″ below the deck. Measure the piston perpendicular to its pin on the skirt. The difference between the two measurements is the piston clearance. If the clearance is within specifications or slightly below (after boring or honing), finish honing is all that is required. If the clearance is excessive, try to obtain a slightly larger piston to bring clearance within specifications. Where this is not possible, obtain the first oversize piston, and hone (or if necessary, bore) the cylinder to size.

Assemble the pistons and connecting rods:

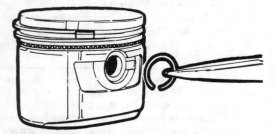

Install the piston pin lock-rings (if used)

Inspect piston pin, connecting rod small end bushing, and piston bore for galling, scoring, or excessive wear. If evident, replace defective part(s). Measure the I.D. of the piston boss and connecting rod small end, and the O.D. of the piston pin. If within specifications, assemble piston pin and rod.
CAUTION: *If piston pin must be pressed in, determine the proper method and use the proper tools; otherwise the piston will distort.*
    Install the lock rings; ensure that they seat properly. If the parts are not within specifications, determine the service method for the type of engine. In some cases, piston and pin are serviced as an assembly when either is defective. Others specify reaming the piston and connecting rods for an oversize pin. If the connecting rod bushing is worn, it may in many cases be replaced. Reaming the piston and replacing the rod bushing are machine shop operations.

Cylinder Block Reconditioning

Procedure	Method

Clean and inspect the camshaft:

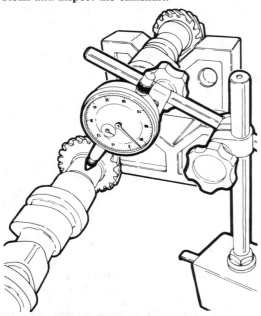

Check the camshaft for straightness

Degrease the camshaft, using solvent, and clean out all oil holes. Visually inspect cam lobes and bearing journals for excessive wear. If a lobe is questionable, check all lobes as indicated below. If a journal or lobe is worn, the camshaft must be regrounded or replaced.

NOTE: *If a journal is worn, there is a good chance that the bushings are worn.* If lobes and journals appear intact, place the front and rear journals in V-blocks, and rest a dial indicator on the center journal. Rotate the camshaft to check straightness. If deviation exceeds .001″, replace the camshaft.

* Check the camshaft lobes with a micrometer, by measuring the lobes from the nose to base and again at 90° (see illustration). The lift is determined by subtracting the second measurement from the first. If all exhaust lobes and all intake lobes are not identical, the camshaft must be reground or replaced.

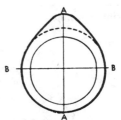

Camshaft lobe measurement

Replace the camshaft bearings:

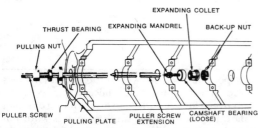

Camshaft bearing removal and installation tool (OHV engines only)

If excessive wear is indicated, or if the engine is being completely rebuilt, camshaft bearings should be replaced as follows: Drive the camshaft rear plug from the block. Assemble the removal puller with its shoulder on the bearing to be removed. Gradually tighten the puller nut until bearing is removed. Remove remaining bearings, leaving the front and rear for last. To remove front and rear bearings, reverse position of the tool, so as to pull the bearings in toward the center of the block. Leave the tool in this position, pilot the new front and rear bearings on the installer, and pull them into position: Return the tool to its original position and pull remaining bearings into position.

NOTE: *Ensure that oil holes align when installing bearings.* Replace camshaft rear plug, and stake it into position to aid retention.

Finish hone the cylinders:

Chuck a flexible drive hone into a power drill, and insert it into the cylinder. Start the hone, and remove it up and down in the cylinder at a rate which will produce approximately a 60° cross-hatch pattern.

NOTE: *Do not extend the hone below the cylinder bore.* After developing the pattern, remove

Cylinder Block Reconditioning

Procedure	Method

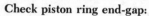

CROSS HATCH PATTERN

50°-60°

Cylinder bore after honing

the hone and recheck piston fit. Wash the cylinders with a detergent and water solution to remove abrasive dust, dry, and wipe several times with a rag soaked in engine oil.

Check piston ring end-gap:

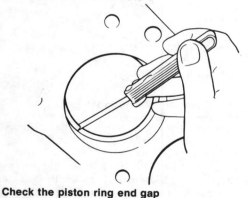

Check the piston ring end gap

Compress the piston rings to be used in a cylinder, one at a time, into that cylinder, and press them approximately 1″ below the deck with an inverted piston. Using feeler gauges, measure the ring end-gap, and compare to specifications. Pull the ring out of the cylinder and file the ends with a fine file to obtain proper clearance.
CAUTION: *If inadequate ring end-gap is utilized, ring breakage will result.*

Install the piston rings:

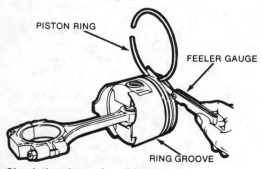

PISTON RING

FEELER GAUGE

RING GROOVE

Check the piston ring side clearance

Inspect the ring grooves in the piston for excessive wear or taper. If necessary, recut the groove(s) for use with an overwidth ring or a standard ring and spacer. If the groove is worn uniformly, overwidth rings, or standard rings and spacers may be installed without recutting. Roll the outside of the ring around the groove to check for burrs or deposits. If any are found, remove with a fine file. Hold the ring in the groove, and measure side clearance. If necessary, correct as indicated above.
NOTE: *Always install any additional spacers above the piston ring.*
The ring groove must be deep enough to allow the ring to seat below the lands (see illustration). In many cases, a "go-no-go" depth gauge will be provided with the piston rings. Shallow grooves may be corrected by recutting, while deep grooves require some type of filler or expander

Cylinder Block Reconditioning

Procedure	Method
	behind the piston. Consult the piston ring supplier concerning the suggested method. Install the rings on the piston, lowest ring first, using a ring expander. **NOTE:** *Position the rings as specified by the manufacturer.* Consult the engine service procedures earlier in this chapter for details concerning specific engines.
Install the camshaft:	Liberally lubricate the camshaft lobes and journals, and install the camshaft. **CAUTION:** *Exercise extreme care to avoid damaging the bearings when inserting the camshaft.* Install and tighten the camshaft thrust plate retaining bolts.
	See the engine service procedures earlier in this chapter for details concerning specific engines.
Check camshaft end-play (OHV engines only): Check the camshaft end-play with a feeler gauge DIAL INDICATOR CAMSHAFT Check the camshaft end-play with a dial indicator	Using feeler gauges, determine whether the clearance between the camshaft boss (or gear) and backing plate is within specifications. Install shims behind the thrust plate, or reposition the camshaft gear and retest endplay. In some cases, adjustment is by replacing the thrust plate. See the engine service procedures earlier in this chapter for details concerning specific engines. * Mount a dial indicator stand so that the stem of the dial indicator rests on the nose of the camshaft, parallel to the camshaft axis. Push the camshaft as far in as possible and zero the gauge. Move the camshaft outward to determine the amount of camshaft endplay. If the endplay is not within tolerance, install shims behind the thrust plate, or reposition the camshaft gear and retest. See the engine service procedures earlier in this chapter for details concerning specific engines.
Install the rear main seal:	See the engine service procedures earlier in this chapter for details concerning specific engines.
Install the crankshaft: INSTALLING BEARING SHELL REMOVING BEARING SHELL **Remove or install the upper bearing insert using a roll-out pin**	Thoroughly clean the main bearing saddles and caps. Place the upper halves of the bearing inserts on the saddles and press into position. **NOTE:** *Ensure that the oil holes align.* Press the corresponding bearing inserts into the main bearing caps. Lubricate the upper main bearings, and lay the crankshaft in position. Place a strip of Plastigage on each of the crankshaft journals, install the main caps, and torque to specifications. Remove the main caps, and compare the Plastigage to the scale on the Plastigage envelope. If clearances are within tolerances, remove the Plastigage, turn the crankshaft 90°, wipe off all oil and retest. If all clearances are correct,

Cylinder Block Reconditioning

Procedure	Method

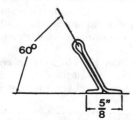

Home-made bearing roll-out pin

remove all Plastigage, thoroughly lubricate the main caps and bearing journals, and install the main caps. If clearances are not within tolerance, the upper bearing inserts may be removed, without removing the crankshaft, using a bearing roll out pin (see illustration). Roll in a bearing that will provide proper clearance, and retest. Torque all main caps, excluding the thrust bearing cap, to specifications. Tighten the thrust bearing cap finger tight. To properly align the thrust bearing, pry the crankshaft the extent of its axial travel several times, the last movement held toward the front of the engine, and torque the thrust bearing cap to specifications. Determine the crankshaft end-play (see below), and bring within tolerance with thrust washers.

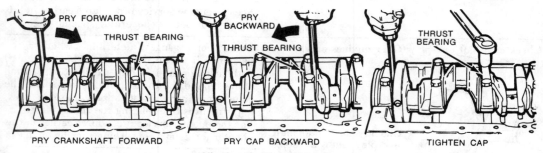

Aligning the thrust bearing

Measure crankshaft end-play:

Mount a dial indicator stand on the front of the block, with the dial indicator stem resting on the nose of the crankshaft, parallel to the crankshaft axis. Pry the crankshaft the extent of its travel rearward, and zero the indicator. Pry the crankshaft forward and record crankshaft end-play. NOTE: *Crankshaft end-play also may be measured at the thrust bearing, using feeler gauges (see illustration).*

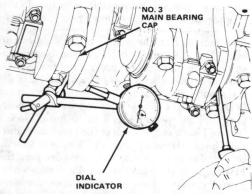

Check the crankshaft end-play with a dial indicator

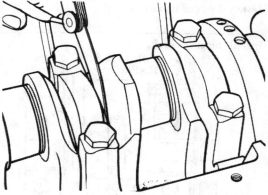

Check the crankshaft end-play with a feeler gauge

Cylinder Block Reconditioning

Procedure	Method

Install the pistons:

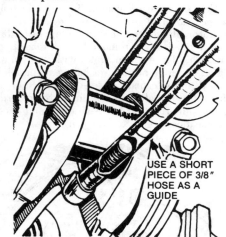

USE A SHORT PIECE OF 3/8" HOSE AS A GUIDE

Use lengths of vacuum hose or rubber tubing to protect the crankshaft journals and cylinder walls during piston installation

RING COMPRESSOR

Install the piston using a ring compressor

Press the upper connecting rod bearing halves into the connecting rods, and the lower halves into the connecting rod caps. Position the piston ring gaps according to specifications (see car section), and lubricate the pistons. Install a ring compresser on a piston, and press two long (8″) pieces of plastic tubing over the rod bolts. Using the tubes as a guide, press the pistons into the bores and onto the crankshaft with a wooden hammer handle. After seating the rod on the crankshaft journal, remove the tubes and install the cap finger tight. Install the remaining pistons in the same manner. Invert the engine and check the bearing clearance at two points (90° apart) on each journal with Plastigage.

NOTE: *Do not turn the crankshaft with Plastigage installed.* If clearance is within tolerances, remove *all* Plastigage, thoroughly lubricate the journals, and torque the rod caps to specifications. If clearance is not within specifications, install different thickness bearing inserts and recheck.

CAUTION: *Never shim or file the connecting rods or caps.* Always install plastic tube sleeves over the rod bolts when the caps are not installed, to protect the crankshaft journals.

Check connecting rod side clearance:

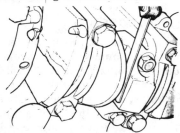

Check the connecting rod side clearance with a feeler gauge

Determine the clearance between the sides of the connecting rods and the crankshaft using feeler gauges. If clearance is below the minimum tolerance, the rod may be machined to provide adequate clearance. If clearance is excessive, substitute an unworn rod, and recheck. If clearance is still outside specifications, the crankshaft must be welded and reground, or replaced.

Inspect the timing chain (or belt):

Visually inspect the timing chain for broken or loose links, and replace the chain if any are found. If the chain will flex sideways, it must be replaced. Install the timing chain as specified. Be sure the timing belt is not stretched, frayed or broken.

NOTE: *If the original timing chain is to be reused, install it in its original position.*

Cylinder Block Reconditioning

Procedure	Method
Check timing gear backlash and runout (OHV engines):  Check the camshaft gear backlash	Mount a dial indicator with its stem resting on a tooth of the camshaft gear (as illustrated). Rotate the gear until all slack is removed, and zero the indicator. Rotate the gear in the opposite direction until slack is removed, and record gear backlash. Mount the indicator with its stem resting on the edge of the camshaft gear, parallel to the axis of the camshaft. Zero the indicator, and turn the camshaft gear one full turn, recording the runout. If either backlash or runout exceed specifications, replace the worn gear(s).  Check the camshaft gear run-out

Completing the Rebuilding Process

Follow the above procedures, complete the rebuilding process as follows:

Fill the oil pump with oil, to prevent cavitating (sucking air) on initial engine start up. Install the oil pump and the pickup tube on the engine. Coat the oil pan gasket as necessary, and install the gasket and the oil pan. Mount the flywheel and the crankshaft vibration damper or pulley on the crankshaft. NOTE: *Always use new bolts when installing the flywheel.* Inspect the clutch shaft pilot bushing in the crankshaft. If the bushing is excessively worn, remove it with an expanding puller and a slide hammer, and tap a new bushing into place.

Position the engine, cylinder head side up. Lubricate the lifters, and install them into their bores. Install the cylinder head, and torque it as specified. Insert the pushrods and install the rocker shaft(s) or position the rocker arms on the pushrods. Adjust the valves.

Install the intake and exhaust manifolds, the carburetor(s), the distributor and spark plugs. Adjust the point gap and the static ignition timing. Mount all accessories and install the engine in the car. Fill the radiator with coolant, and the crankcase with high quality engine oil.

Break-in Procedure

Start the engine, and allow it to run at low speed for a few minutes, while checking for leaks. Stop the engine, check the oil level, and fill as necessary. Restart the engine, and fill the cooling system to capacity. Check the point dwell angle and adjust the ignition timing and the valves. Run the engine at low to medium speed (800–2500 rpm) for approximately ½ hour, and retorque the cylinder head bolts. Road test the car, and check again for leaks.

Follow the manufacturer's recommended engine break-in procedure and maintenance schedule for new engines.

Emission Controls and Fuel System

EMISSION CONTROLS

Positive Crankcase Ventilation

All models are equipped with a positive crankcase ventilation (PCV) system which draws air into the engine through the air cleaner and circulates it through the engine. The air combines with vapors in the crankcase and exits the engine through a metering valve mounted in the rocker arm cover. The air vapor mixture then re-enters the engine through the carburetor or intake manifold and passes into the combustion chambers where it is burned.

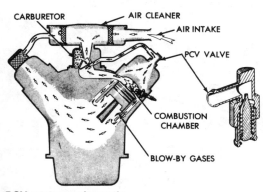

CARBURETOR — AIR CLEANER — AIR INTAKE — PCV VALVE — COMBUSTION CHAMBER — BLOW-BY GASES

PCV system schematic

Evaporative Control System

All vehicles have an Evaporation Control System to reduce evaporation losses from the fuel system. The system has an expansion tank in the main fuel tank. This prevents spillage due to expansion of warm fuel. A special filler cap with a two-way relief valve is used. An internal pressure differential, caused by thermal expansion, opens the valve, as does an external pressure differential caused by fuel usage. Fuel vapors from the carburetor and fuel tank are routed to the crankcase ventilation system. A separator is installed to prevent liquid fuel from entering the crankcase ventilation system.

Evaporation control systems also include a charcoal canister and an overflow limiting valve.

The limiting valve prevents the fuel tank from being overfilled by trapping fuel in the filler when the tank is full. When pressure in the tank becomes greater than the valve operating pressure, the valve opens and allows the gasoline vapors to flow into the charcoal canister.

The charcoal canister is mounted in the engine compartment. It absorbs vapors and retains them until clean air is drawn through a line from it that runs to the PCV valve. Absorption occurs while the car is parked and cleaning occurs when the car engine is running.

NOTE: *Some models are equipped with duel canisters.*

Air Injection System (Air Pump)

A belt-driven air pump, mounted on the front of the engine, is used to inject air into the exhaust ports. This causes oxidation of these gases and a considerable reduction in carbon monoxide and hydrocarbons. The system consists of the pump, a check valve to protect the hoses and pump from hot gases, and a diverter-pressure relief valve assembly. Later models add a vacuum and coolant temperature controlled air switching valve to the system. The switching valve allows air flow to the exhaust ports during warmup, then diverts it to the exhaust manifold or pipe, depending on the engine.

Air Aspirator System

This system is used on some models in place of the air pump system. It utilizes a simple exhaust gas pulsation operated diaphragm valve to draw air from the air cleaner into the exhaust manifold.

Exhaust Gas Recirculation

In order to reduce the emission of oxides of nitrogen (NOx), exhaust gases are ducted from the intake manifold crossover passage to dilute (with inert, oxygen-free gas) the fuel/air mixture. Most engines use an EGR control valve. This valve directs exhaust gas from the crossover passage into the intake manifold. By using either ported-vacuum (varies with throttle opening) or venturi-vacuum signals, the EGR valve is able to proportion the exhaust gas flow to the amount of vacuum present in the carburetor. Thermal switches on the engine and radiator prevent recirculation during engine warmup. All models have a delay timer relay and a solenoid valve to shut off vacuum to the system until the engine has run 30–40 seconds after startup.

Electrically Assisted Choke

There are two types, single and dual stage. Both use an electric assist heating element on the manifold mounted choke coil for faster choke release. The single stage unit applies heat to the choke coil only in summer temperatures, while the dual stage unit applies low heat during warmup and high heat after warmup.

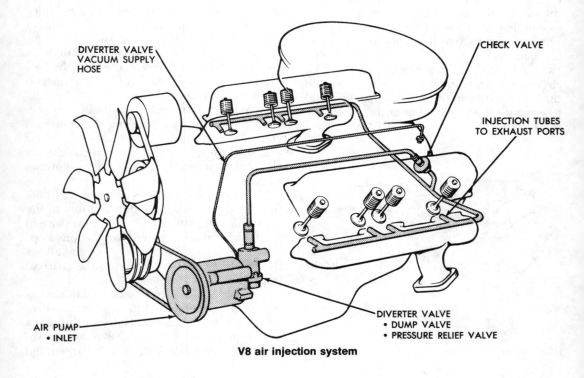

V8 air injection system

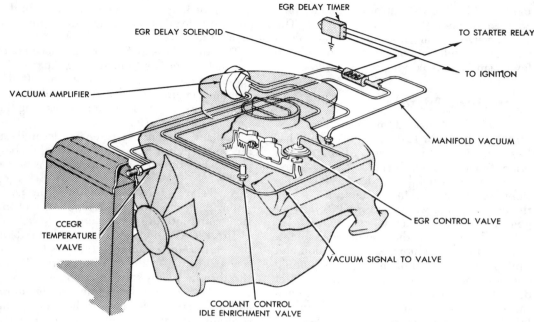

EGR system schematic

OSAC Valve

An orifice spark advance control (OSAC) valve is used on all models to delay distributor vacuum advance for about 15–27 seconds during acceleration.

NOTE: *The amount of time-delay varies slightly from one engine size to another.*

Some models are equipped with "Maximum Cooling" systems and/or air conditioning have a Thermal Ignition Control (TIC) valve to reduce the possibility of engine overheating under heavy load. When coolant temperature at idle reaches 225°F, the TIC valve automatically opens and applies vacuum directly to the distributor, bypassing the OSAC system. Engine idle speed rises and coolant temperature drops. When normal operating temperature is reached, the TIC bypass shuts off. The TIC valve is usually used on Police Package V8s.

Catalytic Converter

These devices are used to oxidize excess carbon monoxide (CO) and hydrocarbons (HC) in the exhaust gases before they can escape out the tailpipe and into the atmosphere. The converter is installed in front of the mufflers, underneath the car and is protected by a heat shield. Many 1977 and later models are equipped with "miniox" converters as well as the main underfloor one.

The expected catalyst life is 50,000 miles, provided that the engine is kept in tune and unleaded fuel is used.

To keep the catalyst from being overheated by an overly rich mixture during deceleration, a catalyst protection system (CPS) is used on some models. The system consists of a throttle positioner solenoid (not to be confused with the idle stop solenoid), a control box, and an engine rpm sensor.

Any time that the engine speed is more than 2,000 rpm while decelerating from highway speeds, the solenoid is energized and keeps the throttle butterfly from fully closing, thus preventing the mixture from becoming too rich.

Coolant Control Idle Enrichment (CCIE) System

The CCIE system is used on most 1975 and later models with automatic transmissions. The system consists of a vacuum-operated valve built into the carburetor, which shuts off the idle circuit air bleeds when vacuum is supplied to its diaphragm.

Depending upon engine applicaton, vacuum is either routed through a coolant controlled vacuum valve or an EGR vacuum control solenoid.

Vacuum is passed to the valve diaphragm below a predetermined temperature, and on models with an EGR control solenoid for only 35 seconds after the engine is started. The CCIE valve action closes off the air bleed passages, which richens the mixture, and allows a smoother cold idle.

Lean Burn System

The Chrysler Corporation Lean Burn System, introduced in 1976 on the Cordoba, has been made available on a number of Aspen/Volaré models for 1978. This system is based on the principle that lower NO_x emissions would occur if the air/fuel ratio inside the cylinder area was raised from its current point (15.5:1) to a much leaner point (18:1).

In order to make the engine workable, a solution to the problems of carburetion and timing had to be found since a lean running engine is not the most efficient in terms of driveability. Chrysler adapted a conventional carburetor to handle the added air coming in, but the real advance of the system is the Spark Control Computer mounted on the air cleaner.

Since a lean burning engine demands precise ignition timing, additional spark control was needed for the distributor. The computer supplies this control by providing an infinitely variable advance curve. Input data is fed instantaneously to the computer by a series of seven sensors located in the engine compartment which monitor timing, water temperature, air temperature, throttle position, idle/off-idle operation, and intake manifold vacuum. The program schedule module of the spark control computer receives the information from the sensors, processes it, and then directs the ignition control module to advance or retard the timing as necessary. This whole process is going on continuously as the engine is running, taking only a thousandth of a second to complete a circuit from sensor to distributor.

The components of the system are as follows: Modified carburetor; Spark Control Computer, consistint of two interacting modules: the Program Schedule Module which is responsible for translating input data, and the Ignition Control Module which transmits data to the distributor to advance or retard the timing; and the following sensors.

Start Pick-up Sensor, located inside the distributor, supplies a signal to the computer providing a fixed timing point which is only used for starting the car. It also has a back-up function of taking over engine timing in case the run pick-up fails. Since the timing in this pick-up is fixed at one point, the engine will be able to run, but not very well.

The Run Pick-up Sensor, also located in the distributor, provides timing data to the computer once the engine is running. It also monitors engine speed and helps the computer decide when the piston is reaching the top of its compression stroke.

Coolant Temperature Sensor, located on the water pump housing, informs the computer when the coolant temperature is below 150°.

Air Temperature Sensor, inside the computer itself, monitors the temperature of the air coming into the air cleaner.

Throttle Position Transducer, located on the carburetor, monitors the position and rate of change of the throttle plates. When the throttle plates start to open and as they continue to open toward full throttle, more and more spark advance is called for by the computer. If the throttle plates are opened quickly even more spark advance is given for about one second. The amount of maximum advance is determined by the temperature of the air coming into the air cleaner. Less advance under acceleration will be given if the air entering the air cleaner is hot, while more advance will be given if the air is cold.

Carburetor Switch Sensor, located on the end of the idle stop solenoid, tells the computer if the engine is at idle or off-idle.

Vacuum Transducer, located on the computer, monitors the amount of intake manifold vacuum present; the more vacuum, the more spark advance to the distributor. In order to obtain this spark advance in the distributor, the carburetor switch sensor has to remain open for a specified amount of time during which the advance will slowly build up to the amount indicated as necessary by the vacuum transducer. If the carburetor switch should close during that time, the advance to the distributor will be cancelled. From here the computer will start with an advance count-down. If the carburetor switch is reopened within a certain amount of time, the advance will continue from a point where the computer decides it should. If the switch is reopened after the computer has counted down to "no advance," the vacuum advance process must start over again.

OPERATION

When you turn the ignition key on, the start pick-up sends its signal to the computer which relays back information for more spark advance during cranking. As soon as the engine starts, the run pick-up takes over and receives more advance for about one minute. This advance is slowly eliminated during the one minute warm-up period. While the engine is cold (coolant temperature below 150° as monitored by the coolant temperature sensor), no more advance will be given to the distributor until the engine reaches normal operating temperature, at which time normal operation of the system will begin.

In normal operation, the basic timing information is relayed by the run pick-up to the computer along with input signals from all the other sensors. From this data the computer determines the maximum allowable advance or retard to be sent to the distributor for any situation.

If either the run pick-up or the computer should fail, the back-up system of the start pick-up takes over. This supplies a fixed timing signal to the distributor which allows the car to be driven until it can be repaired. In this mode, very poor fuel economy and performance will be experienced. If the start pick-up or the ignition control module section of the computer should fail, the engine will not start or run.

Emission Control Troubleshooting

POSITIVE CRANKCASE VENTILATION (PCV) SYSTEM

Valve Test

1. See if there are any deposits in the carburetor passages, the oil filler cap, or the hoses. Clean these as required.

2. Connect a tachometer to the engine.

3. With the engine idling, remove the PCV valve.

NOTE: *If the valve and the hoses are not clogged-up, there should be a hissing sound.*

4. Check the tachometer reading. Place a finger over the valve or hose opening (a suction should be felt).

5. Check the tachometer again. The engine speed should have dropped at least 50 rpm. It should return to normal when the finger is removed from the opening.

6. If the engine does not change speed or if the change is less then 50 rpm, the hose is clogged or the valve is defective. Check the hose first. If the hose is not clogged replace, do not attempt to repair, the PCV valve.

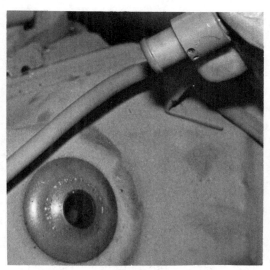

Pull the PCV valve out of the valve cover to test it

7. Test the new valve to make sure that it is operating properly.

NOTE: *There are several commercial PCV valve testers available. Be sure that the one used is suitable for the valve to be tested, as the testers are not universal.*

AIR INJECTION SYSTEM

CAUTION: *Do not hammer on, pry, or bend the pump housing while tightening the drive belt or testing the pump.*

Belt Tension and Air Leaks

1. Check the pump drive belt tension. There should be about ½ in. play in the longest span of belt between pulleys.

2. Turn the pump by hand. If it has seized, the belt will slip, producing noise. Disregard any chirping, squealing, or rolling sounds from inside the pump; these are normal when it is turned by hand.

3. Check the hoses and connections for leaks. Hissing or a blast of air is indicative of a leak. Soapy water, applied lightly around the area in question, is a good method for detecting leaks.

Air Output Test

1. Disconnect the air supply hose at the antibackfire valve.

2. Connect a pressure gauge to the air supply hose.

NOTE: *If there are two hoses plug the second one.*

3. With the engine at normal operating

temperature, increase the idle speed and watch the vacuum gauge.

4. The airflow from the pump should be steady and between 2–6 psi. If it is unsteady or falls below this, the pump is defective and must be replaced.

Pump Noise Diagnosis

The air pump is normally noisy; as engine speed increases, the noise of the pump will rise in pitch. The rolling sound the pump bearings make is normal.

Check Valve Test

1. Before starting the test, check all of the hoses and connections for leaks.

2. Detach the air supply hose(s) from the check valve(s).

3. Insert a probe into the check valve and depress the plate. Release it; the plate should return to its original position against the valve seat. If binding is evident, replace the valve.

4. Repeat Step 3 if two valves are used.

5. With the engine running at normal operating temperature, gradually increase its speed to 1,500 rpm. Check for exhaust gas leakage. If there is any, replace the valve assembly.

NOTE: *Vibration and flutter of the check valve at idle speed is a normal condition and does not mean that the valve should be replaced.*

THERMOSTATICALLY CONTROLLED AIR CLEANER

Air Door Test

1. Remove the air cleaner from the carburetor and allow it to cool to 90°F. Connect a vacuum source with a vacuum gauge to the sensor.

2. Apply 20 in. Hg to the sensor. The door should be in the "heat on" (up) position. If it

remains in the "off" position, test the vacuum motor.

3. Connect the motor to a vacuum source. In addition to the vacuum gauge, a hose clamp and a bleed valve are necessary. Connect them in the following order:

  a. Vacuum source;
  b. Hose clamp (or shut-off valve);
  c. Bleed valve;
  d. Vacuum gauge;
  e. Vacuum motor.

4. Apply 20 in. Hg vacuum to the motor. Use the hose clamp to block the line, so that the motor will retain the vacuum. The door operating motor should retain this amount of vacuum for five minutes. Release the hose clamp.

NOTE: *If the vacuum cannot be built up to the specified amount, the diaphragm has a leak and the valve will require replacement.*

5. By slowly closing the bleed valve, check the operation of the door. The door should open at no less than 5 in. Hg.

ORIFICE SPARK ADVANCE

Control Valve Test

The OSAC valve is located on the air cleaner. Warm the engine to normal operating temperature for this test.

1. Check the vacuum hoses and connections for leaks or plugging.

2. Detach the vacuum line which runs from the distributor to the OSAC valve at the distributor end. Connect a vacuum gauge to this line.

3. Connect a tachometer to the engine. Rapidly open the throttle and then stabilize the engine speed at 2,000 rpm in neutral. When the throttle is rapidly opened the vacuum gauge reading should drop to zero. With the engine speed at a steady 2,000 rpm, it should take about 20 seconds for the vacuum level to rise and then stabilize.

NOTE: *The length of time may vary slightly with different engines; 20 seconds is an approximate figure.*

5. If the vacuum level rises immediately, the valve is defective and must be replaced.

CARBURETOR CONTROLS

Antidieseling Solenoid Test

NOTE: *Antidieseling solenoids are also referred to as "throttle stop" or "idle stop" solenoids.*

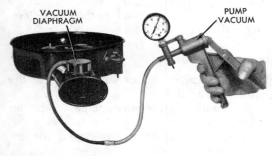

VACUUM
DIAPHRAGM

PUMP
VACUUM

Air door testing

CAUTION: *Cars with catalytic converters have an additional solenoid; this is NOT an antidieseling solenoid, and no attempt to adjust the idle speed with it should be made. See "Catalytic Converter" for details.*

1. Turn the ignition key on and open the throttle. The solenoid plunger should extend (solenoid energized).

2. Turn the ignition off. The plunger should retract, allowing the throttle to close.

NOTE: *With the antidieseling solenoid de-energized, the carburetor idle speed adjusting screw must make contact with the throttle shaft to prevent the throttle plates from jamming in the throttle bore when the engine is turned off.*

3. If the solenoid is functioning properly and the engine is still dieseling, check for one of the following:

    a. High idle or engine shut off speed;

    b. Engine timing not set to specification;

    c. Binding throttle linkage;

    d. Too low an octane fuel being used.

Correct any of these problems, as necessary.

4. If the solenoid fails to function as outlined in Steps 1–2, disconnect the solenoid leads; the solenoid should be de-energized. If it does not, it is jammed and must be replaced.

5. Connect the solenoid to a 12V power source and to ground. Open the throttle so that the plunger can extend. If it does not, the solenoid is defective.

6. If the solenoid is functioning correctly and no other source of trouble can be found, the fault probably lies in the wiring between the solenoid and the ignition switch or in the ignition switch itself. Reconnect the solenoid when finished testing.

Electrically Assisted Choke Test

CAUTION: *Do not immerse the choke heating element in any type of liquid, especially solvent, for any reason.*

NOTE: *A short circuit in the choke wiring or in the heater will show up as a short in the ignition system.*

1. Disconnect the electrical leads from the choke control switch before starting the engine.

2. Connect a test light between the smaller of the two terminals on the choke controls switch and a ground.

Choke control unit identification

3. Start the engine and run it until it reaches normal operating temperature.

4. Apply power from a 12V source to the terminal marked "BAT" on the choke control switch.

5. The test light should light for at least a few seconds or for as long as five minutes. If the light does not come on at all or if it stays on longer than five minutes, replace the switch.

6. Disconnect the test light and reconnect the electrical leads to the choke switch, if it is functioning properly.

7. Detach the lead from the choke switch which runs to the choke heating element.

8. Connect the lead from an ohmmeter to the crimped section at the choke end of the wire, which was removed in Step 7.

CAUTION: *Do not connect the metallic heater housing.*

9. Ground the other ohmmeter test lead to the engine manifold.

10. The meter should indicate a resistance of 4–6 ohms.

11. If the reading is not within specifications, or if it indicates an opened (zero resistance) or a shorted (infinite resistance) heater coil, replace the heater assembly.

NOTE: *The electrically assisted choke does not change any carburetor service procedures. If any parts of the electrically assisted choke are defective, they must be replaced. Adjustment is not possible.*

EVAPORATIVE EMISSION CONTROL SYSTEM

There are several things to check for if a malfunction of the evaporative emission control system is suspected.

1. Leaks may be traced by using an infrared hydrocarbon tester. Run the test probe along the lines and connections. The meter will indicate the presence of a leak by a high hydrocarbon (HC) reading. This method is

much more accurate than a visual inspection which would indicate only the presence of a leak large enough to pass liquid.

2. Leaks may be caused by any of the following, so always check these areas when looking for them:

a. Defective or worn lines;

b. Disconnected or pinched lines;

c. Improperly routed lines;

d. A defective filler cap.

NOTE: *If it becomes necessary to replace any of the lines used in the evaporative emission control system, use only those hoses which are fuel resistant or are marked "EVAP."*

3. If the fuel tank has collapsed, it may be the fault of clogged or pinched vent lines, a defective vapor separator, or a plugged or incorrect fuel filler cap.

4. To test the filler cap, clean it and place it against the mouth. Blow into the relief valve housing if the cap passes pressure with light blowing or if it fails to release with hard blowing, it is defective and must be replaced.

NOTE: *Replace the cap with one marked "pressure/vacuum" only. An incorrect cap will render the system inoperative or damage its components.*

EXHAUST GAS RECIRCULATION (EGR) SYSTEM

EGR System Test

NOTE: *Air temperature should be above 68°F for this test.*

1. Check all of the vacuum hoses which run between the carburetor, intake manifold, EGR valve, and the vacuum amplifier (if so equipped). Replace the hoses and tighten the connections, as required.

2. Allow the engine to warm up. Connect a tachometer to it. Start with the engine idling in neutral and rapidly increase the engine speed to 2,000 rpm.

3. If the EGR valve stem moves (watch the groove on the stem), the valve and the rest of the system are functioning properly. If the stem does not move, proceed with the rest of the EGR system tests.

4. Disconnect the vacuum supply hose from the EGR valve. Apply a vacuum of at least 10 in. Hg to the valve with the engine warmed-up and idling and the transmission Neutral.

NOTE: *A source of more than adequate vacuum is the intake manifold vacuum*

connection. *Run a hose from the EGR valve directly to the connection.*

5. When vacuum is applied to the EGR valve, the engine speed should drop at least 150 rpm. In some cases the engine may even stall. If the engine does not slow down the EGR valve does not operate, the valve is defective or dirty. Replace it or remove the deposits from it.

NOTE: *Always replace the EGR valve gasket when the valve is removed for service, even if the valve itself is not replaced.*

6. If the EGR valve is functioning properly, reconnect its vacuum line and test the temperature control valve.

7. Test the EGR system coolant temperature operated control valve for leaks. The valve is located on either the right or left-side of the radiator top tank.

8. Disconnect the vacuum hose from the EGR coolant temperature operated control valve, then connect a vacuum source and gauge to the valve fitting, in place of the hose.

9. Apply 10 in. Hg of vacuum to the valve. If the valve loses more than 1 in. Hg in one minute, the valve is defective and must be replaced.

10. If everything else is functioning properly, the EGR system does not work and the engine is equipped with a vacuum amplifier, the amplifier is at fault. Replace it and repeat the system test.

NOTE: *Before replacing the amplifier, check the vacuum port in the carburetor. If it is clogged, clean it with solvent; do not use a drill.*

EGR Delay System Test

1. Unfasten the distributor-to-coil lead.

2. Disconnect the vacuum line which runs from the delay solenoid to the vacuum amplier at the amplifier end.

3. Turn the car's ignition switch to "START" and then release it, so that it returns to "RUN."

4. Suck on the end of the disconnected hose; the hose should be blocked.

5. After about 35 seconds from the time that the ignition switch was turned to "START," the solenoid should open, allowing air to flow through the line.

6. If the system isn't working, disconnect the solenoid and connect it directly to a 12-volt power source, making and breaking the circuit several times. If the solenoid works, replace the delay timer.

CHILTON'S
FUEL ECONOMY
& TUNE-UP TIPS

55 WAYS TO IMPROVE FUEL ECONOMY

Tune-up • Spark Plug Diagnosis • Emission Controls

Fuel System • Cooling System • Tires and Wheels

General Maintenance

CHILTON'S FUEL ECONOMY & TUNE-UP TIPS

Fuel economy is important to everyone, no matter what kind of vehicle you drive. The maintenance-minded motorist can save both money and fuel using these tips and the periodic maintenance and tune-up procedures in this Repair and Tune-Up Guide.

There are more than 130,000,000 cars and trucks registered for private use in the United States. Each travels an average of 10-12,000 miles per year, and, and in total they consume close to 70 billion gallons of fuel each year. This represents nearly ⅔ of the oil imported by the United States each year. The Federal government's goal is to reduce consumption 10% by 1985. A variety of methods are either already in use or under serious consideration, and they all affect you driving and the cars you will drive. In addition to "down-sizing", the auto industry is using or investigating the use of electronic fuel delivery, electronic engine controls and alternative engines for use in smaller and lighter vehicles, among other alternatives to meet the federally mandated Corporate Average Fuel Economy (CAFE) of 27.5 mpg by 1985. The government, for its part, is considering rationing, mandatory driving curtailments and tax increases on motor vehicle fuel in an effort to reduce consumption. The government's goal of a 10% reduction could be realized — and further government regulation avoided — if every private vehicle could use just 1 less gallon of fuel per week.

How Much Can You Save?

Tests have proven that almost anyone can make at least a 10% reduction in fuel consumption through regular maintenance and tune-ups. When a major manufacturer of spark plugs sur-

TUNE-UP

1. Check the cylinder compression to be sure the engine will really benefit from a tune-up and that it is capable of producing good fuel economy. A tune-up will be wasted on an engine in poor mechanical condition.

2. Replace spark plugs regularly. New spark plugs alone can increase fuel economy 3%.

3. Be sure the spark plugs are the correct type (heat range) for your vehicle. See the Tune-Up Specifications.

Heat range refers to the spark plug's ability to conduct heat away from the firing end. It must conduct the heat away in an even pattern to avoid becoming a source of pre-ignition, yet it must also operate hot enough to burn off conductive deposits that could cause misfiring.

The heat range is usually indicated by a number on the spark plug, part of the manufacturer's designation for each individual spark plug. The numbers in bold-face indicate the heat range in each manufacturer's identification system.

Periodically, check the spark plugs to be sure they are firing efficiently. They are excellent indicators of the internal condition of your engine.

Manufacturer	Typical Designation
AC	R **45** TS
Bosch (old)	WA **145** T30
Bosch (new)	HR **8** Y
Champion	RBL **15** Y
Fram/Autolite	4**15**
Mopar	P-**62** PR
Motorcraft	BRF-**42**
Prestolite	BP **5** ES-15
NGK	W **16** EP
Nippondenso	14GR **5** 2A

On AC, Bosch (new), Champion, Fram/Autolite, Mopar, Motorcraft and Prestolite, a higher number indicates a hotter plug. On Bosch (old), NGK and Nippondenso, a higher number indicates a colder plug.

4. Make sure the spark plugs are properly gapped. See the Tune-Up Specifications in this book.

5. Be sure the spark plugs are firing efficiently. The illustrations on the next 2 pages show you how to "read" the firing end of the spark plug.

6. Check the ignition timing and set it to specifications. Tests show that almost all cars have incorrect ignition timing by more than 2°.

veyed over 6,000 cars nationwide, they found that a tune-up, on cars that needed one, increased fuel economy over 11%. Replacing worn plugs alone, accounted for a 3% increase. The same test also revealed that 8 out of every 10 vehicles will have some maintenance deficiency that will directly affect fuel economy, emissions or performance. Most of this mileage-robbing neglect could be prevented with regular maintenance.

Modern engines require that all of the functioning systems operate properly for maximum efficiency. A malfunction anywhere wastes fuel. You can keep your vehicle running as efficiently and economically as possible, by being aware of your vehicle's operating and performance characteristics. If your vehicle suddenly develops performance or fuel economy problems it could be due to one or more of the following:

PROBLEM	POSSIBLE CAUSE
Engine Idles Rough	Ignition timing, idle mixture, vacuum leak or something amiss in the emission control system.
Hesitates on Acceleration	Dirty carburetor or fuel filter, improper accelerator pump setting, ignition timing or fouled spark plugs.
Starts Hard or Fails to Start	Worn spark plugs, improperly set automatic choke, ice (or water) in fuel system.
Stalls Frequently	Automatic choke improperly adjusted and possible dirty air filter or fuel filter.
Performs Sluggishly	Worn spark plugs, dirty fuel or air filter, ignition timing or automatic choke out of adjustment.

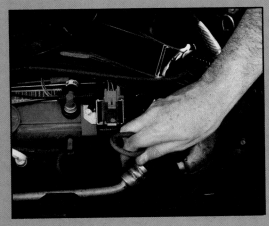

Check spark plug wires on conventional point type ignition for cracks by bending them in a loop around your finger.

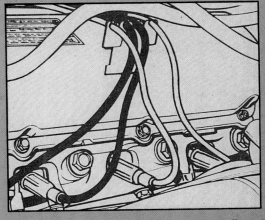

Be sure that spark plug wires leading to adjacent cylinders do not run too close together. (Photo courtesy Champion Spark Plug Co.)

7. If your vehicle does not have electronic ignition, check the points, rotor and cap as specified.

8. Check the spark plug wires (used with conventional point-type ignitions) for cracks and burned or broken insulation by bending them in a loop around your finger. Cracked wires decrease fuel efficiency by failing to deliver full voltage to the spark plugs. One misfiring spark plug can cost you as much as 2 mpg.

9. Check the routing of the plug wires. Misfiring can be the result of spark plug leads to adjacent cylinders running parallel to each other and too close together. One wire tends to

pick up voltage from the other causing it to fire "out of time".

10. Check all electrical and ignition circuits for voltage drop and resistance.

11. Check the distributor mechanical and/or vacuum advance mechanisms for proper functioning. The vacuum advance can be checked by twisting the distributor plate in the opposite direction of rotation. It should spring back when released.

12. Check and adjust the valve clearance on engines with mechanical lifters. The clearance should be slightly loose rather than too tight.

SPARK PLUG DIAGNOSIS

Normal

APPEARANCE: This plug is typical of one operating normally. The insulator nose varies from a light tan to grayish color with slight electrode wear. The presence of slight deposits is normal on used plugs and will have no adverse effect on engine performance. The spark plug heat range is correct for the engine and the engine is running normally.

CAUSE: Properly running engine.

RECOMMENDATION: Before reinstalling this plug, the electrodes should be cleaned and filed square. Set the gap to specifications. If the plug has been in service for more than 10-12,000 miles, the entire set should probably be replaced with a fresh set of the same heat range.

Oil Deposits

APPEARANCE: The firing end of the plug is covered with a wet, oily coating.

CAUSE: The problem is poor oil control. On high mileage engines, oil is leaking past the rings or valve guides into the combustion chamber. A common cause is also a plugged PCV valve, and a ruptured fuel pump diaphragm can also cause this condition. Oil fouled plugs such as these are often found in new or recently overhauled engines, before normal oil control is achieved, and can be cleaned and reinstalled.

RECOMMENDATION: A hotter spark plug may temporarily relieve the problem, but the engine is probably in need of work.

Incorrect Heat Range

APPEARANCE: The effects of high temperature on a spark plug are indicated by clean white, often blistered insulator. This can also be accompanied by excessive wear of the electrode, and the absence of deposits.

CAUSE: Check for the correct spark plug heat range. A plug which is too hot for the engine can result in overheating. A car operated mostly at high speeds can require a colder plug. Also check ignition timing, cooling system level, fuel mixture and leaking intake manifold.

RECOMMENDATION: If all ignition and engine adjustments are known to be correct, and no other malfunction exists, install spark plugs one heat range colder.

Photos Courtesy Fram Corporation

Carbon Deposits

APPEARANCE: Carbon fouling is easily identified by the presence of dry, soft, black, sooty deposits.

CAUSE: Changing the heat range can often lead to carbon fouling, as can prolonged slow, stop-and-start driving. If the heat range is correct, carbon fouling can be attributed to a rich fuel mixture, sticking choke, clogged air cleaner, worn breaker points, retarded timing or low compression. If only one or two plugs are carbon fouled, check for corroded or cracked wires on the affected plugs. Also look for cracks in the distributor cap between the towers of affected cylinders.

RECOMMENDATION: After the problem is corrected, these plugs can be cleaned and reinstalled if not worn severely.

MMT Fouled

APPEARANCE: Spark plugs fouled by MMT (Methycyclopentadienyl Maganese Tricarbonyl) have reddish, rusty appearance on the insulator and side electrode.

CAUSE: MMT is an anti-knock additive in gasoline used to replace lead. During the combustion process, the MMT leaves a reddish deposit on the insulator and side electrode.

RECOMMENDATION: No engine malfunction is indicated and the deposits will not affect plug performance any more than lead deposits (see Ash Deposits). MMT fouled plugs can be cleaned, regapped and reinstalled.

High Speed Glazing

APPEARANCE: Glazing appears as shiny coating on the plug, either yellow or tan in color.

CAUSE: During hard, fast acceleration, plug temperatures rise suddenly. Deposits from normal combustion have no chance to fluff-off; instead, they melt on the insulator forming an electrically conductive coating which causes misfiring.

RECOMMENDATION: Glazed plugs are not easily cleaned. They should be replaced with a fresh set of plugs of the correct heat range. If the condition recurs, using plugs with a heat range one step colder may cure the problem.

Ash (Lead) Deposits

APPEARANCE: Ash deposits are characterized by light brown or white colored deposits crusted on the side or center electrodes. In some cases it may give the plug a rusty appearance.

CAUSE: Ash deposits are normally derived from oil or fuel additives burned during normal combustion. Normally they are harmless, though excessive amounts can cause misfiring. If deposits are excessive in short mileage, the valve guides may be worn.

RECOMMENDATION: Ash-fouled plugs can be cleaned, gapped and reinstalled.

Detonation

APPEARANCE: Detonation is usually characterized by a broken plug insulator.

CAUSE: A portion of the fuel charge will begin to burn spontaneously, from the increased heat following ignition. The explosion that results applies extreme pressure to engine components, frequently damaging spark plugs and pistons.

Detonation can result by over-advanced ignition timing, inferior gasoline (low octane) lean air/fuel mixture, poor carburetion, engine lugging or an increase in compression ratio due to combustion chamber deposits or engine modification.

RECOMMENDATION: Replace the plugs after correcting the problem.

EMISSION CONTROLS

13. Be aware of the general condition of the emission control system. It contributes to reduced pollution and should be serviced regularly to maintain efficient engine operation.

14. Check all vacuum lines for dried, cracked or brittle conditions. Something as simple as a leaking vacuum hose can cause poor performance and loss of economy.

15. Avoid tampering with the emission control system. Attempting to improve fuel econ-

FUEL SYSTEM

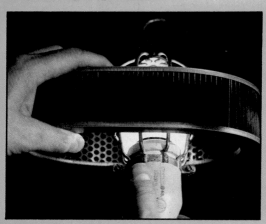 

Check the air filter with a light behind it. If you can see light through the filter it can be reused.

Extremely clogged filters should be discarded and replaced with a new one.

18. Replace the air filter regularly. A dirty air filter richens the air/fuel mixture and can increase fuel consumption as much as 10%. Tests show that ⅓ of all vehicles have air filters in need of replacement.

19. Replace the fuel filter at least as often as recommended.

20. Set the idle speed and carburetor mixture to specifications.

21. Check the automatic choke. A sticking or malfunctioning choke wastes gas.

22. During the summer months, adjust the automatic choke for a leaner mixture which will produce faster engine warm-ups.

COOLING SYSTEM

29. Be sure all accessory drive belts are in good condition. Check for cracks or wear.

30. Adjust all accessory drive belts to proper tension.

31. Check all hoses for swollen areas, worn spots, or loose clamps.

32. Check coolant level in the radiator or expansion tank.

33. Be sure the thermostat is operating properly. A stuck thermostat delays engine warm-up and a cold engine uses nearly twice as much fuel as a warm engine.

34. Drain and replace the engine coolant at least as often as recommended. Rust and scale

TIRES & WHEELS

38. Check the tire pressure often with a pencil type gauge. Tests by a major tire manufacturer show that 90% of all vehicles have at least 1 tire improperly inflated. Better mileage can be achieved by over-inflating tires, but never exceed the maximum inflation pressure on the side of the tire.

39. If possible, install radial tires. Radial tires deliver as much as ½ mpg more than bias belted tires.

40. Avoid installing super-wide tires. They only create extra rolling resistance and decrease fuel mileage. Stick to the manufacturer's recommendations.

41. Have the wheels properly balanced.

omy by tampering with emission controls is more likely to worsen fuel economy than improve it. Emission control changes on modern engines are not readily reversible.

16. Clean (or replace) the EGR valve and lines as recommended.

17. Be sure that all vacuum lines and hoses are reconnected properly after working under the hood. An unconnected or misrouted vacuum line can wreak havoc with engine performance.

23. Check for fuel leaks at the carburetor, fuel pump, fuel lines and fuel tank. Be sure all lines and connections are tight.

24. Periodically check the tightness of the carburetor and intake manifold attaching nuts and bolts. These are a common place for vacuum leaks to occur.

25. Clean the carburetor periodically and lubricate the linkage.

26. The condition of the tailpipe can be an excellent indicator of proper engine combustion. After a long drive at highway speeds, the inside of the tailpipe should be a light grey in color. Black or soot on the insides indicates an overly rich mixture.

27. Check the fuel pump pressure. The fuel pump may be supplying more fuel than the engine needs.

28. Use the proper grade of gasoline for your engine. Don't try to compensate for knocking or "pinging" by advancing the ignition timing. This practice will only increase plug temperature and the chances of detonation or pre-ignition with relatively little performance gain.

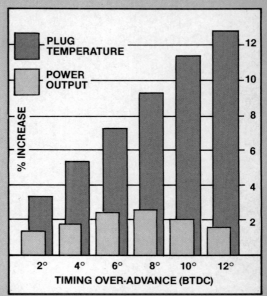

Increasing ignition timing past the specified setting results in a drastic increase in spark plug temperature with increased chance of detonation or preignition. Performance increase is considerably less. (Photo courtesy Champion Spark Plug Co.)

that form in the engine should be flushed out to allow the engine to operate at peak efficiency.

35. Clean the radiator of debris that can decrease cooling efficiency.

36. Install a flex-type or electric cooling fan, if you don't have a clutch type fan. Flex fans use curved plastic blades to push more air at low speeds when more cooling is needed; at high speeds the blades flatten out for less resistance. Electric fans only run when the engine temperature reaches a predetermined level.

37. Check the radiator cap for a worn or cracked gasket. If the cap does not seal properly, the cooling system will not function properly.

42. Be sure the front end is correctly aligned. A misaligned front end actually has wheels going in differed directions. The increased drag can reduce fuel economy by .3 mpg.

43. Correctly adjust the wheel bearings. Wheel bearings that are adjusted too tight increase rolling resistance.

Check tire pressures regularly with a reliable pocket type gauge. Be sure to check the pressure on a cold tire.

GENERAL MAINTENANCE

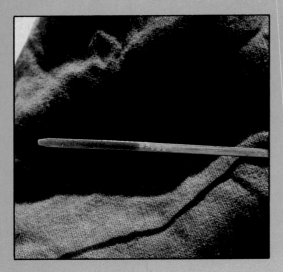

Check the fluid levels (particularly engine oil) on a regular basis. Be sure to check the oil for grit, water or other contamination.

A vacuum gauge is another excellent indicator of internal engine condition and can also be installed in the dash as a mileage indicator.

44. Periodically check the fluid levels in the engine, power steering pump, master cylinder, automatic transmission and drive axle.

45. Change the oil at the recommended interval and change the filter at every oil change. Dirty oil is thick and causes extra friction between moving parts, cutting efficiency and increasing wear. A worn engine requires more frequent tune-ups and gets progressively worse fuel economy. In general, use the lightest viscosity oil for the driving conditions you will encounter.

46. Use the recommended viscosity fluids in the transmission and axle.

47. Be sure the battery is fully charged for fast starts. A slow starting engine wastes fuel.

48. Be sure battery terminals are clean and tight.

49. Check the battery electrolyte level and add distilled water if necessary.

50. Check the exhaust system for crushed pipes, blockages and leaks.

51. Adjust the brakes. Dragging brakes or brakes that are not releasing create increased drag on the engine.

52. Install a vacuum gauge or miles-per-gallon gauge. These gauges visually indicate engine vacuum in the intake manifold. High vacuum = good mileage and low vacuum = poorer mileage. The gauge can also be an excellent indicator of internal engine conditions.

53. Be sure the clutch is properly adjusted. A slipping clutch wastes fuel.

54. Check and periodically lubricate the heat control valve in the exhaust manifold. A sticking or inoperative valve prevents engine warm-up and wastes gas.

55. Keep accurate records to check fuel economy over a period of time. A sudden drop in fuel economy may signal a need for tune-up or other maintenance.

7. If the solenoid doesn't work, replace the solenoid.

8. Reconnect the vacuum lines and the coil after completing the test.

1976 EGR Reminder Light

NOTE: *This light is designed to remind the driver that regularly scheduled service is due; it does not mean that the EGR system is not working properly. This system is only used on cars without a catalytic converter.*

1. After checking the EGR system for proper operation, slide the rubber boot on the EGR reminder odometer up, out of the way.

2. Reset the odometer with a small screwdriver.

3. Slide the boot back down over the odometer. The light will come on again when the next 15,000 mile check-up is due.

REPLACING THE CONVERTER

The converter used is the monolithic (one-piece) type which cannot be refilled.

If the catalyst fails, it will be necessary to replace the entire converter assembly. To do so:

CAUTION: *Allow the converter assembly to cool completely before attempting to service it; catalyst temperatures can reach 1500°–1600° F.*

1. If a grass shield is used, remove the bolts which secure it and lower the shield from underneath the vehicle.

2. Unbolt the converter assembly at the mounting flanges, just as you would a normal exhaust pipe from the manifold.

NOTE: *Support the exhaust pipe while the converter is removed.*

3. Replace the old converter with the new unit.

4. Remove the plastic plugs from the ends of the new converter (if used) and install it in the reverse order of removal, being sure to use all required gaskets to ensure a leak-free fit.

5. Install the grass shields.

LEAN BURN SYSTEM TESTING AND SERVICE

Some of the procedures in this section refer to an adjustable timing light. This is also known as a spark advance tester, i.e., a device which will measure how much spark advance is present going from one point, a base figure, to another. Since precise timing is very important to the Lean Burn System, do not attempt to perform any engine tests calling for an adjustable timing light without the one. In places where a regular timing light can be used, it will be noted in the text.

Troubleshooting

1. Remove the coil wire and hold it about ¼ in. away from an engine ground, then have

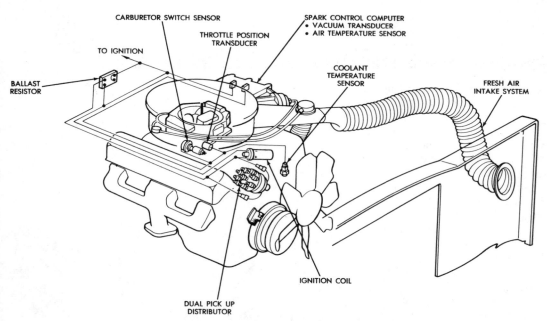

Electronic Lean Burn System Schematic

CHECK HERE FOR SPARK

Checking for spark during cranking

CHECK HERE FOR ARCING

Checking for arcing at coil tower

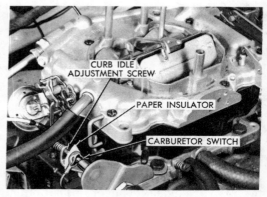

CURB IDLE ADJUSTMENT SCREW

PAPER INSULATOR

CARBURETOR SWITCH

Preparing for power check

someone crank the engine while you check for spark.

2. If you have a good spark, slowly move the coil wire away from the engine and check for arcing at the coil while cranking.

3. If you have good spark and it is not arcing at the coil, check the rest of the parts of the ignition system, if they are alright, the problem is not in the ignition system. Check chapter 11 for trouble-shooting the system.

ENGINE NOT RUNNING—WILL NOT START

1. Check the battery specific gravity; it must be at least 1.220 to deliver the necessary voltage to fire the plugs.

2. Remove the terminal connector from the coolant switch and put a piece of paper or plastic between the curb idle adusting screw and the carburetor switch. This is unnecessary if the screw and switch are not touching.

3. Connect the negative lead of a voltmeter to a good engine ground, turn the ignition switch to the "Run" position and measure the voltage at the carburetor switch terminal. If you receive a reading of more than five volts, go on to Step 7; if not, proceed to the next step.

4. Turn the ignition switch "Off" and disconnect the double terminal connector from the bottom of the Spark Control Computer. Turn the ignition switch back to the "Run" position and measure the voltage at terminal No. 2; if the voltage is not within 1 volt of the voltage you received in Step 3, check the wiring between terminal No. 2 and the igni-

tion switch. If the voltage is correct, go on to the next step.

5. Turn the ignition switch "off" and disconnect the single connector from the bottom of the Spark Control Computer. Using an ohmmeter, check for continuity between terminal No. 7 and the carburetor switch terminal. There should be continuity present, if not, check the wiring.

6. Check for continuity between terminal No. 10 (double connector) and ground. If there is continuity, replace the Spark Control Computer; if not, check the wiring. If the engine still will not start, proceed to the next step.

7. Turn the ignition switch to the "Run" position and check for voltage at terminal No. 1 and ground of the double connector. If you received voltage within 1 volt of that recorded in Step 3, proceed to the next step. If you do not get the correct voltage, check the wiring between the connector and the ignition switch.

8. Turn the ignition switch "Off" and with an ohmmeter, measure resistance between terminals Nos. 5 and 9 of the dual connector. If you do not receive a reading of 150–900 ohms, disconnect the start pick-up leads at the distributor and measure the resistance going into the distributor. If you get

MEASURE VOLTAGE HERE

CARB SWITCH TERMINAL

Power check

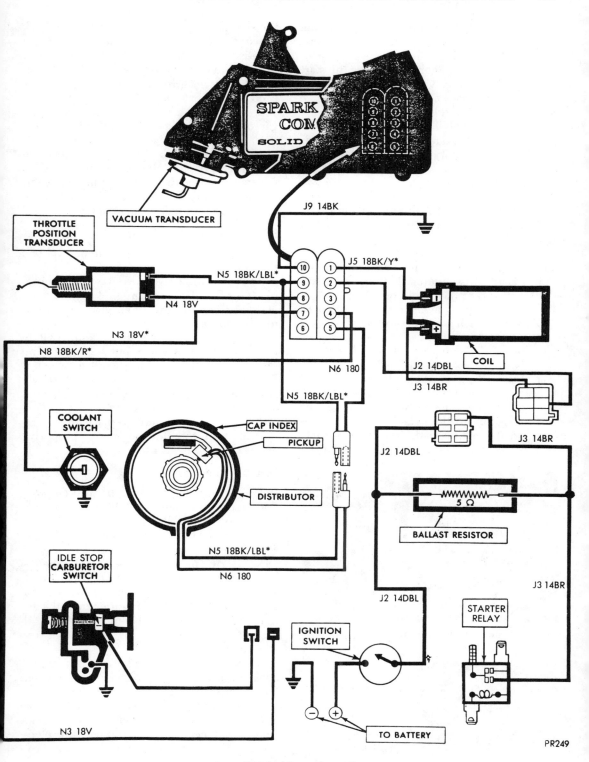

Lean Burn wiring schematic

PR249

a reading of 150–900 ohms here, the wiring between terminals Nos. 5 and 9 and the distributor is faulty. If you still do not get a reading between 150–900 ohms, replace the start pick-up. If you received the proper reading when you initially checked terminals Nos. 5 and 9, proceed to the next step.

9. Connect one lead of an ohmmeter to a good engine ground and with the other lead, check the continuity of both start pick-up leads going into the distributor. If there is not continuity, go on to the next step. If you do get a reading, replace the start pick-up.

10. Remove the distributor cap and check the air gap of the start pick-up coil. Adjust, if necessary, and proceed to the next step.

11. Replace the distributor cap, and start the engine; if it still will not start, replace the Spark Control Computer. If the engine still does not work, put the old one back and re-trace your steps, paying close attention to any wiring which may be shorted.

ENGINE RUNNING BADLY (RUN PICK-UP TESTS)

1. Start the engine and let it run for a couple of minutes. Disconnect the start pick-up lead. If the engine still runs, leave this test and go on to the "Start Timer Advance Test." If the engine died, proceed to Step 2.

2. Disconnect the run pick-up coil from

Checking Run Pick-up at distributor leads

Checking for resistance at throttle transducer terminals

the distributor. Use an ohmmeter to check for continuity at each of the leads going into the distributor. If there is continuity shown, replace the pick-up coil and repeat Step 1. If you do not get a reading of continuity, proceed to the next step.

3. Remove the distributor cap, check the gap of the run pick-up and adjust it if necessary.

4. Reinstall the distributor cap, check the wiring, and try to start the engine. If it does not start, replace the computer and try again. If it still does not start, repeat the test paying close attention to all wiring connections.

Start Timer Advance Test

1. Hook up an *adjustable* timing light to the engine.

2. Have an assistant start the engine, place his foot firmly on the brake, then open and close the throttle, then place the transmission in Drive.

3. Locate the timing signal immediately after the transmission is put in Drive. The meter on the timing light should show about 5–9° advance. This advance should slowly decrease to the basic timing signal after about one minute. If it did not increase the 5–9° or return after one minute, replace the spark control computer. If it did operate properly, proceed to the next test.

Throttle Advance Test

Before performing this test, the throttle position transducer must be adjusted. The adjustments are as follows:

1. The air temperature sensor inside the spark control computer must be cool (below 135°). If the engine is at operating temperature, either turn it off and let it cool down or remove the top of the air cleaner and inject a spray coolant into the computer over tha air temperature sensor for about 15 seconds. If Steps 2–5 take longer than 3–4 minutes, re-cool the sensor.

2. Start the engine and wait about 90 seconds, then connect a jumper wire between the carburetor switch terminal and ground.

3. Disconnect the electrical connector from the transducer and check the timing, adjusting if necessary. Reconnect the electrical connector to the transducer and re-check the timing.

4. If the timing is more than specified on the tune-up decal, loosen the transducer locknut and turn the transducer clockwise until it comes within limits, then turn it an

additional ½ turn clockwise and tighten the locknut.

5. If the timing is at the specified limits, loosen the locknut and turn the transducer counterclockwise until the timing just begins to advance. At that point, turn the transducer ½ turn clockwise and tighten the locknut. After this step you are ready to begin the throttle advance test.

6. Turn the ignition switch "Off" and disconnect the single connector from the bottom of the spark control computer.

7. With an ohmmeter, measure the resistance between terminals Nos. 8 and 9 of the single connector. The measured resistance should be between 60–90 ohms. If it is, go on to the next step, if not, remove the connector from the throttle position transducer and measure the resistance at the transducer terminals. If you now get a reading of 60–90 ohms, check the wiring between the computer terminals and the transducer terminal. If you do not get the 60–90 reading, replace the transducer and proceed to the next step.

8. Reconnect the wiring and turn the switch to the "Run" position without starting the engine. Hook up a voltmeter, negative lead to an engine ground, and touch the positive lead to one terminal of the transducer while opening and closing the throttle all the way. Do the same thing to the other terminal of the transducer. Both terminals should show a 2 volt change when opening and closing the throttle. If not proceed to the next step.

9. Position the throttle linkage on the fast idle cam and ground the carb switch with a jumper wire. Disconnect the wiring connector from the transducer and connect it to a transducer that you know is good.

10. Move the core of the transducer all the way in, start the engine, wait about 90 seconds, and then move the core out about an inch.

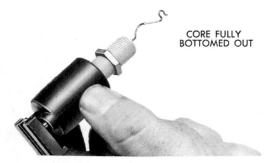

CORE FULLY BOTTOMED OUT

Checking with test transducer

11. Adjust the timing light so that it registers the basic timing signal. The timing light should show the additional amount of advance as given in the "Transducer Advance Specifications" chart in this section. If it is within the specifications, move the core back into the transducer, and the timing should go back to the original position. If the timing did advance and return, go on to the next step. If it did not advance and/or return, replace the spark control computer and try this test over again. If it still fails, replace the transducer.

12. Reset the timing light meter, and have an assistant move the transducer core in and out 5–6 times quickly. The timing should advance 7–12° for about a second and then return to the base figure. If it did not, replace the spark control computer. If you did not get the 2 volt change in reading in Step 8, you should now replace the transducer since you have proved that the spark control computer is not causing it to check out faulty.

13. Remove the test transducer (from Step 9), and reconnect all wiring.

Vacuum Advance Test (Vacuum Transducer)

1. Hook up an adjustable timing light.

2. Turn the ignition switch to the "Run" position, but do not start the engine. Disconnect the idle stop solenoid wire and the wiring connector from the coolant switch. Push the solenoid plunger in all the way, and while holding the throttle linkage open, reconnect the solenoid wire. The solenoid plunger should pop out and when the throttle linkage is released, it should also hold the linkage in place. If it does not, replace the idle stop solenoid.

3. Start the engine and let it warm up; make sure that the transmission is in Neutral and the parking brake is on.

4. Place a small piece of plastic or paper between the carburetor switch and the curb idle adjusting screw; if the screw is not touching the switch, make sure that the fast idle cam is not on or binding; the linkage is not binding, or the throttle stop screw is not overadjusted. Adjust the timing light for the basic timing figure. The meter of the timing light should show 2–5° advance with a minimum of 16 in. of vacuum at the vacuum transducer (checked with a vacuum gauge). If this advance is not present, replace the spark control computer and try the test again. If the advance is present, let the engine run for

about 6–9 minutes, then go on to the next step.

5. After the 6–9 minute waiting period, adjust the timing light so that it registers the basic timing figure. The timing light meter should now register 32–35° of advance. If the advance is not shown, replace the spark control computer and repeat the test; if it is shown, proceed to Step 6.

6. Remove the insulator (paper or plastic) which was installed in Step 4; the timing should return to its base setting. If it does not, make sure that the curb idle adjusting screw is not touching the carburetor switch. If that is alright, turn the engine off and check the wire between terminal No. 7 of the single connector (from the bottom of the spark control computer), and the carburetor switch terminal for a bad connection. If it turns out alright, and the timing still will not return to its base setting, replace the spark control computer.

Coolant Switch Test

1. Connect one lead of the ohmmeter to a good engine ground, the other to the black wire with a tracer in it. Disregard the orange wire if there is one on the switch.

2. If the engine is cold (below 150°), there should be continuity present in the switch. With the thermostat open, and the engine warmed up, there should be no continuity. If either of the conditions in this step are not met, replace the switch.

Lean Burn Timing

This procedure is to set the basic timing signal as shown on the engine tune-up decal in the engine compartment.

1. Connect a jumper wire between the carburetor switch terminal and the ground. Connect a standard timing light to the No. 1 cylinder.

2. Block the wheels and set the parking brake. If the car has an automatic release type parking brake, remove and plug the vacuum line which controls it from the fitting on the rear of the engine.

3. Start and warm the engine up; raise engine speed above 1,500 rpm for a second, then drop the speed and let it idle for a minute or two.

4. With the engine idling at the point specified on the tune-up decal with the transmission in Drive, adjust the timing to the figure given on the tune-up decal.

Idle Speed and Mixture

1. Follow the first three steps under "Lean Burn Timing," then insert an exhaust gas analyzer into the tailpipe.

2. Place the transmission in Drive, the air conditioning and headlights off. Adjust the idle speed to the specification shown on the tune-up decal by turning the idle solenoid speed screw.

3. Adjust the carbon monoxide level to 0.1% with the mixture screws while trying to keep hydrocarbons to a minimum and the idle speed to specification. Turn the screws alternately over their range to coordinate all three factors.

4. Place the transmission in Neutral; disconnect the wire at the idle stop solenoid and adjust the curb idle speed screw to obtain 650 rpm. Reconnect the wire.

5. Remove the air cleaner cover and lift and support the air cleaner assembly high enough to gain access to the fast idle adjustment screw.

6. Place the fast idle speed screw on the highest step of the cam and adjust the idle speed to the specification shown on the tune-up decal.

7. Drop the idle back down to the curb idle position and turn the ignition switch off. Reconnect any hoses or electrical connections taken off in the procedure.

8. If the procedure has to be performed a second time, make sure that you start from the beginning or the readings will be inaccurate.

Removal and Overhaul

None of the components of the Lean Burn System (except the carburetor), are able to be disassembled and repaired. When one part is known to be defective, it is replaced.

The Spark Control Computer is secured by mounting screws inside the air cleaner. To remove the Throttle Position Transducer, loosen the locknut and unscrew it from the mounting bracket, then unsnap the core from the carburetor linkage.

Transducer Advance Specifications

Core Moved Out 1 in.	7–12° @ 75° F
	4–7° @ 104° F
Moved 5–6 Times	7–12°
	(One second duration each time)

Pick-Up Gaps

Start Pick-up	(set to)	0.008 in.
	(check at)	0.010 in.
Run Pick-Up	(set to)	0.012 in.
	(check at)	0.014 in.

IDLE ENRICHMENT SYSTEM TEST

The purpose of the idle enrichment system is to reduce cold engine stalling by use of a metering system related to the basic carburetor instead of the choke. The system enriches carburetor mixtures in the curb idle and fast idle area.

A small vacuum-controlled diaphragm mounted near the top of the carburetor controls idle system air. When control vacuum is applied to the diaphragm, idle system air is reduced. Air losses strengthen the small vacuum signal within the idle system and fuel flow increases. As a result of more fuel and less air, the engine will idle better when cold.

To test the system, proceed as follows:

1. Run the engine to normal operating temperatures.

2. Remove the air cleaner, but *do not* cap any of the vacuum fittings opened by hose removal. The vacuum leakage is needed for the test.

3. Disconnect the hose to the idle enrichment diaphragm at the plastic connector. Remove the plastic connector from the carburetor hose.

4. With the engine running, place the fast idle screw on the lowest step of the fast idle cam.

5. Connect three or four feet of hose to the enrichment diaphragm hose with a suitable connector.

6. Use a hand vacuum pump and apply vacuum to the hose. Listen for a change in engine speed. If the engine speed can be controlled by vacuum, then the system is OK. If the speed cannot be controlled, replace the valve assembly (Holley carburetors) or proceed to the next step (Carter carburetors).

7. Place a finger over the air inlet passage and listen for an engine speed change. If you can control engine speed this way, the diaphragm is leaking or the air valve is stuck open. If speed cannot be controlled this way, the air valve is stuck closed. In either case, clean the air valve, and repeat step six. If

speed control is still absent, replace the diaphragm.

COOLANT CONTROLLED ENGINE VACUUM SWITCH TEST

1. First make sure the vacuum hoses are routed correctly and the engine coolant level is correct.

2. Disconnect the molded connector from the valve. Attach a ⅛ in. hose to the bottom port on the valve.

3. Run the engine to normal operating temperature.

4. With the top tank warm to the touch (but no warmer than 75°F.), blow through the hose. If it is not possible to blow through the valve, then it is defective and must be replaced.

5. Attach a vacuum pump to the bottom port of the valve. Apply 10 in. of vacuum. If the vacuum level drops more than one inch in 15 seconds, replace the valve.

FUEL SYSTEM

Fuel Pump

REMOVAL AND INSTALLATION

1. Disconnect the fuel inlet and outlet lines. Plug the fuel inlet line to prevent emptying the fuel tank.

2. Remove the two fuel pump securing bolts.

3. Remove the fuel pump from the car.

4. Reverse the above steps to install.

TESTING

Fuel pump output can be tested by rigging the pump to discharge into a container. It should pump one quart of fuel in a minute or less, with the engine running at idle speed.

CAUTION: *Use a big container so that it doesn't overflow. Have an assistant ready to stop the engine. Be extremely careful not to spill fuel on hot engine parts.*

Carburetors

The Holley 1945 one barrel carburetor is used on six-cylinder engines. The Carter BBD two barrel is used on the "Super" six cylinder engine and on the 318 cu. in. V8. The Holley 2245 two barrel carburetor is used on the 360 V8. Both the 318 and 360 four barrel engines use the Carter Thermo-Quad carburetor.

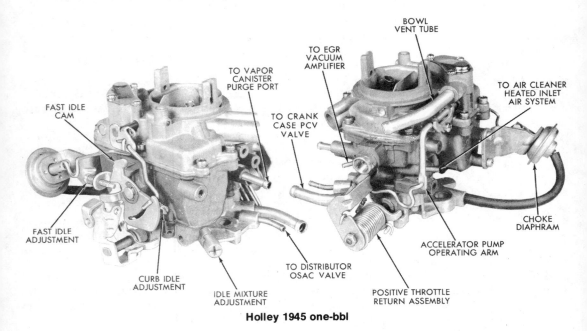

Holley 1945 one-bbl

Carter BBD two-bbl

REMOVAL AND INSTALLATION

1. Remove the air cleaner.
2. Disconnect the fuel and vacuum lines.
It might be a good idea to tag them to avoid confusion when the time comes to put them back.
3. Disconnect the choke rod.
4. Disconnect the accelerator linkage.

5. Disconnect the automatic transmission linkage.
6. Unbolt and remove the carburetor.
7. Remove the base gasket.
8. Before installation, make sure that the carburetor and manifold sealing surfaces are clean.
9. Install a new carburetor base gasket,

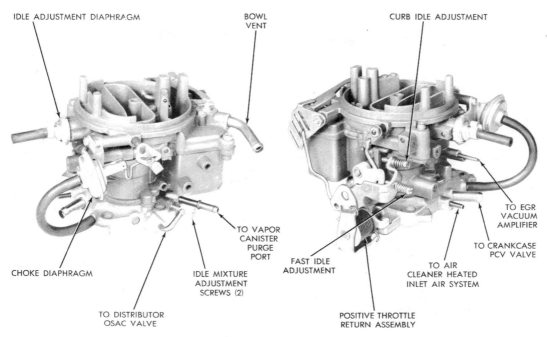

Holley 2245 two-bbl

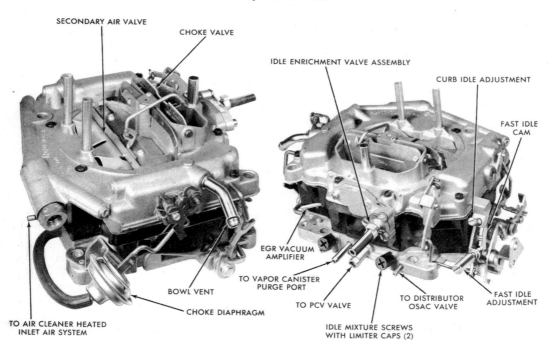

Carter Thermo-Quad Carburetor

making sure that the "top front" marking is correctly located on six-cylinder engines.

10. Install the carburetor and start the fuel and vacuum lines.

11. Bolt down the carburetor evenly.

12. Tighten the fuel and vacuum lines.

13. Connect the accelerator and automatic transmission linkage. If the transmission linkage was disturbed, it will have to be adjusted. The procedure is in this Chapter.

14. Connect the choke rod.

15. Install the air cleaner. Adjust the idle speed and mixture as discribed in Chapter 2.

OVERHAUL

Whenever wear or dirt causes a carburetor to perform poorly, there are two possible solutions to the problem. The simplest is to trade in the old unit for a rebuilt one. The other, cheaper alternative is to buy an overhaul kit and rebuild the original unit. Some of the better overhaul kits contain complete step-by-step instructions along with exploded views and gauges. Other kits, intended for the professional, have only a few general overhaul hints. The second type can be confusing to the novice, especially since a kit may have extra parts so that one kit can cover several variations of the same carburetor. In any event, it is not a good idea to dismantle any carburetor without at least replacing all the gaskets. The carburetor adjustments should all be checked during or after overhaul.

NOTE: *Before you go to the parts store for a rebuilding kit, make sure that you know what make and model your carburetor is. Check for an identification tag or number stamped on the base.*

Efficient carburetion depends greatly on careful cleaning and inspection during overhaul, since dirt, gum, water, or varnish in or on the carburetor parts are often responsible for poor performance.

Overhaul a carburetor in a clean, dust-free area. Carefully disassemble the carburetor, referring often to illustrations. Keep all similar and look-alike parts segregated during disassembly and cleaning to avoid accidental interchange during assembly. Make a note of all jet sizes.

When the carburetor is disassembled, wash all parts (except diaphragms, electric choke units, pump plunger, and any other plastic, leather, fiber, or rubber parts) in clean carburetor solvent. Do not leave parts in the solvent any longer than is necessary to sufficiently loosen the deposits. Excessive cleaning may remove the special finish from the float bowl and choke valve bodies, leaving these parts unfit for service. Rinse all parts in clean solvent and blow them dry with compressed air or allow them to air dry. Wipe clean all cork, plastic, leather, and fiber parts with a clean, lint-free cloth.

Blow out all passages and jets with compressed air and be sure that there are no restrictions or blockages. Never use wire or similar tools to clean jets, fuel passages, or air bleeds. Clean all jets and valves separately to avoid accidental interchange.

Check all parts for wear or damage. If wear or damage is found, replace the defective parts. Especially check the following:

1. Check the float needle and seat for wear. If wear is found, replace the complete assembly.

2. Check the float hinge pin for wear and the float(s) for dents or distortion. Replace the float if fuel has leaked into it.

3. Check the throttle and choke shaft bores for wear or an out-of-round condition. Damage or wear to the throttle arm, shaft, or shaft bore will often require replacement of the throttle body. These parts require a close tolerance of fit; wear may allow air leakage, which could affect starting and idling.

NOTE: *Throttle shafts and bushings are not included in overhaul kits. They can be purchased separately.*

4. Inspect the idle mixture adjusting needles for burrs or grooves. Any such condition requires replacement of the needle, since you will not be able to obtain a satisfactory idle.

5. Test the accelerator pump check valves. They should pass air one way but not the other. Test for proper seating by blowing and sucking on the valve. Replace the valve as necessary. If the valve is satisfactory, wash the valve again to remove breath moisture.

6. Check the bowl cover for warped surfaces with a straightedge.

7. Closely inspect the valves and seats for wear and damage, replacing as necessary.

8. After the carburetor is assembled, check the choke valve for freedom of operation.

Carburetor overhaul kits are recommended for each overhaul. These kits contain all gaskets and new parts to replace those that deteriorate most rapidly. Failure to replace all parts supplied with the kit (especially gaskets) can result in poor performance later.

Some carburetor manufacturers supply overhaul kits of three basic types: minor repair; major repair; and gasket kits. Basically, they contain the following:

Minor Repair Kits:
- All gaskets
- Float needle valve
- All diaphragms
- Spring for the pump diaphragm

Major Repair Kits:

- All jets and gaskets
- All diaphragms
- Float needle valve
- Volume control screw
- Pump ball valve
- Float
- Some cover hold-down screws and washers

Gasket Kits:

- All gaskets

After cleaning and checking all components, reasemble the carburetor, using new parts and referring to illustrations. When reassembling, make sure that all screws and jets are tight in their seats, but do not over-tighten as the tips will be distorted. Tighten all screws gradually, in rotation. Do not tighten needle valves into their seats; uneven jetting will result. Always use new gaskets. Be sure to adjust the float level when reassembling.

THROTTLE AND AUTOMATIC TRANSMISSION LINKAGE ADJUSTMENTS

Throttle linkage adjustments are rarely required unless the transmission linkage has been disturbed. However, it is a good idea to check that the throttle valve(s) open all the way when the accelerator pedal is held all the way down. This is occasionally the source of poor performance on new cars.

All Automatic Transmission

1. Lubricate the friction points of the linkage.
2. Disconnect the choke at the carburetor or otherwise make sure that the throttle is off the fast idle cam.
3. Loosen the adjustment swivel lockscrew at the transmission.
4. The swivel must be free to slide along the flat end of the throttle rod.
5. Hold the transmission lever firmly forward against its internal stop and tighten the swivel lockscrew. The adjustment is completed and linkage slack removed by the preload spring.
6. Pull the transmission throttle rod slowly back and release it. It should go back forward slowly.
7. Loosen the cable clamp nut. Adjust the position of the outer cable in the clamp so that all slack is removed. Move the outer cable away from the carburetor to do this. Move the outer cable back ¼ in. to allow slack at idle.

All Manual Transmission

1. Lubricate the friction points of the throttle linkage.
2. Disconnect the choke at the carburetor and make sure that the throttle is off the fast idle cam.

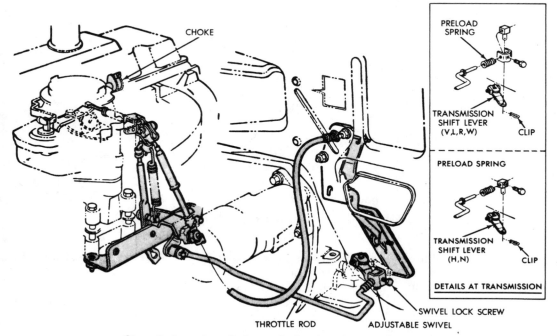

Six cylinder automatic transmission throttle rod adjustment

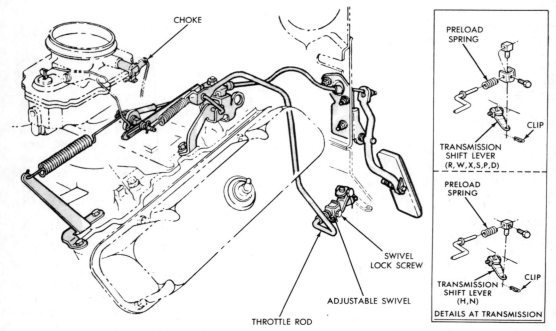

V8 automatic transmission throttle rod adjustment

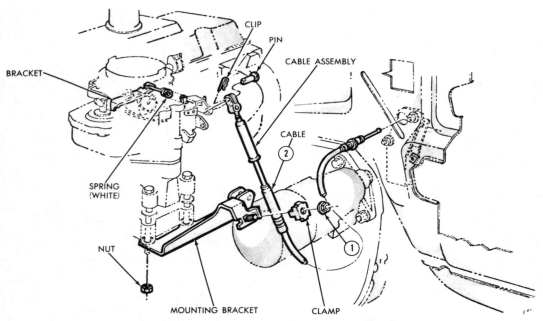

Six cylinder manual transmission throttle rod adjustment

3. Loosen the cable clamp nut. Adjust the cable by moving the cable housing so that there is about ¼ in. of slack in the cable at idle.

4. Tighten the cable clamp nut.

5. Reconnect the choke and check the linkage for free movement.

HOLLEY CARBURETOR ADJUSTMENTS

NOTE: *Most of these adjustments require that measurements be made in thousandths of an inch, using some sort of gauge. Drill bits are ideal for this purpose.*

Model 1945

The model 1945 carburetor is a concentric downdraft single-barrel carburetor with an internal float bowl which completely surrounds the venturi. The unit uses dual nitrophyl floats which permit operation at extreme angles. It is used on six-cylinder engines.

Float Level

1. Remove the float bowl cover and invert the bowl. Hold the retaining spring in place.
2. Place a straightedge across the surface of the bowl. It should just clear the toes of the floats by the specified measurement.
3. If adjustment is necessary, bend the float tang to obtain the correct adjustment.

Fast Idle

1. Remove the air cleaner and disconnect the vacuum lines to the heated air control and the OSAC (Orifice Spark Advance Control) valve. If there is no OSAC valve, disconnect the hose to the distributor and the EGR hose. Cap all carburetor vacuum fittings.
2. With the engine off, transmission in

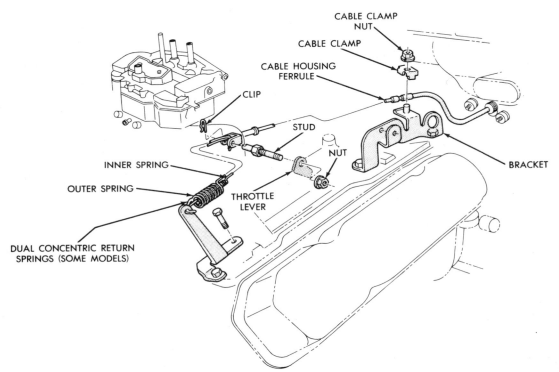

V8 manual transmission throttle rod adjustment

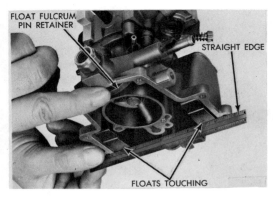

Holley 1945—float level check

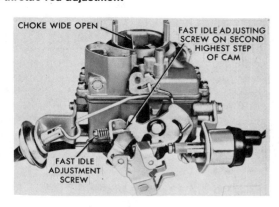

Holley 1945—fast idle adjustment

Neutral and the parking brake set, open the throttle and close the choke.

3. Close the throttle. This will place the fast idle speed screw on the highest step.

4. Move the fast idle cam until the screw drops to the second highest speed step.

5. Start the engine and stabilize the engine speed. Rotate the idle speed screw to obtain the specified setting.

Choke Unloader

1. Hold the throttle valves wide-open and insert the specified gauge between the upper edge of the choke valve and the inner wall of the air horn.

2. Place slight pressure against the control lever and attempt to remove the gauge. There should be a slight drag as the gauge is being withdrawn. If adjustment is necessary, bend the unloader tang on the throttle lever until the correct opening has been obtained.

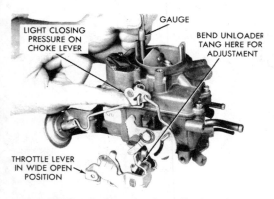

Holley 1945—choke unloader adjustment

MODEL 2245

The model 2245 carburetor is a two-barrel unit used on 360 cubic inch engines. The carburetor uses four fuel metering systems. The Idle and Idle Enrichment System provides the correct mixture for idle and low-speed performance; the Accelerator Pump System furnishes additional fuel during acceleration; the Main Metering System gives an economical mixture for normal cruising conditions; and the Power Enrichment System enriches the mixture when high power output is desired.

Float Level

1. Invert the air horn so that the weight of the float is forcing the metering needle against its seat.

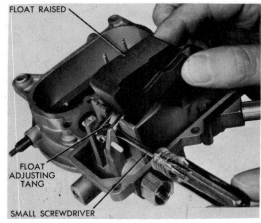

Holley 2245—float level adjustment

2. Measure the distance from the top of the float and the float stop. The clearance should be the same as given in the "Specifications" chart. Make certain that the gauge is level when making the measurement.

3. If adjustment is necessary, bend the float adjusting tab toward or away from the needle. A narrow-bladed screwdriver may be used to bend the tab.

4. Check the float drop by holding the air horn upright. The bottom edge of the float should be parallel to the underside of the air horn. If an adjustment is necessary, bend the tang on the float arm.

Fast Idle Cam Position

1. Position the fast idle speed adjusting screw on the second highest notch on the fast idle cam. Move the choke valve toward the closed position by applying light pressure on the choke shaft lever.

2. Insert the correct gauge between the top of the choke valve and the wall of the air horn.

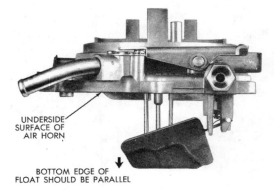

Holley 2245—checking float drop

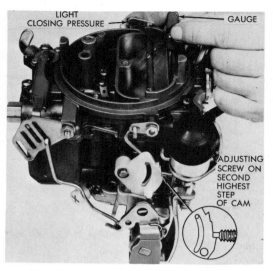

Holley 2245—fast idle cam position adjustment

An adjustment will be necessary if there is not a slight drag when the gauge is removed.

3. If an adjustment is necessary, bend the fast idle connector rod at the angle.

Vacuum Kick

1. The adjustment must be made with some type of vacuum source. If the adjustment is made with the engine running, disconnect the fast idle linkage to allow the choke to close to the kick position with the engine at curb idle. If an auxiliary vacuum source is to be used, open the throttle valves and move the choke to the closed position. Release the throttle first and then the choke.

2. If an auxiliary vacuum source is used, disconnect the vacuum hose from the carburetor and connect it to the hose from the vacuum supply with a small length of extra hose. Apply a vacuum of 15 in. or more of mercury.

3. Insert the correct gauge (see "Specifica-

tions" chart) between the top of the choke valve and the wall of the air horn. Apply pressure to the choke rod without distorting the diaphragm link. The cylindrical stem of the diaphragm will extend as the internal spring is compressed. This spring must be fully compressed for proper measurement of the vacuum kick adjustment.

4. If a slight drag is not felt when the gauge is removed, adjustment is necessary. Adjust the diaphragm link to obtain the correct choke valve opening. Adjustments can be made by carefully opening or closing the U-bend in the link.

CAUTION: *Do not twist or bend the diaphragm.*

5. Connect the vacuum hose to the correct carburetor fitting. Replace the linkage.

6. Make the following check. With no vacuum source attached to the diaphragm, the choke valve should move freely between open and closed positions. If the movement is not free, examine the linkage for misalignment or interferences caused by the bending operation.

Choke Unloader (Wide Open Kick)

1. Place the throttle valves in the wide-open position and insert the proper gauge between the upper edge of the choke valve and the inner wall of the air horn.

2. While holding pressure on the shaft lever, a slight drag should be felt as the gauge is removed.

3. If an adjustment is necessary, bend the unloader tang on the throttle lever.

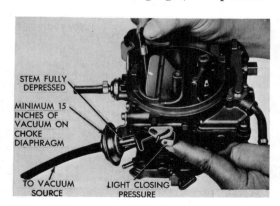

Holley 2245—vacuum kick adjustment

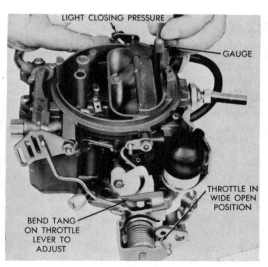

Holley 2245—choke unloader adjustment

Accelerator Pump

1. Back off the curb idle adjusting screw and open the choke valve so that the fast idle cam allows the throttle valves to be completely seated in their bores.

NOTE: *Make certain that the pump connector rod is placed in the correct slot of the accelerator pump rocker arm. On manual transmission models, it is the first slot next to the retaining nut.*

2. Close the throttle valves and measure the distance from the top of the air horn to the end of the plunger shaft. See "Specifications" chart.

3. If adjustment is needed, bend the pump operating rod at its loop.

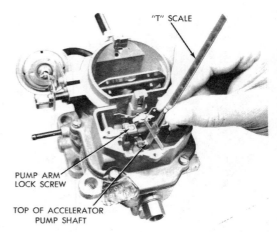

Carter BBD—accelerator pump stroke adjustment

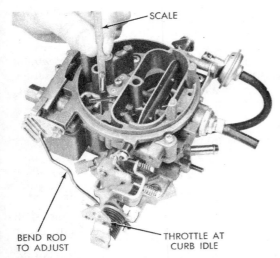

Holley 2245—accelerator pump adjustment

CARTER CARBURETOR ADJUSTMENTS

NOTE: *Most of these adjustments require that measurements be made in thousandths of an inch, using some sort of gauge. Drill bits are ideal for this purpose.*

Model BBD

The BBD carburetor is a two-barrel unit. This is sometimes called a Ball & Ball carburetor. It is used on 318 cu. in. V8s and the "Super" six cylinder.

Accelerator Pump

1. Back off the idle adjusting screw. Open the choke valve so that the fast idle cam allows the throttle valves to close. Be sure that the accelerator pump "S" link is in the outer hole of the pump arm.

2. With the throttle valves closed tightly, measure the distance between the top of the air horn and the top of the pump plunger shaft. If the dimension is not as specified, loosen the pump arm adjusting lockscrew (near the plunger shaft) and rotate the sleeve to obtain the correct dimension.

Fast Idle Cam Position

1. With the fast idle speed adjusting screw contacting the second highest speed step on the fast idle cam, move the choke valve toward the closed position with light pressure on the choke shaft lever.

2. Insert the specified drill (refer to "Specifications"), between the choke valve and the wall of the air horn. An adjustment will be necessary if a slight drag is not obtained as the drill is being removed.

3. If an adjustment is required, bend the fast idle connector rod at the lower angle.

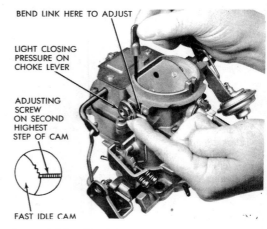

Carter BBD—fast idle cam position adjustment

Choke Unloader (Wide Open Kick)

1. Hold the throttle valves in the wide open position. Insert the specified drill (see "Specifications") between the upper edge of the choke valve and the inner wall of the air horn.

2. With a finger lightly pressing against the choke lever, a slight drag should be felt as the drill is being withdrawn. If an adjustment is necessary, bend the unloader tang on the throttle lever until the correct opening has been obtained.

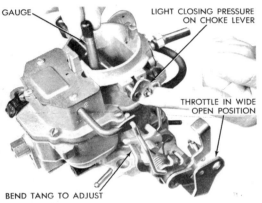

Carter BBD—choke unloader adjustment

Fast Idle Speed

1. Disconnect and plug the connections for the heated air control and OSAC valve or distributor. With the engine off and the transmission in Park or Neutral position, open the throttle slightly.

2. Close the choke valve until the fast idle screw can be positioned on the highest speed step of the fast idle cam.

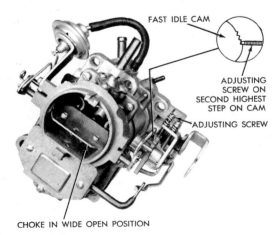

Carter BBD—fast idle speed adjustment

3. Start the engine and let the idle stabilize. Turn the fast idle speed screw in or out to obtain the specified speed.

4. Stopping the engine between adjustments is not necessary. However, reposition the fast idle speed screw on the cam after each speed adjustment to provide the correct throttle closing torque.

Vacuum Kick

1. If the adjustment is to be made with the engine running, disconnect the fast idle linkage to allow the choke to close to the kick position with engine at curb idle. If an auxiliary vacuum source is to be used, open the throttle valves (engine not running) and move the choke to the closed position. Release the throttle first, then release the choke.

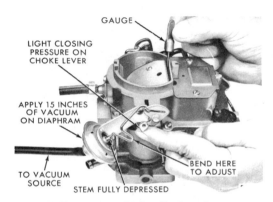

Carter BBD—vacuum kick adjustment

2. When using an auxiliary vacuum source, disconnect the vacuum hose from the carburetor and connect it to the hose from the vacuum supply with a small length of tube to act as a fitting. Removal of the hose from the diaphragm may require sufficient force to damage the diaphragm. Apply a vacuum of 15 or more in. of mercury.

3. Insert the specified drill (refer to "Specifications") between the choke valve and the upper wall of the air horn. Apply sufficient closing pressure on the lever to which the choke rod attaches to provide a minimum choke valve opening without distortion of the diaphragm link. Note that the cylindrical stem of the diaphragm will extend as the internal spring is compressed. This spring must be fully compressed for proper measurement of the vacuum kick of adjustment.

4. An adjustment will be necessary if a slight drag is not obtained as the drill is being removed. Shorten or lengthen the dia-

Holley Model 2245 Specifications

Year	Carb.* Part No.	Float Level (in.)	Accelerator Pump Adjustment (in.)	Bowl Vent Clearance (in.)	Fast Idle (rpm)	Choke Unloader Clearance (in.)	Vacuum Kick (in.)	Fast Idle Cam Position (in.)	Choke
1975	R-7226-A	.190	.250	.015	1600	.170	.150	.110	Fixed
	R-7211-A	.190	.250	.015	1600	.170	.150	.110	Fixed
	R-7027-A	.190	.250	.015	1600	.170	.150	.110	Fixed
1976	R-7364-A	.190	.265	.025	1600	.170	.150	.110	Fixed
	R-7366-A	.190	.265	.025	1600	.170	.150	.110	Fixed
1977	R-7671-A	.190	.265	.025	1700	.170	.110	.110	Fixed
1978	R-7991-A	.188	.265	.025	1600	.170	.110	.110	Fixed
	R-8326-A	.188	.265	.025	1600	.170	.110	.110	Fixed
1979	R-8450-A	.188	.266	.025	1600	.170	.110	.110	Fixed
	R-8774-A	.188	.266	.025	1600	.170	.110	.110	Fixed

*Located on a tag attached to the carburetor.

Carter BBD Specifications

Year	Model ④	Float Level (in.)	Accelerator Pump Travel (in.)	Bowl Vent (in.)	Choke Unloader (in.)	Choke Vacuum Kick	Fast Idle Cam Position	Fast Idle Speed (rpm)	Automatic Choke Adjustment
1976	8071S	¼	0.500 ①	—	0.280	0.130	0.070	1500	Fixed
	8069S	¼	0.500 ①	—	0.310	0.070	0.070	1200	Fixed
	8070S	¼	0.500 ①	—	0.310	0.110	0.070	1500	Fixed
	8077S, 8099S	¼	0.500 ①	—	0.280	0.110	0.070	1250	Fixed
	8072S	¼	0.500 ①	—	0.310	0.070	0.070	1500	Fixed
1977	8087S	¼	0.469 ①	—	0.280	0.100	0.070	1600	Fixed
	8089S	¼	0.469 ①	—	0.280	0.130	0.070	1600	Fixed
	8090S	¼	0.469 ①	—	0.280	0.130	0.070	1700	Fixed
	8127S	¼	0.469 ①	—	0.280	0.110	0.070	1500	Fixed
	8093S	¼	0.469 ①	—	0.310	0.130	0.070	1400	Fixed
	8094S	¼	0.469 ①	—	0.310	0.070	0.070	1400	Fixed

Carter BBD Specifications (cont.)

Year	Model ④	Float Level (in.)	Accelerator Pump Travel (in.)	Bowl Vent (in.)	Choke Unloader (in.)	Choke Vacuum Kick	Fast Idle Cam Position	Fast Idle Speed (rpm)	Automatic Choke Adjustment
	8096S	¼	0.469 ①	—	0.310	0.110	0.070	1500	Fixed
	8126S	¼	0.469 ①	—	0.310	0.110	0.070	1500	Fixed
1978	8136S	¼	0.500 ①	0.080	0.280	0.110	0.070	1500	Fixed
	8137S	¼	0.500 ①	0.080	0.280	0.100	0.070	1600	Fixed
	8177S	¼	0.500 ①	0.080	0.280	0.100	0.070	1600	Fixed
	8175S	¼	0.500 ①	0.080	0.280	0.160	0.070	1400	Fixed
	8143S	¼	0.500 ①	0.080	0.280	0.150	0.070	1500	Fixed
1979	8198S	¼	0.500 ①	0.080	0.280	0.100	0.070	1600	Fixed
	8199S	¼	0.500 ①	0.080	0.280	0.100	0.070	1600	Fixed
1980	8233S	¼	0.500 ①	0.080	0.280	0.130	0.070	1500	Fixed
	8235S	¼	0.500 ①	0.080	0.280	0.130	0.070	1700	Fixed
	8237S	¼	0.500 ①	0.080	0.280	0.110	0.070	1500	Fixed
	8239S	¼	0.500 ①	0.080	0.280	0.110	0.070	1500	Fixed
	8286S	¼	0.500 ①	0.080	0.280	0.100	0.070	1400	Fixed

Holley Model 1945 Specifications

Year	Carb. Part No. ②	Float Level (in.)	Accelerator Pump Adjustment (in.)	Bowl Vent Clearance (in.)	Fast Idle (rpm)	Choke Unloader Clearance (in.)	Vacuum Kick (in.)	Fast Idle Cam Position (in.)	Choke
1976	R-7356-A	①	2.22	.060	1600	.250	.110	.080	Fixed
	R-7357-A	①	2.65	.060	1700	.250	.100	.080	Fixed
	R-7360-A	①	2.22	—	1600	.250	.110	.080	Fixed
	R-7361-A	.046	2.65	—	1700	.250	.100	.080	Fixed
	R-7363-A	.046	2.65	—	1700	.250	.100	.080	Fixed
	R-7823-A	①	2.22	.070	1600	.250	.110	.080	Fixed
	R-7824-A	①	2.33	.105	1700	.250	.100	.080	Fixed
1977	R-7632-A	①	2.22	.060	1400	.250	.110	.080	Fixed
	R-7633-A	①	2.33	.060	1700	.250	.110	.080	Fixed
	R-7635-A	①	2.33	—	1700	.250	.110	.080	Fixed
	R-7744-A	①	2.33	.060	1700	.250	.130	.080	Fixed
	R-7745-A	①	2.22	.060	1600	.250	.150	.080	Fixed
	R-7746-A	①	2.33	.060	1700	.250	.110	.080	Fixed
	R-7764-A	①	2.22	.060	1700	.250	.110	.080	Fixed

Holley Model 1945 Specifications (cont.)

Year	Part								
1977	R-7765-A	①	2.33	.060	1700	.250	.110	.080	Fixed
1978	R-7988-A	①	2.22	.062	1400	.250	.110	.080	Fixed
	R-7989-A	①	2.33	.062	1600	.250	.110	.080	Fixed
	R-8008-A	①	2.33	.062	1700	.250	.110	.080	Fixed
	R-8010-A	①	2.33	.062	1500	.250	.130	.080	Fixed
	R-8394-A	①	2.33	.062	1700	.250	.110	.080	Fixed
1979	R-8727-A	①	1.615④	1/16	1600	.250	.110	.080	Fixed
	R-8680-A	①	1.615④	1/16	1500	.250	.130	.080	Fixed
	R-8555-A	①	1.70③	1/16	1400	.250	.110	.080	Fixed
	R-8727-A	①	1.615④	1/16	1600	.250	.110	.080	Fixed
	R-8680-A	①	1.615④	1/16	1500	.250	.130	.080	Fixed
1980	R-8718-A	①	1.70③	1/16	1400	.250	.150	.090	Fixed
	R-8831-A	①	1.615④	1/16	1600	.250	.140	.090	Fixed
	R-8832-A	①	1.70③	1/16	1400	.250	.110	.090	Fixed
	R-8833-A	①	1.615④	1/16	1600	.250	.110	.090	Fixed

① Flush with the top of the bowl cover gasket, plus or minus 1/32
② Located on a tag attached to the carburetor.
③ Position #1
④ Position #2

phragm link to obtain the correct choke opening. Length changes should be made carefully by bending the U-bend provided in the diaphragm link.

CAUTION: *Do not apply twisting or bending force to the diaphragm.*

5. Reinstall the vacuum hose on the correct carburetor fitting. Return the fast idle linkage to its original condition if it was disturbed, as suggested in Step 1.

6. Make the following check: With no vacuum applied to the diaphragm, the choke valve should move freely between the open and closed positions. If its movement is not free, examine the linkage for misalignment or interference caused by the bending operation. Repeat the adjustment if necessary to provide proper link operation.

Float Level

1. Invert the carburetor so that the weight of the floats is the only force on the needle and seat.

2. Use a T-scale to check the float level. Measure the area from the surface of the fuel bowl to the crown of each float at center.

3. To adjust, hold the floats on the bottom of the bowl and bend the float lip to give the specified dimension.

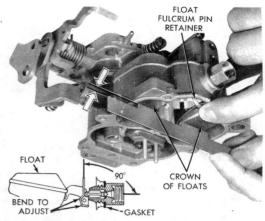

Carter BBD—checking float setting

Fuel Tank

REMOVAL AND INSTALLATION

1. Block the front wheels, raise the rear of the car and support with jackstands.

2. Drain the fuel from the tank. If there is no drain plug, remove the fuel line and drain into a suitable safe container.

3. Remove all lines and hoses from the tank. Remove the filler neck attachment.

4. Support the tank and remove the nuts and bolts securing the mounting straps.

5. Lower the tank slowly, and remove from under the car.

6. Installation is the reverse of removal.

Chassis Electrical

HEATER

On non-air conditioned cars, it is necessary to remove the heater assembly to remove either the blower motor or the heater core. Use the following procedure.

REMOVAL AND INSTALLATION

CAUTION: *This is a major disassembly operation.*

1. Disconnect the battery ground cable and drain the coolant.

2. Disconnect the heater hoses at the firewall. Plug the core tubes to prevent spillage.

3. Slide the front seat all the way back.

4. Remove the core tube firewall seals and retainer.

5. Remove the instrument cluster bezel by removing the four screws along the lower edge, placing the automatic transmission selector in 1, and pulling out to detach the upper edge clips.

6. Remove the instrument panel upper cover by removing the mounting screws at the top inner surface of the glove box, at the brow above the instrument cluster, at the left end cap mounting, at the right side of the pad brow, and in the defroster outlets.

7. Remove the steering column cover

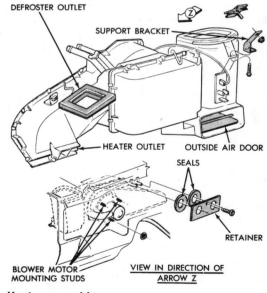

Heater assembly

(the instrument panel piece under the column).

8. Remove the right intermediate side cowl trim panel. Remove the lower instrument panel (the part with the glove box). Remove the instrument panel center to lower reinforcement.

9. Remove the right vent control cable,

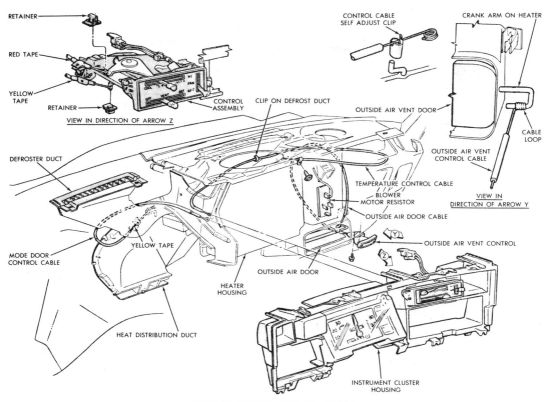

Heater control cable assembly

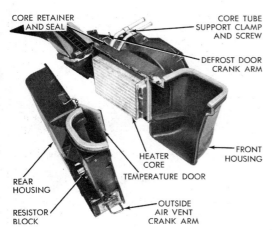

Heater core removal

Use the following procedure to remove the core or blower motor.

1. Remove the heater assembly from the car.

2. Remove the retainer clips and separate the housing halves.

3. Remove the screw attaching the seal retainer and seal around the core tubes. Remove the core tube support clamp.

4. Slide the core out.

5. Remove the blower vent tube and the blower mounting nuts. Remove the blower motor.

Heater Blower

REMOVAL AND INSTALLATION

Air Conditioned Cars

The blower motor is removed from inside the car.

1. Disconnect the motor wiring.

2. Remove the motor mounting nuts from the bottom of the recirculation housing.

3. Separate the lower blower motor housing from the upper housing.

4. Remove the mounting plate screws and

the temperature, and heating mode door control cables from the unit.

10. Disconnect the blower motor resistor block wiring.

11. Remove the mounting nuts on the engine side of the firewall.

12. Remove the heater support-to-plenum bracket.

13. Remove the heater unit.

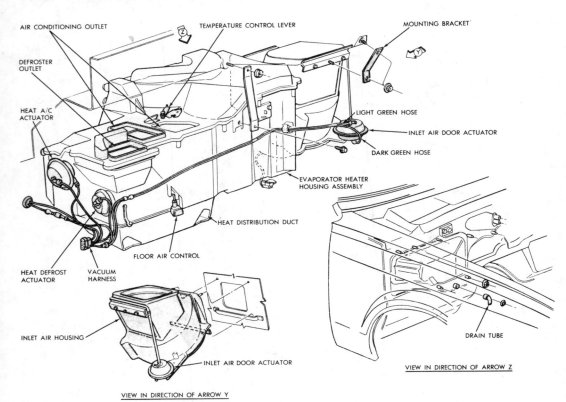

AIR CONDITIONING OUTLET

DEFROSTER OUTLET

HEAT A/C ACTUATOR

HEAT DEFROST ACTUATOR

VACUUM HARNESS

INLET AIR HOUSING

FLOOR AIR CONTROL

HEAT DISTRIBUTION DUCT

TEMPERATURE CONTROL LEVER

MOUNTING BRACKET

LIGHT GREEN HOSE

INLET AIR DOOR ACTUATOR

DARK GREEN HOSE

EVAPORATOR HEATER HOUSING ASSEMBLY

INLET AIR DOOR ACTUATOR

VIEW IN DIRECTION OF ARROW Y

DRAIN TUBE

VIEW IN DIRECTION OF ARROW Z

Air conditioning and heater assembly

remove the mounting plate and blower motor.

Heater Core
REMOVAL AND INSTALLATION
Air Conditioned Cars

CAUTION: *This job requires that the air conditioning system be evacuated. Have this done by a professional if you are not*

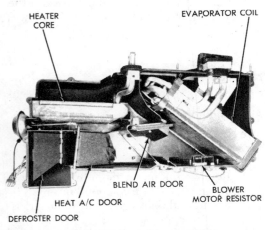

HEATER CORE

EVAPORATOR COIL

BLEND AIR DOOR

HEAT A/C DOOR

DEFROSTER DOOR

BLOWER MOTOR RESISTOR

Evaporator and heater housing assembly

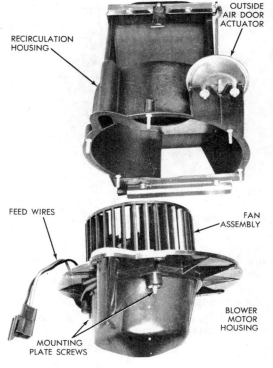

RECIRCULATION HOUSING

OUTSIDE AIR DOOR ACTUATOR

FEED WIRES

FAN ASSEMBLY

BLOWER MOTOR HOUSING

MOUNTING PLATE SCREWS

Blower motor assembly

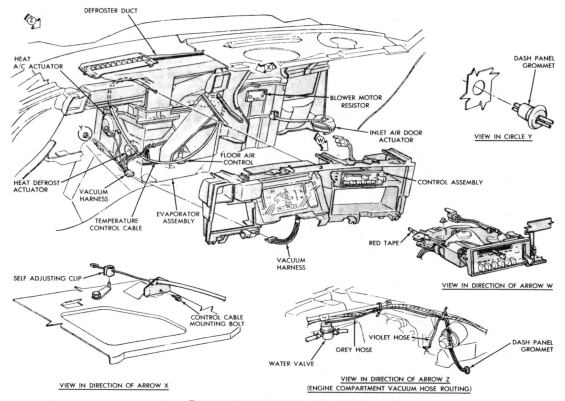

Evaporative assembly and controls

familiar with air conditioning service, and then remove the heater core.

1. Discharge the air conditioning system.

2. Disconnect the battery ground cable, drain the coolant, remove the air cleaner, and disconnect the heater hoses. Plug the core tubes to prevent spillage.

3. Remove the H-type expansion valve.

4. Slide the front seat all the way back.

5. Remove the instrument cluster bezel assembly by removing the four screws along the lower edge, placing the automatic transmission selector in 1, and pulling out to detach the upper edge clips.

6. Remove the instrument panel upper cover by removing the mounting screws at the top inner surface of the glove box, at the brow above the instrument cluster, at the left end cap mounting, at the right side of the pad brow, and in the defroster outlets.

7. Remove the steering column cover (the instrument panel piece under the column).

8. Remove the right intermediate side cowl trim panel. Remove the lower instrument panel (the part with the glove box).

Remove the instrument panel center to lower reinforcement.

9. Remove the floor console, if any.

10. Remove the right center air distribution duct. Detach the locking tab on the defroster duct.

11. Disconnect the temperature control cable from the housing. Disconnect the blower motor resistor block wiring.

12. Detach the vacuum lines from the water valve and tee in the engine compartment. Detach the wiring from the evaporator housing. Remove the vacuum lines from the inlet air housing and disconnect the vacuum harness coupling.

13. Remove the drain tube in the engine compartment. Remove the mounting nuts from the firewall.

14. Remove the hanger strap from the rear of the evaporator and plenum stud.

15. Roll the unit back so that the pipes clear and remove it.

16. Remove the blend air door lever from the shaft. Remove the screws and lift off the top cover. Lift the heater core out.

17. Reverse the procedure for installation.

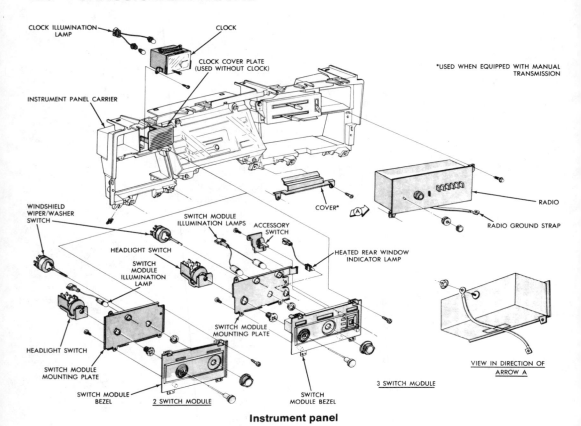

Instrument panel

Have the air conditioning system recharged and checked for leaks. Refill the cooling system.

RADIO

Removal and Installation

1. Disconnect the battery ground cable.
2. Remove the instrument cluster bezel by removing the four screws along the lower edge, placing the automatic transmission selector in the 1 position, and pulling the bezel out to detach the clips along the top edge.
3. Remove the radio mounting screws.
4. Pull the radio out of the panel and disconnect the wiring and the antenna cable.
5. Remove the radio.
6. Installation is the reverse of removal.

WINDSHIELD WIPERS

When your wiper blades wear out, you can either replace the entire wiper blade assembly or just the rubber inserts. The wiper arms can also be replaced if necessary.

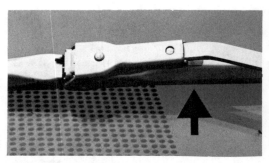

The release lever is under the arm (arrow)

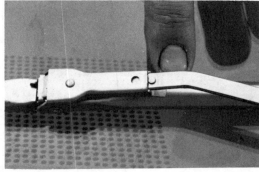

Press down on the lever to release the blade assembly

Wiper Blades

REMOVAL AND INSTALLATION

1. Non-concealed wipers usually have a release lever under the arm. Push the lever, wiggle the blade, and pull it off. Just push the blade back onto the arm to replace.

2. To replace the blade inserts, push the release button on the end bridge to release it from the center bridge. Sometimes there is an end clip on replacement inserts; if so, remove it. Slide the old insert out of the claws of the two bridges. Slide the new insert into place, install the end clip, if any, and re-assemble the blade.

Wiper Arms

REMOVAL AND INSTALLATION

CAUTION: *Make sure to position the arm so that the blade doesn't hit the edge of the windshield when running at top speed. This would produce annoying noise and a strain on the motor.*

Lift the arm and look for a spring retainer at the bottom. If there is one, hold it out of the way with a screwdriver. Wiggle the arm and pull it off. To replace, just push it on, making sure that the latch is out of the way.

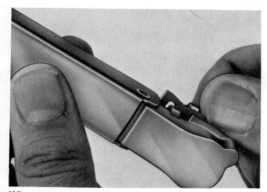

Wiper arm removal

Motor

REMOVAL AND INSTALLATION

1. Disconnect the battery ground cable.
2. Remove the wiper arms.
3. Remove the cowl screen.
4. Hold the motor crank with a wrench while removing the crank arm nut.
5. Remove the three mounting nuts and the motor.
6. Position the motor on the three studs on the dash panel. Be sure that the rubber

Wiper motor (arrow)

gasket and spacers between the motor and dash panel are correctly positioned.

7. Install the 3 nuts that retain the motor to the dash panel and connect the wiring to the motor. Don't forget to install the ground strap under 1 nut.

8. Match the flats on the crank arm with those on the motor shaft. Start the crank arm nut carefully so that the crank arm stays in the correct position.

9. While holding the crank arm with one wrench, tighten the nut to 8 ft. lbs.

10. Reconnect the battery ground cable and test the wipers.

11. Install the cowl screen. Be careful that the screen doesn't pinch the washer hoses.

12. Install the windshield wiper arms and blades.

INSTRUMENT CLUSTER

REMOVAL AND INSTALLATION

1. Disconnect battery ground cable. Make sure the gearshift lever is in Park.

2. Remove the four screws which are located in the lower edge of the instrument cluster bezel. Disconnect speedometer cable.

3. The bezel is retained by clips along the upper edge. Pull the bezel toward while disengaging the clips to remove the bezel.

4. Installation is in the reverse order of removal.

HEADLIGHTS

REMOVAL AND INSTALLATION

1. Remove the headlight cover (surrounding trim panel).

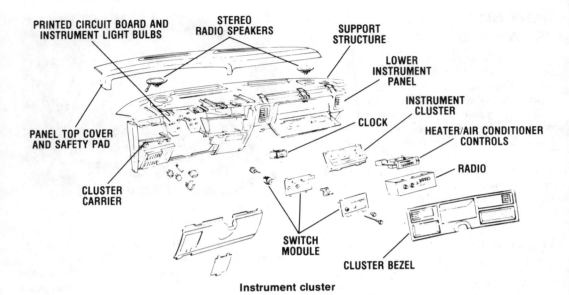

PRINTED CIRCUIT BOARD AND
INSTRUMENT LIGHT BULBS

STEREO
RADIO SPEAKERS

SUPPORT
STRUCTURE

LOWER
INSTRUMENT
PANEL

INSTRUMENT
CLUSTER

CLOCK

HEATER/AIR CONDITIONER
CONTROLS

RADIO

PANEL TOP COVER
AND SAFETY PAD

CLUSTER
CARRIER

SWITCH
MODULE

CLUSTER BEZEL

Instrument cluster

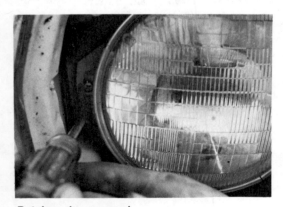

Trim cover removal

Rotate the ring to remove it

Retainer ring removal

2. Loosen the screws holding the headlight retainer ring in place.

NOTE: *The screws directly above and to one side of the headlight are for adjusting the vertical and horizontal headlight aim.*

Don't confuse these with the retaining ring screws.

3. Rotate the retainer ring to disengage the ring from the screws. Remove the ring.

4. Pull the headlight out and pull the wire plug off the back.

There are currently only 3 types of round headlights commonly in use on U.S. cars:

    a. Four-lamp system high beam.

    b. Four-lamp system combined high and low beam;

    c. Two-lamp system combined high and low beam.

Knowing this, you can check your required headlight number against the "Light Bulb Specifications" chart and charge off to the discount or auto parts store.

NOTE: *If your two-lamp system takes a 6014 headlight, don't buy the 6012 headlight. This is an older headlight that is*

Pull on the plug, not the wires, when removing the headlight

being phased out. It isn't as bright as a 6014, though it will interchange.

5. Push the plug onto the new headlight. Position the headlight. There are lugs on the headlight to make it impossible to put it in wrong.

6. Replace the retainer ring and tighten the screws.

7. Replace the headlight cover.

Speedometer Cable Core
REMOVAL AND INSTALLATION

1. Reach up behind the cluster and disconnect the cable.

2. Remove the cable from its casing. If the cable is broken, raise the car and disconnect the cable from the transmission. Pull the cable from the casing.

3. Install the new cable into the casing. Connect the transmission (if disconnected). Engage the cable with the drive head and push in. Secure the cable.

CIRCUIT PROTECTION

Fuses and Flashers

The fuses and flashers are located under the instrument panel on most models.

Fuse Link

The fuse link is a short length of insulated wire contained in the alternator wiring harness, between the alternator and the starter

relay. The fuse link is several wire gauge sizes smaller than the other wires in the harness. If a booster battery is connected incorrectly to the car battery or if some component of the charging system is shorted to ground, the fuse link melts and protects the alternator. The fuse link is attached to the starter relay. The insulation on the wire reads: FUSE LINK. A melted fuse link can usually be identified by cracked or bubbled insulation. If it is difficult to determine if the fuse link is melted, connect a test light to both ends of the wire. If the fuse link is not melted, the test light will light showing that an open circuit does not exist in the wire.

FUSE LINK REPLACEMENT

1. Disconnect the negative battery cable.

2. Disconnect the eyelet of the fuse link from the starter relay.

3. Cut the other end of the fuse link from the wiring harness at the splice.

4. Connect the eyelet end of a new fuse link to the starter relay.

NOTE: *Use only an original equipment type fuse link. Under no conditions should standard wire be substituted.*

5. Splice the open end of the new fuse link into the wiring harness.

6. Solder the splice with rosin-core solder and wrap the splice with electrical tape. This slice must be soldered.

7. Connect the negative battery cable.

8. Start the engine, to check to see that the new connections complete the circuit.

WIRING DIAGRAMS

Wiring diagrams have been left out of this book. As cars have become more complex, and available with longer and longer option lists, wiring diagrams have grown in size and complexity also. It has become virtually impossible to provide a readable reproduction in a reasonable number of pages. Information on ordering wiring diagrams from the vehicle manufacturer can be found in the owners manual.

Clutch and Transmission

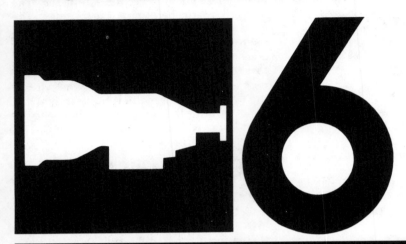

MANUAL TRANSMISSION

CROSS-OVER BLADE IN NEUTRAL

Two manual transmissions are available on the Aspen and Volaré, a 3-speed and 4-speed. The 4-speed transmission features an overdrive high gear for better fuel economy.

LINKAGE ADJUSTMENT

Column Shift

1. Loosen both shift rod swivels at the ends of the two long rods from the column.
2. Make sure the transmission levers are in the neutral or middle positions.
3. Move the column shift lever into neutral to line up the locating slots in the bottom of the steering column shift housing and the bearing housing. Install a tool into the slot to hold the lever in place.
4. Place a screwdriver between the cross-over blade (between the two column levers) and the second-third (the upper one) lever so that both lever pins are engaged by the cross-over blade.
5. Tighten both swivel bolts to 125 in. lbs.
6. Remove the gearshift housing locating tool.
7. Remove the screwdriver.
8. Shift through all gears to check the adjustment and cross-over (through neutral) smoothness.

Holding crossover blade in neutral position

9. Check that the ignition switch will lock with the shift lever in reverse only, without applying any pressure to the shift lever.

Three-Speed Floorshift

1. Make an alignment tool out of $^1/_{16}$ in. thick metal. It should be ⅝ in. wide and 2⅜ in. long.

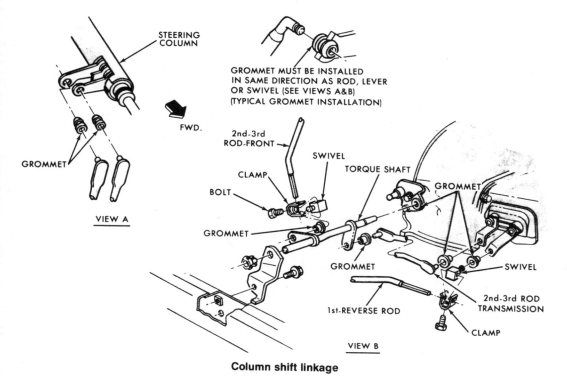

Column shift linkage

2. Detach the shift rod swivels.

3. From under the car, insert the alignment tool through the shifter levers and the shifter to hold the levers in the neutral positions.

4. Place both shift levers on the transmission side cover in the neutral or middle position.

5. Adjust the swivels so that they can be installed freely in the shifter lever holes.

6. Remove the alignment tool and check the shifting action.

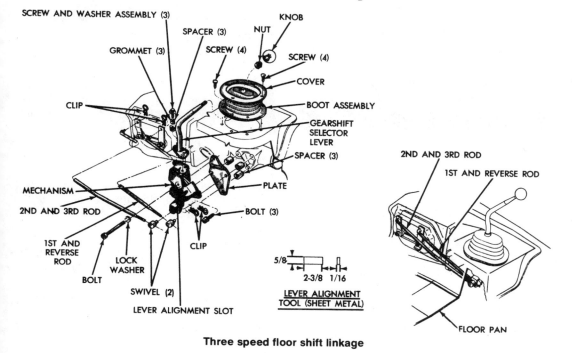

Three speed floor shift linkage

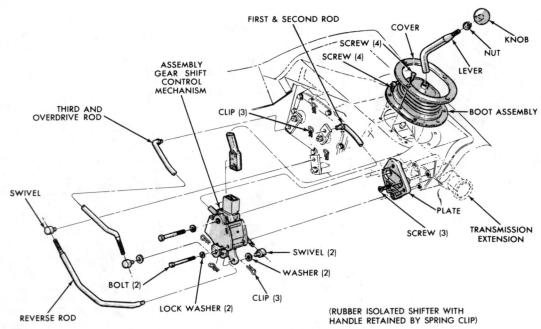

FIRST & SECOND ROD
COVER
KNOB
NUT
SCREW (4)
SCREW (4)
LEVER
ASSEMBLY GEAR SHIFT CONTROL MECHANISM
CLIP (3)
THIRD AND OVERDRIVE ROD
BOOT ASSEMBLY
SWIVEL
PLATE
SCREW (3)
TRANSMISSION EXTENSION
SWIVEL (2)
WASHER (2)
BOLT (2)
CLIP (3)
REVERSE ROD
LOCK WASHER (2)
(RUBBER ISOLATED SHIFTER WITH HANDLE RETAINED BY SPRING CLIP)

Four speed floor shift linkage

Four-Speed Floorshift

1. Remove all the shift rods from the transmission shift levers.

2. Place all the transmission shift levers in their neutral positions.

3. From under the car, insert a ¼ in. rod or drill bit about 2¼ in. long through the shifter levers and the shifter to hold the levers in the neutral positions.

4. Adjust the shift rods so that they can be installed freely in the shifter lever holes.

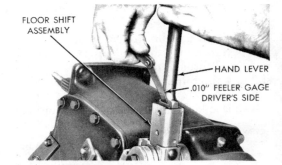

FLOOR SHIFT ASSEMBLY

HAND LEVER
.010" FEELER GAGE DRIVER'S SIDE

Floor shift lever removal

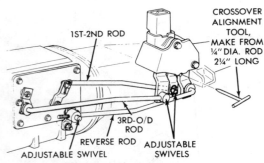

1ST-2ND ROD
CROSSOVER ALIGNMENT TOOL, MAKE FROM ¼" DIA. ROD 2¼" LONG
3RD-O/D ROD
REVERSE ROD
ADJUSTABLE SWIVELS
ADJUSTABLE SWIVEL

Four speed linkage adjustment

5. Remove the aligning tool and check the shifting action.

REMOVAL AND INSTALLATION

1. Raise and support the car safely.

2. Drain the transmission. If it doesn't

have a drain plug, you can get most of the lubricant out by using a suction gun at the fill hole. Remove the shift rods from the transmission levers.

3. After marking both parts for reassembly, detach the driveshaft and the rear universal joint.

CAUTION: *Don't nick or scratch the ground surface on the sliding spline yoke.*

4. Disconnect the speedometer cable and back-up light switch. Remove the console, if necessary, and unbolt the shifter from the extension housing on floor-shift models. The shift level unbolts from the shifter.

5. Unfasten the transmission extension housing from the center crossmember and jack up the engine and transmission about 1 in.

6. Remove the center crossmember.

7. On some models it may be necessary to disconnect or loosen the exhaust system and position it to one side to gain clearance in order to remove the transmission.

8. Support the transmission on a jack. Remove the bolts which secure the transmission to the clutch housing.

9. Slide the transmission toward the rear until the input shaft clears the clutch disc. Lower the transmission and remove it from the car.

10. Installation is the reverse of removal. Lubricate the input shaft pilot bearing in the flywheel and the bearing retainer pilot (for the clutch release sleeve). Do not lubricate the clutch splines or the clutch release levers. Torque the transmission to clutch housing bolts to 50 ft. lbs.

CLUTCH

All models use a coil spring type clutch. The larger diameter clutches have centrifugal rollers which exert a force between the pressure plate and cover to increase the load on the disc at high engine speeds.

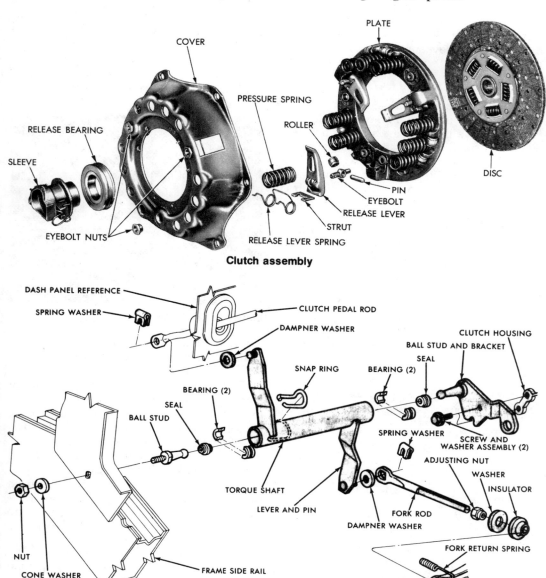

Clutch assembly

Clutch linkage

NOTE: *It is normal for the centrifugal rollers to rattle before the cover is installed.*

FREE-PLAY ADJUSTMENT

1. Check that the rubber pedal stop is in good shape.
2. Under the car, turn the self-locking adjustment nut on the release fork operating rod to get about $5/32$ in. free movement at the end of the fork. If the nut won't turn readily, the swivel is probably binding in the release fork. Tap it to free it.
3. Check the adjustment by making sure that you have 1 in. of free-play at the pedal. The easiest way to measure this is to hold a yardstick alongside the clutch pedal and press the pedal down until you can feel resistance.

REMOVAL AND INSTALLATION

1. Remove the transmission.
2. Remove the clutch housing pan.
3. Remove the spring washer which secures the clutch fork rod to the torque shaft lever and remove the fork rod.
4. Disconnect the fork return spring at the fork. Disconnect the torque shaft return spring. If so equipped, at the torque shaft assembly.
5. Remove the clutch release (throwout) bearing from the clutch release fork. Remove the release fork and boot from the clutch housing.
6. Using a metal punch, mark the clutch cover (pressure plate) and the flywheel to indicate their correct positions for reassembly.
7. Loosen the clutch cover (pressure plate) securing bolts one or two turns at a time in succession to prevent warping the clutch cover.

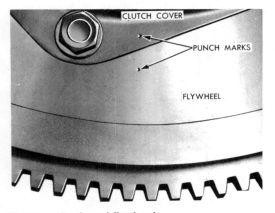

Marking clutch and flywheel

8. Remove the bolts and take out the clutch disc and pressure plate. Do not get any grease or oil on the pressure plate or the clutch disc.
9. Lubricate the pilot bearing in the end of the crankshaft with about half a teaspoon of high temperature grease. Place the grease deep in the cavity. If the bearing is damaged, it will have to be removed with a puller and a new one driven in.
10. Clean the surfaces of the flywheel and pressure plate with fine sandpaper. Check the pressure plate carefully for possible replacement.
11. Place the clutch disc and pressure plate in position and insert a clutch disc aligning tool (dummy shaft) through the clutch disc hub and into the pilot bearing.

NOTE: *The springs on the clutch disc should be facing away from the flywheel when the disc is properly installed.*

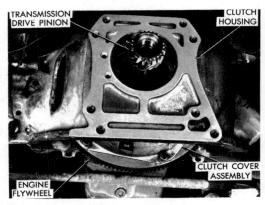

Clutch disc alignment

12. Align the punch marks that were made before the removal on the flywheel and the pressure plate.
13. Install the pressure plate securing bolts and tighten them one to two turns at a time in an alternating sequence. Tighten $5/16$ in. bolts to 17 ft. lbs. and ⅜ in. bolts to 30 ft. lbs. Remove the clutch alignment tool.
14. Pack the throwout bearing sleeve and the release fork pads with grease. If the bearing is noisy or worn, it must be pressed off the sleeve and a new one pressed on.
15. Insert the throwout bearing into the bellhousing and place the fork fingers under the throwout bearing retaining springs.
16. Reverse steps 1–6 to finish installation. Do not lubricate the transmission splines.
17. Adjust clutch pedal free-play.

AUTOMATIC TRANSMISSION

All models use the Torqueflite automatic transmission. There are three versions: A-904, A-904LA, and the A-727.

This section covers in-car automatic transmission service that can readily be handled by the owner. The most common automatic transmission difficulties are those caused by need for band or linkage adjustments or dirty fluid. Though the factory doesn't recommend any periodic fluid changes except for heavy service, it is a good idea to change the fluid and filter whenever periodic transmission adjustments are done. Refer to Chapter 1 for the fluid and filter changing procedure, transmission identification, and the required intervals for adjustments. Throttle linkage adjustments are covered in Chapter 4.

KICK-DOWN BAND ADJUSTMENT

The kick-down band adjusting screw is located on the left-hand side of the transmission case near the throttle lever shaft.

1. Loosen the locknut and back it off about 5 turns. Be sure that the adjusting screw is free in the case.

2. Torque the adjusting screw to exactly 72 in. lbs.

3. Back off the adjusting screw 2 turns on A904; 2½ turns on A727 and the 1980 A904. Hold the adjusting screw and tighten the lock nut to 35 ft. lbs.

LOW-REVERSE BAND ADJUSTMENT

The pan must be removed from the transmission to gain access to the Low-Reverse band adjusting screw. An in. lb torque wrench is also necessary for accurate adjustment.

1. Drain the transmission and remove the pan. See Chapter 1 for the procedure.

2. Loosen the band adjusting screw locknut and back it off about 5 turns. Be sure that the adjusting screw turns freely in the lever.

3. Torque the adjusting screw to exactly 72 in. lbs. On A-904 transmissions with a six-cylinder engine, torque the adjusting screw to exactly 41 in. lbs.

4. Back off the adjusting screw A904; 4 turns on V8 models or 7 turns on six-cylinder models, except the A727 which requires 2 turns. Keep the screw from turning and tighten the locknut.

5. Install the pan using a new gasket. Refill the transmission with the Dexron fluid.

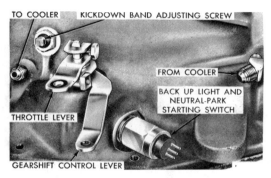

Kickdown band adjustment screw location

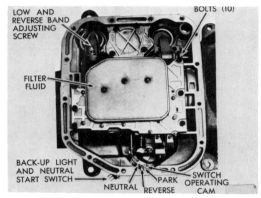

Automatic transmission—pan removed

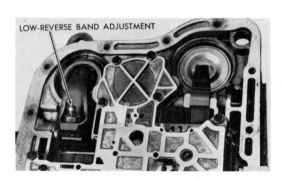

Low-reverse band adjusting screw

NEUTRAL SAFETY/BACKUP LIGHT SWITCH REPLACEMENT

The neutral safety switch is mounted in the transmission case. When the gearshift lever is placed in either the Park or Neutral position, a cam, which is attached to the transmission throttle lever inside the transmission, contacts the neutral safety switch and provides a ground to complete the starter solenoid circuit.

The back-up lamp switch is incorporated into the neutral safety switch. The center ter-

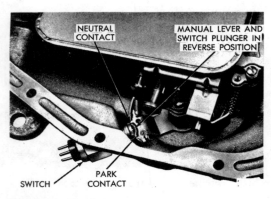

Neutral start switch

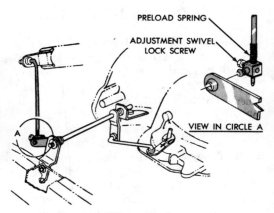

Column gearshift linkage

minal is for the neutral safety switch and the two outer terminals are for the back-up lamps.

There is no adjustment for the switch. If a malfunction occurs, first check to make sure that the transmission gear shift linkage is properly adjusted. If the malfunction continues, the switch must be removed and replaced.

To remove the switch, disconnect the electrical leads and unscrew the switch from the transmission. Use a drain pan to catch the transmission fluid that drains out of the mounting hole. Install a new switch using a new seal and refill the transmission to the proper level.

SHIFT LINKAGE ADJUSTMENT

1. Under the car, loosen the adjustable rod swivel lock bolt.

2. Put the floorshift or column shift lever into Park.

3. Move the transmission shift lever all the way to the rear.

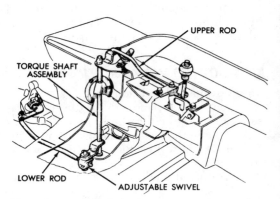

Console gearshift linkage

4. Tighten the swivel lock bolt (torque is 90 in. lbs) without putting any pressure on the linkage.

5. The shift effort must be free and the detents should feel crisp. All gate stops must be positive. It should be possible to start the engine in Park and Neutral only.

Drive Train

DRIVELINE

The driveshaft is a one-piece tubular shaft with two universal joints, one at each end. The front joint yoke serves as a slip yoke on the transmission output shaft. The rear universal joint is the type that must be disassembled to be removed. The rear axle is a live, or solid, type. Numerous rear axle ratios and several rear axles have been used, depending on the application. See Chapter 1 for rear axle identification. In addition, a limited-slip feature has been available. feature has been available. Chrysler calls this Sure-Grip.

Driveshaft and U-Joints
REMOVAL AND INSTALLATION

You can avoid loss of lubricant from the rear of the transmission by raising the rear of the car before removing the driveshaft.

1. Match mark the driveshaft, U-joint and pinion flange before dissassembly. These

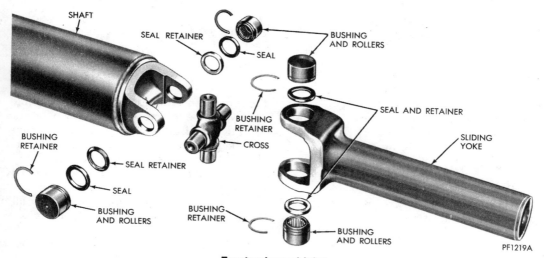

SHAFT

SEAL RETAINER

SEAL

BUSHING AND ROLLERS

BUSHING RETAINER

BUSHING RETAINER

CROSS

SEAL AND RETAINER

SLIDING YOKE

BUSHING RETAINER

SEAL RETAINER

SEAL

BUSHING AND ROLLERS

BUSHING RETAINER

BUSHING AND ROLLERS

PF1219A

Front universal joint

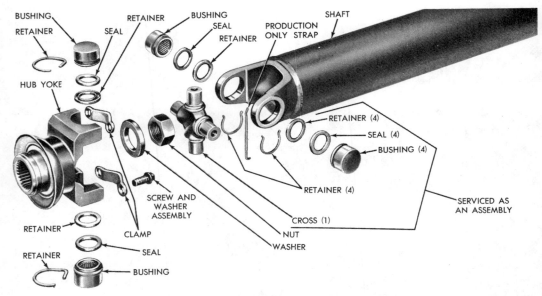

BUSHING
RETAINER
RETAINER
SEAL
RETAINER
BUSHING
SEAL
RETAINER
PRODUCTION
ONLY STRAP
SHAFT
HUB YOKE
RETAINER (4)
SEAL (4)
BUSHING (4)
RETAINER (4)
SERVICED AS
AN ASSEMBLY
SCREW AND
WASHER
ASSEMBLY
RETAINER
CLAMP
SEAL
RETAINER
BUSHING
CROSS (1)
NUT
WASHER

Rear universal joint

marks must be realigned during reassembly to maintain the balance of the driveline. Failure to align them may result in excessive vibration.

2. Remove both of the clamps from the differential pinion yoke and slide the driveshaft forward slightly to disengage the U-joint from the pinion yoke. Tape the two loose U-joint bearings together to prevent them from falling off.

CAUTION: *Do not disturb the bearing assembly retaining strap. Never allow the driveshaft to hang from either of the U-joints. Always support the unattached end of the shaft to prevent damage to the joints.*

3. Lower the rear end of the driveshaft and gently slide the front yoke/driveshaft assembly rearward disengaging the assembly from the transmission output shaft. Be careful not to damage the splines or the surface which the output shaft seal rides on.

4. Check the transmission output shaft seal for signs of leakage.

5. Installation is the reverse of removal. Be sure to align the match marks. The torque for the clamp bolts is 170 in. lbs.

U-JOINT OVERHAUL

1. Remove the driveshaft.

2. To remove the bearings from the yoke, first remove the bearing retainer snap rings located at the base or open end of each bearing cap.

3. Pressing on one of the bearings, drive

U-joint disassembly

U-joint assembly

the bearing in toward the center of the joint. This will force the cross to push the opposite bearing out of the universal joint. This step may be performed using a hammer and suitable drift or a vise and sockets of pieces of pipe. However installation of bearings must be done using the vise or a press.

4. After the bearing has been pushed all the way out of the yoke, pull up the cross slightly and pack some washers under it. Then press on the end of the cross from which the bearing was just removed to force

the first bearing out of the yoke. Repeat steps 3 and 4 to remove the remaining two bearings.

5. If a grease fitting is supplied with the new U-joint assembly, install it. If no fitting is supplied, make sure that the joint is amply greased. Pack grease in the recesses in the end of the cross.

6. To reassemble start both bearing cups into the yoke at the same time and hold the cross carefully in the fingers in its installed position. Be careful not to knock any rollers out of position.

7. Squeeze both bearings in a vise or press, moving the bearings into place. Continually check for free movement of the cross in the bearings as they are pressed into the yoke. If there is a sudden increase in the force needed to press the bearings into place, or the cross starts to bind, the bearings are cocked in the yoke. They must be removed and restarted in the yoke. Failure to do so will greatly reduce the life of the bearing. Repeat steps 6 and 7 to reinstall the remaining two bearings.

REAR AXLE
Axle Shaft
REMOVAL AND INSTALLATION

NOTE: *This procedure also covers axle bearing replacement.*

7¼ In. Axle

NOTE: *Whenever this axle assembly is serviced, both the brake support plate gaskets and the inner axle shaft oil seal must be renewed. There is no provision for adjusting the axle shaft end-play.*

REMOVAL

1. Raise the rear of the car and remove the wheels.
2. Detach the clips which secure the brake drum to the axle shaft studs and remove the brake drum.
3. Disconnect the brake lines at the wheel cylinders and block off the lines.
4. Through the access hole in the axle shaft flange, remove the axle shaft retaining nuts.
5. Attach a puller or slide hammer to the axle shaft flange and remove the axle shaft.

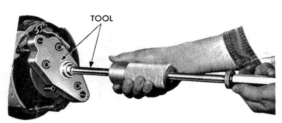

7¼ in. axle shaft removal

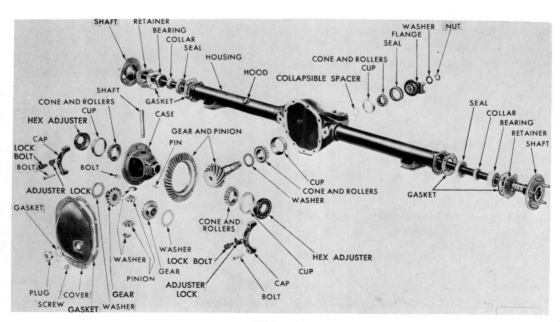

7¼ in. axle

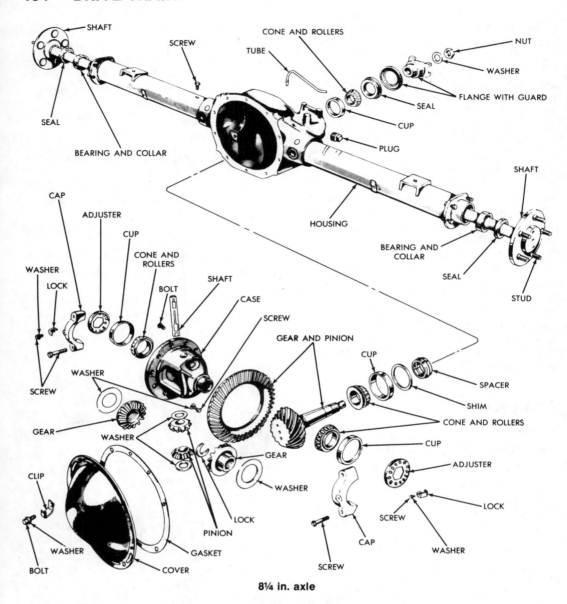

8¼ in. axle

6. Remove the brake assembly from the axle housing.

7. Remove the axle shaft oil seal from the axle housing.

CAUTION: *Never use a torch or other heat source as an aid in removing any axle shaft components; this will result in serious damage to the axle assembly.*

OVERHAUL

1. Place the axle shaft housing retaining collar in a vise. With a chisel, cut deeply into the retaining collar at 90° intervals. Remove the bearing with a puller.

2. To assemble the axle shaft, replace the

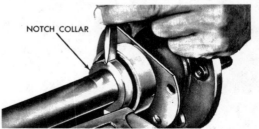

Removing axle shaft collar

retainer plate, bearing, and bearing retainer collar on the axle shaft, using a press.

INSTALLATION

1. Insert new axle shaft oil seals in the axle housing and lightly grease the outside diameter of the bearing.

2. Replace the foam gasket on the studs of the axle housing and install the brake support plate assembly on the axle housing studs. Refit the outer gasket.

3. Very carefully slide the axle shaft assembly through the oil seal and engage the splines of the differential side gear. Using a non-metallic hammer, lightly tap the end of the axle shaft to position the axle shaft bearing in the recess of the axle housing. Install the retainer plate over the axle housing studs and torque the securing nuts to 35 ft. lbs.

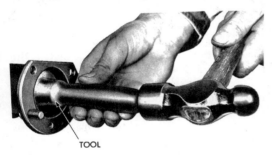

TOOL

Installing oil seal—7¼ in. axle

4. Reconnect the brake lines to the wheel cylinders and bleed the hydraulic system.

5. Install the brake drum and retaining clips.

6. Replace the rear wheels and lower the car.

8¼ In. Axle

NOTE: *There is no provision for axle shaft end-play adjustment on this axle.*

REMOVAL

1. Raise the vehicle and remove the rear wheels.

2. Clean all dirt from the housing cover and remove the housing cover to drain the lubricant.

3. Remove the brake drum.

4. Rotate the differential case until the differential pinion shaft lockscrew can be removed. Remove the lockscrew and pinion shaft.

5. Push the axle shafts toward the center of the vehicle and remove the C-locks from the grooves on the axle shafts.

6. Pull the axle shafts from the housing, being careful not to damage the bearing which remains in the housing.

7. Inspect the axle shaft bearings and replace any doubtful parts. Whenever the axle shaft is replaced, the bearings should also be replaced.

8. Remove the axle shaft seal from the bore in the housing, using the button end of the axle shaft.

9. Remove the axle shaft bearing from the housing. Do not reuse the bearing or the seal.

10. Check the bearing shoulder in the axle housing for imperfections. These should be corrected with a file or polish.

INSTALLATION

1. Clean the axle shaft bearing cavity.

2. Install the axle shaft bearing in the cav-

TOOL   TOOL

Removing axle shaft bearing—8¼ in. axle

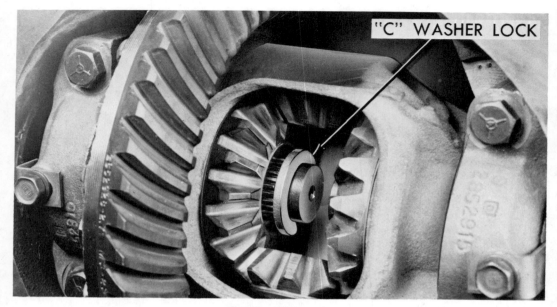

"C" WASHER LOCK

C-lock—8¼ in. axle

ity. Be sure that the bearing is not cocked and that it is seated firmly against the shoulder.

3. Install the axle shaft bearing seal. It should be seated beyond the end of the flange face.

4. Insert the axle shaft, making sure that the splines do not damage the seal. Be sure that the splines are properly engaged with the differential side gear splines.

5. Install the C-locks in the grooves on the axle shafts. Pull the shafts outward so that the C-locks seat in the counterbore of the differential side gears.

6. Install the differential pinion shaft through the case and pinions. Install the lockscrew and secure it in position.

7. Clean the housing and gasket surfaces. Install the cover and a new gasket.

NOTE: *Replacement gaskets may not be available for differential covers. In this case, the use of gel type nonsticking sealant is recommended. See Chapter 1.*

Be sure that the rear axle ratio identification tag is replaced under one of the cover bolts. Refill the axle with the specified lubricant.

8. Install the brake drum and wheel.

9. Lower the vehicle to the ground and test the operation of the brakes.

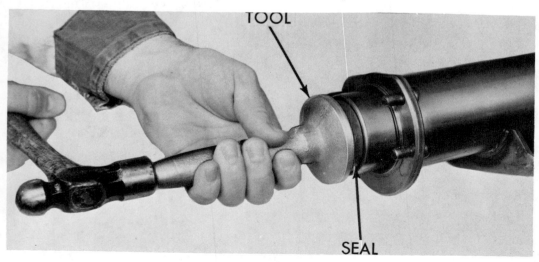

TOOL

SEAL

Axle seal installation—8¼ in. axle

Suspension and Steering

FRONT SUSPENSION

The Aspen/Volaré front suspension is of a unique design. Transverse torsion bars are used on these cars in place of the traditional Chrysler longitudinal torsion bars. The torsion bars react on the outboard ends of the lower control arms. The torsion bars are anchored in the front crossmember opposite the wheel on which they react. Upper and lower control arms locate the wheel spindle. A stabilizer bar is used to resist front roll and to act as the lower control arm strut.

Torsion Bars
REMOVAL AND INSTALLATION

The torsion bars are not interchangeable from right to left. They are marked with an R or an L, according to their location.

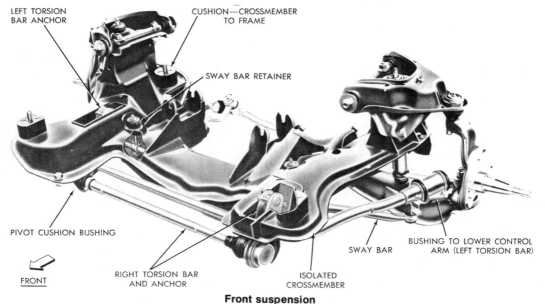

LEFT TORSION BAR ANCHOR

CUSHION—CROSSMEMBER TO FRAME

SWAY BAR RETAINER

PIVOT CUSHION BUSHING

FRONT

RIGHT TORSION BAR AND ANCHOR

ISOLATED CROSSMEMBER

SWAY BAR

BUSHING TO LOWER CONTROL ARM (LEFT TORSION BAR)

Front suspension

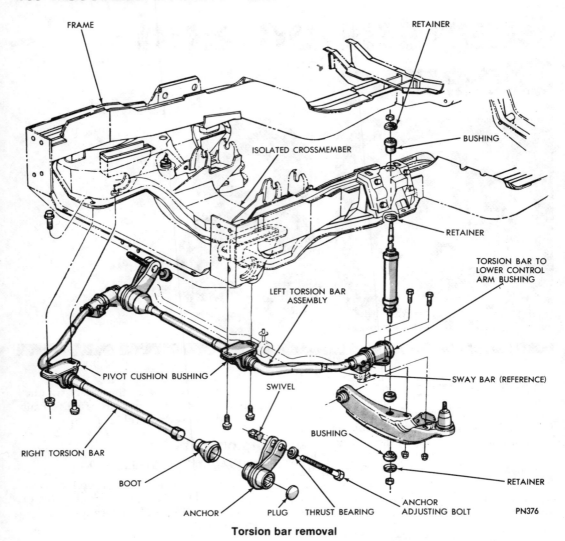

Torsion bar removal

1. Raise the car so that the front suspension hangs free.

2. Release the load on the torsion bar by turning the anchor adjusting bolts counterclockwise.

3. Remove the adjusting bolt on the bar to be removed.

4. Raise the lower control arms until there is 2⅞ in. clearance between the crossmember ledge at the jounce bumper and the torsion bar bushing on the lower control arm.

5. Unbolt the sway bar from the control arm.

6. Unbolt the torsion bar pivot bushing from the crossmember. Remove the bar and anchor assembly from the crossmember.

7. Check the seals on the bar for damage. If corrosion is evident, replace the bar assembly. Touch up any paint nicks or scratches. Check the adjusting bolt and swivel for corrosion or damage. Replace them if necessary.

8. Slide the balloon seal over the end of the bar with the cupped end toward the hex.

9. Coat the hex end of the bar with high-temperature waterproof grease.

10. Install the hex end of the bar into the anchor bracket. The ears of the bracket should be nearly straight up.

11. Install the bar anchor bracket assembly into the crossmember anchor retainer. Install the adjusting bolt and bearing. Attach the pivot bushing to the crossmember, finger tight.

12. Support the lower control arms at the height specified in Step 4 and install the torsion bar bushing to lower control arm bolts. Tighten them to 50 ft lbs.

Anchor adjusting bolt (arrow)

13. Check that the anchor bracket is fully seated in the crossmember. Tighten the pivot bushing bolts to 75 ft lbs.

14. Put the balloon seal over the anchor bracket.

15. Install a new sway bar end bolt and tighten to 50 ft lbs.

16. Load the bar by turning the adjusting bolt clockwise. Lower the car and adjust the front end height.

Shock Absorbers

TESTING

To test the shock absorbers, bounce the front of the car up and down a few times. When released, the car should return to its normal ride height and stop bouncing immediately. If the shocks are worn, they should be replaced in pairs to provide equal damping. Heavy-duty replacements are available to provide a more stable and slightly firmer ride.

REMOVAL AND INSTALLATION

Sometimes this job is easier with the wheel and tire removed. If you remove one shock at a time, you won't have any problem installing all the parts.

1. Remove the nut and retainer from the top of the shock.

2. Remove the lower nut and retainer from the shock.

NOTE: *Steps 1 and 2 sound easy, but very often the retaining nuts are rusted in place. Penetrating oil helps, and very often you have to find a way to stop the shock absorber shaft from turning while you remove the top nut.*

3. Fully compress the shock and remove it downward.

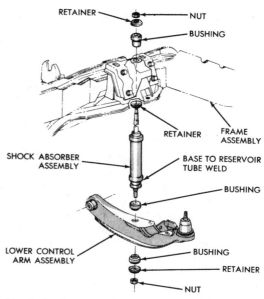

Front shock assembly

4. If the upper bushing needs to be replaced, it can be cut or pried out. To install the new one, wet it and start it into the bracket hole with a twisting motion. Tap it into position with a hammer.

5. Purge the new shock of air by extending it in its normal position and compressing it while inverted. Do this several times. It is normal for there to be more resistance to extension than to compression.

6. Compress the new shock and insert the upper end through the lower retainer, the bushing, and the upper retainer. Tighten the nut to 25 ft lbs.

NOTE: *All retainers must be installed with the concave side in contact with the rubber bushing.*

7. Align the lower mount and install the nut and bolt finger tight. Tighten the nut to

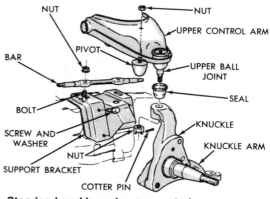

Steering knuckle and upper control arm

35 ft lbs with the weight of the car on the wheels.

Ball Joints

The ball joints are the suspension pivots at the outer (steering knuckle) ends of the upper and lower control arms.

INSPECTION

NOTE: *Before performing the inspection, make sure the wheel bearings are adjusted correctly (Chapter 9) and that the control arm bushings are in good condition.*

1. Place a jack under the lower control arm as close to the wheel as possible.
2. Raise the car until there is 1-2 in. of clearance under the wheel.

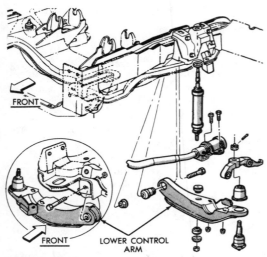

Lower control arm

3. Insert a bar under the wheel and pry upward. If the wheel raises noticeably the ball joints are worn. Determine if the upper or lower ball joint is worn by visual inspection while prying on the wheel.

NOTE: *Due to the distribution of forces in the suspension, the lower ball joint is usually the defective joint. The manufacturer's limit for lower ball joint play, measured at the joint, is 0.030 in. This limit may not agree with your state's inspection regulations.*

REMOVAL AND INSTALLATION
Upper Ball Joint

1. Raise the car by placing a jack stand under the lower control arm as close to the wheel as possible.

Ball joint removal

2. Remove the nut that attaches the upper ball joint to the steering knuckle. Loosen the ball joint stud from the steering knuckle. Ball joint removal tools are available at auto parts stores and large mail order houses to press the ball joint out. Follow the manufacturer's directions for operating the tool. Never strike the ball joint stud.

3. Unscrew the upper ball joint from the upper control arm and remove it from the vehicle.

4. Position a new ball joint on the upper control arm and screw the joint into the arm. Be careful not to cross thread the joint in the arm. Torque to 125 ft. lbs.

5. Position a new seal on the ball joint stud and install the seal in the ball joint making sure the seal is fully seated on the ball joint housing.

6. Position the ball joint stud in the steering knuckle and install the retaining nut. Torque the nut to 100 ft lbs.

7. Lubricate the ball joint.

8. Lower the car.

Lower Ball Joint

1. Remove the lower control arm rebound bumper.

2. Raise the vehicle so that the front suspension drops to the downward limit of its travel. Position jackstands beneath the front frame for extra support.

3. Remove the wheel and tire assembly.

4. Remove the brake caliper from its mounts and tie it up out of the way so that there is no strain on the flexible brake hose.

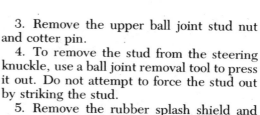

Front sway bar

5. Remove the hub and rotor assembly, splash shield, and lower shock absorber mounting nut and bolt.

6. Unload the torsion bar by rotating the adjusting bolt counterclockwise.

7. Remove the upper ball joint stud cotter pin and nut. Use a ball joint removal tool to press the ball joint out. Never strike the ball joint stud.

8. Press the ball joint out of the lower control arm.

9. Press the new ball joint into the lower control arm.

10. Place a new seal over the ball joint. Press the retainer portion of the seal down over the ball joint housing until it locks into position.

11. Insert the ball joint stud through the opening in the knuckle arm and install the stud retaining nut. Tighten to 100 ft lbs. Install the cotter pin and lubricate the ball joint.

12. Load the torsion bar by rotating the adjusting bolt clockwise.

13. Install the shock absorber nut and bolt, the splash shield, hub and rotor assembly, and brake caliper. Install the wheel and tire assembly.

14. Adjust the front wheel bearings. Remove the jackstands and lower the car. Install the rebound bumper. Adjust the front suspension height and alignment.

Upper Control Arm
REMOVAL AND INSTALLATION

1. Jack up the car and support it under the lower control arm as near to the wheel as possible.

2. Remove the wheel and tire.

3. Remove the upper ball joint stud nut and cotter pin.

4. To remove the stud from the steering knuckle, use a ball joint removal tool to press it out. Do not attempt to force the stud out by striking the stud.

5. Remove the rubber splash shield and remove the control arm pivot shaft bolts and nuts. Remove the control arm from the car.

6. Installation is the reverse of removal. It will be necessary to realign the front end and check front suspension height. Tighten the upper ball joint stud nut to 100 ft. lbs. and the pivot shaft nuts to 150 ft. lbs.

Lower Control Arm
REMOVAL AND INSTALLATION

1. Raise the car and remove the wheel.

2. Remove the brake caliper and wire it up.

3. Remove the lower shock absorber attachment.

4. Remove the hub, rotor and splash shield.

5. Unload both torsion bars by turning the adjusting bolts counterclockwise.

CAUTION: *Unload both bars even if you are removing only one control arm.*

6. Raise the lower control arm until there is 2⅞ in. clearance between the crossmember ledge at the jounce bumper and the torsion bar bushing on the lower control arm. Unbolt the torsion bar bushing on the lower control arm. Unbolt the torsion bar bushing from the control arm.

7. Separate the lower ball joint from steering knuckle arm.

8. Remove the lower control arm pivot bolt and the control arm.

9. Position the control arm, install the pivot bolt, and make the flange nut finger tight.

10. Install the ball joint stud in the steering knuckle arm, tighten the nut to 100 ft lbs, and install a new cotter pin.

11. Hold the control arm at the height used in Step 6. Tighten the torsion bar bushing bolts to 50 ft lbs. Tighten the control arm pivot bolt to 100 ft lbs.

12. Replace the shock absorber and tighten the lower nut to 35 ft lbs.

13. Replace the brake assembly. Tighten the caliper bolts to 15 lbs.

14. Turn the adjusting screws clockwise to load the torsion bars.

15. Lower the car and adjust suspension height and wheel alignment.

Height adjustment. The inset is for Aspen/Volaré

Front End Height Adjustment

The front end height should be checked whenever suspension components are replaced and before front end alignment.

1. Bounce the front of the car several times, releasing it on a downward bounce.

2. Measure from the lowest point of the lower control arm inner pivot bushing to the floor. This should be between 10⅛–10¼ in.

3. Adjust by turning the long bolts at the ends of the torsion bars. The left side bolt adjusts the right side height and vice-versa.

4. Maximum side-to-side variation is ⅛ in.

Front End Alignment

Only caster, camber, and toe-in settings are adjustable. Specifications for steering axis inclination and wheel pivot ratio are useful only in detecting damaged components. Caster and camber cannot be set accurately without professional equipment. Toe-in can be adjusted with some degree of success without any special equipment. Front end height should be checked before adjusting front end alignment.

CASTER ADJUSTMENT

Caster is the backward or forward tilt from the vertical of the steering knuckle centerline at the top, measured in degrees. A steering knuckle centerline tilted backward at the top has positive (+) caster, while one tilted forward has negative (−) caster. Most American cars have negative or zero caster to reduce steering effort. Positive caster produces

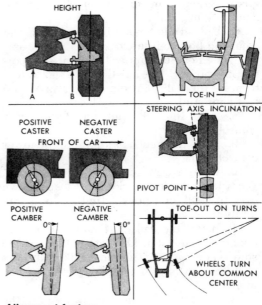

Alignment factors

greater directional stability and requires greater steering effort, since it also increases the self-centering effect at the steering wheel.

Caster is adjusted by loosening either one of the upper control arm pivot bar adjusting bolts and moving the pivot bar. The bolts should be tightened to 150 ft. lbs. after adjustment.

CAMBER ADJUSTMENT

Camber is the inward or outward tilt, measured in degrees, of the wheel at the top. A wheel tilted out at the top has positive (+)

Wheel Alignment Specifications

Year	Caster Range (deg)	Caster Pref Setting (deg)	Camber Range (deg)	Camber Pref Setting (deg)	Toe-in (in.)	Steering Axis Inclin. (deg)	Wheel Pivot Ratio (deg) Inner Wheel	Wheel Pivot Ratio (deg) Outer Wheel
'76–'79	1½P to 3¾P	2½P	②	①	1/16 to ¼	8	20	18
'80	1¼P–3¾P	2½P ± 1	¼N–1¼P	½P ± ½	1/8 ± 1/16	8	20	18

① Left wheel—½P; Right wheel—¼P
② Left wheel—0 to 1P; Right wheel—¼N to ¾P
N Negative   P Positive

camber. A wheel tilted in has negative (−) camber. Camber has a great effect on tire wear.

Camber is adjusted by loosening both the upper control arm pivot bar adjusting bolts and moving both ends of the pivot bar equal amounts. The bolts should be tightened to 150 ft. lbs. after adjustment. Caster should always be rechecked after setting camber.

TOE-IN ADJUSTMENT

Toe-in is the amount, measured in inches, that the centerlines of the wheels are closer together at the front than at the rear. Virtually all cars, except some with front wheel drive, are set with toe-in. Front wheel drive cars usually require toe-out to prevent excessive toe-in under power.

Toe-in must be checked after caster and camber have been adjusted, but it can be adjusted without checking the other two settings.

Toe-in is adjusted at the tie-rod sleeves. The wheels must be straight-ahead when adjusting toe-in.

1. Loosen the clamp bolts on the tie-rod sleeves.

2. Rotate the sleeves equally (in opposite directions) to obtain the correct measurement. If the sleeves are not adjusted equally, the steering wheel will be crooked.

NOTE: *If your steering wheel is already crooked, it can be straightened by turning the sleeves equally in the same direction.*

3. Toe-in can be determined by measuring the distance between the centers of the tire treads, front and rear.

4. When the adjustment is complete, turn the U of the clamps down and tighten the bolts to 11 ft. lbs. A torque wrench isn't essential here, but don't overtighten the clamps.

REAR SUSPENSION

Springs

REMOVAL AND INSTALLATION

1. Raise and support the car and remove the wheels. Position jack stands under the axle to remove the weight of the rear axle from the springs.

2. Disconnect the rear shock absorbers at the bottom attaching bolts. Lower the axle assembly to allow the rear springs to hang free.

3. Remove the U-bolt nuts and remove the U-bolts and plate. Remove the nuts which secure the front spring hanger to the body mounting bracket.

4. Remove the rear spring hanger bolts and let the spring drop far enough to allow the front spring hanger bolts to be removed.

5. Remove the front pivot bolt from the front spring hanger.

6. Remove the shackle nuts and remove the shackle from the rear of the spring.

7. To start installation, assemble the

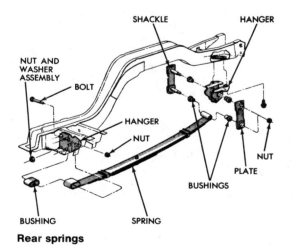

Rear springs

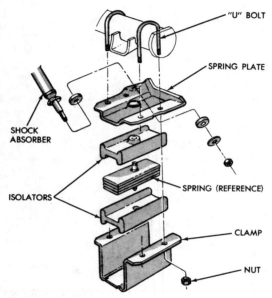

Rear spring isolator

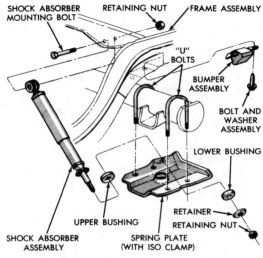

Rear shock assembly

shackle and bushings in the rear of the spring and hanger. Start the shackle bolt nut. Do not lubricate the rubber bushings and do not tighten the bolt nut.

8. Install the front spring hanger to the front spring eye and insert the pivot bolt and nut but do not tighten them.

9. Install the rear spring hanger to the body bracket and tighten the bolts to 30 ft. lbs.

10. Raise the spring and insert the bolts in the spring hanger mounting bracket holes. Tighten the bracket nuts to 30 ft. lbs.

11. Position the axle assembly so it is correctly aligned with the spring center bolt.

12. Position the center bolt over the lower spring plate. Insert the U-bolt and nut and tighten the nuts to 45 ft. lbs.

13. Install the shock absorbers. Tighten to lower mount to 35 ft. lbs.

14. Lower the car. Tighten the pivot bolts to 125 ft. lbs. and shackle nuts to 40 ft. lbs.

15. If springs were replaced, check the front suspension height and adjust if necessary.

Shock Absorbers

TESTING

To test the shock absorbers, bounce the rear of the car up and down a few times. When released, the car should return to its normal ride height and stop bouncing immediately.

If the shocks are worn, they should both be replaced to provide equal damping.

Heavy-duty replacements are available to provide a more stable and slightly firmer ride. Air adjustable shock absorbers can be used to maintain a level ride with heavy loads.

CAUTION, *Air adjustable shock absorbers should not be used to raise the car to provide clearance for outsize rear tires. The results of a sudden pressure loss underway could be disastrous.*

REMOVAL AND INSTALLATION

1. Raise the car and support it under the rear axle to relieve the load from the shock absorber.

2. Remove the nut which attaches the shock to the spring mounting plate stud and then pull the shock from the stud.

3. At the upper mount, remove the shock attaching bolt and nut and remove the shock from the car.

4. Purge the new shock of air by extending it in its normal position and compressing it while inverted. Do this several times. It is normal for there to be more resistance to extension than to compression.

5. To install the shock, position it so the upper bolt may be inserted. Hand tighten the nut and bolt.

6. Align the shock with the spring mounting plate stud, install the retainer, nut, and washer, and hand tighten the nut.

7. Lower the car and tighten the upper nut to 70 ft. lbs. and the lower to 35 ft. lbs.

STEERING

A worm and recirculating ball type steering gear is used with the manual steering system.

Power steering is an option on all models. Hydraulic power is provided by a constant displacement type, belt driven pump. A collapsible, energy-absorbing steering column is used. No service operations involving removal or dissassembly of the steering column are given here. Such critical and delicate operations should be entrusted to qualified service personnel.

Steering Wheel
REMOVAL AND INSTALLATION

NOTE, *All models are equipped with collapsible steering columns. A sharp blow or excessive pressure on the column will cause it to collapse. Do not hammer on the steering wheel.*

1. Disconnect the ground cable from the battery.

2. Remove the padded center assembly. This center assembly is often held on only by spring clips. There are usually holes in the back of the wheel so the pad can be pushed off. However, on some deluxe interiors it is held on by screws behind the arms of the wheel.

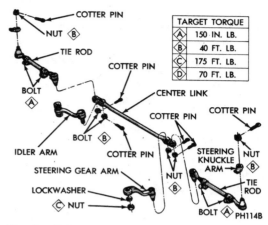

TARGET TORQUE	
Ⓐ	150 IN. LB.
Ⓑ	40 FT. LB.
Ⓒ	175 FT. LB.
Ⓓ	70 FT. LB.

Steering linkage

3. Remove the large center nut. Mark the steering wheel and steering shaft so that the wheel may be replaced in its original position. In most cases, the wheel can only go on one way.

4. Using a puller, pull the steering wheel from the steering shaft. It is possible to make a puller by drilling two holes in a piece of steel exactly the same distance apart as the two threaded holes on either side of the large nut. Drill another hole in the center of the piece the same diameter as the steering shaft. Find a bolt of a slightly smaller diame-

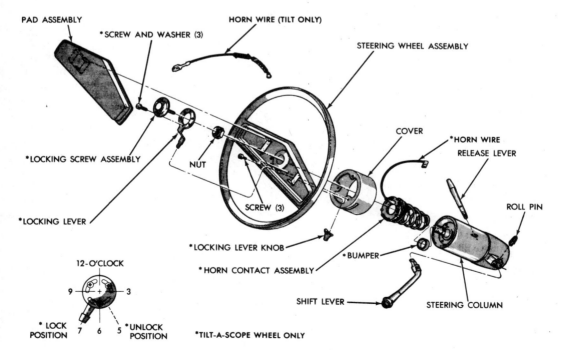

Steering wheel disassembled

ter than the steering shaft. Place the puller over the steering shaft and thread the two bolts into the holes in the wheel. Tighten the two bolts, and then tighten the center bolt to draw the wheel off the shaft.

5. Reverse the above procedure to install the wheel. When placing the wheel on the shaft, make sure the tires are straight ahead and the match marks are aligned. Tighten the nut to 60 ft. lbs.

Turn Signal Switch

REMOVAL AND INSTALLATION

1. Disconnect the battery ground cable.
2. Remove the steering wheel.
3. Remove the steering column cover.
4. With tilting steering wheel, remove the shift position indicator, unbolt the steering column from the lower instrument panel reinforcement and the mounting bracket from the column wiring trough.
   CAUTION: *Support the steering column to prevent damage.*
5. With standard column, unsnap the wiring trough from the column.
6. Position the automatic transmission column shift lever fully clockwise. Set the tilting steering wheel at its midpoint.
7. Disconnect the harness wire connector.
8. Remove the turn signal lever screw and the lever. If the car has speed control, just let the lever hang; don't remove it.
9. Remove the upper bearing retainer screws.
10. Pull the switch gently from the column while guiding the wires through the column opening.
11. Installation is the reverse of removal. Tighten the mounting bracket to steering column bolts to 10 ft. lbs. and the bracket bolts to 9 ft. lbs.

Ignition Switch and/or Ignition Lock Cylinder

REMOVAL AND INSTALLATION

Standard Steering Column

1. Disconnect the negative battery cable and remove the steering wheel.
2. On vehicles equipped with a column shift, pry the lever out of the grommet with a screwdriver.
3. Remove the steering shaft lower coupling at the wormshaft roll pin.
4. Disconnect the wiring connectors at

the steering column jacket. Disconnect the horn wire.

5. Disconnect the turn signal lever by removing the retaining bolt located in the column housing, next to the steering column.
6. Disconnect the transmission indicator pointer from the shifter housing. Remove the nuts attaching the steering column bracket to the instrument panel support.
7. Remove the column through the passenger compartment.
8. Remove the ignition buzzer switch retaining screw and lift out the switch.
9. Remove the two retaining screws and the lock lever guide plate to expose the lock cylinder release hole.
10. Place the cylinder in the "Lock" position and remove the key.
11. Insert a small screwdriver into the release hole and push it in to release the spring loaded lock retainer. Pull the lock cylinder out of the housing at the same time.
12. Remove the retaining screws and the ignition switch assembly. Pull the lock lever and spring assembly out of the housing.
13. Reverse the above for installation.

Tilt Steering Column

1. Disconnect the negative battery cable.
2. Remove the steering wheel.
3. Remove the three attaching screws and remove the shaft lock cover.
4. Remove the screws that attach the tilt control lever and the turn signal lever to the steering column and then remove the levers.
5. Push in the hazard warning knob and unscrew the knob from the turn signal switch. Remove the ignition key lamp assembly.
6. Depress the lock plate to gain access to the lock plate retaining snap-ring. Remove the snap-ring from the steering shaft.
7. Remove the lock plate, cancelling cam, and spring.
8. Remove the three turn signal switch attaching screws, place the shift lever in the Low (L) position, and pull the switch and wires as far upward as possible.
9. With the ignition lock cylinder in the "Lock" position, insert a small screwdriver into the lock release slot in the housing cover.
10. Press down with the screwdriver to release the spring latch at the bottom of the slot and pull the lock cylinder from the housing.

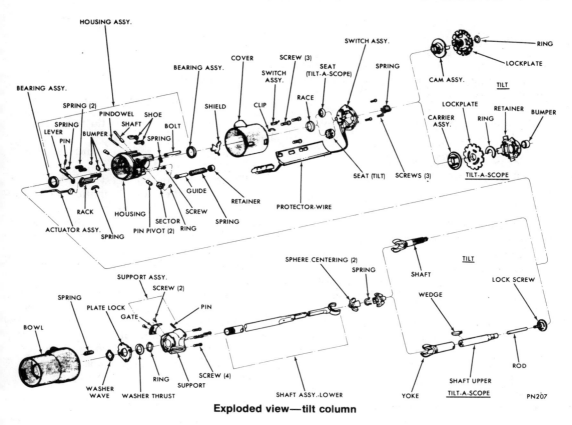

Exploded view—tilt column

The following steps are for ignition switch replacement only.

11. Remove the three screws that attach the upper steering column housing to the steering column and remove the housing.

12. Install the column tilt control lever and move the column to the full "Up" position.

13. Insert a screwdriver into the slot in the spring retainer and press the retainer in approximately $3/16$ in. Turn the retainer approximately 1/8 turn to the left until the ears align with the grooves in the housing. Remove the spring retainer, spring, and guide.

14. Push the steering shaft inward to enable removal of the inner race and seat. Remove the race and seat.

15. Make sure the ignition switch is in the "Lock" position, then remove the wire connector from the ignition switch and remove the screws that attach the ignition switch to the outside of the steering column.

16. Lift the ignition switch from the column and twist it to disengage the switch actuating rod from the rack. Remove the switch.

17. To install the ignition lock cylinder, insert the cylinder into the housing with the cylinder in the "Lock" position and the key *removed.*

18. Move the cylinder into the housing until it contacts the switch actuator. Move the switch actuator rod up and down to align the parts. When the parts are aligned, the cylinder will move inward and lock into place.

The following steps are for ignition switch installation only.

19. With the ignition switch in the "Lock" position, insert the actuating rod into the steering column.

20. Twist the switch and rod assembly as required to engage the actuating rod with the rack. Make sure the ignition lock cylinder is in the "Lock" position.

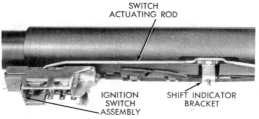

Ignition switch

21. Install the ignition switch mounting screws but do not tighten them.

22. Move the ignition switch downward, away from the steering wheel, and tighten the switch mounting screws. Make sure that the ignition switch has not moved out of the lock detent.

23. Attach the switch wiring connector.

Power Steering Pump

REMOVAL AND INSTALLATION

1. Loosen the pump mounting bolts and remove the power steering belt.

2. Disconnect the hoses at the pump. Be careful not to get any dirt in the hoses.

3. Remove the pump bolts and remove the pump with the bracket.

4. To install the pump, place it in position and install the mounting bolts. Tighten them to 30 ft. lbs.

5. Install the belt and tighten the bolts.

6. Connect the pressure and return hoses. Replace the O-ring on the pressure hose, if so equipped.

7. Fill the pump with the power steering fluid specified in Chapter 1.

8. Start the engine and rotate the steering wheel from stop to stop several times to bleed the system. Check the pump fluid level and fill it as required. Make certain the hoses are away from the exhaust manifold and are not kinked.

Tie-Rod Ends

REMOVAL AND INSTALLATION

1. Loosen the tie rod adjuster sleeve clamp nuts.

2. Remove the tie rod end stud nut and cotter pin.

3. If the outer tie rod end is being removed, remove the stud from the steering knuckle. If the inner tie rod end is being removed, remove the stud from the center link. The studs on all the tie rod ends fit in a tapered hole. They can be removed with a ball joint removal tool available at auto parts stores.

4. Unscrew the tie rod end from the threaded sleeve. The threads may be left or right-hand threads. Count the number of turns required to remove it.

5. To install, reverse the above. Turn the tie rod end in as many turns as was needed to remove it. This will give approximately correct toe-in.

6. Tighten the stud nuts to 40 ft. lbs. and install new cotter pins.

7. Set the toe-in as explained earlier in this chapter.

Brakes

All Volaré and Aspen models are equipped with front disc brakes and rear drum brakes. A split hydraulic system is used, with independent circuits for the front and rear brakes. The brakes on all models are self-adjusting.

HYDRAULIC SYSTEM

Master Cylinder
REMOVAL AND INSTALLATION

1. Disconnect the brake lines from the master cylinder. Plug the outlets in the master cylinder.

2. Remove the nuts that attach the master cylinder to the firewall or power brake booster.

3. On models with standard brakes, disconnect the pushrod from the brake pedal.

4. Slide the master cylinder straight out and off the firewall or brake booster.

5. Reverse the procedure to install the master cylinder. When reconnecting the brake lines, start the fitting with your fingers and turn the fitting in several threads before using a wrench. This will prevent cross threading. If difficulty is encountered with threading the fittings, bend the brake line slightly so that the fitting enters the hole

squarely. If a fluid leak occurs tighten the fitting, check for a damaged seat or tubing end, or look for a hairline crack in the tubing.

6. Bleed the brake system after installation is complete.

OVERHAUL

If the master cylinder leaks externally, or if the pedal sinks while being held down, the master cylinder is probably worn. There are three possible solutions:

 a. Buy a new master cylinder.

 b. Trade the old one in on a rebuilt unit.

 c. Rebuild the old one with a rebuilding kit.

Overhaul is as follows:

NOTE: *Front and rear refer to the locations of the positions in the cylinder, not to the brakes they operate.*

1. Clean the outside of the cylinder. Remove the cover and drain the fluid. It should not be reused.

2. Remove the secondary (front) piston retainer screw from inside the reservoir. Remove the snap-ring from the end of the cylinder bore.

3. Remove the rear (primary) and front (secondary) pistons. If the front piston sticks in the cylinder, air pressure may be used to

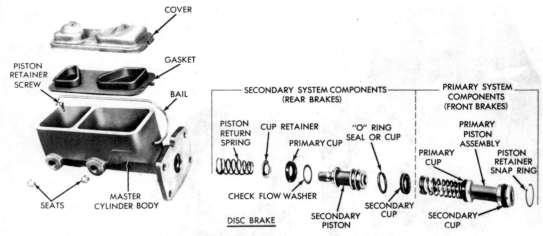

Master cylinder-exploded view

remove it. Always use new rubber cups if air pressure was used.

4. Note the position of the rubber cups and springs and remove them from the pistons and from the bore. Don't remove the primary (middle) cup of the primary (rear) piston. Replace the entire piston if the cup is worn.

5. Remove the tube seats, using an easy out or a screw threaded into the seat. Unless the seat is damaged it is not absolutely necessary to remove it.

6. Remove the residual pressure valves, if any, and springs found under the seats.

7. Clean the inside of the master cylinder with brake fluid or denatured alcohol.

8. Closely inspect the inside of the master cylinder. Polish the inside of the bore with crocus cloth. If there is rust or pit marks it will be necessary to use a hone. Discard the master cylinder if scores or pits cannot be eliminated by honing of 0.002 in. or less.

NOTE: *If the bore of an aluminum cylinder is scored, the cylinder must be replaced.*

9. Do not reuse old rubber parts and be sure to use all the new parts supplied in the rebuilding kit.

10. Before assembly, thoroughly lubricate all parts (especially seals) with clean brake fluid.

11. Replace the primary cup on the front end of the secondary (front) piston with the lip away from the piston.

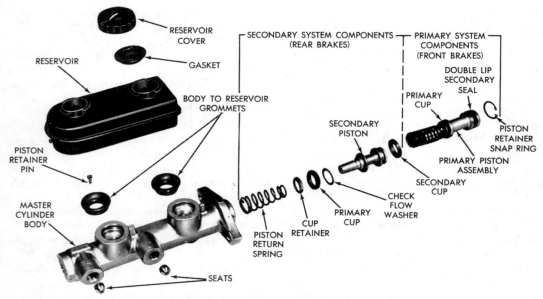

Components of the aluminum master cylinder

12. Carefully slide the O-ring over the rear of the piston and into the second land.

13. Slowly work the rear secondary cup over the piston and position it in the rear land. The lip must face to the rear.

14. Slide the cup retainer over the front piston stem with the cup lip facing away from the piston.

15. Replace the small end of the pressure spring into the retainer.

16. Position the assembly in the bore. Be sure the cups are not canted.

17. Slowly work the secondary cup over the back of the rear (primary) piston with the cup lip facing forward.

18. Position the spring retainer in the center of the rear piston assembly. It should be over the shoulder of the front piston. Position the piston assembly in the bore. Slowly work the cup lips into the bore, then seat the piston assembly.

19. Hold the pistons in the seated position. Install the snap-ring. Insert the piston retaining screw and tighten it securely.

20. Replace the residual pressure valves, if any, and spring. Position them in the outlet and install the tube seats.

21. Before installing a new or reconditioned master cylinder, it will be necessary to bleed it.

   a. Insert bleeding tubes from the tube seats into the reservoirs and fill both brake reservoirs with brake fluid.

   b. Insert a dowel pin into the depression in the piston or operate the pushrod and push in and release the piston. It will return under its own spring pressure. Repeat this operation until all of the air bubbles are expelled.

   c. Remove the bleeding tubes, and install the cover and the gasket.

22. Install the master cylinder on the car.

Brake Warning Systems

Four-wheel drum brake models have a pressure differential switch to alert the driver when one of the two brake circuits loses pressure. On disc-drum models, this switch is combined with a pressure metering valve to limit pressure to the rear brakes and prevent rear wheel locking. Both types are located in the engine compartment, usually on the frame rail. These valves reset themselves automatically after the malfunction is corrected and the brakes used. They do not interfere with normal system bleeding; however, if pressure bleeding is attempted on disc brake cars, a spring clip must be used to hold the metering valve stem out.

CAUTION: *Never push the metering valve stem in. The valve will be damaged and the front brakes will be disabled.*

Bleeding

The purpose of bleeding the brakes is to expel air trapped in the hydraulic system. The system must be bled whenever the pedal feels spongy, indicating that compressible air has entered the system. It must also be bled whenever the system has been opened or leaking. You will need a helper for this job.

The customary procedure is to start with the wheel farthest away from the master cylinder and work in. In other words, right rear - right front - left front.

1. Clean the bleed screw at each wheel.

2. Attach a small rubber hose to one of the bleed screws and place the end in a container of brake fluid.

3. Fill the master cylinder with brake fluid. Check the level often during bleeding. Pump up the brake pedal and hold it.

4. Open the bleed screw about one-quarter turn, press the brake pedal down and hold it, close the bleed screw, and slowly release the pedal. Continue until no more air bubbles are forced from the cylinder on application of the brake pedal.

5. Repeat the procedure on the remaining wheel cylinders.

Disc brakes may be bled in the same manner as drum brakes, except that the disc should be rotated to make sure that the piston has returned to the unapplied position when bleeding is completed and the bleed screw closed.

FRONT DISC BRAKES

A sliding caliper front disc brake is used on all models. A single hydraulic piston is used, this acts on the inboard brake shoe. When the brake pedal is depressed, the piston forces the inside brake shoe or pad into contact with the disc. Increasing force against the disc causes the caliper to slide towards the disc and bring the outboard shoe into contact. The caliper slides on machined grooves or "ways" in the adapter that is bolted to the steering knuckle. Retaining spring clips keep the caliper from moving vertically.

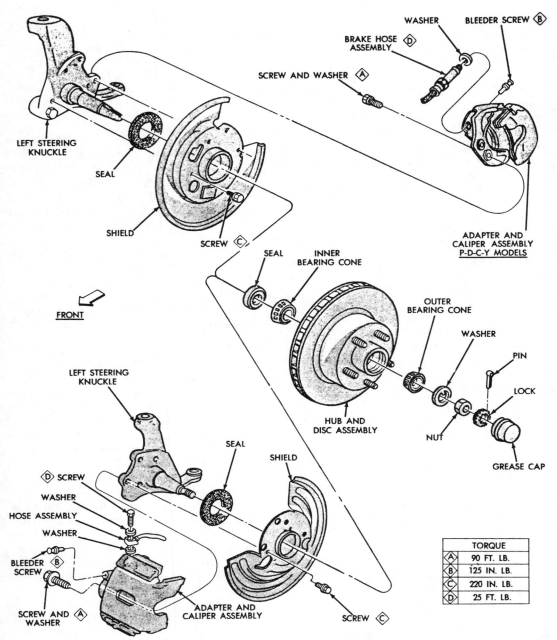

WASHER   BLEEDER SCREW Ⓑ

BRAKE HOSE Ⓓ
ASSEMBLY

SCREW AND WASHER Ⓐ

LEFT STEERING
KNUCKLE

SEAL

SHIELD

SCREW Ⓒ

FRONT

SEAL   INNER
BEARING CONE

ADAPTER AND
CALIPER ASSEMBLY
P-D-C-Y MODELS

LEFT STEERING
KNUCKLE

OUTER
BEARING CONE

WASHER

PIN

LOCK

Ⓓ SCREW

WASHER

HOSE ASSEMBLY

WASHER

BLEEDER Ⓑ
SCREW

SEAL

SHIELD

HUB AND
DISC ASSEMBLY

NUT

GREASE CAP

SCREW AND Ⓐ
WASHER

ADAPTER AND
CALIPER ASSEMBLY

SCREW Ⓒ

TORQUE	
Ⓐ	90 FT. LB.
Ⓑ	125 IN. LB.
Ⓒ	220 IN. LB.
Ⓓ	25 FT. LB.

Exploded view—sliding caliper assembly

Brake Pads

INSPECTION

A visual inspection of the brake pads, calipers, and brake lines is recommended every several thousand miles.

1. Jack up the front of the car and support it on stands. Remove the front wheels.

2. Check the rubber brake lines to the calipers for breaks or cracks. Check the metal brake lines for rust or damage from rocks or other road debris.

3. Examine the surfaces of the disc for deep scoring or grooves.

4. Inspect the brake pads. The outside pads are normally thinner than the inside pads. Replace the brake pads if they are worn to within $1/32$ in. of the disc.

5. Check the caliper for signs of brake fluid leakage. The caliper will have to be re-

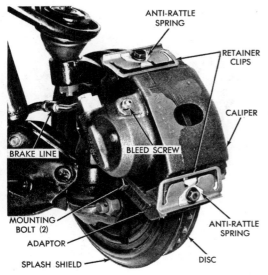

Caliper assembly—front view

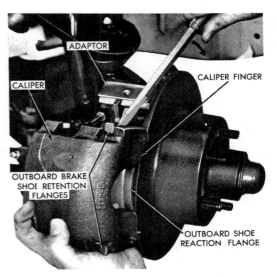

Removing outboard pad

moved and rebuilt or replaced if any leakage is evident.

REMOVAL AND INSTALLATION

Brake pads should always be replaced in full axle sets, that is they should be renewed on both sides at the same time. Original equipment replacement sets contain four brake pads, new retainer clips, and O-rings. Always reinstall the anti-rattle springs under the retaining clip bolts, they prevent annoying brake squeaks and rattles.

1. Jack up the front of the car and support it with stands under the front crossmember. Remove the front wheels.

2. Remove the caliper retaining clips and anti-rattle springs.

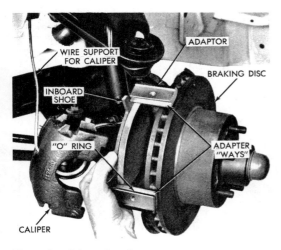

Removing inboard pad

3. Slowly remove the caliper from the disc by sliding it out and away. It's not necessary to disconnect the brake line from the caliper.

4. Support the caliper, so as not to put a strain on the flexible brake line.

5. Remove the outside pad by using a screwdriver to pry between the pad and the caliper. Don't gouge the disc.

6. Remove the inside pad.

7. Wire the caliper to the front suspension for support. Don't let it hang by the brake line.

8. Check for piston boot damage and fluid leaks. Any damage will require disassembly of the caliper.

9. Check the sliding surfaces on the caliper and the adaptor. If they are rusty, remove the rubber O-ring and carefully wire brush the corrosion.

10. Install new O-rings on the caliper adaptor.

11. Remove about half of the fluid from the front chamber of the master cylinder. This will prevent an overflow when the new, thicker pads are installed.

12. Carefully push the piston back into the caliper bore. A large pair of sliding pliers are handy for this job. Be careful not to damage the rubber piston boot.

13. Slide the new outboard pad into the caliper recess.

NOTE: *There should be no free-play between the brake pad flanges and the caliper. This can cause brake pad rattling. Should free-play exist as shown by vertical pad movement after installation, remove the pad from the caliper and tap the flanges down to make a slight interference fit.*

14. Install the outboard pad by snapping it into place with your hand. If it is necessary to use a C-clamp to install the pad, use the old pads to protect the new pad from damage.

15. Install new O-rings on the adapter. Put the inside pad in place by positioning the pad on the adaptor with its flanges in the adapter "ways."

16. Carefully slide the caliper assembly into place in the adapter and over the disc. Align the caliper on the adapter.

CAUTION: *Don't pull the dust boot out of its groove when sliding the piston and boot over the inside pad.*

17. Install the anti-rattle springs and retaining clips and tighten the screws to 15 ft. lbs. The springs go over the retaining clips.

18. Step on the brake pedal several times until you feel a firm pedal. Refill the master cylinder. Bleed the brakes if the pedal doesn't come up.

19. Install the wheels and tighten the lug nuts to 85 ft. lbs. in a criss-cross pattern.

20. Lower car and road test.

Calipers

REMOVAL AND INSTALLATION

Follow steps 1 through 6 of "Brake Pad Removal." Disconnect the brake line and remove the caliper. Installation is the reverse of removal. Bleed the brakes.

OVERHAUL

1. Remove the caliper assembly from the car *without* disconnecting the hydraulic line.

2. Support the caliper assembly on the upper control arm and surround it with shop

WOODEN OR PLASTIC STICK

PISTON BORE

PISTON SEAL

Removing piston seal

towels to absorb any brake fluid. Slowly depress the brake pedal until the piston is pushed out of its bore.

CAUTION: *Do not use compressed air to force the piston from its bore; injury could result.*

3. Disconnect the brake line from the caliper and plug it to prevent fluid loss.

4. Mount the caliper in a soft-jawed vise and clamp lightly. Do not tighten the vise too much or the caliper will become distorted.

5. Work the dust boot out with your fingers.

6. Use a small pointed *wooden* or *plastic* stick to work the piston seal out of the groove in the bore. Discard the seal.

CAUTION: *Using a screwdriver or other metal tool could scratch the piston bore.*

7. Using the same wooden or plastic stick, press the outer bushings out of the housing. Discard the old bushings. remove the inner bushings in the same manner. Discard them as well.

8. Clean all parts in denatured alcohol or

CALIPER

PISTON SEAL

PISTON DUST BOOT

PISTON BORE

Removing dust boot

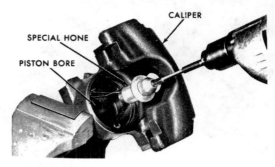

CALIPER

SPECIAL HONE

PISTON BORE

Honing piston bore

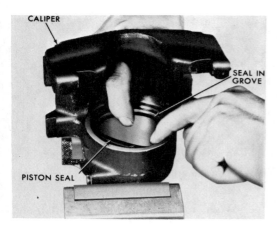

Installing piston seal

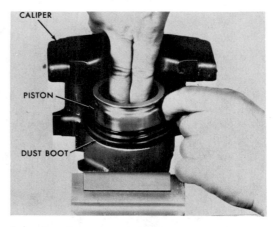

Inserting piston through dust boot

brake fluid. Blow out all bores and passages with compressed air.

9. Inspect the piston and bore for scoring or pitting. Replace the piston if necessary. Bores with light scratches or corrosion may be cleaned with crocus cloth. Bores with deep scratches may be honed if you do not increase the bore diameter more than 0.002 in. Replace the housing if the bore must be enlarged beyond this.

NOTE: *Black stains are caused by piston seals and are harmless.*

10. If the bore had to be honed, clean its grooves with a stiff, non-metallic rotary brush. Clean the bore twice by flushing it out with brake fluid and drying it with a soft, lint-free cloth.

Caliper assembly is as follows:

1. Clamp the caliper in a soft-jawed vise; do not overtighten.

2. Dip a new piston seal in brake fluid or the lubricant supplied with the rebuilding

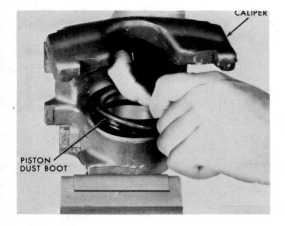

Installing piston dust boot

kit. Position the new seal in one area of its groove and gently work it into place with clean fingers, so that it is correctly seated. Do not use an old seal.

3. Coat a new boot with brake fluid or lubricant (as above), leaving a generous amount inside.

4. Insert the boot in the caliper and work it into the groove, using your fingers only. The boot will snap into place once it is correctly positioned. Run your forefinger around the inside of the boot to make sure that it is correctly seated.

5. Install the bleed screw in its hole and plug the fluid inlet on the caliper.

6. Coat the piston with brake fluid or lubricant. Spread the boot with your fingers and work the piston into the boot.

7. Depress the piston; this will force the boot into its groove on the piston. Remove the plug and bottom the piston in the bore.

8. Compress the flanges of new guide pin bushings and work them into place by pressing *in* on the bushings with your fingertips, until they are seated. Make sure that the flanges cover the housing evenly on all sides.

9. Install the caliper on the car as previously outlined.

Brake Disc

REMOVAL AND INSTALLATION

The brake disc and hub are removed at the same time.

1. Raise and support the car and remove the tire and wheel.

2. Remove the caliper from the disc but do not disconnect the brake line. Support the caliper.

Brake disc showing minimum thickness

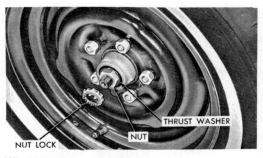

Wheel bearing adjustment

3. Remove the grease cap, cotter pin, nut lock, nut, thrust washer, and outer wheel bearing.

4. Slide the disc off the spindle.

5. Reverse the procedure to install the disc. Adjust the wheel bearing. Tighten wheel lug nuts to 85 ft. lbs.

INSPECTION

1. With the wheel removed, check to see that there is no grease or other foreign material on the disc. If the disc is badly scored replace or refinish it. The minimum disc thickness is cast into the hub.

2. Measure the thickness of the disc with a micrometer at 12 points around the disc, 1 in. from the disc's edge. Any variation of more than 0.0005 in. means that the disc should be replaced.

3. Using a dial indicator, check the disc run out on both sides with the wheel bearing adjusted to zero endplay. Run out should be no greater than 0.004 in. If the run out exceeds this figure the disc should be refinished or replaced. Make sure the wheel bearing is properly adjusted when making this measurement.

Wheel Bearings
ADJUSTMENT

1. Raise the front wheel off the floor.

2. Remove the grease cap. You can pry it off with a screw driver or grab it with a pair of water pump pliers.

3. Remove the cotter pin and the nut lock.

4. While turning the wheel, tighten the nut to 240–300 in. lbs.

5. Back the adjusting nut off completely, then tighten it finger tight. Install the nut lock and the cotter pin.

6. Coat the inside of the cap with grease (don't fill it) and replace the cap.

NOTE: *Correct adjustment should result in 0.001–0.003 in. end-play.*

REMOVAL, PACKING, AND INSTALLATION

1. Raise and support the car. Remove the wheel.

2. Remove the caliper.

3. Remove the disc and the outer bearing.

4. Remove the inner bearing.

5. To remove the bearing cone if necessary, drive the inner seal out of the hub and drive the cone out with a ¾ in. diameter non-metallic rod. Install the new cone and install the new seal with the lip inward.

6. Clean the bearings thoroughly in a safe solvent. Check their condition, but don't spin them any more than is absolutely necessary.

7. Clean the spindle and apply a light coat of grease on all polished surfaces.

8. Pack both wheel bearings using wheel bearing grease made for disc brakes. Ordinary grease will melt and ooze out, ruining the pads. Place a healthy glob of grease in the palm of one hand and force the edge of the bearing into it so that the grease fills the bearing. Do this until the whole bearing is (ugh!) packed. Grease packing tools are available to make this job a lot less messy.

9. Fill the hub grease cavity with grease even with the inner diameter of the bearing cups. Replace the hub and adjust the bearings.

10. Replace the caliper.

11. Replace the wheel.

REAR DRUM BRAKES

Brake Drums

REMOVAL AND INSTALLATION

1. Remove the rear plug from the brake adjusting access hole on the inside of the wheel.

2. Slide a thin screwdriver through the hole and position the adjusting lever away from the adjusting notches on the star sheel.

3. Insert an adjusting tool or screwdriver into the brake adjusting hole and engage the star wheel. Pry downward with the tool to back off the brake adjustment.

4. Remove the rear wheel and tire. Remove clips (if any) from the wheel studs and discard them.

5. Remove the drum from the axle. The drum simply slips from the axle leaving the wheel studs in place in the axle. However, the drum will sometimes be rusted in place. To break the rust, strike the drum sharply several times with a soft hammer on the corner. Strike the drum in several places around its circumference. Do not strike the drum on the edge of the open side as this may cause cracks.

6. Installation is the reverse of the removal procedure.

INSPECTION

1. Drum run out (out of round) and diameter should be measured. Drum diameter should not vary more than 0.002 in. and run

MAXIMUM DIAMETER MARKING

Drum showing maximum diameter

out should not exceed 0.006 in. Do not reface a drum more than 0.060 inches over its standard diameter.

NOTE: *The maximum safe inside diameter is marked on the drum.*

2. Check the drum for large cracks and scores. Replace the drum if necessary.

3. If the brake linings are wearing more on one edge than the other then the drum may be "bell" shaped and will have to be replaced or resurfaced.

Brake Shoes

INSPECTION

The brake drums must be removed to inspect the linings. If they are worn to $1/32$ in. or less at any point, the front linings must all be replaced.

NOTE: *This may not agree with your state's inspection specifications.*

REMOVAL AND INSTALLATION

Remove the wheel and brake drum and proceed as follows:

NOTE: *If you are not thoroughly familiar with the procedures involved in brake replacement, disassemble and assemble one side at a time, leaving the other wheel intact, as a reference.*

1. Remove the shoe return springs using a brake spring service tool. Detach the adjusting cable eye from the anchor and unhook the other end from the lever. Remove the cable, overload spring, guide and anchor plate.

2. Detach the adjusting lever from the

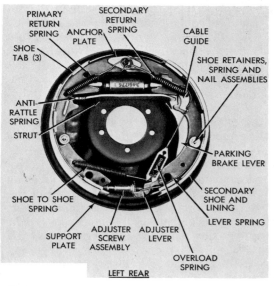

PRIMARY RETURN SPRING
SECONDARY RETURN SPRING
ANCHOR PLATE
CABLE GUIDE
SHOE TAB (3)
SHOE RETAINERS, SPRING AND NAIL ASSEMBLIES
ANTI-RATTLE SPRING
STRUT
PARKING BRAKE LEVER
SECONDARY SHOE AND LINING
LEVER SPRING
SHOE TO SHOE SPRING
SUPPORT PLATE
ADJUSTER SCREW ASSEMBLY
ADJUSTER LEVER
OVERLOAD SPRING
LEFT REAR

Drum brake assembly

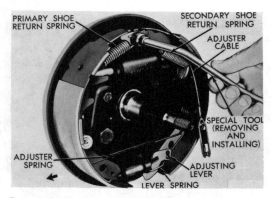

Removing the brake shoe return springs

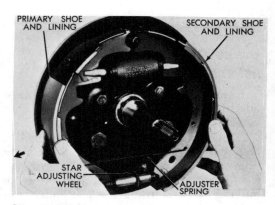

Shoe installation

spring, and separate the spring from the pivot. Remove the spring completely from the secondary shoe web and unfasten it from the primary shoe web.

3. With the anchor ends of both shoes spread apart, remove the parking brake lever strut, as well as the anti-rattle spring.

4. Detach the parking brake cable from the parking brake lever.

5. Remove the retainers, springs, and nails from the shoe. Extract both shoes from the pushrods, and lift them out. remove the star wheel assembly from the shoes.

6. Put a thin film of high temperature grease at the six shoe tab contact areas on the support plate.

7. Lubricate the pivot on the inner side of the secondary shoe web, and install the parking brake lever on it. Fasten the lever with its washer and horseshoe clip.

8. Connect the parking brake cable to the lever. Slip the secondary shoe next to the support plate, while engaging the shoe web with the pushrod, and push it against the anchor.

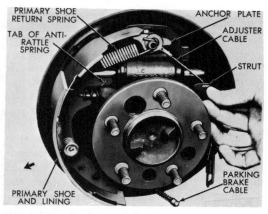

Removing the parking brake cable

9. Position the parking brake strut behind the hub and slide it into the slot in the lever. Fit the anti-rattle spring over the free end of the strut.

10. Position the primary shoe, engage it in the pushrod and with the free end of the parking brake strut. Place the anchor plate over the anchor and fit the eye of the adjustment cable over the anchor. Connect the primary shoe return spring to its web and fit its other end over the anchor.

11. Place the cable guide in the secondary shoe web. Hold it in this position while engaging the secondary shoe return spring, which goes through the guide and into the web. Put its other end over the anchor.

NOTE: *Be sure that the cable guide stays flat against the web, and that the secondary shoe return spring overlaps that of the primary.*

Squeeze the spring loops around the anchor, with pliers, until they are parallel.

12. Place the star wheel assembly between the shoes, with the star wheel assembly adjacent to the secondary shoe. The left rear star wheel is plated and marked with an "L."

13. Place the adjustment lever spring over the pivot pin on the shoe web and fit the lever under the spring, but over the pin. To lock the lever, push it toward the rear.

14. Install the shoe retaining nails, retainers, and spring. Thread the adjusting cable over the guide. Hook the end of the overload spring in the adjustment lever, making sure that the cable remains tight against the anchor and is aligned with the guide.

15. Install the brake drum and adjust the brakes. Initial adjustment is the same as for front drum brakes.

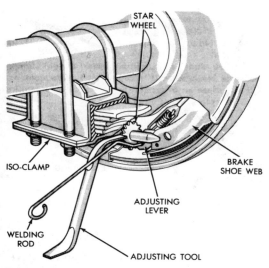

Brake adjustment

INITIAL BRAKE ADJUSTMENT

Although the brakes are self adjusting, it is best to make an initial adjustment after backing off the adjuster to remove the brake drum or after shoe replacement.

1. Raise the wheels to be adjusted so that they are free to spin.

2. Remove the rear adjusting hole cover from the backing plate.

3. Make sure the parking brake is fully released.

4. Insert an adjusting tool or screwdriver in the hole until it contacts the star wheel. Lift the handle of the tool upward, rotating the star wheel, until there is a slight drag felt when the tire is rotated.

5. Insert a piece of welding rod or a thin screwdriver into the adjustment hole. Push against the adjusting lever and hold it away from the star wheel. Back off on the star wheel until no drag is felt. Replace the adjusting hole cover.

6. Repeat on the other wheel.

Wheel Cylinders
REMOVAL AND INSTALLATION

1. Raise and support the car and remove the wheel and tire.

2. Remove the brake drum and brake shoes.

3. Remove the brake line from the cylinder.

4. Unfasten the wheel cylinder attaching bolts and remove the cylinder from its support.

5. Installation is the reverse of removal. Bleed the brakes after installing the cylinder.

OVERHAUL

1. Pry the boots off either end of the cylinder and remove the pushrods. Push in on one of the pistons to force out the other piston, its cup, the spring, and the piston itself.

2. Wash the pistons, the wheel sylinder housing, and the spring in fresh brake fluid. Dry them with compressed air.

3. Inspect the cylinder bore wall for signs of wear. If it is badly scored or pitted, the entire cylinder should be replaced. Light scratches or corrosion can be removed with crocus cloth or a hone.

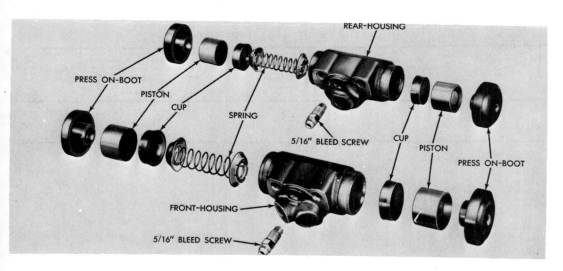

Wheel cylinder—exploded view

4. Dip the pistons and new cups in clean brake fluid. Coat the cylinder wall with brake fluid.

5. Place the spring in the cylinder bore. Position the cups in either end of the cylinder with open end of the cups facing inward (toward each other).

6. Place the pistons in either end of the cylinder bore with the recessed ends facing outward. Slide the pistons into the bore until the ends are flush with the end of the bore. Open the bleeder to relieve any pressure.

7. Fit the boots over the ends of the cylinder and push down until each boot is seated.

PARKING BRAKE

Cable

ADJUSTMENT

1. Rear brakes must be in adjustment before adjusting parking brakes. Raise and support the rear wheels. Release the parking brake lever and loosen the cable adjusting nut under the car.

2. Tighten the cable adjusting nut until a light drag is felt while rotating the wheel. Loosen the cable adjusting nut until both rear wheels can be rotated freely, then back off the cable adjusting nut two full turns.

3. Apply the parking brake several times and test to see that the rear wheels rotate freely.

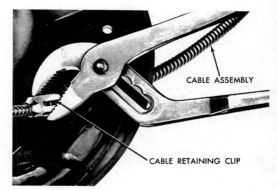

CABLE ASSEMBLY

CABLE RETAINING CLIP

Removing brake cable

REMOVAL AND INSTALLATION

1. Raise and support the car and remove the rear wheels.

2. Disconnect the brake cable from the adjuster connector.

3. Remove the retaining clip from the brake cable bracket at the end of the outer cable.

4. Remove the brake drum from the rear axle.

5. Remove the brake shoe retaining springs and return springs.

6. Remove the brake shoe strut and spring from the brake support and disconnect the brake cable from the operating arm.

7. Compress the retainers on the end of the brake cable housing and remove the cable from the support.

8. Installation is the reverse of removal.

Brake Specifications
(All measurements are given in inches)

Year	Master Cylinder Diameter	Wheel Cylinder Diameter		Disc or Drum Diameter	
		Disc	Drum	Front Disc	Rear Drum
All	1.03	2.75	$15/16$	10.98	10 (Sedan) 11 (Wagon)

Body

You can repair most minor auto body damage yourself. Minor damage usually falls into one of several categories: (1) small scratches and dings in the paint that can be repaired without the use of body filler, (2) deep scratches and dents that require body filler, but do not require pulling, or hammering metal back into shape and (3) rust-out repairs. The repair sequences illustrated in this chapter are typical of these types of repairs. If you want to get involved in more complicated repairs including pulling or hammering sheet metal back into shape, you will probably need more detailed instructions. Chilton's *Minor Auto Body Repair, 2nd Edition* is a comprehensive guide to repairing auto body damage yourself.

TOOLS AND SUPPLIES

The list of tools and equipment you may need to fix minor body damage ranges from very basic hand tools to a wide assortment of specialized body tools. Most minor scratches, dings and rust holes can be fixed using an electric drill, wire wheel or grinder attachment, half-round plastic file, sanding block, various grades of sandpaper (#36, which is coarse through #600, which is fine) in both wet and dry types, auto body plastic,

primer, touch-up paint, spreaders, newspaper and masking tape.

Most manufacturers of auto body repair products began supplying materials to professionals. Their knowledge of the best, most-used products has been translated into body repair kits for the do-it-yourselfer. Kits are available from a number of manufacturers and contain the necessary materials in the required amounts for the repair identified on the package.

Kits are available for a wide variety of uses, including:

• Rusted out metal
• All purpose kit for dents and holes
• Dents and deep scratches
• Fiberglass repair kit
• Epoxy kit for restyling.

Kits offer the advantage of buying what you need for the job. There is little waste and little chance of materials going bad from not being used. The same manufacturers also merchandise all of the individual products used—spreaders, dent pullers, fiberglass cloth, polyester resin, cream hardener, body filler, body files, sandpaper, sanding discs and holders, primer, spray paint, etc.

CAUTION: *Most of the products you will be using contain harmful chemicals, so be extremely careful. Always read the complete label before opening the containers. When* *you put them away for future use, be sure they are out of children's reach!*

Most auto body repair kits contain all the materials you need to do the job right in the kit. So, if you have a small rust spot or dent you want to fix, check the contents of the kit before you run out and buy any additional tools.

ALIGNING BODY PANELS

Doors

There are several methods of adjusting doors. Your vehicle will probably use one of those illustrated.

Whenever a door is removed and is to be reinstalled, you should matchmark the position of the hinges on the door pillars. The holes of the hinges and/or the hinge attaching points are usually oversize to permit alignment of doors. The striker plate is also moveable, through oversize holes, permitting up-and-down, in-and-out and fore-and-aft movement. Fore-and-aft movement is made by adding or subtracting shims from behind the striker and pillar post. The striker should be adjusted so that the door closes fully and remains closed, yet enters the lock freely.

DOOR HINGES

Don't try to cover up poor door adjustment with a striker plate adjustment. The gap on each side of the door should be equal and uniform and there should be no metal-to-metal contact as the door is opened or closed.

1. Determine which hinge bolts must be loosened to move the door in the desired direction.

2. Loosen the hinge bolt(s) just enough to allow the door to be moved with a padded pry bar.

3. Move the door a small amount and check the fit, after tightening the bolts. Be sure that there is no bind or interference with adjacent panels.

4. Repeat this until the door is properly positioned, and tighten all the bolts securely.

Hood, Trunk or Tailgate

As with doors, the outline of hinges should be scribed before removal. The hood and trunk can be aligned by loosening the hinge bolts in their slotted mounting holes and moving the hood or trunk lid as necessary.

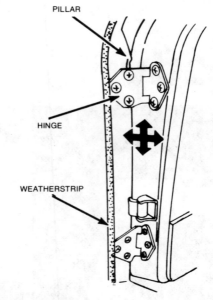

Door hinge adjustment

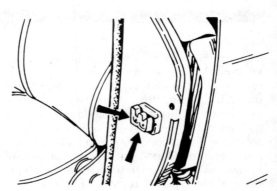

Move the door striker as indicated by arrows

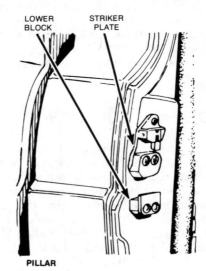

Striker plate and lower block

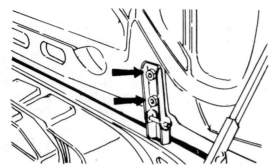

Loosen the hinge boots to permit fore-and-aft and horizontal adjustment

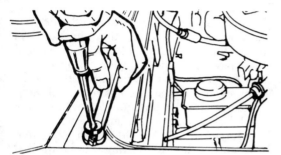

The hood is adjusted vertically by stop-screws at the front and/or rear

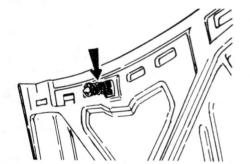

The hood pin can be adjusted for proper lock engagement

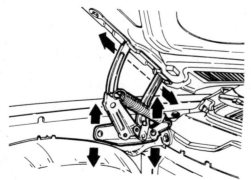

The height of the hood at the rear is adjusted by loosening the bolts that attach the hinge to the body and moving the hood up or down

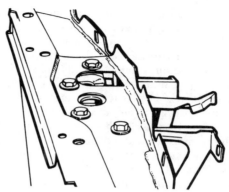

The base of the hood lock can also be repositioned slightly to give more positive lock engagement

The hood and trunk have adjustable catch locations to regulate lock engagement. Bumpers at the front and/or rear of the hood provide a vertical adjustment and the hood lockpin can be adjusted for proper engagement.

The tailgate on the station wagon can be adjusted by loosening the hinge bolts in their slotted mounting holes and moving the tailgate on its hinges. The latchplate and latch striker at the bottom of the tailgate opening can be adjusted to stop rattle. An adjustable bumper is located on each side.

RUST, UNDERCOATING, AND RUSTPROOFING

Rust

Rust is an electrochemical process. It works on ferrous metals (iron and steel) from the inside out due to exposure of unprotected surfaces to air and moisture. The possibility of rust exists practically nationwide—anywhere humidity, industrial pollution or chemical salts are present, rust can form. In coastal areas, the problem is high humidity and salt air; in snowy areas, the problem is chemical salt (de-icer) used to keep the roads clear, and in industrial areas, sulphur dioxide is present in the air from industrial pollution and is changed to sulphuric acid when it rains. The rusting process is accelerated by high temperatures, especially in snowy areas, when vehicles are driven over slushy roads and then left overnight in a heated garage.

Automotive styling also can be a contributor to rust formation. Spot welding of panels creates small pockets that trap moisture and form an environment for rust formation. Fortunately, auto manufacturers have been working hard to increase the corrosion protection of their products. Galvanized sheet metal enjoys much wider use, along with the increased use of plastic and various rust retardant coatings. Manufacturers are also designing out areas in the body where rust-forming moisture can collect.

To prevent rust, you must stop it before it gets started. On new vehicles, there are two ways to accomplish this.

First, the car or truck should be treated with a commercial rustproofing compound. There are many different brands of franchised rustproofers, but most processes involve spraying a waxy "self-healing" compound under the chassis, inside rocker panels, inside doors and fender liners and similar places where rust is likely to form. Prices for a quality rustproofing job range from $100–$250, depending on the area, the brand name and the size of the vehicle.

Ideally, the vehicle should be rustproofed as soon as possible following the purchase. The surfaces of the car or truck have begun to oxidize and deteriorate during shipping. In addition, the car may have sat on a dealer's lot or on a lot at the factory, and once the rust has progressed past the stage of light, powdery surface oxidation rustproofing is not likely to be worthwhile. Professional rustproofers feel that once rust has formed, rustproofing will simply seal in moisture already present. Most franchised rustproofing operations offer a 3–5 year warranty against rust-through, but will not support that warranty if the rustproofing is not applied within three months of the date of manufacture.

Undercoating should not be mistaken for rustproofing. Undercoating is a black, tar-like substance that is applied to the underside of a vehicle. Its basic function is to deaden noises that are transmitted from under the car. It simply cannot get into the crevices and seams where moisture tends to collect. In fact, it may clog up drainage holes and ventilation passages. Some undercoatings also tend to crack or peel with age and only create more moisture and corrosion attracting pockets.

The second thing you should do immediately after purchasing the car is apply a paint sealant. A sealant is a petroleum based product marketed under a wide variety of brand names. It has the same protective properties as a good wax, but bonds to the paint with a chemically inert layer that seals it from the air. If air can't get at the surface, oxidation cannot start.

The paint sealant kit consists of a base coat and a conditioning coat that should be applied every 6–8 months, depending on the manufacturer. The base coat must be applied before waxing, or the wax must first be removed.

Third, keep a garden hose handy for your car in winter. Use it a few times on nice days during the winter for underneath areas, and it will pay big dividends when spring arrives. Spraying under the fenders and other areas which even car washes don't reach will help remove road salt, dirt and other build-ups which help breed rust. Adjust the nozzle to a high-force spray. An old brush will help break up residue, permitting it to be washed away more easily.

It's a somewhat messy job, but worth it in the long run because rust often starts in those hidden areas.

At the same time, wash grime off the door sills and, more importantly, the under portions of the doors, plus the tailgate if you have a station wagon or truck. Applying a coat of wax to those areas at least once before and once during winter will help fend off rust.

When applying the wax to the under parts of the doors, you will note small drain holes. These holes often are plugged with undercoating or dirt. Make sure they are cleaned out to prevent water build-up inside the doors. A small punch or penknife will do the job.

Water from the high-pressure sprays in car washes sometimes can get into the housings for parking and taillights, so take a close look. If they contain water merely loosen the retaining screws and the water should run out.

Repairing Scratches and Small Dents

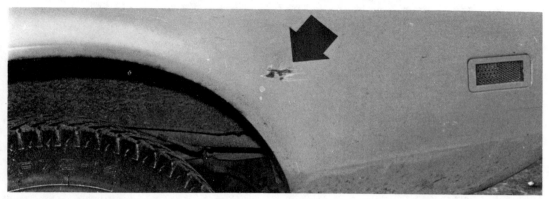

Step 1. This dent (arrow) is typical of a deep scratch or minor dent. If deep enough, the dent or scratch can be pulled out or hammered out from behind. In this case no straightening is necessary

Step 2. Using an 80-grit grinding disc on an electric drill grind the paint from the surrounding area down to bare metal. This will provide a rough surface for the body filler to grab

Step 3. The area should look like this when you're finished grinding

Step 4. Mix the body filler and cream hardener according to the directions

Step 5. Spread the body filler evenly over the entire area. Be sure to cover the area completely

Step 6. Let the body filler dry until the surface can just be scratched with your fingernail

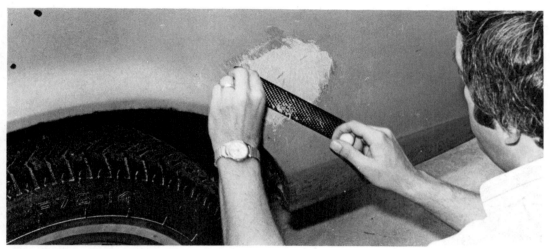

Step 7. Knock the high spots from the body filler with a body file

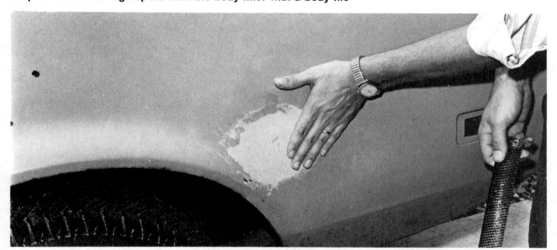

Step 8. Check frequently with the palm of your hand for high and low spots. If you wind up with low spots, you may have to apply another layer of filler

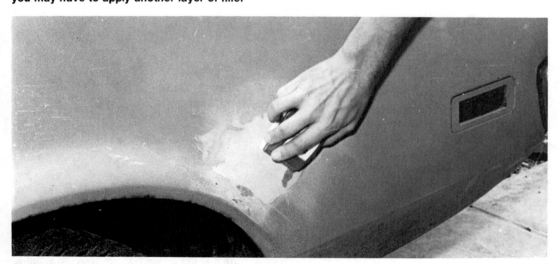

Step 9. Block sand the entire area with 320 grit paper

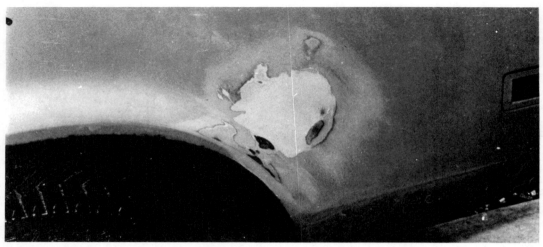

Step 10. When you're finished, the repair should look like this. Note the sand marks extending 2—3 inches out from the repaired area

Step 11. Prime the entire area with automotive primer

Step 12. The finished repair ready for the final paint coat. Note that the primer has covered the sanding marks (see Step 10). A repair of this size should be able to be spotpainted with good results

REPAIRING RUST HOLES

One thing you have to remember about rust: even if you grind away all the rusted metal in a panel, and repair the area with any of the kits available, *eventually* the rust will return. There are two reasons for this. One, rust is a chemical reaction that causes pressure under the repair from the inside out. That's how the blisters form. Two, the back side of the panel (and the repair) is wide open to moisture, and unpainted body filler acts like a sponge. That's why the best solution to rust problems is to remove the rusted panel and install a new one or have the rusted area cut out and a new piece of sheet metal welded in its place. The trouble with welding is the expense; sometimes it will cost more than the car or truck is worth.

One of the better solutions to do-it-yourself rust repair is the process using a fiberglass cloth repair kit (shown here). This will give a strong repair that resists cracking and moisture and is relatively easy to use. It can be used on large or small holes and also can be applied over contoured surfaces.

Step 1. Rust areas such as this are common and are easily fixed

Step 2. Grind away all traces of rust with a 24-grit grinding disc. Be sure to grind back 3—4 inches from the edge of the hole down to bare metal and be sure all traces of rust are removed

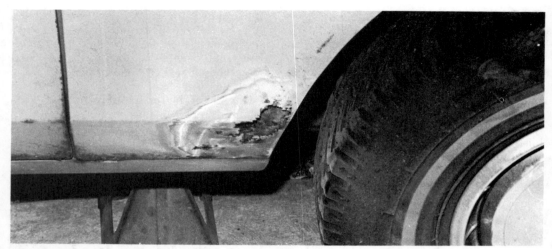

Step 3. Be sure all rust is removed from the edges of the metal. The edges must be ground back to un-rusted metal

Step 4. If you are going to use release film, cut a piece about 2″ larger than the area you have sanded. Place the film over the repair and mark the sanded area on the film. Avoid any unnecessary wrinkling of the film

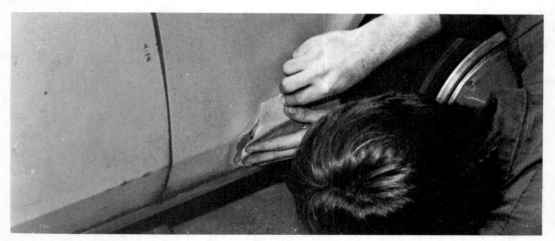

Step 5. Cut 2 pieces of fiberglass matte. One piece should be about 1″ smaller than the sanded area and the second piece should be 1″ smaller than the first. Use sharp scissors to avoid loose ends

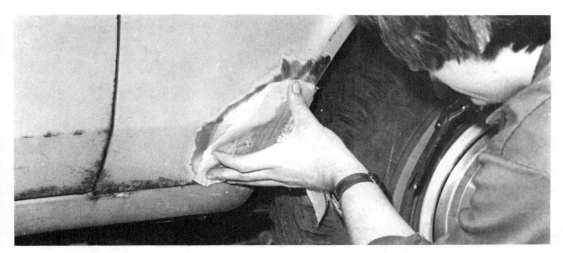

Step 6. Check the dimensions of the release film and cloth by holding them up to the repair area

Step 7. Mix enough repair jelly and cream hardener in the mixing tray to saturate the fiberglass material or fill the repair area. Follow the directions on the container

Step 8. Lay the release sheet on a flat surface and spread an even layer of filler, large enough to cover the repair. Lay the smaller piece of fiberglass cloth in the center of the sheet and spread another layer of repair jelly over the fiberglass cloth. Repeat the operation for the larger piece of cloth. If the fiberglass cloth is not used, spread the repair jelly on the release film, concentrated in the middle of the repair

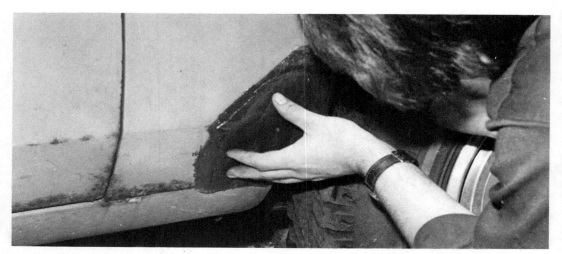

Step 9. Place the repair material over the repair area, with the release film facing outward

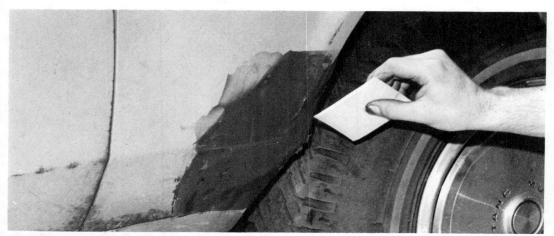

Step 10. Use a spreader and work from the center outward to smooth the material, following the body contours. Be sure to remove all air bubbles

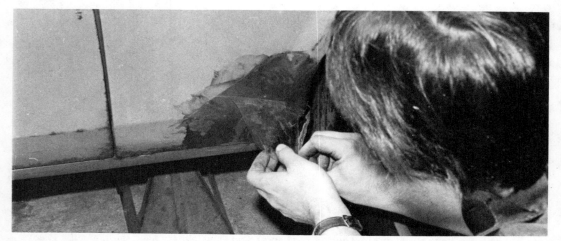

Step 11. Wait until the repair has dried tack-free and peel off the release sheet. The ideal working temperature is 65—90° F. Cooler or warmer temperatures or high humidity may require additional curing time

Step 12. Sand and feather-edge the entire area. The initial sanding can be done with a sanding disc on an electric drill if care is used. Finish the sanding with a block sander

Step 13. When the area is sanded smooth, mix some topcoat and hardener and apply it directly with a spreader. This will give a smooth finish and prevent the glass matte from showing through the paint

Step 14. Block sand the topcoat with finishing sandpaper

Step 15. To finish this repair, grind out the surface rust along the top edge of the rocker panel

Step 16. Mix some more repair jelly and cream hardener and apply it directly over the surface

Step 17. When it dries tack-free, block sand the surface smooth

Step 18. If necessary, mask off adjacent panels and spray the entire repair with primer. You are now ready for a color coat

AUTO BODY CARE

There are hundreds—maybe thousands—of products on the market, all designed to protect or aid your car's finish in some manner. There are as many different products as there are ways to use them, but they all have one thing in common—the surface must be clean.

Washing

The primary ingredient for washing your car is water, preferably "soft" water. In many areas of the country, the local water supply is "hard" containing many minerals. The little rings or film that is left on your car's surface after it has dried is the result of "hard" water.

Since you usually can't change the local water supply, the next best thing is to dry the surface before it has a chance to dry itself.

Into the water you usually add soap. Don't use detergents or common, coarse soaps. Your car's paint never truly dries out, but is always evaporating residual oils into the air. Harsh detergents will remove these oils, causing the paint to dry faster than normal. Instead use warm water and a non-detergent soap made especially for waxed surfaces or a liquid soap made for waxed surfaces or a liquid soap made for washing dishes by hand.

Other products that can be used on painted surfaces include baking soda or plain soda water for stubborn dirt.

Wash the car completely, starting at the top, and rinse it completely clean. Abrasive grit should be loaded off under water pressure; scrubbing grit off will scratch the finish. The best washing tool is a sponge, cleaning mitt or soft towel. Whichever you choose, replace it often as each tends to absorb grease and dirt.

Other ways to get a better wash include:

• Don't wash your car in the sun or when the finish is hot.

• Use water pressure to remove caked-on dirt.

• Remove tree-sap and bird effluence immediately. Such substances will eat through wax, polish and paint.

One of the best implements to dry your car is a turkish towel or an old, soft bath towel. Anything with a deep nap will hold any dirt in suspension and not grind it into the paint.

Harder cloths will only grind the grit into the paint making more scratches. Always start drying at the top, followed by the hood and trunk and sides. You'll find there's always more dirt near the rocker panels and wheelwells which will wind up on the rest of the car if you dry these areas first.

Cleaners, Waxes and Polishes

Before going any farther you should know the function of various products.

Cleaners—remove the top layer of dead pigment or paint.

Rubbing or polishing compounds—used to remove stubborn dirt, get rid of minor scratches, smooth away imperfections and partially restore badly weathered paint.

Polishes—contain no abrasives or waxes; they shine the paint by adding oils to the paint.

Waxes—are a protective coating for the polish.

CLEANERS AND COMPOUNDS

Before you apply any wax, you'll have to remove oxidation, road film and other types of pollutants that washing alone will not remove.

The paint on your car never dries completely. There are always residual oils evaporating from the paint into the air. When enough oils are present in the paint, it has a healthy shine (gloss). When too many oils evaporate the paint takes on a whitish cast known as oxidation. The idea of polishing and waxing is to keep enough oil present in the painted surface to prevent oxidation; but when it occurs, the only recourse is to remove the top layer of "dead" paint, exposing the healthy paint underneath.

Products to remove oxidation and road film are sold under a variety of generic names—polishes, cleaner, rubbing compound, cleaner/polish, polish/cleaner, self-polishing wax, pre-wax cleaner, finish restorer and many more. Regardless of name there are two types of cleaners—abrasive cleaners (sometimes called polishing or rubbing compounds) that remove oxidation by grinding away the top layer of "dead" paint, or chemical cleaners that dissolve the "dead" pigment, allowing it to be wiped away.

Abrasive cleaners, by their nature, leave thousands of minute scratches in the finish, which must be polished out later. These should only be used in extreme cases, but are usually the only thing to use on badly oxidized paint finishes. Chemical cleaners are much milder but are not strong enough for severe cases of oxidation or weathered paint.

The most popular cleaners are liquid or paste abrasive polishing and rubbing compounds. Polishing compounds have a finer abrasive grit for medium duty work. Rubbing compounds are a coarser abrasive and for heavy duty work. Unless you are familiar with how to use compounds, be very careful. Excessive rubbing with any type of compound or cleaner can grind right through the paint to primer or bare metal. Follow the directions on the container—depending on type, the cleaner may or may not be OK for your paint. For example, some cleaners are not formulated for acrylic lacquer finishes.

When a small area needs compounding or heavy polishing, it's best to do the job by hand. Some people prefer a powered buffer for large areas. Avoid cutting through the paint along styling edges on the body. Small, hand operations where the compound is applied and rubbed using cloth folded into a thick ball allow you to work in straight lines along such edges.

To avoid cutting through on the edges when using a power buffer, try masking tape. Just cover the edge with tape while using power. Then finish the job by hand with the tape removed. Even then work carefully. The paint tends to be a lot thinner along the sharp ridges stamped into the panels.

Whether compounding by machine or by hand, only work on a small area and apply the compound sparingly. If the materials are spread too thin, or allowed to sit too long, they dry out. Once dry they lose the ability to deliver a smooth, clean finish. Also, dried out polish tends to cause the buffer to stick in one spot. This in turn can burn or cut through the finish.

WAXES AND POLISHES

Your car's finish can be protected in a number of ways. A cleaner/wax or polish/cleaner followed by wax or variations of each all provide good results. The two-step approach (polish followed by wax) is probably slightly better but consumes more time and effort. Properly fed with oils, your paint should never need cleaning, but despite the best polishing job, it won't last unless it's protected with wax. Without wax, polish must be renewed at least once a month to prevent oxidation. Years ago (some still swear by it today), the best wax was made from the Brazilian palm, the Carnuba, favored for its vegetable base and high melting point. However, modern synthetic waxes are harder, which means they protect against moisture better, and chemically inert silicone is used for a long lasting protection. The only problem with silicone wax is that it penetrates all layers of paint. To repaint or touch up a panel or car protected by silicone wax, you have to completely strip the finish to avoid "fish-eyes."

Under normal conditions, silicone waxes will last 4–6 months, but you have to be careful of wax build-up from too much waxing. Too thick a coat of wax is just as bad as no wax at all; it stops the paint from breathing.

Combination cleaners/waxes have become popular lately because they remove the old layer of wax plus light oxidation, while putting on a fresh coat of wax at the same time. Some cleaners/waxes contain abrasive cleaners which require caution, although many cleaner/waxes use a chemical cleaner.

Applying Wax or Polish

You may view polishing and waxing your car as a pleasant way to spend an afternoon, or as a boring chore, but it has to be done to keep the paint on your car. Caring for the paint doesn't require special tools, but you should follow a few rules.

1. Use a good quality wax.

2. Before applying any wax or polish, be sure the surface is completely clean. Just because the car looks clean, doesn't mean it's ready for polish or wax.

3. If the finish on your car is weathered, dull, or oxidized, it will probably have to be compounded to remove the old or oxidized paint. If the paint is simply dulled from lack of care, one of the non-abrasive cleaners known as polishing compounds will do the trick. If the paint is severely scratched or really dull, you'll probably have to use a rubbing compound to prepare the finish for waxing. If you're not sure which one to use, use the polishing compound, since you can easily ruin the finish by using too strong a compound.

4. Don't apply wax, polish or compound in direct sunlight, even if the directions on the can say you can. Most waxes will not cure properly in bright sunlight and you'll probably end up with a blotchy looking finish.

5. Don't rub the wax off too soon. The result will be a wet, dull looking finish. Let the wax dry thoroughly before buffing it off.

6. A constant debate among car enthusiasts is how wax should be applied. Some maintain pastes or liquids should be applied in a circular motion, but body shop experts have long thought that this approach results in barely detectable circular abrasions, especially on cars that are waxed frequently. They advise rubbing in straight lines, especially if any kind of cleaner is involved.

7. If an applicator is not supplied with the wax, use a piece of soft cheesecloth or very soft lint-free material. The same applies to buffing the surface.

SPECIAL SURFACES

One-step combination cleaner and wax formulas shouldn't be used on many of the special surfaces which abound on cars. The one-step materials contain abrasives to achieve a clean surface under the wax top coat. The abrasives are so mild that you could clean a car every week for a couple of years without fear of rubbing through the paint. But this same level of abrasiveness might, through repeated use, damage decals used for special trim effects. This includes wide stripes, wood-grain trim and other appliques.

Painted plastics must be cleaned with care. If a cleaner is too aggressive it will cut through the paint and expose the primer. If bright trim such as polished aluminum or chrome is painted, cleaning must be performed with even greater care. If rubbing compound is being used, it will cut faster than polish.

Abrasive cleaners will dull an acrylic finish. The best way to clean these newer finishes is with a non-abrasive liquid polish. Only dirt and oxidation, not paint, will be removed.

Taking a few minutes to read the instructions on the can of polish or wax will help prevent making serious mistakes. Not all preparations will work on all surfaces. And some are intended for power application while others will only work when applied by hand.

Don't get the idea that just pouring on some polish and then hitting it with a buffer will suffice. Power equipment speeds the operation. But it also adds a measure of risk. It's very easy to damage the finish if you use the wrong methods or materials.

Caring for Chrome

Read the label on the container. Many products are formulated specifically for chrome, but others contain abrasives that will scratch the chrome finish. If it isn't recommended for chrome, don't use it.

Never use steel wool or kitchen soap pads to clean chrome. Be careful not to get chrome cleaner on paint or interior vinyl surfaces. If you do, get it off immediately.

Troubleshooting

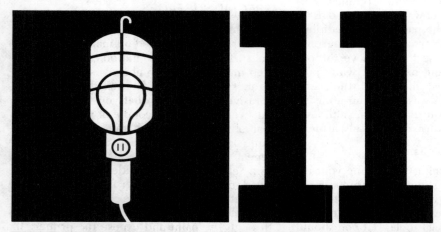

11

This section is designed to aid in the quick, accurate diagnosis of automotive problems. While automotive repairs can be made by many people, accurate troubleshooting is a rare skill for the amateur and professional alike.

In its simplest state, troubleshooting is an exercise in logic. It is essential to realize that an automobile is really composed of a series of systems. Some of these systems are interrelated; others are not. Automobiles operate within a framework of logical rules and physical laws, and the key to troubleshooting is a good understanding of all the automotive systems.

This section breaks the car or truck down into its component systems, allowing the problem to be isolated. The charts and diagnostic road maps list the most common problems and the most probable causes of trouble. Obviously it would be impossible to list every possible problem that could happen along with every possible cause, but it will locate MOST problems and eliminate a lot of unnecessary guesswork. The systematic format will locate problems within a given system, but, because many automotive systems are interrelated, the solution to your particular problem may be found in a number of systems on the car or truck.

USING THE TROUBLESHOOTING CHARTS

This book contains all of the specific information that the average do-it-yourself mechanic needs to repair and maintain his or her car or truck. The troubleshooting charts are designed to be used in conjunction with the specific procedures and information in the text. For instance, troubleshooting a point-type ignition system is fairly standard for all models, but you may be directed to the text to find procedures for troubleshooting an individual type of electronic ignition. You will also have to refer to the specification charts throughout the book for specifications applicable to your car or truck.

TOOLS AND EQUIPMENT

The tools illustrated in Chapter 1 (plus two more diagnostic pieces) will be adequate to troubleshoot most problems. The two other tools needed are a voltmeter and an ohmmeter. These can be purchased separately or in combination, known as a VOM meter.

In the event that other tools are required, they will be noted in the procedures.

Troubleshooting Engine Problems

See Chapters 2, 3, 4 for more information and service procedures.

Index to Systems

System	To Test	Group
Battery	Engine need not be running	1
Starting system	Engine need not be running	2
Primary electrical system	Engine need not be running	3
Secondary electrical system	Engine need not be running	4
Fuel system	Engine need not be running	5
Engine compression	Engine need not be running	6
Engine vacuum	Engine must be running	7
Secondary electrical system	Engine must be running	8
Valve train	Engine must be running	9
Exhaust system	Engine must be running	10
Cooling system	Engine must be running	11
Engine lubrication	Engine must be running	12

Index to Problems

Problem: Symptom	Begin at Specific Diagnosis, Number ____
Engine Won't Start:	
Starter doesn't turn	1.1, 2.1
Starter turns, engine doesn't	2.1
Starter turns engine very slowly	1.1, 2.4
Starter turns engine normally	3.1, 4.1
Starter turns engine very quickly	6.1
Engine fires intermittently	4.1
Engine fires consistently	5.1, 6.1
Engine Runs Poorly:	
Hard starting	3.1, 4.1, 5.1, 8.1
Rough idle	4.1, 5.1, 8.1
Stalling	3.1, 4.1, 5.1, 8.1
Engine dies at high speeds	4.1, 5.1
Hesitation (on acceleration from standing stop)	5.1, 8.1
Poor pickup	4.1, 5.1, 8.1
Lack of power	3.1, 4.1, 5.1, 8.1
Backfire through the carburetor	4.1, 8.1, 9.1
Backfire through the exhaust	4.1, 8.1, 9.1
Blue exhaust gases	6.1, 7.1
Black exhaust gases	5.1
Running on (after the ignition is shut off)	3.1, 8.1
Susceptible to moisture	4.1
Engine misfires under load	4.1, 7.1, 8.4, 9.1
Engine misfires at speed	4.1, 8.4
Engine misfires at idle	3.1, 4.1, 5.1, 7.1, 8.4

Sample Section

Test and Procedure	Results and Indications	Proceed to
4.1—Check for spark: Hold each spark plug wire approximately ¼″ from ground with gloves or a heavy, dry rag. Crank the engine and observe the spark.	→ If no spark is evident:	→**4.2**
	→ If spark is good in some cases:	→**4.3**
	→ If spark is good in all cases:	→**4.6**

Specific Diagnosis

This section is arranged so that following each test, instructions are given to proceed to another, until a problem is diagnosed.

Section 1—Battery

Test and Procedure	Results and Indications	Proceed to
1.1—Inspect the battery visually for case condition (corrosion, cracks) and water level.	If case is cracked, replace battery:	**1.4**
	If the case is intact, remove corrosion with a solution of baking soda and water (**CAUTION:** *do not get the solution into the battery*), and fill with water:	**1.2**

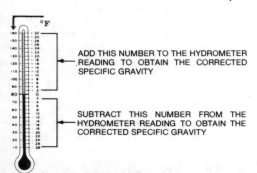

DIRT ON TOP OF BATTERY
CORROSION
PLUGGED VENT
LOOSE CABLE OR POSTS
CRACKS
LOW WATER LEVEL

Inspect the battery case

Test and Procedure	Results and Indications	Proceed to
1.2—Check the battery cable connections: Insert a screwdriver between the battery post and the cable clamp. Turn the headlights on high beam, and observe them as the screwdriver is gently twisted to ensure good metal to metal contact.	If the lights brighten, remove and clean the clamp and post; coat the post with petroleum jelly, install and tighten the clamp:	**1.4**
	If no improvement is noted:	**1.3**

TESTING BATTERY CABLE CONNECTIONS USING A SCREWDRIVER

Test and Procedure	Results and Indications	Proceed to
1.3—Test the state of charge of the battery using an individual cell tester or hydrometer.	If indicated, charge the battery. **NOTE:** *If no obvious reason exists for the low state of charge (i.e., battery age, prolonged storage), proceed to:*	**1.4**

°F

ADD THIS NUMBER TO THE HYDROMETER READING TO OBTAIN THE CORRECTED SPECIFIC GRAVITY

SUBTRACT THIS NUMBER FROM THE HYDROMETER READING TO OBTAIN THE CORRECTED SPECIFIC GRAVITY

Specific Gravity (@ 80° F.)

Minimum	Battery Charge
1.260	100% Charged
1.230	75% Charged
1.200	50% Charged
1.170	25% Charged
1.140	Very Little Power Left
1.110	Completely Discharged

The effects of temperature on battery specific gravity (left) and amount of battery charge in relation to specific gravity (right)

Test and Procedure	Results and Indications	Proceed to
1.4—Visually inspect battery cables for cracking, bad connection to ground, or bad connection to starter.	If necessary, tighten connections or replace the cables:	**2.1**

Section 2—Starting System
See Chapter 3 for service procedures

Test and Procedure	Results and Indications	Proceed to

Note: Tests in Group 2 are performed with coil high tension lead disconnected to prevent accidental starting.

2.1—Test the starter motor and solenoid: Connect a jumper from the battery post of the solenoid (or relay) to the starter post of the solenoid (or relay).	If starter turns the engine normally:	**2.2**
	If the starter buzzes, or turns the engine very slowly:	**2.4**
	If no response, replace the solenoid (or relay).	**3.1**
	If the starter turns, but the engine doesn't, ensure that the flywheel ring gear is intact. If the gear is undamaged, replace the starter drive.	**3.1**
2.2—Determine whether ignition override switches are functioning properly (clutch start switch, neutral safety switch), by connecting a jumper across the switch(es), and turning the ignition switch to "start".	If starter operates, adjust or replace switch:	**3.1**
	If the starter doesn't operate:	**2.3**
2.3—Check the ignition switch "start" position: Connect a 12V test lamp or voltmeter between the starter post of the solenoid (or relay) and ground. Turn the ignition switch to the "start" position, and jiggle the key.	If the lamp doesn't light or the meter needle doesn't move when the switch is turned, check the ignition switch for loose connections, cracked insulation, or broken wires. Repair or replace as necessary:	**3.1**
	If the lamp flickers or needle moves when the key is jiggled, replace the ignition switch.	**3.3**

Checking the ignition switch "start" position

STARTER RELAY
(IF EQUIPPED)

2.4—Remove and bench test the starter, according to specifications in the engine electrical section.	If the starter does not meet specifications, repair or replace as needed:	**3.1**
	If the starter is operating properly:	**2.5**
2.5—Determine whether the engine can turn freely: Remove the spark plugs, and check for water in the cylinders. Check for water on the dipstick, or oil in the radiator. Attempt to turn the engine using an 18″ flex drive and socket on the crankshaft pulley nut or bolt.	If the engine will turn freely only with the spark plugs out, and hydrostatic lock (water in the cylinders) is ruled out, check valve timing:	**9.2**
	If engine will not turn freely, and it is known that the clutch and transmission are free, the engine must be disassembled for further evaluation:	**Chapter 3**

Section 3—Primary Electrical System

Test and Procedure	Results and Indications	Proceed to
3.1—Check the ignition switch "on" position: Connect a jumper wire between the distributor side of the coil and ground, and a 12V test lamp between the switch side of the coil and ground. Remove the high tension lead from the coil. Turn the ignition switch on and jiggle the key.	If the lamp lights:	**3.2**
	If the lamp flickers when the key is jiggled, replace the ignition switch:	**3.3**
	If the lamp doesn't light, check for loose or open connections. If none are found, remove the ignition switch and check for continuity. If the switch is faulty, replace it:	**3.3**

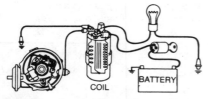

Checking the ignition switch "on" position

3.2—Check the ballast resistor or resistance wire for an open circuit, using an ohmmeter. See Chapter 3 for specific tests.	Replace the resistor or resistance wire if the resistance is zero. **NOTE:** *Some ignition systems have no ballast resistor.*	**3.3**

 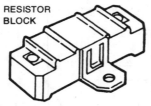

RESISTOR BLOCK

CALIBRATED RESISTANCE LEAD

Two types of resistors

3.3—On point-type ignition systems, visually inspect the breaker points for burning, pitting or excessive wear. Gray coloring of the point contact surfaces is normal. Rotate the crankshaft until the contact heel rests on a high point of the distributor cam and adjust the point gap to specifications. On electronic ignition models, remove the distributor cap and visually inspect the armature. Ensure that the armature pin is in place, and that the armature is on tight and rotates when the engine is cranked. Make sure there are no cracks, chips or rounded edges on the armature.	If the breaker points are intact, clean the contact surfaces with fine emery cloth, and adjust the point gap to specifications. If the points are worn, replace them. On electronic systems, replace any parts which appear defective. If condition persists:	**3.4**

Test and Procedure	Results and Indications	Proceed to
3.4—On point-type ignition systems, connect a dwell-meter between the distributor primary lead and ground. Crank the engine and observe the point dwell angle. On electronic ignition systems, conduct a stator (magnetic pickup assembly) test. See Chapter 3.	On point-type systems, adjust the dwell angle if necessary. **NOTE:** *Increasing the point gap decreases the dwell angle and vice-versa.*	**3.6**
	If the dwell meter shows little or no reading;	**3.5**
	On electronic ignition systems, if the stator is bad, replace the stator. If the stator is good, proceed to the other tests in Chapter 3.	

WIDE GAP   NARROW GAP

CLOSE   OPEN   SMALL DWELL   LARGE DWELL

NORMAL DWELL   INSUFFICIENT DWELL   EXCESSIVE DWELL

Dwell is a function of point gap

3.5—On the point-type ignition systems, check the condenser for short: connect an ohmeter across the condenser body and the pigtail lead.	If any reading other than infinite is noted, replace the condenser	**3.6**

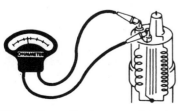

OHMMETER

Checking the condenser for short

3.6—Test the coil primary resistance: On point-type ignition systems, connect an ohmmeter across the coil primary terminals, and read the resistance on the low scale. Note whether an external ballast resistor or resistance wire is used. On electronic ignition systems, test the coil primary resistance as in Chapter 3.	Point-type ignition coils utilizing ballast resistors or resistance wires should have approximately 1.0 ohms resistance. Coils with internal resistors should have approximately 4.0 ohms resistance. If values far from the above are noted, replace the coil.	**4.1**

OHMMETER

Check the coil primary resistance

Section 4—Secondary Electrical System
See Chapters 2–3 for service procedures

Test and Procedure	Results and Indications	Proceed to
4.1—Check for spark: Hold each spark plug wire approximately ¼″ from ground with gloves or a heavy, dry rag. Crank the engine, and observe the spark.	If no spark is evident:	**4.2**
	If spark is good in some cylinders:	**4.3**
	If spark is good in all cylinders:	**4.6**

Check for spark at the plugs

4.2—Check for spark at the coil high tension lead: Remove the coil high tension lead from the distributor and position it approximately ¼″ from ground. Crank the engine and observe spark. **CAUTION: This test should not be performed on engines equipped with electronic ignition.**	If the spark is good and consistent:	**4.3**
	If the spark is good but intermittent, test the primary electrical system starting at 3.3:	**3.3**
	If the spark is weak or non-existent, replace the coil high tension lead, clean and tighten all connections and retest. If no improvement is noted:	**4.4**
4.3—Visually inspect the distributor cap and rotor for burned or corroded contacts, cracks, carbon tracks, or moisture. Also check the fit of the rotor on the distributor shaft (where applicable).	If moisture is present, dry thoroughly, and retest per 4.1:	**4.1**
	If burned or excessively corroded contacts, cracks, or carbon tracks are noted, replace the defective part(s) and retest per 4.1:	**4.1**
	If the rotor and cap appear intact, or are only slightly corroded, clean the contacts thoroughly (including the cap towers and spark plug wire ends) and retest per 4.1:	
	If the spark is good in all cases:	**4.6**
	If the spark is poor in all cases:	**4.5**

Inspect the distributor cap and rotor

Test and Procedure	Results and Indications	Proceed to
4.4—Check the coil secondary resistance: On point-type systems connect an ohmmeter across the distributor side of the coil and the coil tower. Read the resistance on the high scale of the ohmmeter. On electronic ignition systems, see Chapter 3 for specific tests.	The resistance of a satisfactory coil should be between 4,000 and 10,000 ohms. If resistance is considerably higher (i.e., 40,000 ohms) replace the coil and retest per 4.1. **NOTE: *This does not apply to high performance coils.***	

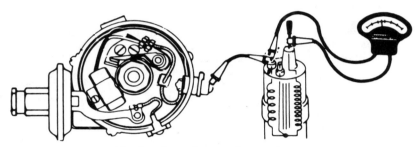

Testing the coil secondary resistance

Test and Procedure	Results and Indications	Proceed to
4.5—Visually inspect the spark plug wires for cracking or brittleness. Ensure that no two wires are positioned so as to cause induction firing (adjacent and parallel). Remove each wire, one by one, and check resistance with an ohmmeter.	Replace any cracked or brittle wires. If any of the wires are defective, replace the entire set. Replace any wires with excessive resistance (over $8000\,\Omega$ per foot for suppression wire), and separate any wires that might cause induction firing.	4.6

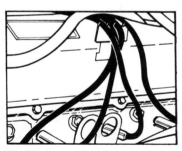

Misfiring can be the result of spark plug leads to adjacent, consecutively firing cylinders running parallel and too close together

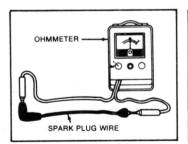

On point-type ignition systems, check the spark plug wires as shown. On electronic ignitions, do not remove the wire from the distributor cap terminal; instead, test through the cap

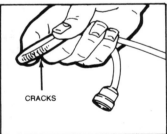

Spark plug wires can be checked visually by bending them in a loop over your finger. This will reveal any cracks, burned or broken insulation. Any wire with cracked insulation should be replaced

Test and Procedure	Results and Indications	Proceed to
4.6—Remove the spark plugs, noting the cylinders from which they were removed, and evaluate according to the color photos in the middle of this book.	See following.	**See following.**

Test and Procedure	Results and Indications	Proceed to
4.7—Examine the location of all the plugs.	The following diagrams illustrate some of the conditions that the location of plugs will reveal.	4.8

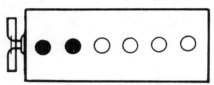

Two adjacent plugs are fouled in a 6-cylinder engine, 4-cylinder engine or either bank of a V-8. This is probably due to a blown head gasket between the two cylinders

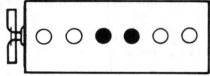

The two center plugs in a 6-cylinder engine are fouled. Raw fuel may be "boiled" out of the carburetor into the intake manifold after the engine is shut-off. Stop-start driving can also foul the center plugs, due to overly rich mixture. Proper float level, a new float needle and seat or use of an insulating spacer may help this problem

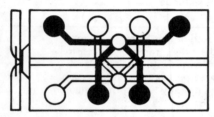

An unbalanced carburetor is indicated. Following the fuel flow on this particular design shows that the cylinders fed by the right-hand barrel are fouled from overly rich mixture, while the cylinders fed by the left-hand barrel are normal

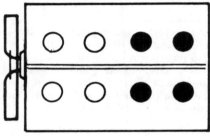

If the four rear plugs are overheated, a cooling system problem is suggested. A thorough cleaning of the cooling system may restore coolant circulation and cure the problem

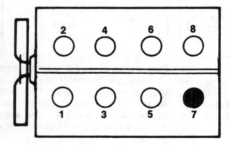

Finding one plug overheated may indicate an intake manifold leak near the affected cylinder. If the overheated plug is the second of two adjacent, consecutively firing plugs, it could be the result of ignition cross-firing. Separating the leads to these two plugs will eliminate cross-fire

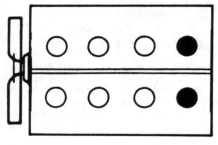

Occasionally, the two rear plugs in large, lightly used V-8's will become oil fouled. High oil consumption and smoky exhaust may also be noticed. It is probably due to plugged oil drain holes in the rear of the cylinder head, causing oil to be sucked in around the valve stems. This usually occurs in the rear cylinders first, because the engine slants that way

Test and Procedure	Results and Indications	Proceed to
4.8—Determine the static ignition timing. Using the crankshaft pulley timing marks as a guide, locate top dead center on the compression stroke of the number one cylinder.	The rotor should be pointing toward the No. 1 tower in the distributor cap, and, on electronic ignitions, the armature spoke for that cylinder should be lined up with the stator.	**4.8**
4.9—Check coil polarity: Connect a voltmeter negative lead to the coil high tension lead, and the positive lead to ground (**NOTE: Reverse the hook-up for positive ground systems**). Crank the engine momentarily.	If the voltmeter reads up-scale, the polarity is correct:	**5.1**
	If the voltmeter reads down-scale, reverse the coil polarity (switch the primary leads):	**5.1**

Checking coil polarity

Section 5—Fuel System
See Chapter 4 for service procedures

Test and Procedure	Results and Indications	Proceed to
5.1—Determine that the air filter is functioning efficiently: Hold paper elements up to a strong light, and attempt to see light through the filter.	Clean permanent air filters in solvent (or manufacturer's recommendation), and allow to dry. Replace paper elements through which light cannot be seen:	**5.2**
5.2—Determine whether a flooding condition exists: Flooding is identified by a strong gasoline odor, and excessive gasoline present in the throttle bore(s) of the carburetor.	If flooding is not evident:	**5.3**
	If flooding is evident, permit the gasoline to dry for a few moments and restart.	
	If flooding doesn't recur:	**5.7**
	If flooding is persistent:	**5.5**

If the engine floods repeatedly, check the choke butterfly flap

5.3—Check that fuel is reaching the carburetor: Detach the fuel line at the carburetor inlet. Hold the end of the line in a cup (not styrofoam), and crank the engine.	If fuel flows smoothly:	**5.7**
	If fuel doesn't flow (**NOTE: Make sure that there is fuel in the tank**), or flows erratically:	**5.4**

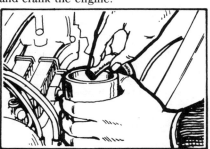

Check the fuel pump by disconnecting the output line (fuel pump-to-carburetor) at the carburetor and operating the starter briefly

Test and Procedure	Results and Indications	Proceed to
5.4—Test the fuel pump: Disconnect all fuel lines from the fuel pump. Hold a finger over the input fitting, crank the engine (with electric pump, turn the ignition or pump on); and feel for suction.	If suction is evident, blow out the fuel line to the tank with low pressure compressed air until bubbling is heard from the fuel filler neck. Also blow out the carburetor fuel line (both ends disconnected):	**5.7**
	If no suction is evident, replace or repair the fuel pump: **NOTE:** *Repeated oil fouling of the spark plugs, or a no-start condition, could be the result of a ruptured vacuum booster pump diaphragm, through which oil or gasoline is being drawn into the intake manifold (where applicable).*	**5.7**
5.5—Occasionally, small specks of dirt will clog the small jets and orifices in the carburetor. With the engine cold, hold a flat piece of wood or similar material over the carburetor, where possible, and crank the engine.	If the engine starts, but runs roughly the engine is probably not run enough. If the engine won't start:	**5.9**
5.6—Check the needle and seat: Tap the carburetor in the area of the needle and seat.	If flooding stops, a gasoline additive (e.g., Gumout) will often cure the problem:	**5.7**
	If flooding continues, check the fuel pump for excessive pressure at the carburetor (according to specifications). If the pressure is normal, the needle and seat must be removed and checked, and/or the float level adjusted:	**5.7**
5.7—Test the accelerator pump by looking into the throttle bores while operating the throttle. **Check for gas at the carburetor by looking down the carburetor throat while someone moves the accelerator**	If the accelerator pump appears to be operating normally:	**5.8**
	If the accelerator pump is not operating, the pump must be reconditioned. Where possible, service the pump with the carburetor(s) installed on the engine. If necessary, remove the carburetor. Prior to removal:	**5.8**
5.8—Determine whether the carburetor main fuel system is functioning: Spray a commercial starting fluid into the carburetor while attempting to start the engine.	If the engine starts, runs for a few seconds, and dies:	**5.9**
	If the engine doesn't start:	**6.1**

Test and Procedure	Results and Indications	Proceed to
5.9—Uncommon fuel system malfunctions: See below:	If the problem is solved: If the problem remains, remove and recondition the carburetor.	6.1

Condition	Indication	Test	Prevailing Weather Conditions	Remedy
Vapor lock	Engine will not restart shortly after running.	Cool the components of the fuel system until the engine starts. Vapor lock can be cured faster by draping a wet cloth over a mechanical fuel pump.	Hot to very hot	Ensure that the exhaust manifold heat control valve is operating. Check with the vehicle manufacturer for the recommended solution to vapor lock on the model in question.
Carburetor icing	Engine will not idle, stalls at low speeds.	Visually inspect the throttle plate area of the throttle bores for frost.	High humidity, 32–40° F.	Ensure that the exhaust manifold heat control valve is operating, and that the intake manifold heat riser is not blocked.
Water in the fuel	Engine sputters and stalls; may not start.	Pump a small amount of fuel into a glass jar. Allow to stand, and inspect for droplets or a layer of water.	High humidity, extreme temperature changes.	For droplets, use one or two cans of commercial gas line anti-freeze. For a layer of water, the tank must be drained, and the fuel lines blown out with compressed air.

Section 6—Engine Compression

See Chapter 3 for service procedures

6.1—Test engine compression: Remove all spark plugs. Block the throttle wide open. Insert a compression gauge into a spark plug port, crank the engine to obtain the maximum reading, and record.	If compression is within limits on all cylinders: If gauge reading is extremely low on all cylinders: If gauge reading is low on one or two cylinders: (If gauge readings are identical and low on two or more adjacent cylinders, the head gasket must be replaced.)	7.1 6.2 6.2

Checking compression

6.2—Test engine compression (wet): Squirt approximately 30 cc. of engine oil into each cylinder, and retest per 6.1.	If the readings improve, worn or cracked rings or broken pistons are indicated: If the readings do not improve, burned or excessively carboned valves or a jumped timing chain are indicated: NOTE: *A jumped timing chain is often indicated by difficult cranking.*	See Chapter 3 7.1

Section 7—Engine Vacuum
See Chapter 3 for service procedures

Test and Procedure	Results and Indications	Proceed to
7.1—Attach a vacuum gauge to the intake manifold beyond the throttle plate. Start the engine, and observe the action of the needle over the range of engine speeds.	See below.	**See below**

INDICATION: normal engine in good condition

Proceed to: 8.1

Normal engine
Gauge reading: steady, from 17–22 in./Hg.

INDICATION: sticking valves or ignition miss

Proceed to: 9.1, 8.3

Sticking valves
Gauge reading: intermittent fluctuation at idle

INDICATION: late ignition or valve timing, low compression, stuck throttle valve, leaking carburetor or manifold gasket

Proceed to: 6.1

Incorrect valve timing
Gauge reading: low (10–15 in./Hg) but steady

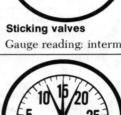

INDICATION: improper carburetor adjustment or minor intake leak.

Proceed to: 7.2

Carburetor requires adjustment
Gauge reading: drifting needle

INDICATION: ignition miss, blown cylinder head gasket, leaking valve or weak valve spring

Proceed to: 8.3, 6.1

Blown head gasket
Gauge reading: needle fluctuates as engine speed increases

INDICATION: burnt valve or faulty valve clearance. Needle will fall when defective valve operates

Proceed to: 9.1

Burnt or leaking valves
Gauge reading: steady needle, but drops regularly

INDICATION: choked muffler, excessive back pressure in system

Proceed to: 10.1

Clogged exhaust system
Gauge reading: gradual drop in reading at idle

INDICATION: worn valve guides

Proceed to: 9.1

Worn valve guides
Gauge reading: needle vibrates excessively at idle, but steadies as engine speed increases

White pointer = steady gauge hand

Black pointer = fluctuating gauge hand

Test and Procedure	Results and Indications	Proceed to
7.2—Attach a vacuum gauge per 7.1, and test for an intake manifold leak. Squirt a small amount of oil around the intake manifold gaskets, carburetor gaskets, plugs and fittings. Observe the action of the vacuum gauge.	If the reading improves, replace the indicated gasket, or seal the indicated fitting or plug: If the reading remains low:	**8.1** **7.3**
7.3—Test all vacuum hoses and accessories for leaks as described in 7.2. Also check the carburetor body (dashpots, automatic choke mechanism, throttle shafts) for leaks in the same manner.	If the reading improves, service or replace the offending part(s): If the reading remains low:	**8.1** **6.1**

Section 8—Secondary Electrical System
See Chapter 2 for service procedures

Test and Procedure	Results and Indications	Proceed to
8.1—Remove the distributor cap and check to make sure that the rotor turns when the engine is cranked. Visually inspect the distributor components.	Clean, tighten or replace any components which appear defective.	**8.2**
8.2—Connect a timing light (per manufacturer's recommendation) and check the dynamic ignition timing. Disconnect and plug the vacuum hose(s) to the distributor if specified, start the engine, and observe the timing marks at the specified engine speed.	If the timing is not correct, adjust to specifications by rotating the distributor in the engine: (Advance timing by rotating distributor opposite normal direction of rotor rotation, retard timing by rotating distributor in same direction as rotor rotation.)	**8.3**
8.3—Check the operation of the distributor advance mechanism(s): To test the mechanical advance, disconnect the vacuum lines from the distributor advance unit and observe the timing marks with a timing light as the engine speed is increased from idle. If the mark moves smoothly, without hesitation, it may be assumed that the mechanical advance is functioning properly. To test vacuum advance and/or retard systems, alternately crimp and release the vacuum line, and observe the timing mark for movement. If movement is noted, the system is operating.	If the systems are functioning: If the systems are not functioning, remove the distributor, and test on a distributor tester:	**8.4** **8.4**
8.4—Locate an ignition miss: With the engine running, remove each spark plug wire, one at a time, until one is found that doesn't cause the engine to roughen and slow down.	When the missing cylinder is identified:	**4.1**

Section 9—Valve Train
See Chapter 3 for service procedures

Test and Procedure	Results and Indications	Proceed to
9.1—Evaluate the valve train: Remove the valve cover, and ensure that the valves are adjusted to specifications. A mechanic's stethoscope may be used to aid in the diagnosis of the valve train. By pushing the probe on or near push rods or rockers, valve noise often can be isolated. A timing light also may be used to diagnose valve problems. Connect the light according to manufacturer's recommendations, and start the engine. Vary the firing moment of the light by increasing the engine speed (and therefore the ignition advance), and moving the trigger from cylinder to cylinder. Observe the movement of each valve.	Sticking valves or erratic valve train motion can be observed with the timing light. The cylinder head must be disassembled for repairs.	**See Chapter 3**
9.2—Check the valve timing: Locate top dead center of the No. 1 piston, and install a degree wheel or tape on the crankshaft pulley or damper with zero corresponding to an index mark on the engine. Rotate the crankshaft in its direction of rotation, and observe the opening of the No. 1 cylinder intake valve. The opening should correspond with the correct mark on the degree wheel according to specifications.	If the timing is not correct, the timing cover must be removed for further investigation.	**See Chapter 3**

Section 10—Exhaust System

Test and Procedure	Results and Indications	Proceed to
10.1—Determine whether the exhaust manifold heat control valve is operating: Operate the valve by hand to determine whether it is free to move. If the valve is free, run the engine to operating temperature and observe the action of the valve, to ensure that it is opening.	If the valve sticks, spray it with a suitable solvent, open and close the valve to free it, and retest. If the valve functions properly: If the valve does not free, or does not operate, replace the valve:	**10.2** **10.2**
10.2—Ensure that there are no exhaust restrictions: Visually inspect the exhaust system for kinks, dents, or crushing. Also note that gases are flowing freely from the tailpipe at all engine speeds, indicating no restriction in the muffler or resonator.	Replace any damaged portion of the system:	**11.1**

Section 11—Cooling System
See Chapter 3 for service procedures

Test and Procedure	Results and Indications	Proceed to
11.1—Visually inspect the fan belt for glazing, cracks, and fraying, and replace if necessary. Tighten the belt so that the longest span has approximately ½″ play at its midpoint under thumb pressure (see Chapter 1).	Replace or tighten the fan belt as necessary:	**11.2**

Checking belt tension

Test and Procedure	Results and Indications	Proceed to
11.2—Check the fluid level of the cooling system.	If full or slightly low, fill as necessary:	**11.5**
	If extremely low:	**11.3**
11.3—Visually inspect the external portions of the cooling system (radiator, radiator hoses, thermostat elbow, water pump seals, heater hoses, etc.) for leaks. If none are found, pressurize the cooling system to 14–15 psi.	If cooling system holds the pressure:	**11.5**
	If cooling system loses pressure rapidly, reinspect external parts of the system for leaks under pressure. If none are found, check dipstick for coolant in crankcase. If no coolant is present, but pressure loss continues:	**11.4**
	If coolant is evident in crankcase, remove cylinder head(s), and check gasket(s). If gaskets are intact, block and cylinder head(s) should be checked for cracks or holes.	
	If the gasket(s) is blown, replace, and purge the crankcase of coolant:	**12.6**
	NOTE: *Occasionally, due to atmospheric and driving conditions, condensation of water can occur in the crankcase. This causes the oil to appear milky white. To remedy, run the engine until hot, and change the oil and oil filter.*	
11.4—Check for combustion leaks into the cooling system: Pressurize the cooling system as above. Start the engine, and observe the pressure gauge. If the needle fluctuates, remove each spark plug wire, one at a time, noting which cylinder(s) reduce or eliminate the fluctuation.	Cylinders which reduce or eliminate the fluctuation, when the spark plug wire is removed, are leaking into the cooling system. Replace the head gasket on the affected cylinder bank(s).	

Pressurizing the cooling system

Test and Procedure	Results and Indications	Proceed to
11.5—Check the radiator pressure cap: Attach a radiator pressure tester to the radiator cap (wet the seal prior to installation). Quickly pump up the pressure, noting the point at which the cap releases.	If the cap releases within ± 1 psi of the specified rating, it is operating properly:	**11.6**
	If the cap releases at more than ± 1 psi of the specified rating, it should be replaced:	**11.6**

Checking radiator pressure cap

Test and Procedure	Results and Indications	Proceed to
11.6—Test the thermostat: Start the engine cold, remove the radiator cap, and insert a thermometer into the radiator. Allow the engine to idle. After a short while, there will be a sudden, rapid increase in coolant temperature. The temperature at which this sharp rise stops is the thermostat opening temperature.	If the thermostat opens at or about the specified temperature:	**11.7**
	If the temperature doesn't increase: (If the temperature increases slowly and gradually, replace the thermostat.)	**11.7**
11.7—Check the water pump: Remove the thermostat elbow and the thermostat, disconnect the coil high tension lead (to prevent starting), and crank the engine momentarily.	If coolant flows, replace the thermostat and retest per 11.6:	**11.6**
	If coolant doesn't flow, reverse flush the cooling system to alleviate any blockage that might exist. If system is not blocked, and coolant will not flow, replace the water pump.	

Section 12—Lubrication
See Chapter 3 for service procedures

Test and Procedure	Results and Indications	Proceed to
12.1—Check the oil pressure gauge or warning light: If the gauge shows low pressure, or the light is on for no obvious reason, remove the oil pressure sender. Install an accurate oil pressure gauge and run the engine momentarily.	If oil pressure builds normally, run engine for a few moments to determine that it is functioning normally, and replace the sender.	—
	If the pressure remains low:	**12.2**
	If the pressure surges:	**12.3**
	If the oil pressure is zero:	**12.3**
12.2—Visually inspect the oil: If the oil is watery or very thin, milky, or foamy, replace the oil and oil filter.	If the oil is normal:	**12.3**
	If after replacing oil the pressure remains low:	**12.3**
	If after replacing oil the pressure becomes normal:	—

Test and Procedure	Results and Indications	Proceed to
12.3—Inspect the oil pressure relief valve and spring, to ensure that it is not sticking or stuck. Remove and thoroughly clean the valve, spring, and the valve body.	If the oil pressure improves: If no improvement is noted:	— **12.4**
12.4—Check to ensure that the oil pump is not cavitating (sucking air instead of oil): See that the crankcase is neither over nor underfull, and that the pickup in the sump is in the proper position and free from sludge.	Fill or drain the crankcase to the proper capacity, and clean the pickup screen in solvent if necessary. If no improvement is noted:	**12.5**
12.5—Inspect the oil pump drive and the oil pump:	If the pump drive or the oil pump appear to be defective, service as necessary and retest per 12.1: If the pump drive and pump appear to be operating normally, the engine should be disassembled to determine where blockage exists:	**12.1** **See Chapter 3**
12.6—Purge the engine of ethylene glycol coolant: Completely drain the crankcase and the oil filter. Obtain a commercial butyl cellosolve base solvent, designated for this purpose, and follow the instructions precisely. Following this, install a new oil filter and refill the crankcase with the proper weight oil. The next oil and filter change should follow shortly thereafter (1000 miles).		

TROUBLESHOOTING EMISSION CONTROL SYSTEMS

See Chapter 4 for procedures applicable to individual emission control systems used on specific combinations of engine/transmission/model.

TROUBLESHOOTING THE CARBURETOR
See Chapter 4 for service procedures

Carburetor problems cannot be effectively isolated unless all other engine systems (particularly ignition and emission) are functioning properly and the engine is properly tuned.

Condition	Possible Cause
Engine cranks, but does not start	1. Improper starting procedure 2. No fuel in tank 3. Clogged fuel line or filter 4. Defective fuel pump 5. Choke valve not closing properly 6. Engine flooded 7. Choke valve not unloading 8. Throttle linkage not making full travel 9. Stuck needle or float 10. Leaking float needle or seat 11. Improper float adjustment
Engine stalls	1. Improperly adjusted idle speed or mixture **Engine hot** 2. Improperly adjusted dashpot 3. Defective or improperly adjusted solenoid 4. Incorrect fuel level in fuel bowl 5. Fuel pump pressure too high 6. Leaking float needle seat 7. Secondary throttle valve stuck open 8. Air or fuel leaks 9. Idle air bleeds plugged or missing 10. Idle passages plugged **Engine Cold** 11. Incorrectly adjusted choke 12. Improperly adjusted fast idle speed 13. Air leaks 14. Plugged idle or idle air passages 15. Stuck choke valve or binding linkage 16. Stuck secondary throttle valves 17. Engine flooding—high fuel level 18. Leaking or misaligned float
Engine hesitates on acceleration	1. Clogged fuel filter 2. Leaking fuel pump diaphragm 3. Low fuel pump pressure 4. Secondary throttle valves stuck, bent or misadjusted 5. Sticking or binding air valve 6. Defective accelerator pump 7. Vacuum leaks 8. Clogged air filter 9. Incorrect choke adjustment (engine cold)
Engine feels sluggish or flat on acceleration	1. Improperly adjusted idle speed or mixture 2. Clogged fuel filter 3. Defective accelerator pump 4. Dirty, plugged or incorrect main metering jets 5. Bent or sticking main metering rods 6. Sticking throttle valves 7. Stuck heat riser 8. Binding or stuck air valve 9. Dirty, plugged or incorrect secondary jets 10. Bent or sticking secondary metering rods. 11. Throttle body or manifold heat passages plugged 12. Improperly adjusted choke or choke vacuum break.
Carburetor floods	1. Defective fuel pump. Pressure too high. 2. Stuck choke valve 3. Dirty, worn or damaged float or needle valve/seat 4. Incorrect float/fuel level 5. Leaking float bowl

Condition	Possible Cause
Engine idles roughly and stalls	1. Incorrect idle speed 2. Clogged fuel filter 3. Dirt in fuel system or carburetor 4. Loose carburetor screws or attaching bolts 5. Broken carburetor gaskets 6. Air leaks 7. Dirty carburetor 8. Worn idle mixture needles 9. Throttle valves stuck open 10. Incorrectly adjusted float or fuel level 11. Clogged air filter
Engine runs unevenly or surges	1. Defective fuel pump 2. Dirty or clogged fuel filter 3. Plugged, loose or incorrect main metering jets or rods 4. Air leaks 5. Bent or sticking main metering rods 6. Stuck power piston 7. Incorrect float adjustment 8. Incorrect idle speed or mixture 9. Dirty or plugged idle system passages 10. Hard, brittle or broken gaskets 11. Loose attaching or mounting screws 12. Stuck or misaligned secondary throttle valves
Poor fuel economy	1. Poor driving habits 2. Stuck choke valve 3. Binding choke linkage 4. Stuck heat riser 5. Incorrect idle mixture 6. Defective accelerator pump 7. Air leaks 8. Plugged, loose or incorrect main metering jets 9. Improperly adjusted float or fuel level 10. Bent, misaligned or fuel-clogged float 11. Leaking float needle seat 12. Fuel leak 13. Accelerator pump discharge ball not seating properly 14. Incorrect main jets
Engine lacks high speed performance or power	1. Incorrect throttle linkage adjustment 2. Stuck or binding power piston 3. Defective accelerator pump 4. Air leaks 5. Incorrect float setting or fuel level 6. Dirty, plugged, worn or incorrect main metering jets or rods 7. Binding or sticking air valve 8. Brittle or cracked gaskets 9. Bent, incorrect or improperly adjusted secondary metering rods 10. Clogged fuel filter 11. Clogged air filter 12. Defective fuel pump

TROUBLESHOOTING FUEL INJECTION PROBLEMS

Each fuel injection system has its own unique components and test procedures, for which it is impossible to generalize. Refer to Chapter 4 of this Repair & Tune-Up Guide for specific test and repair procedures, if the vehicle is equipped with fuel injection.

TROUBLESHOOTING ELECTRICAL PROBLEMS

See Chapter 5 for service procedures

For any electrical system to operate, it must make a complete circuit. This simply means that the power flow from the battery must make a complete circle. When an electrical component is operating, power flows from the battery to the component, passes through the component causing it to perform its function (lighting a light bulb), and then returns to the battery through the ground of the circuit. This ground is usually (but not always) the metal part of the car or truck on which the electrical component is mounted.

Perhaps the easiest way to visualize this is to think of connecting a light bulb with two wires attached to it to the battery. If one of the two wires attached to the light bulb were attached to the negative post of the battery and the other were attached to the positive post of the battery, you would have a complete circuit. Current from the battery would flow to the light bulb, causing it to light, and return to the negative post of the battery.

The normal automotive circuit differs from this simple example in two ways. First, instead of having a return wire from the bulb to the battery, the light bulb returns the current to the battery through the chassis of the vehicle. Since the negative battery cable is attached to the chassis and the chassis is made of electrically conductive metal, the chassis of the vehicle can serve as a ground wire to complete the circuit. Secondly, most automotive circuits contain switches to turn components on and off as required.

Every complete circuit from a power source must include a component which is using the power from the power source. If you were to disconnect the light bulb from the wires and touch the two wires together (don't do this) the power supply wire to the component would be grounded before the normal ground connection for the circuit.

Because grounding a wire from a power source makes a complete circuit—less the required component to use the power—this phenomenon is called a short circuit. Common causes are: broken insulation (exposing the metal wire to a metal part of the car or truck), or a shorted switch.

Some electrical components which require a large amount of current to operate also have a relay in their circuit. Since these circuits carry a large amount of current, the thickness of the wire in the circuit (gauge size) is also greater. If this large wire were connected from the component to the control switch on the instrument panel, and then back to the component, a voltage drop would occur in the circuit. To prevent this potential drop in voltage, an electromagnetic switch (relay) is used. The large wires in the circuit are connected from the battery to one side of the relay, and from the opposite side of the relay to the component. The relay is normally open, preventing current from passing through the circuit. An additional, smaller, wire is connected from the relay to the control switch for the circuit. When the control switch is turned on, it grounds the smaller wire from the relay and completes the circuit. This closes the relay and allows current to flow from the battery to the component. The horn, headlight, and starter circuits are three which use relays.

It is possible for larger surges of current to pass through the electrical system of your car or truck. If this surge of current were to reach an electrical component, it could burn it out. To prevent this, fuses, circuit breakers or fusible links are connected into the current supply wires of most of the major electrical systems. When an electrical current of excessive power passes through the component's fuse, the fuse blows out and breaks the circuit, saving the component from destruction.

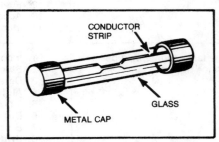

Typical automotive fuse

A circuit breaker is basically a self-repairing fuse. The circuit breaker opens the circuit the same way a fuse does. However, when either the short is removed from the circuit or the surge subsides, the circuit breaker resets itself and does not have to be replaced as a fuse does.

A fuse link is a wire that acts as a fuse. It is normally connected between the starter relay and the main wiring harness. This connection is usually under the hood. The fuse link (if installed) protects all the

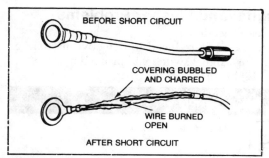

Most fusible links show a charred, melted insulation when they burn out

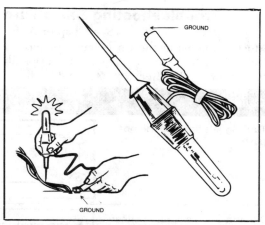

The test light will show the presence of current when touched to a hot wire and grounded at the other end

chassis electrical components, and is the probable cause of trouble when none of the electrical components function, unless the battery is disconnected or dead.

Electrical problems generally fall into one of three areas:

1. The component that is not functioning is not receiving current.

2. The component itself is not functioning.

3. The component is not properly grounded.

The electrical system can be checked with a test light and a jumper wire. A test light is a device that looks like a pointed screwdriver with a wire attached to it and has a light bulb in its handle. A jumper wire is a piece of insulated wire with an alligator clip attached to each end.

If a component is not working, you must follow a systematic plan to determine which of the three causes is the villain.

1. Turn on the switch that controls the inoperable component.

2. Disconnect the power supply wire from the component.

3. Attach the ground wire on the test light to a good metal ground.

4. Touch the probe end of the test light to the end of the power supply wire that was disconnected from the component. If the component is receiving current, the test light will go on.

NOTE: *Some components work only when the ignition switch is turned on.*

If the test light does not go on, then the problem is in the circuit between the battery and the component. This includes all the switches, fuses, and relays in the system. Follow the wire that runs back to the battery. The problem is an open circuit between the

battery and the component. If the fuse is blown and, when replaced, immediately blows again, there is a short circuit in the system which must be located and repaired. If there is a switch in the system, bypass it with a jumper wire. This is done by connecting one end of the jumper wire to the power supply wire into the switch and the other end of the jumper wire to the wire coming out of the switch. If the test light lights with the jumper wire installed, the switch or whatever was bypassed is defective.

NOTE: *Never substitute the jumper wire for the component, since it is required to use the power from the power source.*

5. If the bulb in the test light goes on, then the current is getting to the component that is not working. This eliminates the first of the three possible causes. Connect the power supply wire and connect a jumper wire from the component to a good metal ground. Do this with the switch which controls the component turned on, and also the ignition switch turned on if it is required for the component to work. If the component works with the jumper wire installed, then it has a bad ground. This is usually caused by the metal area on which the component mounts to the chassis being coated with some type of foreign matter.

6. If neither test located the source of the trouble, then the component itself is defective. Remember that for any electrical system to work, all connections must be clean and tight.

Troubleshooting Basic Turn Signal and Flasher Problems
See Chapter 5 for service procedures
Most problems in the turn signals or flasher system can be reduced to defective flashers or bulbs, which are easily replaced. Occasionally, the turn signal switch will prove defective.
F = Front   R = Rear   ● = Lights off   ○ = Lights on

Condition		Possible Cause
Turn signals light, but do not flash	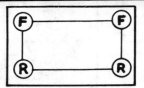	Defective flasher
No turn signals light on either side	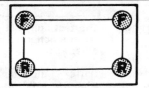	Blown fuse. Replace if defective. Defective flasher. Check by substitution. Open circuit, short circuit or poor ground.
Both turn signals on one side don't work		Bad bulbs. Bad ground in both (or either) housings.
One turn signal light on one side doesn't work	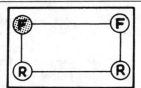	Defective bulb. Corrosion in socket. Clean contacts. Poor ground at socket.
Turn signal flashes too fast or too slowly	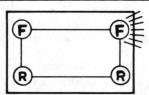	Check any bulb on the side flashing too fast. A heavy-duty bulb is probably installed in place of a regular bulb. Check the bulb flashing too slowly. A standard bulb was probably installed in place of a heavy-duty bulb. Loose connections or corrosion at the bulb socket.
Indicator lights don't work in either direction		Check if the turn signals are working. Check the dash indicator lights. Check the flasher by substitution.
One indicator light doesn't light		On systems with one dash indicator: See if the lights work on the same side. Often the filaments have been reversed in systems combining stoplights with taillights and turn signals. Check the flasher by substitution. On systems with two indicators: Check the bulbs on the same side. Check the indicator light bulb. Check the flasher by substitution.

Troubleshooting Lighting Problems

See Chapter 5 for service procedures

Condition	Possible Cause
One or more lights don't work, but others do	1. Defective bulb(s) 2. Blown fuse(s) 3. Dirty fuse clips or light sockets 4. Poor ground circuit
Lights burn out quickly	1. Incorrect voltage regulator setting or defective regulator 2. Poor battery/alternator connections
Lights go dim	1. Low/discharged battery 2. Alternator not charging 3. Corroded sockets or connections 4. Low voltage output
Lights flicker	1. Loose connection 2. Poor ground. (Run ground wire from light housing to frame) 3. Circuit breaker operating (short circuit)
Lights "flare"—Some flare is normal on acceleration—If excessive, see "Lights Burn Out Quickly"	High voltage setting
Lights glare—approaching drivers are blinded	1. Lights adjusted too high 2. Rear springs or shocks sagging 3. Rear tires soft

Troubleshooting Dash Gauge Problems

Most problems can be traced to a defective sending unit or faulty wiring. Occasionally, the gauge itself is at fault. See Chapter 5 for service procedures.

Condition	Possible Cause
COOLANT TEMPERATURE GAUGE	
Gauge reads erratically or not at all	1. Loose or dirty connections 2. Defective sending unit. 3. Defective gauge. To test a bi-metal gauge, remove the wire from the sending unit. Ground the wire for an instant. If the gauge registers, replace the sending unit. To test a magnetic gauge, disconnect the wire at the sending unit. With ignition ON gauge should register COLD. Ground the wire; gauge should register HOT.
AMMETER GAUGE—TURN HEADLIGHTS ON (DO NOT START ENGINE). NOTE REACTION	
Ammeter shows charge Ammeter shows discharge Ammeter does not move	1. Connections reversed on gauge 2. Ammeter is OK 3. Loose connections or faulty wiring 4. Defective gauge

Condition	Possible Cause

OIL PRESSURE GAUGE

Condition	Possible Cause
Gauge does not register or is inaccurate	1. On mechanical gauge, Bourdon tube may be bent or kinked. 2. Low oil pressure. Remove sending unit. Idle the engine briefly. If no oil flows from sending unit hole, problem is in engine. 3. Defective gauge. Remove the wire from the sending unit and ground it for an instant with the ignition ON. A good gauge will go to the top of the scale. 4. Defective wiring. Check the wiring to the gauge. If it's OK and the gauge doesn't register when grounded, replace the gauge. 5. Defective sending unit.

ALL GAUGES

Condition	Possible Cause
All gauges do not operate All gauges read low or erratically All gauges pegged	1. Blown fuse 2. Defective instrument regulator 3. Defective or dirty instrument voltage regulator 4. Loss of ground between instrument voltage regulator and frame 5. Defective instrument regulator

WARNING LIGHTS

Condition	Possible Cause
Light(s) do not come on when ignition is ON, but engine is not started Light comes on with engine running	1. Defective bulb 2. Defective wire 3. Defective sending unit. Disconnect the wire from the sending unit and ground it. Replace the sending unit if the light comes on with the ignition ON. 4. Problem in individual system 5. Defective sending unit

Troubleshooting Clutch Problems

It is false economy to replace individual clutch components. The pressure plate, clutch plate and throwout bearing should be replaced as a set, and the flywheel face inspected, whenever the clutch is overhauled. See Chapter 6 for service procedures.

Condition	Possible Cause
Clutch chatter	1. Grease on driven plate (disc) facing 2. Binding clutch linkage or cable 3. Loose, damaged facings on driven plate (disc) 4. Engine mounts loose 5. Incorrect height adjustment of pressure plate release levers 6. Clutch housing or housing to transmission adapter misalignment 7. Loose driven plate hub
Clutch grabbing	1. Oil, grease on driven plate (disc) facing 2. Broken pressure plate 3. Warped or binding driven plate. Driven plate binding on clutch shaft
Clutch slips	1. Lack of lubrication in clutch linkage or cable (linkage or cable binds, causes incomplete engagement) 2. Incorrect pedal, or linkage adjustment 3. Broken pressure plate springs 4. Weak pressure plate springs 5. Grease on driven plate facings (disc)

Troubleshooting Clutch Problems (cont.)

Condition	Possible Cause
Incomplete clutch release	1. Incorrect pedal or linkage adjustment or linkage or cable binding 2. Incorrect height adjustment on pressure plate release levers 3. Loose, broken facings on driven plate (disc) 4. Bent, dished, warped driven plate caused by overheating
Grinding, whirring grating noise when pedal is depressed	1. Worn or defective throwout bearing 2. Starter drive teeth contacting flywheel ring gear teeth. Look for milled or polished teeth on ring gear.
Squeal, howl, trumpeting noise when pedal is being released (occurs during first inch to inch and one-half of pedal travel)	Pilot bushing worn or lack of lubricant. If bushing appears OK, polish bushing with emery cloth, soak lube wick in oil, lube bushing with oil, apply film of chassis grease to clutch shaft pilot hub, reassemble. NOTE: Bushing wear may be due to misalignment of clutch housing or housing to transmission adapter
Vibration or clutch pedal pulsation with clutch disengaged (pedal fully depressed)	1. Worn or defective engine transmission mounts 2. Flywheel run out. (Flywheel run out at face not to exceed 0.005") 3. Damaged or defective clutch components

Troubleshooting Manual Transmission Problems
See Chapter 6 for service procedures

Condition	Possible Cause
Transmission jumps out of gear	1. Misalignment of transmission case or clutch housing. 2. Worn pilot bearing in crankshaft. 3. Bent transmission shaft. 4. Worn high speed sliding gear. 5. Worn teeth or end-play in clutch shaft. 6. Insufficient spring tension on shifter rail plunger. 7. Bent or loose shifter fork. 8. Gears not engaging completely. 9. Loose or worn bearings on clutch shaft or mainshaft. 10. Worn gear teeth. 11. Worn or damaged detent balls.
Transmission sticks in gear	1. Clutch not releasing fully. 2. Burred or battered teeth on clutch shaft, or sliding sleeve. 3. Burred or battered transmission mainshaft. 4. Frozen synchronizing clutch. 5. Stuck shifter rail plunger. 6. Gearshift lever twisting and binding shifter rail. 7. Battered teeth on high speed sliding gear or on sleeve. 8. Improper lubrication, or lack of lubrication. 9. Corroded transmission parts. 10. Defective mainshaft pilot bearing. 11. Locked gear bearings will give same effect as stuck in gear.
Transmission gears will not synchronize	1. Binding pilot bearing on mainshaft, will synchronize in high gear only. 2. Clutch not releasing fully. 3. Detent spring weak or broken. 4. Weak or broken springs under balls in sliding gear sleeve. 5. Binding bearing on clutch shaft, or binding countershaft. 6. Binding pilot bearing in crankshaft. 7. Badly worn gear teeth. 8. Improper lubrication. 9. Constant mesh gear not turning freely on transmission mainshaft. Will synchronize in that gear only.

Condition	Possible Cause
Gears spinning when shifting into gear from neutral	1. Clutch not releasing fully. 2. In some cases an extremely light lubricant in transmission will cause gears to continue to spin for a short time after clutch is released. 3. Binding pilot bearing in crankshaft.
Transmission noisy in all gears	1. Insufficient lubricant, or improper lubricant. 2. Worn countergear bearings. 3. Worn or damaged main drive gear or countergear. 4. Damaged main drive gear or mainshaft bearings. 5. Worn or damaged countergear anti-lash plate.
Transmission noisy in neutral only	1. Damaged main drive gear bearing. 2. Damaged or loose mainshaft pilot bearing. 3. Worn or damaged countergear anti-lash plate. 4. Worn countergear bearings.
Transmission noisy in one gear only	1. Damaged or worn constant mesh gears. 2. Worn or damaged countergear bearings. 3. Damaged or worn synchronizer.
Transmission noisy in reverse only	1. Worn or damaged reverse idler gear or idler bushing. 2. Worn or damaged mainshaft reverse gear. 3. Worn or damaged reverse countergear. 4. Damaged shift mechanism.

TROUBLESHOOTING AUTOMATIC TRANSMISSION PROBLEMS

Keeping alert to changes in the operating characteristics of the transmission (changing shift points, noises, etc.) can prevent small problems from becoming large ones. If the problem cannot be traced to loose bolts, fluid level, misadjusted linkage, clogged filters or similar problems, you should probably seek professional service.

Transmission Fluid Indications

The appearance and odor of the transmission fluid can give valuable clues to the overall condition of the transmission. Always note the appearance of the fluid when you check the fluid level or change the fluid. Rub a small amount of fluid between your fingers to feel for grit and smell the fluid on the dipstick.

If the fluid appears:	It indicates:
Clear and red colored	Normal operation
Discolored (extremely dark red or brownish) or smells burned	Band or clutch pack failure, usually caused by an overheated transmission. Hauling very heavy loads with insufficient power or failure to change the fluid often result in overheating. Do not confuse this appearance with newer fluids that have a darker red color and a strong odor (though not a burned odor).
Foamy or aerated (light in color and full of bubbles)	1. The level is too high (gear train is churning oil) 2. An internal air leak (air is mixing with the fluid). Have the transmission checked professionally.
Solid residue in the fluid	Defective bands, clutch pack or bearings. Bits of band material or metal abrasives are clinging to the dipstick. Have the transmission checked professionally.
Varnish coating on the dipstick	The transmission fluid is overheating

TROUBLESHOOTING DRIVE AXLE PROBLEMS

First, determine when the noise is most noticeable.

Drive Noise: Produced under vehicle acceleration.

Coast Noise: Produced while coasting with a closed throttle.

Float Noise: Occurs while maintaining constant speed (just enough to keep speed constant) on a level road.

External Noise Elimination

It is advisable to make a thorough road test to determine whether the noise originates in the rear axle or whether it originates from the tires, engine, transmission, wheel bearings or road surface. Noise originating from other places cannot be corrected by servicing the rear axle.

ROAD NOISE

Brick or rough surfaced concrete roads produce noises that seem to come from the rear axle. Road noise is usually identical in Drive or Coast and driving on a different type of road will tell whether the road is the problem.

TIRE NOISE

Tire noise can be mistaken as rear axle noise, even though the tires on the front are at fault. Snow tread and mud tread tires or tires worn unevenly will frequently cause vibrations which seem to originate elsewhere; *temporarily, and for test purposes only,* inflate the tires to 40–50 lbs. This will significantly alter the noise produced by the tires, but will not alter noise from the rear axle. Noises from the rear axle will normally cease at speeds below 30 mph on coast, while tire noise will continue at lower tone as speed is decreased. The rear axle noise will usually change from drive conditions to coast conditions, while tire noise will not. Do not forget to lower the tire pressure to normal after the test is complete.

ENGINE/TRANSMISSION NOISE

Determine at what speed the noise is most pronounced, then stop in a quiet place. With the transmission in Neutral, run the engine through speeds corresponding to road speeds where the noise was noticed. Noises produced with the vehicle standing still are coming from the engine or transmission.

FRONT WHEEL BEARINGS

Front wheel bearing noises, sometimes confused with rear axle noises, will not change when comparing drive and coast conditions. While holding the speed steady, lightly apply the footbrake. This will often cause wheel bearing noise to lessen, as some of the weight is taken off the bearing. Front wheel bearings are easily checked by jacking up the wheels and spinning the wheels. Shaking the wheels will also determine if the wheel bearings are excessively loose.

REAR AXLE NOISES

Eliminating other possible sources can narrow the cause to the rear axle, which normally produces noise from worn gears or bearings. Gear noises tend to peak in a narrow speed range, while bearing noises will usually vary in pitch with engine speeds.

Noise Diagnosis

The Noise Is:	Most Probably Produced By:
1. Identical under Drive or Coast	Road surface, tires or front wheel bearings
2. Different depending on road surface	Road surface or tires
3. Lower as speed is lowered	Tires
4. Similar when standing or moving	Engine or transmission
5. A vibration	Unbalanced tires, rear wheel bearing, unbalanced driveshaft or worn U-joint
6. A knock or click about every two tire revolutions	Rear wheel bearing
7. Most pronounced on turns	Damaged differential gears
8. A steady low-pitched whirring or scraping, starting at low speeds	Damaged or worn pinion bearing
9. A chattering vibration on turns	Wrong differential lubricant or worn clutch plates (limited slip rear axle)
10. Noticed only in Drive, Coast or Float conditions	Worn ring gear and/or pinion gear

Troubleshooting Steering & Suspension Problems

Condition	Possible Cause
Hard steering (wheel is hard to turn)	1. Improper tire pressure 2. Loose or glazed pump drive belt 3. Low or incorrect fluid 4. Loose, bent or poorly lubricated front end parts 5. Improper front end alignment (excessive caster) 6. Bind in steering column or linkage 7. Kinked hydraulic hose 8. Air in hydraulic system 9. Low pump output or leaks in system 10. Obstruction in lines 11. Pump valves sticking or out of adjustment 12. Incorrect wheel alignment
Loose steering (too much play in steering wheel)	1. Loose wheel bearings 2. Faulty shocks 3. Worn linkage or suspension components 4. Loose steering gear mounting or linkage points 5. Steering mechanism worn or improperly adjusted 6. Valve spool improperly adjusted 7. Worn ball joints, tie-rod ends, etc.
Veers or wanders (pulls to one side with hands off steering wheel)	1. Improper tire pressure 2. Improper front end alignment 3. Dragging or improperly adjusted brakes 4. Bent frame 5. Improper rear end alignment 6. Faulty shocks or springs 7. Loose or bent front end components 8. Play in Pitman arm 9. Steering gear mountings loose 10. Loose wheel bearings 11. Binding Pitman arm 12. Spool valve sticking or improperly adjusted 13. Worn ball joints
Wheel oscillation or vibration transmitted through steering wheel	1. Low or uneven tire pressure 2. Loose wheel bearings 3. Improper front end alignment 4. Bent spindle 5. Worn, bent or broken front end components 6. Tires out of round or out of balance 7. Excessive lateral runout in disc brake rotor 8. Loose or bent shock absorber or strut
Noises (see also "Troubleshooting Drive Axle Problems")	1. Loose belts 2. Low fluid, air in system 3. Foreign matter in system 4. Improper lubrication 5. Interference or chafing in linkage 6. Steering gear mountings loose 7. Incorrect adjustment or wear in gear box 8. Faulty valves or wear in pump 9. Kinked hydraulic lines 10. Worn wheel bearings
Poor return of steering	1. Over-inflated tires 2. Improperly aligned front end (excessive caster) 3. Binding in steering column 4. No lubrication in front end 5. Steering gear adjusted too tight
Uneven tire wear (see "How To Read Tire Wear")	1. Incorrect tire pressure 2. Improperly aligned front end 3. Tires out-of-balance 4. Bent or worn suspension parts

HOW TO READ TIRE WEAR

The way your tires wear is a good indicator of other parts of the suspension. Abnormal wear patterns are often caused by the need for simple tire maintenance, or for front end alignment.

Excessive wear at the center of the tread indicates that the air pressure in the tire is consistently too high. The tire is riding on the center of the tread and wearing it prematurely. Occasionally, this wear pattern can result from outrageously wide tires on narrow rims. The cure for this is to replace either the tires or the wheels.

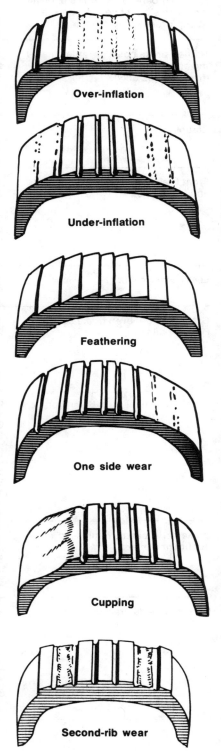

Over-inflation

Under-inflation

Feathering

One side wear

Cupping

Second-rib wear

This type of wear usually results from consistent under-inflation. When a tire is under-inflated, there is too much contact with the road by the outer treads, which wear prematurely. When this type of wear occurs, and the tire pressure is known to be consistently correct, a bent or worn steering component or the need for wheel alignment could be indicated.

Feathering is a condition when the edge of each tread rib develops a slightly rounded edge on one side and a sharp edge on the other. By running your hand over the tire, you can usually feel the sharper edges before you'll be able to see them. The most common causes of feathering are incorrect toe-in setting or deteriorated bushings in the front suspension.

When an inner or outer rib wears faster than the rest of the tire, the need for wheel alignment is indicated. There is excessive camber in the front suspension, causing the wheel to lean too much putting excessive load on one side of the tire. Misalignment could also be due to sagging springs, worn ball joints, or worn control arm bushings. Be sure the vehicle is loaded the way it's normally driven when you have the wheels aligned.

Cups or scalloped dips appearing around the edge of the tread almost always indicate worn (sometimes bent) suspension parts. Adjustment of wheel alignment alone will seldom cure the problem. Any worn component that connects the wheel to the suspension can cause this type of wear. Occasionally, wheels that are out of balance will wear like this, but wheel imbalance usually shows up as bald spots between the outside edges and center of the tread.

Second-rib wear is usually found only in radial tires, and appears where the steel belts end in relation to the tread. It can be kept to a minimum by paying careful attention to tire pressure and frequently rotating the tires. This is often considered normal wear but excessive amounts indicate that the tires are too wide for the wheels.

Troubleshooting Disc Brake Problems

Condition	Possible Cause
Noise—groan—brake noise emanating when slowly releasing brakes (creep-groan)	Not detrimental to function of disc brakes—no corrective action required. (This noise may be eliminated by slightly increasing or decreasing brake pedal efforts.)
Rattle—brake noise or rattle emanating at low speeds on rough roads, (front wheels only).	1. Shoe anti-rattle spring missing or not properly positioned. 2. Excessive clearance between shoe and caliper. 3. Soft or broken caliper seals. 4. Deformed or misaligned disc. 5. Loose caliper.
Scraping	1. Mounting bolts too long. 2. Loose wheel bearings. 3. Bent, loose, or misaligned splash shield.
Front brakes heat up during driving and fail to release	1. Operator riding brake pedal. 2. Stop light switch improperly adjusted. 3. Sticking pedal linkage. 4. Frozen or seized piston. 5. Residual pressure valve in master cylinder. 6. Power brake malfunction. 7. Proportioning valve malfunction.
Leaky brake caliper	1. Damaged or worn caliper piston seal. 2. Scores or corrosion on surface of cylinder bore.
Grabbing or uneven brake action—Brakes pull to one side	1. Causes listed under "Brakes Pull". 2. Power brake malfunction. 3. Low fluid level in master cylinder. 4. Air in hydraulic system. 5. Brake fluid, oil or grease on linings. 6. Unmatched linings. 7. Distorted brake pads. 8. Frozen or seized pistons. 9. Incorrect tire pressure. 10. Front end out of alignment. 11. Broken rear spring. 12. Brake caliper pistons sticking. 13. Restricted hose or line. 14. Caliper not in proper alignment to braking disc. 15. Stuck or malfunctioning metering valve. 16. Soft or broken caliper seals. 17. Loose caliper.
Brake pedal can be depressed without braking effect	1. Air in hydraulic system or improper bleeding procedure. 2. Leak past primary cup in master cylinder. 3. Leak in system. 4. Rear brakes out of adjustment. 5. Bleeder screw open.
Excessive pedal travel	1. Air, leak, or insufficient fluid in system or caliper. 2. Warped or excessively tapered shoe and lining assembly. 3. Excessive disc runout. 4. Rear brake adjustment required. 5. Loose wheel bearing adjustment. 6. Damaged caliper piston seal. 7. Improper brake fluid (boil). 8. Power brake malfunction. 9. Weak or soft hoses.

Troubleshooting Disc Brake Problems (cont.)

Condition	Possible Cause
Brake roughness or chatter (pedal pumping)	1. Excessive thickness variation of braking disc. 2. Excessive lateral runout of braking disc. 3. Rear brake drums out-of-round. 4. Excessive front bearing clearance.
Excessive pedal effort	1. Brake fluid, oil or grease on linings. 2. Incorrect lining. 3. Frozen or seized pistons. 4. Power brake malfunction. 5. Kinked or collapsed hose or line. 6. Stuck metering valve. 7. Scored caliper or master cylinder bore. 8. Seized caliper pistons.
Brake pedal fades (pedal travel increases with foot on brake)	1. Rough master cylinder or caliper bore. 2. Loose or broken hydraulic lines/connections. 3. Air in hydraulic system. 4. Fluid level low. 5. Weak or soft hoses. 6. Inferior quality brake shoes or fluid. 7. Worn master cylinder piston cups or seals.

Troubleshooting Drum Brakes

Condition	Possible Cause
Pedal goes to floor	1. Fluid low in reservoir. 2. Air in hydraulic system. 3. Improperly adjusted brake. 4. Leaking wheel cylinders. 5. Loose or broken brake lines. 6. Leaking or worn master cylinder. 7. Excessively worn brake lining.
Spongy brake pedal	1. Air in hydraulic system. 2. Improper brake fluid (low boiling point). 3. Excessively worn or cracked brake drums. 4. Broken pedal pivot bushing.
Brakes pulling	1. Contaminated lining. 2. Front end out of alignment. 3. Incorrect brake adjustment. 4. Unmatched brake lining. 5. Brake drums out of round. 6. Brake shoes distorted. 7. Restricted brake hose or line. 8. Broken rear spring. 9. Worn brake linings. 10. Uneven lining wear. 11. Glazed brake lining. 12. Excessive brake lining dust. 13. Heat spotted brake drums. 14. Weak brake return springs. 15. Faulty automatic adjusters. 16. Low or incorrect tire pressure.

Condition	Possible Cause
Squealing brakes	1. Glazed brake lining. 2. Saturated brake lining. 3. Weak or broken brake shoe retaining spring. 4. Broken or weak brake shoe return spring. 5. Incorrect brake lining. 6. Distorted brake shoes. 7. Bent support plate. 8. Dust in brakes or scored brake drums. 9. Linings worn below limit. 10. Uneven brake lining wear. 11. Heat spotted brake drums.
Chirping brakes	1. Out of round drum or eccentric axle flange pilot.
Dragging brakes	1. Incorrect wheel or parking brake adjustment. 2. Parking brakes engaged or improperly adjusted. 3. Weak or broken brake shoe return spring. 4. Brake pedal binding. 5. Master cylinder cup sticking. 6. Obstructed master cylinder relief port. 7. Saturated brake lining. 8. Bent or out of round brake drum. 9. Contaminated or improper brake fluid. 10. Sticking wheel cylinder pistons. 11. Driver riding brake pedal. 12. Defective proportioning valve. 13. Insufficient brake shoe lubricant.
Hard pedal	1. Brake booster inoperative. 2. Incorrect brake lining. 3. Restricted brake line or hose. 4. Frozen brake pedal linkage. 5. Stuck wheel cylinder. 6. Binding pedal linkage. 7. Faulty proportioning valve.
Wheel locks	1. Contaminated brake lining. 2. Loose or torn brake lining. 3. Wheel cylinder cups sticking. 4. Incorrect wheel bearing adjustment. 5. Faulty proportioning valve.
Brakes fade (high speed)	1. Incorrect lining. 2. Overheated brake drums. 3. Incorrect brake fluid (low boiling temperature). 4. Saturated brake lining. 5. Leak in hydraulic system. 6. Faulty automatic adjusters.
Pedal pulsates	1. Bent or out of round brake drum.
Brake chatter and shoe knock	1. Out of round brake drum. 2. Loose support plate. 3. Bent support plate. 4. Distorted brake shoes. 5. Machine grooves in contact face of brake drum (Shoe Knock). 6. Contaminated brake lining. 7. Missing or loose components. 8. Incorrect lining material. 9. Out-of-round brake drums. 10. Heat spotted or scored brake drums. 11. Out-of-balance wheels.

Troubleshooting Drum Brakes (cont.)

Condition	Possible Cause
Brakes do not self adjust	1. Adjuster screw frozen in thread. 2. Adjuster screw corroded at thrust washer. 3. Adjuster lever does not engage star wheel. 4. Adjuster installed on wrong wheel.
Brake light glows	1. Leak in the hydraulic system. 2. Air in the system. 3. Improperly adjusted master cylinder pushrod. 4. Uneven lining wear. 5. Failure to center combination valve or proportioning valve.

Appendix

General Conversion Table

Multiply by	To convert	To	
2.54	Inches	Centimeters	.3937
30.48	Feet	Centimeters	.0328
.914	Yards	Meters	1.094
1.609	Miles	Kilometers	.621
6.45	Square inches	Square cm.	.155
.836	Square yards	Square meters	1.196
16.39	Cubic inches	Cubic cm.	.061
28.3	Cubic feet	Liters	.0353
.4536	Pounds	Kilograms	2.2045
3.785	Gallons	Liters	.264
.068	Lbs./sq. in. (psi)	Atmospheres	14.7
.138	Foot pounds	Kg. m.	7.23
1.014	H.P. (DIN)	H.P. (SAE)	.9861
—	To obtain	From	Multiply by

Note: 1 cm. equals 10 mm.; 1 mm. equals .0394".

Conversion—Common Fractions to Decimals and Millimeters

Common Fractions	Decimal Fractions	Millimeters (approx.)	Common Fractions	Decimal Fractions	Millimeters (approx.)	Common Fractions	Decimal Fractions	Millimeters (approx.)
1/128	.008	0.20	11/32	.344	8.73	43/64	.672	17.07
1/64	.016	0.40	23/64	.359	9.13	11/16	.688	17.46
1/32	.031	0.79	3/8	.375	9.53	45/64	.703	17.86
3/64	.047	1.19	25/64	.391	9.92	23/32	.719	18.26
1/16	.063	1.59	13/32	.406	10.32	47/64	.734	18.65
5/64	.078	1.98	27/64	.422	10.72	3/4	.750	19.05
3/32	.094	2.38	7/16	.438	11.11	49/64	.766	19.45
7/64	.109	2.78	29/64	.453	11.51	25/32	.781	19.84
1/8	.125	3.18	15/32	.469	11.91	51/64	.797	20.24
9/64	.141	3.57	31/64	.484	12.30	13/16	.813	20.64
5/32	.156	3.97	1/2	.500	12.70	53/64	.828	21.03
11/64	.172	4.37	33/64	.516	13.10	27/32	.844	21.43
3/16	.188	4.76	17/32	.531	13.49	55/64	.859	21.83
13/64	.203	5.16	35/64	.547	13.89	7/8	.875	22.23
7/32	.219	5.56	9/16	.563	14.29	57/64	.891	22.62
15/64	.234	5.95	37/64	.578	14.68	29/32	.906	23.02
1/4	.250	6.35	19/32	.594	15.08	59/64	.922	23.42
17/64	.266	6.75	39/64	.609	15.48	15/16	.938	23.81
9/32	.281	7.14	5/8	.625	15.88	61/64	.953	24.21
19/64	.297	7.54	41/64	.641	16.27	31/32	.969	24.61
5/16	.313	7.94	21/32	.656	16.67	63/64	.984	25.00
21/64	.328	8.33						

Conversion—Millimeters to Decimal Inches

mm	inches	mm	inches	mm	inches	mm	inches	mm	inches
1	.039 370	31	1.220 470	61	2.401 570	91	3.582 670	210	8.267 700
2	.078 740	32	1.259 840	62	2.440 940	92	3.622 040	220	8.661 400
3	.118 110	33	1.299 210	63	2.480 310	93	3.661 410	230	9.055 100
4	.157 480	34	1.338 580	64	2.519 680	94	3.700 780	240	9.448 800
5	.196 850	35	1.377 949	65	2.559 050	95	3.740 150	250	9.842 500
6	.236 220	36	1.417 319	66	2.598 420	96	3.779 520	260	10.236 200
7	.275 590	37	1.456 689	67	2.637 790	97	3.818 890	270	10.629 900
8	.314 960	38	1.496 050	68	2.677 160	98	3.858 260	280	11.032 600
9	.354 330	39	1.535 430	69	2.716 530	99	3.897 630	290	11.417 300
10	.393 700	40	1.574 800	70	2.755 900	100	3.937 000	300	11.811 000
11	.433 070	41	1.614 170	71	2.795 270	105	4.133 848	310	12.204 700
12	.472 440	42	1.653 540	72	2.834 640	110	4.330 700	320	12.598 400
13	.511 810	43	1.692 910	73	2.874 010	115	4.527 550	330	12.992 100
14	.551 180	44	1.732 280	74	2.913 380	120	4.724 400	340	13.385 800
15	.590 550	45	1.771 650	75	2.952 750	125	4.921 250	350	13.779 500
16	.629 920	46	1.811 020	76	2.992 120	130	5.118 100	360	14.173 200
17	.669 290	47	1.850 390	77	3.031 490	135	5.314 950	370	14.566 900
18	.708 660	48	1.889 760	78	3.070 860	140	5.511 800	380	14.960 600
19	.748 030	49	1.929 130	79	3.110 230	145	5.708 650	390	15.354 300
20	.787 400	50	1.968 500	80	3.149 600	150	5.905 500	400	15.748 000
21	.826 770	51	2.007 870	81	3.188 970	155	6.102 350	500	19.685 000
22	.866 140	52	2.047 240	82	3.228 340	160	6.299 200	600	23.622 000
23	.905 510	53	2.086 610	83	3.267 710	165	6.496 050	700	27.559 000
24	.944 880	54	2.125 980	84	3.307 080	170	6.692 900	800	31.496 000
25	.984 250	55	2.165 350	85	3.346 450	175	6.889 750	900	35.433 000
26	1.023 620	56	2.204 720	86	3.385 820	180	7.086 600	1000	39.370 000
27	1.062 990	57	2.244 090	87	3.425 190	185	7.283 450	2000	78.740 000
28	1.102 360	58	2.283 460	88	3.464 560	190	7.480 300	3000	118.110 000
29	1.141 730	59	2.322 830	89	3.503 903	195	7.677 150	4000	157.480 000
30	1.181 100	60	2.362 200	90	3.543 300	200	7.874 000	5000	196.850 000

To change decimal millimeters to decimal inches, position the decimal point where desired on either side of the millimeter measurement shown and reset the inches decimal by the same number of digits in the same direction. For example, to convert 0.001 mm to decimal inches, reset the decimal behind the 1 mm (shown on the chart) to 0.001; change the decimal inch equivalent (0.039″ shown) to 0.000039″.

Tap Drill Sizes

Screw & Tap Size	National Fine or S.A.E. Threads Per Inch	Use Drill Number
No. 5	44	37
No. 6	40	33
No. 8	36	29
No. 10	32	21
No. 12	28	15
¼	28	3
5/16	24	1
3/8	24	Q
7/16	20	W
½	20	29/64
9/16	18	33/64
5/8	18	37/64
¾	16	11/16
7/8	14	13/16
1⅛	12	1 3/64
1¼	12	1 11/64
1½	12	1 27/64

Tap Drill Sizes

Screw & Tap Size	National Coarse or U.S.S. Threads Per Inch	Use Drill Number
No. 5	40	39
No. 6	32	36
No. 8	32	29
No. 10	24	25
No. 12	24	17
¼	20	8
5/16	18	F
3/8	16	5/16
7/16	14	U
½	13	27/64
9/16	12	31/64
5/8	11	17/32
¾	10	21/32
7/8	9	49/64
1	8	7/8
1⅛	7	63/64
1¼	7	1 7/64
1½	6	1 11/32

Decimal Equivalent Size of the Number Drills

Drill No.	Decimal Equivalent	Drill No.	Decimal Equivalent	Drill No.	Decimal Equivalent
80	.0135	53	.0595	26	.1470
79	.0145	52	.0635	25	.1495
78	.0160	51	.0670	24	.1520
77	.0180	50	.0700	23	.1540
76	.0200	49	.0730	22	.1570
75	.0210	48	.0760	21	.1590
74	.0225	47	.0785	20	.1610
73	.0240	46	.0810	19	.1660
72	.0250	45	.0820	18	.1695
71	.0260	44	.0860	17	.1730
70	.0280	43	.0890	16	.1770
69	.0292	42	.0935	15	.1800
68	.0310	41	.0960	14	.1820
67	.0320	40	.0980	13	.1850
66	.0330	39	.0995	12	.1890
65	.0350	38	.1015	11	.1910
64	.0360	37	.1040	10	.1935
63	.0370	36	.1065	9	.1960
62	.0380	35	.1100	8	.1990
61	.0390	34	.1110	7	.2010
60	.0400	33	.1130	6	.2040
59	.0410	32	.1160	5	.2055
58	.0420	31	.1200	4	.2090
57	.0430	30	.1285	3	.2130
56	.0465	29	.1360	2	.2210
55	.0520	28	.1405	1	.2280
54	.0550	27	.1440		

Decimal Equivalent Size of the Letter Drills

Letter Drill	Decimal Equivalent	Letter Drill	Decimal Equivalent	Letter Drill	Decimal Equivalent
A	.234	J	.277	S	.348
B	.238	K	.281	T	.358
C	.242	L	.290	U	.368
D	.246	M	.295	V	.377
E	.250	N	.302	W	.386
F	.257	O	.316	X	.397
G	.261	P	.323	Y	.404
H	.266	Q	.332	Z	.413
I	.272	R	.339		

Anti-Freeze Chart

Temperatures Shown in Degrees Fahrenheit +32 is Freezing

Quarts of ETHYLENE GLYCOL Needed for Protection to Temperatures Shown Below

Cooling System Capacity Quarts	1	2	3	4	5	6	7	8	9	10	11	12	13	14
10	+24°	+16°	+4°	−12°	−34°	−62°								
11	+25	+18	+8	−6	−23	−47								
12	+26	+19	+10	0	−15	−34	−57°							
13	+27	+21	+13	+3	−9	−25	−45							
14			+15	+6	−5	−18	−34							
15			+16	+8	0	−12	−26							
16		+17	+10	+2	−8	−19	−34	−52°						
17		+18	+12	+5	−4	−14	−27	−42						
18		+19	+14	+7	0	−10	−21	−34	−50°					
19		+20	+15	+9	+2	−7	−16	−28	−42					
20			+16	+10	+4	−3	−12	−22	−34	−48°				
21				+17	+12	+6	0	−9	−17	−28	−41			
22				+18	+13	+8	+2	−6	−14	−23	−34	−47°		
23				+19	+14	+9	+4	−3	−10	−19	−29	−40		
24				+19	+15	+10	+5	0	−8	−15	−23	−34	−46°	
25				+20	+16	+12	+7	+1	−5	−12	−20	−29	−40	−50°
26					+17	+13	+8	+3	−3	−9	−16	−25	−34	−44
27					+18	+14	+9	+5	−1	−7	−13	−21	−29	−39
28					+18	+15	+10	+6	+1	−5	−11	−18	−25	−34
29					+19	+16	+12	+7	+2	−3	−8	−15	−22	−29
30					+20	+17	+13	+8	+4	−1	−6	−12	−18	−25

For capacities over 30 quarts divide true capacity by 3. Find quarts Anti-Freeze for the 1/3 and multiply by 3 for quarts to add.

For capacities under 10 quarts multiply true capacity by 3. Find quarts Anti-Freeze for the tripled volume and divide by 3 for quarts to add.

To Increase the Freezing Protection of Anti-Freeze Solutions Already Installed

Number of Quarts of ETHYLENE GLYCOL Anti-Freeze Required to Increase Protection

Cooling System Capacity Quarts	From +20° F. to					From +10° F. to					From 0° F. to			
	0°	−10°	−20°	−30°	−40°	0°	−10°	−20°	−30°	−40°	−10°	−20°	−30°	−40°
10	1¾	2¼	3	3½	3¾	¾	1½	2¼	2¾	3¼	¾	1½	2	2½
12	2	2¾	3½	4	4½	1	1¾	2½	3¼	3¾	1	1¾	2½	3¼
14	2¼	3¼	4	4¾	5½	1¼	2	3	3¾	4½	1	2	3	3½
16	2½	3½	4½	5¼	6	1¼	2½	3½	4¼	5¼	1¼	2¼	3¼	4
18	3	4	5	6	7	1½	2¾	4	5	5¾	1½	2½	3¾	4¾
20	3¼	4½	5¾	6¾	7½	1¾	3	4¼	5½	6½	1½	2¾	4¼	5¼
22	3½	5	6¼	7¼	8¼	1¾	3¼	4¾	6	7¼	1¾	3¼	4½	5½
24	4	5½	7	8	9	2	3½	5	6½	7½	1¾	3½	5	6
26	4¼	6	7½	8¾	10	2	4	5½	7	8¼	2	3¾	5½	6¾
28	4½	6¼	8	9½	10½	2¼	4¼	6	7½	9	2	4	5¾	7¼
30	5	6¾	8½	10	11½	2½	4½	6½	8	9½	2¼	4¼	6¼	7¾

Test radiator solution with proper hydrometer. Determine from the table the number of quarts of solution to be drawn off from a full cooling system and replace with undiluted anti-freeze, to give the desired increased protection. For example, to increase protection of a 22-quart cooling system containing Ethylene Glycol (permanent type) anti-freeze, from +20° F. to −20° F. will require the replacement of 6¼ quarts of solution with undiluted anti-freeze.

Index

Chilton's Repair & Tune-Up Guides

The complete line covers domestic cars, imports, trucks, vans, RV's and 4-wheel drive vehicles.

CODE	TITLE	CODE	TITLE
#7199	AMC 75–82; all models	#7171	Ford Vans 61–82
#7165	Alliance 1983	#7165	Fuego 82–83
#7323	Aries 81–82	#6935	GM Sub-compact 71–81 inc. Vega, Monza,
#7344	Arrow 78–83		Astre, Sunbird, Starfire & Skyhawk
#7193	Aspen/Volaré 76–80	#7311	Granada 78–83
#5902	Audi 70–73	#7204	Honda 73–82
#7028	Audi 4000/5000 77–81	#5912	International Scout 67–73
#6337	Audi Fox 73–75	#7136	Jeep CJ 1945–81
#5807	Barracuda 65–72	#6739	Jeep Wagoneer, Commando, Cherokee 66–79
#7203	Blazer 69–82	#7203	Jimmy 69–82
#5576	BMW 59–70	#7059	J-2000 1982
#7315	BMW 70–82	#7165	Le Car 76–83
#7308	Buick 75–83 all full sized models	#7323	Le Baron 1982
#7307	Buick Century/Regal 75–83	#7055	Lynx 81–82 inc. EXP & LN-7
#7045	Camaro 67–81	#6634	Maverick/Comet 70–77
#7317	Camaro 82–83	#7198	Mazda 71–82
#6695	Capri 70–77	#7031	Mazda RX-7 79–81
#7195	Capri 79–82	#6065	Mercedes-Benz 59–70
#7059	Cavalier 1982	#5907	Mercedes-Benz 68–73
#7309	Celebrity 82–83	#6809	Mercedes-Benz 74–79
#7309	Century 82–83	#7318	Mercury 68–83 all full sized models
#5807	Challenger 65–72	#7194	Mercury Mid-Size 71–82 inc. Continental,
#7343	Challenger (Import) 71–83		Cougar, XR-7 & Montego
#7344	Champ 78–83	#7173	MG 61–80
#6316	Charger/Coronet 71–75	#7311	Monarch 75–80
#7162	Chevette 76–82 inc. diesel	#7405	Mustang 65–73
#7313	Chevrolet 68–83 all full sized models	#6812	Mustang II 74–78
#7167	Chevrolet/GMC Pick-Ups 70–82	#7195	Mustang 79–82
#7169	Chevrolet/GMC Vans 67–82	#6841	Nova 69–79
#7310	Chevrolet S-10/GMC S-15 Pick-Ups 82–83	#7308	Oldsmobile 75–83 all full sized models
#7051	Chevy Luv 72–81 inc. 4wd	#7335	Omega 80–83
#7056	Chevy Mid-Size 64–81 inc. El Camino,	#7191	Omni/Horizon 78–82
	Chevelle, Laguna, Malibu & Monte Carlo	#6575	Opel 71–75
#6841	Chevy II 62–79	#5982	Peugeot 70–74
#7309	Ciera 82–83	#7335	Phoenix 80–83
#7059	Cimarron 1982	#7027	Pinto/Bobcat 71–80
#7335	Citation 80–83	#8552	Plymouth 68–76 full sized models
#7343	Colt 71–83	#7168	Plymouth Vans 67–82
#7194	Continental 1982	#7308	Pontiac 75–83 all full sized models
#6691	Corvair 60–69 inc. Turbo	#7309	Pontiac 6000 82–83
#6576	Corvette 53–62	#5822	Porsche 69–73
#7192	Corvette 63–82	#7048	Porsche 924 & 928 77–81 inc. Turbo
#7405	Cougar 65–73	#7323	Reliant 81–82
#7190	Cutlass 70–82	#7165	Renault 75–83
#6324	Dart/Demon 68–76	#7383	S-10 Blazer 82–83
#5790	Datsun 61–72	#7383	S-15 Jimmy 82–83
#7196	Datsun F10, 310, Nissan Stanza 77–82	#5988	Saab 69–75
#7170	Datsun 200SX, 510, 610, 710, 810 73–82	#7344	Sapporo 78–83
#7197	Datsun 1200, 210/Nissan Sentra 73–82	#5821	Satellite/Roadrunner, Belvedere, GTX 68–73
#7172	Datsun Z & ZX 70–82	#7059	Skyhawk 1982
#7050	Datsun Pick-Ups 70–81 inc. 4wd	#7335	Skylark 80–83
#6554	Dodge 68–77 all full sized models	#7208	Subaru 70–82
#7323	Dodge 400 1982	#5905	Tempest/GTO/LeMans 68–73
#6486	Dodge Charger 67–70	#5795	Toyota 66–70
#7168	Dodge Vans 67–82	#7314	Toyota Celica & Supra 71–83
#7032	Dodge D-50/Plymouth Arrow Pick-Ups 77–81	#7316	Toyota Corolla, Carina, Tercel, Starlet 70–83
#7055	Escort 81–82 inc. EXP & LN-7	#7044	Toyota Corona, Cressida, Crown, Mark II 70–81
#6320	Fairlane/Torino 62–75	#7035	Toyota Pick-Ups 70–81
#7312	Fairmont 78–83	#5910	Triumph 69–73
#7042	Fiat 69–81	#7162	T-1000 1982
#6846	Fiesta 78–80	#6326	Valiant/Duster 68–76
#7046	Firebird 67–81	#5796	Volkswagen 49–71
#7345	Firebird 82–83	#6837	Volkswagen 70–81
#7059	Firenza 1982	#7339	Volkswagen Front Wheel Drive 74–83 inc.
#7318	Ford 68–83 all full sized models		Dasher, GTI, Jetta, Quantum, Pick-Up,
#7140	Ford Bronco 66–81		Rabbit, Scirocco
#7341	Ford Courier 72–82	#6529	Volvo 56–69
#7194	Ford Mid-Size 71–82 inc. Torino, Gran Torino,	#7040	Volvo 70–80
	Ranchero, Elite, LTD II & Thunderbird	#7312	Zephyr 78–83
#7166	Ford Pick-Ups 65–82 inc. 4wd		

Chilton's Repair & Tune-Up Guides are available at your local retailer or by mailing a check or money order for **$10.95** plus **$1.00** to cover postage and handling to:

Chilton Book Company
Dept. DM
Radnor, PA 19089

NOTE: When ordering be sure to include your name & address, book code & title.